Stranded 40 years in the past by a spell of
Chief Sitting Bull, General George Custer and the
Seventh Cavalry join Davy Crockett to
win independence for Texas.

CUSTER
AND
CROCKETT

———

AFTER THE ALAMO

by Gregory Urbach

Custer and Crockett

Acknowledgements
Cover by Doug Stambaugh
Matthew Bernstein, story editor
Spanish translations courtesy of Claudia R. Colville
Art contributions by Kwei-lin Lum

Dedicated to the memory of
Thomas Ward Custer
1845-1876

In 1862, 16-year-old Thomas Ward Custer enlisted in the Union army as a private, successively earning the brevet ranks of lieutenant, captain, major, and lieutenant colonel. Barely 20-years-old when the Civil War ended, he had fought at Stones River, Missionary Ridge, the Atlanta Campaign, Cedar Creek, Five Forks, Namozine Church, and Sayler's Creek. In 1865, he won the Medal of Honor twice for gallantry.

Custer and Crockett

After the Alamo by Doug Stambaugh

Table of Contents

History Matters

Our revisionist culture has made George Custer the great villain of the Indian Wars, but this is lazy history. Without doubt, Custer was egotistical, prickly to criticism, and annoying to many. So was General George Patton, but Patton lived to be sixty years old while George Custer died at thirty-six. Had he lived to 1898, Custer might have commanded American troops in the Spanish-American War and joined the ranks of Grant, Pershing and Eisenhower. Perhaps it would have been Custer who charged up San Juan Hill instead of Teddy Roosevelt. But that was not meant to be.

There is a story about Custer that you will never hear from his critics. In 1869, while searching for two kidnapped women in the Texas panhandle, Custer's troops were poised to assault a Cheyenne village. He had overwhelming strength, but rather than attack, he rode into the village with only an interpreter at his side. Chief Medicine Arrow insulted him, refused to release the prisoners, and could easily have killed him, but Custer patiently negotiated. Eventually, the prisoners were released, and there was no battle. In fact, Custer made more agreements with Indians than he fought wars. If seeking blame for broken treaties, we should look to the corrupt politicians in Washington, not the poorly paid soldiers serving on a violent frontier.

History matters because it's complicated. In September of 1962 at Rice University, President John F. Kennedy said, "We choose to go to the moon. We choose to go to the moon in this decade and do the other things, not because they are easy, but because they are hard, because that goal will serve to organize and measure the best of our energies and skills, because that challenge is one that we are willing to accept, one we are unwilling to postpone, and one which we intend to win."

Kennedy understood that the challenges of our world cannot be reduced to a few trite phrases. The 1830s, and really, much of America's early history were a product of hard choices. Generosity had to be measured against the lives of those you loved, and the future you hoped to build. If some failed the expectations of modern society, it should be remembered that their educations were often limited, their experiences more brutal, their life expectancy much shorter, and their idealism more pronounced. Judging people of the past by our own standards is never fair, and usually leads to flawed interpretations. You cannot learn from the past if you don't place the culture in perspective.

I will take a moment to harken back to that professor from Dominguez Hills mentioned in *Custer at the Alamo*. In a television college course on the history of the Mexican-American border, this instructor claimed David Crockett came from Kentucky, was forced to flee the United States, brought slaves with him to Texas, and was an enemy of indigenous peoples. None of these assertions are true, but it's what these young people were taught. This professor's goal was indoctrinate his students, not educate them, and in the process subvert history to serve a political agenda. It's fortunate that the great majority of educators in this country take a more responsible approach, and we should thank them, for their task is not an easy one.

Custer and Crockett is not a history book, it's an adventure story. But I like to think the research that has gone into this work might inspire further investigations into the characters and the times in which they lived.

Greg Urbach
Reseda, California

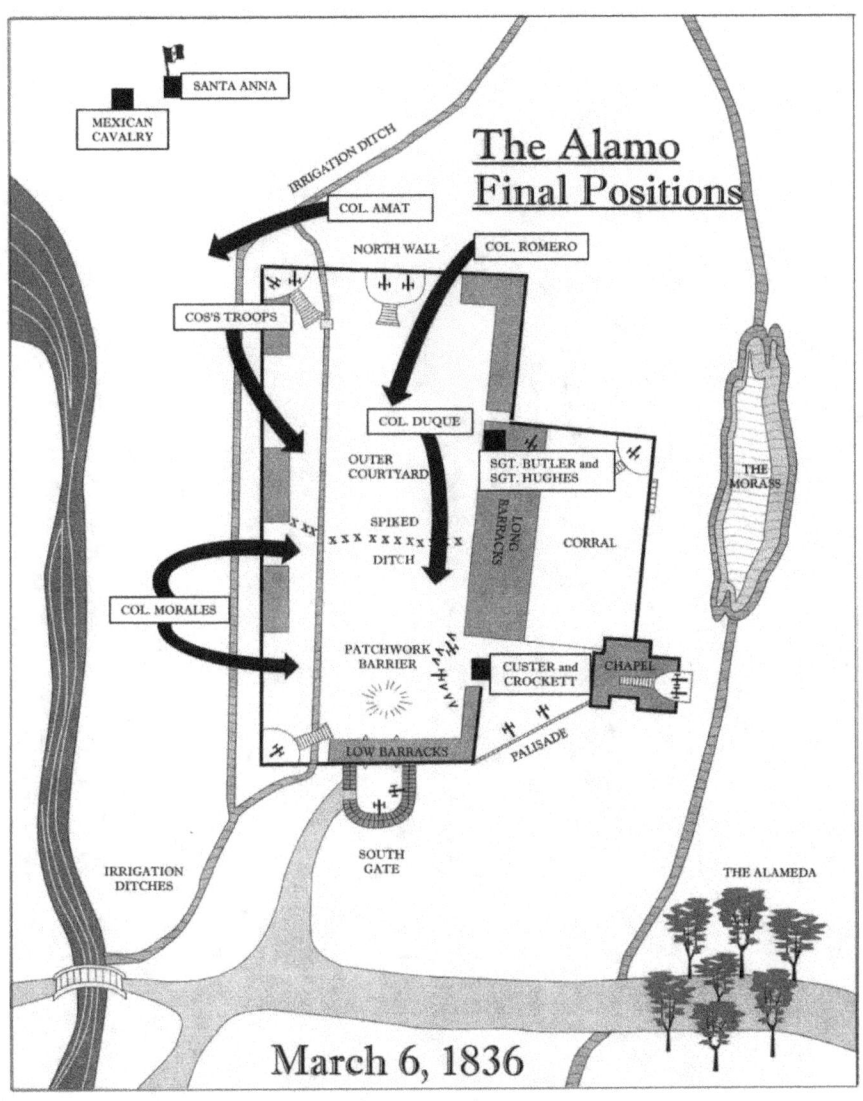

Custer's Victory at the Alamo

**"One crowded hour of glorious life
is worth an age without a name."**

Sir Walter Scott

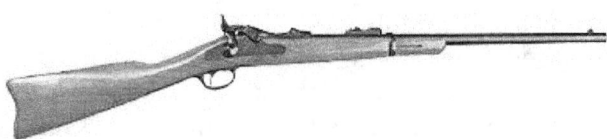

**Chapter One
THE ROAD TO GOLIAD**

We had defeated the white soldiers at the Little Big Horn. Hundreds of wasichu lay dead on the hills across the river from our village, the bodies stripped and sent scarred into the next world. Two of the Cheyenne women claimed the Long Hair lay among them, a man of great courage and little wisdom. The circles of the People celebrated. Our cousins, the Northern Cheyenne, claimed much of the glory. Perhaps too much. Of the Lakota nation, there were the Oglala of Crazy Horse, Lame Deer's Miniconjou, as well as the Sans Arc, Brule, and many others. And my own people, the Hunkpapa. Some said the Arapaho had joined our battle, but I did not see them fight.

All that was gained would be for nothing. Seeking a vision at the Sun Dance on the Rosebud, I had cut a hundred strips of flesh from my arms that the future might be revealed. What truth could Wakan Tanka offer to save us from the white man? The answer held no hope, for the People were doomed. Our way of life would perish on the reservations through disease and starvation. But I would not accept this judgment. I prayed for a new path- a trail not taken that might lead to a better world.

My prayer was answered, or so I believed. Lifted among gray clouds

1

with many birds scouting my path, I returned to the world of my youth. I was no longer Tatanka Iyotake, a leader of the Strong Hearts. No longer a medicine chief of the Great Sioux Nation. I was a boy again, learning and eager. Sage and solemn. My sister, who had died, lived once more, and the future of my people was yet to be decided.

The ways of Wakan Tanka can be strange. My new path would be even stranger.

————————

March 17th, 1836

"General, sir! Colonel Custer's respects. Says thar's a Mex'ikan army up ahead. At the river crossing," Corporal Jimmy Allen reported, offering a brisk salute.

His white-legged Sorrel was lathered from a hard ride, his blue cotton shirt and rawhide britches thick with trail dust. Though only nineteen, Allen had proven himself at the Alamo, possibly saving my life. But he was still a youngster.

"Did my little brother say how many Mex'ikans?" I asked, disguising my disappointment. For I had hoped to take the enemy unawares.

"A lot, sir. Hell of a lot. I'm supposed to warn Doctor Lord," Allen said, quickly galloping off.

"What the hell are you looking at, Crockett?" I said, seeing the old bear hunter giving me the eye. The lanky former congressman, now fifty years old, was dressed in stained brown leathers and spoke with a Tennessee drawl.

"Just a mite curious, George. How's you gonna deploy 'gainst a hell of a lot of Mex'ikans?" Crockett responded, smiling the whole time.

"The Seventh still needs work on our communication skills, I'll grant you that," I said. "But the answer is always the same. I will look for a weakness in the enemy position and attack."

"Odds don't worry you none?"

"The odds never worry me. If they did, I wouldn't have turned Stuart back at Gettysburg, and the United States would have become two nations."

"And you was what? Twenty-three? Saved the whole damn country all by yer'self? Hell, I didn't save the whole damn country 'til I was mid-forty," Crockett mused, giving his mount a soft kick.

As word spread down the line, the entire column gradually picked up the pace. Hundreds of horses, wagons, oxen, and even a few cattle. Each troop rode under their own red and white swallowtail guidon, but the Stars and Stripes guidon that we had brought with us to Texas had been retired, for this Texas was not part of the United States. We had adopted a new symbol, the Buffalo Flag, a white banner with green stripe along the bottom and a bison proudly painted on the field. I gave Traveller a nudge. The big spotted gray stallion shook his head but complied.

"And how'd you do that, Davy? Jumping the Mississippi or riding a bolt of lightning?" I asked.

"Told Andy Jackson his Indian removal policy was nothin' less than murder," Crockett responded. "Couldn't stop him from doin' it, but the country knows I'm right. Someday thar'll be a reckonin'."

I knew from my own history that wasn't true. The last Cherokee tribes in the east would be driven to Oklahoma on the Trail of Tears. A death march. And Andrew Jackson would retire as one of America's greatest presidents. There was a time I wouldn't have cared, but much had changed since then.

"Slow? Slow, where are you?" I called.

The young Indian boy we had found on the windswept Texas plains during our journey south was soon riding at my side, sitting Vic like he'd done it all his life. I was a bit jealous, as Vic was my favorite warhorse.

The boy's heavy fur coat was pulled up against the March cold, but he wore no hat. His long black hair was held back with a red headband. The dark eyes gazed with curiosity.

"Yes, General," Slow said in his Lakota accent.

"President Crockett was remarking on the plight of the Cherokee," I said. "There seems nothing we can do to help them. Have you any ideas?"

"Many speak of the *Tsalagi*. Their lodges lay north along the Red River, among the Texas hills," Slow said, having listened to many stories. But a month before, he had barely heard of the Cherokee.

"Most still live in the United States," I said.

"Their days are done," Slow pronounced.

"Is this the word of the Great Spirit?" I asked in jest.

"It is the history of your people. Do you think I have not asked

3

these questions of Butler and Hughes?" he answered.

Smart kid. I shouldn't have teased him.

"Ya gots any suggestions?" Crockett asked, leaning across me to look at Slow. I pushed him back.

"The *Tsalagiyi Nvdagi* must choose a new path. They can be friends or enemies," Slow replied.

"An' if they be enemies?" Crockett said.

"Then General Custer will attack. There will be no mercy," Slow declared.

"For God's Sake, son, I don't go attacking without mercy," I protested, for it had never been my way. Despite some unflattering press notices.

"Your ways of mercy come to an end, as the former lives of the *Tsalagiyi Nvdagi* come to an end. They have no choice. Either do you," Slow said.

"We've got some trouble up ahead. I want you to stay with the supply wagons. Protect Morning Star and Isabella for me," I urged.

"These soldiers from Mexico, have they come so far to die?" Slow asked.

"They want to defend their country," I answered.

"Warriors of the People fight for our families. We fight for our hunting grounds," Slow remarked. "Do these soldiers not live far away? Beyond the big desert?"

"They do," I admitted.

"Then they are fools," Slow decided.

He pulled Vic up, waited for E Company to pass by, and then rode to the rear of the column where his sister Morning Star was riding with Isabella Seguin.

"Kinda blood-thirsty, don't ya think?" Crockett observed.

"Sioux," I replied, for it said all that was needed.

We rode on for another hour through rolling foothills. I did not deploy the regiment, for we were still a good ten miles from Goliad. And dividing the command without knowing the enemy's whereabouts seemed unwise. I'd learned that such tactics do not always work out for the best.

The trail ran south parallel with the San Antonio River, which was somewhere off to our right. Low sage covered mountains rose on the left. My five companies, along with the wagons and artillery, were strung out for two miles.

Just after noon, Sergeant James Butler rode toward us at a steady gait. Jimmy was a true veteran. Thirty-two years old, five and a half feet tall, he had gray eyes, sandy hair, and the ruddy complexion of a cavalryman. His civilian occupation had been New York farmer before enlisting in the army. After the Alamo, I had offered him a lieutenant's commission. His reply was that of a proud non-commissioned officer, in language that may not be repeated here.

"Colonel Custer's respects, sir," Butler said, not bothering to salute. "We got a Mexican army 'bout three miles up ahead blocking the river crossing. Mostly light infantry. Tom's guessing its General Urrea, but we never did find out where Santa Anna went after he retreated from Béjar. We saw a few elements of Sesma's cavalry."

"Colonel Custer's suggestions?" I inquired, suspecting he had some.

"Says it might be good to scout the fords to the left, maybe cross downriver and make contact with Fannin," Butler said.

"What direction does this river run? How deep? How fast? Is the enemy spread out or concentrated?" I asked, my voice higher when excited.

"Can't say for sure, but probably a good ford every few miles, running west to east, then turns south."

"The river will not be deep until the spring thaw," Captain Juan Seguin said, riding a spirited mustang.

The son of my new business partner, Erasmo Seguin, Juan was just a few months short of thirty. Lanky, smart and easy-going. Of French and Mexican descent, his family was prominent in San Antonio and respected throughout Texas. Formally an officer in Houston's army, Seguin's knowledge of the terrain was proving indispensable.

"Captain, please report to General Keogh. Have your rangers seek Urrea's right flank," I ordered.

"*Si, General Custer. Gracias,*" Seguin said, waving his company to follow.

"Voss," I summoned.

The twenty-six year old corporal came running. Blond-haired, blue-eyed with a light complexion, Voss served well as my regimental trumpeter.

"Yes, sir," Voss reported in his Hanoverian accent.

"*Officer's Call,*" I ordered, letting Voss blow the bugle. There could be no harm if the enemy already knew we were coming.

Within a few minutes, Crockett, Algernon Smith and Bill Cooke were in attendance, accompanied by John Baugh, Almaron Dickenson and Mario Sepulveda. Captain Nathaniel Brister, leading B Company, was still a mile back. My officer were a combination of the original Seventh Cavalry and men who had served me at the Alamo.

Colonel Juan Almonte rode up a moment later, still uncomfortable acting as my adjutant. Abducted into my service following General Castrillón's surrender, Almonte was in his early thirties, an intelligent staff officer born in Nocupétaro. He had lived for a time in New Orleans and spoke perfect English. His father, the Mexican patriot José María Morelos, had been executed for treason twenty years before.

"We have a situation," I explained. "Seems Tom got stopped at the ford and can't get across without our help."

"Maybe Crockett can fly us across?" Cooke teased.

"No time for comedy, Canada. This could be serious," I said. "If Urrea has a free hand to hold the river crossings, Goliad must already have fallen."

"We're too late?" Baugh asked.

"Urrea may be using a holding force to delay us while pressing La Bahia," Keogh suggested.

"We've had no word from Fort Defiance," Baugh mentioned, though with the countryside swarming with cavalry patrols, messages might have been intercepted.

"Gentlemen, we will attack," I ordered. "Captain Dickenson, bring the artillery up to support Colonel Custer at the ford. Captain Sepulveda, have your teamsters hurry the train along. I don't want Dickenson's guns running out of ammunition. Myles, I want you to probe toward the left. Cross the river where you can and find their line of supply. Burn whatever you can't bring back."

Being a true Irishman, Keogh's face lit up like a Christmas pudding.

"And you, General Custer?" Mark Kellogg asked.

I didn't even know Kellogg was riding with the command. The last I'd heard, the former reporter for the *Bismarck Tribune* had gone to Gonzales. In his early forties, Kellogg wore a rumpled blue suit, tall leather boots, and a yellow straw hat. His dark brown eyes were always filled with a smirking challenge.

"What are you doing here? Thought you were looking for Houston?" I inquired.

"Houston is getting ready to fall back on San Felipe, when he's not getting drunk," Kellogg said. "I didn't see much point in staying around."

"Do you know his plans?" I asked.

"The Brazos Convention is standing by their declaration of independence," Kellogg reported. "Trouble is, they don't have any money, and they fight with each other more than anything else. That doesn't answer my question, general. What are you doing to do?"

"We'll branch off to the right. See if we can take the enemy in flank," I replied, tightening my belt.

The Goliad Road was the primary avenue from the port town of Copano to San Antonio, wide enough for wagons. The countryside to the west was less promising. Rolling hills and tangled thickets stretched as far as the eye could see. But there were buffalo trails, and I was leading a cavalry outfit. Anyplace the buffalo could go, the Seventh could go, too.

"Crockett, keep the column moving forward. E Company, you're with me," I said, seeing a worn path.

The forty of us followed the narrow trail through thick brush, then into a long valley. Portions were swampy due to the recent rain. A mile on, I led the command into the woods, scouting the best path. A few scattered shots were heard in the distance.

"Call the company forward, but quietly," I said to my color bearer.

"One company to turn their flank, General?" Sergeant Hughes asked, waiting for a chance to unfurl our colors.

Bobby Hughes had been my color bearer for several years now. Thirty-six years old, standing at my own height of 5'9", and a bit stocky for a cavalryman, he had the deep blue eyes and bushy brown hair of one born in Dublin. Though most of the non-commissioned officers carried Springfields, Hughes kept a Henry lever-action 16-shot repeating rifle in his saddle sheath.

"We'll just need to see what they've got, Bobby. Should be a small holding force," I answered.

"And if it ain't?" Butler said.

"Tom has a hundred men. So does Keogh. Crockett is coming up with two hundred more. The enemy should have more to worry

7

about than gadflies like us."

"General George Armstrong Custer? A gadfly?" Sergeant Butler said.

"That's what General Grant called me," I replied.

The trail took a turn south toward the river, passing through a large meadow. I saw birds but no game. The firing from downriver intensified from scattered reports to an occasional volley. And then an artillery shot.

"That can't be Dickenson, sir. There hasn't been enough time," Butler said.

He was right. A final line of trees separated my command from the San Antonio River, the underbrush thick except where the buffalo trails crept though. I looked back along our line moving in column of twos through the woods, knowing there was barely enough space. The men did not look afraid, but they understood the situation.

"Let us go first, sir," Voss said, coming up with Private Watson. Corporal French and Private Knecht crowded forward, too.

"Can't let our general get shot by a sentry," French said.

His impertinence irked me. Was I letting discipline get too lax?

"Dismount. Horse holders to the rear. Rifles at the ready," I said, for we were all sensing an unseen danger.

"Look, sir. Two rifle companies, at least. And they're getting ready to cross," Sergeant Hughes said, pointing through the trees at the far bank fifty yards away.

I counted sixty to seventy Mexican infantry in full battle dress. Half a dozen officers rode along their line keeping order on worn horses. They had no artillery but appeared well armed. Nor did they look concerned. This was a veteran force.

"It's an ambush," Butler said, checking the chamber on his .45 caliber 1874 Sharps carbine.

"There's more coming up through the trees. They're holding Tom at the Goliad Road while sending out units to turn our flanks," Hughes guessed. "This Urrea fellow ain't no slouch."

"Indeed he isn't," I agreed.

I tried to picture the terrain in my mind like I had at Yellow Tavern. The Rebs had been seeking our flanks, but we refused to give ground. Jeb Stuart got himself killed trying to press an impossible position.

"Private Watson, go back the way we came. Report to Colonel Custer. Tell him the enemy is attacking in force and to consolidate his position," I ordered. "Have Keogh recalled. I don't want to take on Urrea's army advancing through these woods."

"Yes, sir," Watson said, disappearing almost instantly. A reliable young man.

"Bobby, Jimmy, it appears we'll be the ones holding the river crossing. Tie the horses in the trees and spread the company along this growth."

"Ammunition ain't gonna last long," Butler warned.

"Don't know that we have a choice. Get moving, Jimmy," I answered.

I took a position in the center of the line, readying my Remington Rolling Block .50 caliber hunting rifle. I only had twenty rounds, but the Remington had the best range in the army. Eight hundred yards on a good day, while the British Brown Bess carried by the Mexican soldiers were barely accurate at fifty. And I had a plan. What troubled me was the lack of warning. If Fannin knew such a large force was nearing Goliad, why hadn't he sent word? Was his command wiped out?

The enemy paused on the river's edge, waiting for the rear column to catch up. They had a small meadow to work in, unlike the north bank that had trees right down to the water's edge. A decisive advantage for a defensive force, or so I hoped. But none of my doubts were revealed, for a successful commander never projects anything but confidence.

The Mexicans finally formed up. Downstream, the firing was now general. Cannon and rifle fire echoed through the trees. Smoke began to drift along the skyline. This was no skirmish, but a significant engagement, and I desperately wished to be at the ford. But I had stumbled into my own obligation, and Tom would know how to handle anything Urrea threw at him.

"We're ready, sir. And so are they. Reckon we should kill the officers first?" Butler asked.

"You bagged yourself a general at the Alamo. Isn't one enough, Jimmy?" I asked, for I had seen the fatal shot that killed Cos on the north wall.

"Ain't a full hand without some colonels and captains," he replied.

"Kill the officers first," I agreed, for that was a conclusion I'd already reached. A leaderless army was less likely to make an effective attack under stressful conditions.

The first private was just stepping into the water, a short fellow in a red tunic, white cross straps over his chest, a tall back shako hat, and white trousers now grimy from the trail dust. His leather shoes were badly worn, and it looked like he hadn't shaved in a week. I estimated the river at forty feet wide and about four feet deep. The enemy would need to hold their muskets and powder above their shoulders to keep them dry.

"Okay, Jimmy, you have the first shot," I granted.

Butler's rifle bucked, the loud crack scaring birds from the tree tops, and a gray-haired major toppled from his black stallion, a bullet through his chest. I shot the captain riding next to him, then chambered another round and killed the sergeant major standing at their side. Hughes shot a lieutenant, a sergeant, and the color bearer in rapid succession. And then my entire troop opened fire on the surprised enemy, twelve of them falling in wounded piles.

The majority of the bewildered Mexicans retreated into the trees, and most kept going, heading toward whatever camp they had come from. But one brave unit refused to flee. A surviving officer rallied a platoon of sharpshooters dressed in white. Possibly some of the famous Cazadores. Though the river was now shrouded in gun smoke, I could see the sergeants arranging a line of forty men, half kneeling and half standing behind them. Belatedly, I realized they carried Baker rifles. A fusillade of lead tore through the trees, felling several of my men.

This was not an ordinary force we were facing. We had captured two score of Baker rifles in San Antonio, an English weapon only used by elite corps. I'd heard that some of them were even made in the Tower of London. The .625 caliber model had an accurate range of 100 yards, far better than a Brown Bess, though they were slower to reload. With our own .45 caliber ammunition in short supply, a company armed with Baker rifles would be a boon.

A series of scattered shots caused several of the sharpshooters to fall, but they were quickly reloading, protected by a cloud of musket smoke. I ignored the officers and began targeting the rank and file, for they knew their business and needed no orders. After two additional exchanges, a handful of survivors finally fled into the forest, leaving half their unit on the field.

"You okay, Jimmy? How about you, Bobby?" I called out.

"Well enough, General," Hughes said, having walked our line checking for casualties. "We gots three wounded, but none too bad."

"Should we cross over and take their equipment?" Butler asked.

We needed all the powder we could find, and I wanted those Baker rifles now lying on the beach. But I feared some of the enemy may still be lingering in the trees, and from the sound of heavy guns downstream, my regiment was fully engaged.

"Leave six men to cover the ford," I said. "Corporal French can have the command. Or would you rather be a sergeant, Henry?"

"Sergeant sounds fine, sir. Long as you don't try to make me no officer," French answered, much to Butler's delight. Like Butler and Hughes, French was a sturdy veteran. Strong, lean and swarthy from duty on the plains. A good man in a fight.

"It's not like being an officer is such a bad thing," I protested.

"Ain't no good thing, neither," Butler said, slapping French on the shoulder.

"Men, find your horses. We're moving out," I said, running for Traveller.

The sturdy stallion was unperturbed by the recent battle, munching flowers and casually relieving himself. I didn't wait for the troop, but mounted up and rode out, anxious to discover what was happening on the Goliad Road.

Cannon fire, but not just the Mexican 4-pounders. They were being answered by Dickenson's 6-pounders, both guns active. It made me hopeful, for I sensed no panic.

Butler rode past me, then Hughes. Traveller was a good horse, but he wasn't Vic. It made me sorry I'd loaned him to Slow. Half the troop was ahead of me when we regained the main road, turning right for the sound of the guns. We met Mitch Bouyer a mile later.

Bouyer was my most valuable scout, the half breed son of a French Canadian trader and Santee Sioux squaw. He'd been loaned to me by General Terry for the Little Big Horn march, and stayed with the command to the end. Bouyer and I didn't always get along, for he could be crusty and insubordinate, but his faults were few compared to his virtues.

11

"Lots of Mex'cans," he reported. "Tommy took a chunk a high ground. Kan't find Keogh, and Seguin took off with the T'janos."

"Deserted?" I asked.

"Nah, don't think thar's no desertin'. But they's a disappeared."

"What about the supply train?"

"Ole Davy got 'em in right enough," Bouyer said. "I'm s'pposed to take you off to the left. Lower piece of the road takin' fire."

We followed Bouyer down into a shallow valley and back up a gentle series of lightly wooded hills, close enough to hear the musket balls ripping through the trees. A hundred yards back of the river, we came to a dry creek bed filled with our wagons, and just beyond, a low ridge where fifty men were lying down along the crest. A tent had been set up for the wounded. Younger members of our command were carrying ammunition to the artillery set just behind the hill, Brister directing fire while Dickenson kept the guns in action. The position seemed organized and under control.

"Welcome back, George. 'Fraid ya was gonna miss the fightin'," Crockett said, helping a wounded man down from the hill. His ammunition belt was empty, and he wouldn't be the only one.

"Big army?" I asked.

"Not so big as the Alamo, but plenty big enough," Crockett answered, moving on.

I ran past the artillery toward the top of the hill, kneeling in a shallow ravine just below the crest. There were fewer trees here, a gentle wind scattering the smoke of battle. Two companies of the Seventh were nearby, all using muskets captured in San Antonio. It was good not to waste our .45 ammunition.

"What's the situation, Tom?" I inquired, drawing one of my Webley Bulldogs.

"Doing fine, Autie," he answered, face smudged with powder. "About six hundred infantry. Some of Semsa's cavalry. We caught them crossing the river. Or they caught us. Kinda hard to tell which."

"Keogh?"

"Off on the left looking for their flank. Seguin is behind the lines somewhere with his rangers."

"What's the plan?" I asked.

"Our artillery has them stopped. Now that the command is drawn up, we'll press their position," Tom said. "Sepulveda, order your boys down behind those fallen trees near the road. Prepare for volley fire."

"Who is the general now?" I asked.

"It's what you would have done," Tom said, lowering his head.

"Maybe. If I'd been given the chance," I answered, walking back down the hill toward a small clump of oaks that had become our headquarters.

A long spiny branch was hung with a swallow tail Seventh Cavalry guidon and the silken gold flag of the New Orleans Greys. We had left the Alamo's double-starred flag back in San Antonio, the tattered banner only fit for a museum.

My aide-de-camp, Major William Cooke, had drawn a map of the position and was dispatching Tom's orders. New members of the command were acting as orderlies, running to and fro. The sweet sound of cannon fire echoed off the hill.

"What do you need, General?" Cooke asked, briefly looking up from his memo book. Now thirty years old, and known at Queen's Own due to his Canadian birth, Cooke had served me loyally since joining the Seventh ten years before. Without doubt the tall young man, famous for his long sideburns, was my most efficient officer.

"Ammunition for my revolvers," I replied.

"Third wagon," Cooke said.

I expected him, or an orderly, to fetch the bullets for me, but everyone was busy. I went to find the ammunition boxes myself.

"Hello, George," a lilting voice greeted.

It was Isabella, her sleeves rolled up and blood on her blue cotton skirt. Her hands were filled with bandages for the wounded.

"You're awful close to the battle, *dulce paloma*," I said in surprise.

"This is Texas," she replied. "Women do not shrink from their duties here. Sweet dove or not."

I looked around, saw everyone was preoccupied, and gave her a quick peck on the cheek. The lovely senorita blushed.

I heard the volley of Sepulveda's men, followed by shouting and a brief lull. Something was happening, so I grabbed a handful of ammunition and ran back up the hill, loading the pistols as I went. Voss and Private Donnelly of F Company had a nice spot among the rocks, so I knelt between them.

"They're backing off, sir," Voss said, holding his fire.

The ground across the river was rough, strewn with deep ruts. I saw no wagons, no cannon, and only a few horses. Of the six hundred that had faced Tom, only a few dozen were left.

"Let's go!" I shouted, jumping to my feet with both pistols drawn.

I ran down the hill to the water's edge, firing several times and watching with glee as the enemy fled. Then noticed I was alone.

"Autie, get back up here, you damn fool!" Tom yelled from the hilltop.

The command was spread out along the crest, still holding their positions. Tom's sergeants were keeping the men in line, refusing to let them advance. Bullets kicked up dirt at my feet, and a shot whistled near my ear. Butler ran down the slope, grabbing my arm to pull me back.

"Damn it, Tom! What the hell?" I cursed. "We had them on the run."

"And we're going to let them go," Tom calmly replied. "Those woods are a maze of narrow trails."

"We can run them to ground," I protested.

"That's what Grant thought at the Wilderness."

"These aren't Lee's boys. They're half-starved conscripts."

"I'm not taking the command forward without reconnaissance," he insisted.

"*You* aren't going to?"

"I have command of the field," Tom replied.

As much as I wanted to object, I had too much respect for Tom to call him out. Especially in front of the men. But I intended to have a serious conversation later.

It took an hour to reform. Urrea had fallen back in good order. Baugh told me they were headed south, possibly toward Refugio. A logical place to resupply.

Late in the day, we finally crossed a shallow ford of the San Antonio River, making room in the wagons for the wounded. Sergeant French reported, having captured thirty much needed Baker rifles on his portion of the battlefield. And proving the soundness of my judgment in promoting him. Captain Seguin was still absent, but Keogh returned. His command looked beat up, their uniforms dusty and tattered.

"'Twas a hell of a thing," Keogh said, digging through his saddlebags for his flask. At least he didn't drink while in combat like

Reno had.

"Unable to ford the river?" I asked.

"Nah, didn't need to. We skirted a bend an' found a couple hundred Mexicans spread out along the river road. Pretty ornery, too. Looked like they'd been marchin' all night," Keogh said. "We took too much fire to make a crossing. Lost Captain Carey. Sergeant Pico. Couple others."

"Goliad must have fallen. No other excuse for Fannin not warning us," I said.

"Guess we'll know soon enough," Keogh replied. "What does Tommy think?"

"He's busy organizing the wagons. Half of the ammunition for the Springfields is gone," I answered. "I'm going on. Take your company to the right. Follow Urrea for a few miles in case he decides to turn back. I'll see you at Fort Defiance."

"Yes, sir," Keogh said, offering a salute before riding out.

"On to Goliad, sir?" Hughes asked.

"Yes. We'll take point with F Company. Tell Colonel Custer to catch up soon as he can," I instructed, giving Traveller a nudge.

———————

The muddy road rising from the river was heavily wooded, leading into a broad winter meadow. Beyond the meadow, on a low plain, was Presidio La Bahia. The old Spanish fort had been renamed Fort Defiance by Texas rebels after capturing it the previous October. Unlike the adobe buildings that were typical of west Texas, this compound was made of stone. With eight foot walls for defense and several bastions for cannon, the fort looked like a defensible position. A long single-story headquarters fronted the west side of the enclosure, and a tall church rose above the northwest corner. A white silk flag with a single blue star flew from the roof. Through my binoculars, I read the words *Liberty or Death* painted on the fabric. The wind had not been kind to their banner, much of it ragged along the edges.

I heard pounding hooves behind me.

"Reporting, Autie," Tom said, riding to my side on his winded Athena.

The brown Kentucky thoroughbred looked tired, as were all the horses, and in need of extra care. Even Traveller was drooping his head.

"Bad?"

"Twelve dead, twenty-eight wounded. Doctor Lord needs dry quarters for a hospital," Tom said.

"We're almost there."

"That's not a Mexican flag flying over the fort," Tom observed. "Is it a trap?"

"No, I don't think so. Urrea must have bypassed them to ambush us. I'm surprised we haven't seen Fannin yet," I said, seeing no activity near the gate.

The plateau upon which Fort Defiance rested had been cleared of trees for the most part, the land used for grazing and farming. And to establish a field of fire should the fort be threatened. Thick forest grew to the west and south. Below the fort, on a gently sloping hill, were three dozen thatched adobe houses, but the residents had apparently fled. All I saw were a few broken down wagons and a barking dog. The chicken coops were empty.

"Voss, call up C Troop," Tom suddenly ordered.

Voss blew the *Advance* before I could object.

"What's that for?" I asked.

"Being careful, Autie. Just being careful," Tom said.

Tom turned Athena around to ride back down the line, alerting the men for action.

I reached the base of the hill, stopping two hundred yards from the northwest corner of the fort. Half a dozen men, presumably Fannin and his officers, were watching from the bastion. Butler and Hughes rode up, followed by the elusive Juan Seguin.

"Captain Seguin, I was getting worried about you," I chided.

"We have scouted the trail, sir. General Urrea was camped five miles south of here, but never attacked La Bahia. They are retreating," he reported.

"Did you run into messengers from Fannin?" I asked.

"No, sir. None," Seguin replied.

Crockett rushed up on his borrowed black stallion, his best friend right next him riding a brown Spanish mare. Micajah Autry was a thin middle-aged Quaker from North Carolina who had ridden to San Antonio along with several volunteers calling themselves the

Tennessee Boys. Which was odd, for few of them were actually from Tennessee.

"What's wrong, George?" Crockett asked. He looked weary and was rubbing a sore shoulder. Was the bear hunter getting old?

"We're not getting a friendly reception," I speculated, for the gate remained closed even after our banners were recognized.

"I'll see to it," Crockett said, giving his mount a kick. Only Autry followed, the rest of my staff waiting at the foot of the hill.

Tom returned with C Troop, now armed with our new Baker rifles. Except for Tom and Cooke, who held 1873 .44-40 Winchester rifles. My officers didn't seem surprised by the situation.

Half a mile away, on the far side of the meadow, I saw my scouts return with E Company. Bouyer and Smith dismounted, watching for my reaction. I raised a hand to keep them still.

Perhaps I was tired, but gradually it dawned on me that Fannin's men had not sortied out to support our attack, though they had pleaded with us to come to their aid but a week before. Had there had been a change of heart?

Crockett reached the bastion, looking up at the officers on the wall and making gestures. We were too far back to hear the conservation, though I detected some frustration on Crockett's part. I saw no other activity in the fort. The pasture was surprisingly quiet, as if waiting for some drama.

A few minutes later, Crockett came back, walking his horse by the reins. I went to meet him partway, leaving Traveller with Voss.

"Fannin's a right nervous. Says he'll meet with da two of us, and Mister Seguin," Crockett reported. "Wants the rest of the battalion to camp in the village outside the walls."

"What kind of bull is this? We just fought a battle for that son of a bitch," Butler said, cocking his Sharps.

"Colonel Crockett, my compliments to Colonel Fannin. Tell him we'll be along shortly," I said, giving Crockett an encouraging glance.

"General!" Butler protested.

"Quiet down, Jimmy. I'm still the senior officer here."

Butler settled down, but his opinion was widely shared, making the men angry.

Crockett left his horse with my hired Negro, John Armstrong, and trudged back up the hill where a six-pounder was poking over the wall.

"Autie, we can't . . ." Tom started to say.

"I have a plan," I interrupted.

"That's more like it," Cooke said.

"Okay, this is what I want," I whispered. "The moment Captain Seguin and I enter the gate, bring the entire command forward on the double. No noise, no bugles. Just come on quick. Major Baugh, they have a blind spot near the low wall behind the church. Send your men over if you can. Butler, Hughes, you'll follow me though the gate. What do you say, Juan? Willing to enter the lion's den?"

"My honor, General," Seguin agreed, checking his matched pair of silver flintlock pistols. My sidearms were ready, both Webleys reloaded. A fine Spanish saber hung at my side.

Cooke had C Troop's guidon waved to the soldiers across the meadow. Smith gave a subtle nod and pulled E Company back into the woods for instructions. Crockett finished his talk with the men on the wall and moved to his right where a heavy oak door provided entrance between the corner bastion and the headquarters.

"How well do you know Fannin?" I asked Seguin.

"We served together at the siege of Béjar," Seguin said. "Governor Robinson tried to appoint him commander of our forces over Houston during the feud with Smith. There has been much confusion ever since. I think Fannin is a brave man, but he has not been able to control his soldiers."

"Let's go, Captain," I said to Seguin, leaving our horses behind.

Crockett and Autry waited at the portal as the heavy door swung inward. Seguin and I quickly caught up. Voss and my two sergeants followed twenty paces behind. Inside was Colonel James Fannin, medium height with thinning sandy hair and vivid blue eyes. His blue woolen uniform was smartly pressed, a jaunty red sash tied around his waist. I guessed him in his early thirties, about Tom's age. Four of his officers stood by, well-dressed but not in a military fashion. They looked more like unsuccessful lawyers than soldiers.

Beyond the small group, on the parade ground of the large compound, were dozens of worn tents, supply wagons, livestock, and perhaps three hundred loitering militia. I guessed the area at three acres, and noticed wooden ramparts built inside the walls serving as firing platforms. Such ramparts certainly would have benefited the

18

Alamo when we needed them.

"Mr. Custer, I assume?" Fannin said in a Georgia accent, extending his hand.

I drew my saber, putting the point to his throat. Seguin produced both pistols, pointing at Fanning's lieutenants. Before they could finish gasping with astonishment, Hughes, Butler and Voss charged through the gate, Colts drawn.

"Sir!" Fannin shouted in indignation.

Crockett seemed equally shocked, but it couldn't be helped. Soon the pounding of shod hooves announced the arrival of C Troop, the men jumping from their horses and pouring through the gate. Gradually, the volunteers in the plaza noticed Fannin's predicament, but none knew what to do. And many seemed not to care. Tom and Cooke appeared on the bastion to my left, climbing over the wall next to the six-pounder and aiming their Winchesters.

"Call your sergeants together," I ordered.

Fannin stood frozen, unable to utter a sound. His subordinates seemed confused, looking to Crockett for direction.

"Reckon you boys should do as General Custer says," Crockett urged.

Fannin's adjutant proved to be a burly New Hampshirite named Joe Chadwick, who went to deliver the summons. Chadwick seemed a straightforward fellow, neither ruffled nor unduly alarmed. I knew him to be a topographical engineer, and like Fannin, a drop-out from West Point.

"Crockett, I must protest," Fannin said, finally gathering himself.

"Ya kinda brought this on yourself, Jimmie," Crockett said.

As my men continued to filter into the fort, Chadwick brought a dozen sergeants forward. Or presumed sergeants, for none wore anything resembling uniforms except a few of the New Orleans Greys.

"Colonel Fannin, you requested our help, and now keep us from these walls. I will have an immediate explanation," I demanded, though I needed none. The answer was obvious. I lowered the sword, but kept it ready.

"We have orders from President Burnett to ignore your authority, sir. The provisional government has reformed under the declaration of March 2nd," he said. "General Houston has reached Gonzales at the head of a thousand men. He will be here in a few days."

19

"Sam don't got no thousand men," Crockett said. "Our man Kellogg saw him just last week. There's barely two hundred volunteers, and most a them don't got no horses."

"Houston ordered us to fall back to Victoria," Chadwick said with the bearing of a gentleman. His accent was educated.

"Then you had best get moving," Tom said, coming down the ramp with his rifle pointed at Fannin's gut. It was a bit melodramatic, but effective.

"We can't leave for several more days. We're still waiting for oxen to move the cannon," Fannin explained, nervously fingering the hilt of his silver-plated sword.

"We also have men in the field," Chadwick added. "Colonel Ward and Captain King are evacuating colonists from Refugio."

"Dr. Grant was killed at Agua Dulce. Most of his men are missing. We can't retreat until we know they've retired in good order," Fannin said, seeking to defend his actions.

Their excuses did not impress me. I walked out into the compound for a better view of the fort, seeing five small artillery pieces. Most were 4-pounders, easy to use and effective at short range. Several ammunition carts stood nearby loaded with powder and shot. When a wagon gate opened on the south side, Smith rode in with E Company, forming a line before a row of workshops. Sergeant French climbed up on the wall to make his presence known, holding the troop's guidon.

"Colonel Fannin, we will have a talk in your office," I said, putting the sword away. "Mr. Chadwick, lead your militia outside the fort."

"Fort Defiance is our station, sir!" Fannin objected.

"Colonel Custer, help these gentlemen with their kit," I instructed. "Weapons and knapsacks only. We'll need the wagons for our wounded."

"Yes, General," Tom said with a salute. "Hughes, French, lend a hand."

Fannin looked fit to kill, but surrounded as he was, could hardly do more than frown. Chadwick took the situation for what it was, ordering the sergeants to round up their men. Some were New Orleans Greys, friends of those who had served with me at the Alamo. Others were recently arrived militia from the states calling themselves the Georgia Battalion, Alabama Red Rovers, and Mobile

20

Grays. But few showed any unit discipline, coming and going as they pleased.

The headquarters was better arrayed than I expected, with maplewood furniture, a conference table, and colorful knitted curtains. The plaster walls were painted yellow. Woven carpets protected from the cold stone floor. Inside the doorway, I found racks for spare arms. Of which there were few. I understood that until the previous fall, the fort had been held by the Mexican army and largely stripped of supplies by the conquering Texans before laying siege to Béjar.

I sat in Fannin's high-backed chair, making him stand before me. Knowing what I did of another time, one that had not yet happened, it was hard for me to forget that Fannin had gotten his entire command massacred after surrendering at Coleto Creek. Urrea had offered honorable terms, or so it seemed, but he was overruled by Santa Anna. On a bright Palm Sunday morning in 1836, four hundred of Fannin's men had been marched out of the fort and shot.

I did not associate Fannin's failure with my own at the Little Big Horn, for in my fevered dreams of a grass covered Montana ridge, there was no surrender. Only the massacre.

"Colonel Fannin, you know the Béjar Declaration does not acknowledge the Brazos convention, nor does it tolerate the ratification of a slave constitution. You subscribed to this in your letter requesting the Seventh Cavalry's assistance," I sternly rebuked.

"The situation changed. Houston and—"

"Houston isn't here, and Urrea was," Cooke interrupted. "We saved your damned butt. Is this how you show gratitude?"

"We could have held. Fort Defiance is well manned. We have cannon," Fannin replied.

"Enough to hold off a thousand veteran Mexican troops? I think not," I disagreed.

"We were about to fall back on Victoria. Plenty of supplies there," he answered.

"I do not wish to delay you. You may withdraw with your volunteers. You will travel with what you can carry," I decided.

"But our cannon? Our wagons?" he angrily said.

"Those belong to the Seventh Cavalry. And sir, if I ever find you under arms against my command again, I promise to put you up

21

against the nearest tree and shoot you. Do I make myself clear?" I said, giving him my coldest stare.

"You may have the upper hand now, Mister Custer, but it won't last," Fannin vowed. "Thousands of volunteers are flowing in from the United States. Thousands upon thousands. From Alabama and Louisiana. Georgia and South Carolina. It won't matter how many browns, blacks and renegade whites you got. Or traitors like Crockett. It won't matter how good your guns are. Texas will become a son of the South whether you like it or not."

I suspected he had good cause for his opinion, but that was tomorrow's battle. There was enough on my plate already.

"Bill, get this son of a bitch out of my sight," I said.

Cooke hustled the frustrated man from the headquarters and all the way to the gate without letting him gather his personal effects. I heartily approved.

"Not so good makin' friends today," Crockett said, having watched silently from the corner.

"Fannin makes his living selling slaves. I should have realized he'd be reluctant to give up his profession," I replied.

"Seems mighty confident, in a frightened rabbit sort a way," Crockett remarked.

"I notice he didn't seem too pleased with you," I remarked.

"Ain't worried 'bout it," Crockett said. "Only man e'er stayed mad at me was Andy Jackson, an' only then 'cuz I met him halfway."

"Many of the invaders he spoke of are coming from Tennessee, David. If you're having second thoughts, now's the time to say so."

"Ain't got no second thoughts, George. Wouldn't be here if I did. A man's got to know what's right, then go ahead," he said.

"Amen to that."

We walked out into the busy courtyard. The wagon gate was still open and most of the former garrison was slowly departing, their gear carried in bedrolls slung over their shoulders. Tom was smiling.

"Eighty-eight horses, ten oxen, score of cattle, a few sheep, and a thousand chickens," he reported. "Not much in the way of arms, but a nice stash of powder. Dr. Lord has taken over their hospital."

"There is flour, too. The women of the fort have been busy making bread," Seguin said, a warm wheat loaf in his hand. He offered to share but I declined.

"What's going on over there?" I said, pointing to a conspiratorial group of militia.

"That's Baugh talking to the New Orleans Greys. There's about thirty of them. He thinks they should sign up with us, but being Southerners, I wouldn't count on it," Tom said.

"Will Baugh stay if the Greys don't?" I asked.

"Hope so. John's a good man," Tom replied.

"What about Brister? He's a Grey, too."

"Nat's more interested in gold than slaves. I think he'll stand fast," Tom guessed.

"Keep an eye on them. If they leave, make sure they don't take any of our guns with them," I said, walking up the stone steps to the bastion overlooking the river road.

Our wagons finished the climb from the ford, and the artillery pieces were placed below the bastion aimed at the village where Fannin was reorganizing his evicted army. Lieutenant Sepulveda and his Zacatecan militia would keep a close watch on our former allies. A few minutes later, I saw our civilian contingent arriving, Slow in the lead riding Vic followed by Isabella and Morning Star on their spirited mares. Kellogg was with them, no doubt telling of his adventure to Gonzales.

Señor Erasmo Seguin, a short but stout *don* in his early fifties, was driving a two-wheeled cart pulled by a cooperative donkey. Ten of his vaqueros rode alongside him. Seguin waved when he saw me on the wall, the smile reminding me of my father. Hughes took down Fannin's banner and replaced it with our own, a white flag with a large black buffalo embroidered in the middle.

My regimental staff took over the headquarters, settling the women in the officer's quarters where the large fireplace would keep the room warm. Our servants moved next to the kitchen, cooking scrounged victuals. The first action I decided on was to rename Fort Defiance back to Presidio de La Bahia, for I would not defend a monument to Fannin's arrogance.

"Not a bad post," Tom said as I began a tour of the compound.

"Not good, either," Cooke said, making notes in his memo pad.

"Good for holding off a small force. Or Indians," I speculated.

"Hard to defend against a professional army. Should we blow it up?"

"No need for that," Cooke said. "If a Mexican force takes it, we can always take it back. If we want it. In the meantime, La Bahia is a valuable relay post between San Antonio and the coast."

I nodded agreement. The fort posed no threat to my anticipated operations, and could still prove an asset. And with west Texas being largely a wasteland threatened by the Comanche, the local population still needed such protections.

"We'll rest here until the wounded can be moved," I decided. "Have Seguin send out his scouts. It would be nice to know what our enemies are doing."

I walked the entire perimeter of the fort, inspecting the near empty warehouses, studying the stone bastions, and even spent a few minutes in the old church, where I noticed Slow speaking with a Spanish priest. By late afternoon, we saw Fannin's men drifting off to the east. The New Orleans Greys were going with him.

"Sorry, General," Major Baugh said, carrying his backpack.

He alone had come to explain his departure. The rest of Fannin's command was skulking off into the woods. Baugh handed back the Colt .45 I had given him.

"Leaving us?" I asked, tucking the pistol in my belt.

"'Fraid so, sir. The boys think we should stick with our own," Baugh said.

"John, I came to admire you at the Alamo. You're a brave man," I said, shaking his hand.

"Wish I could stay, sir," he replied.

"Don't get caught in arms against the Seventh," Tom warned with a frown. "Best tell your friends, too."

"Appreciate the advice, Colonel," Baugh said, doffing his cap and walking off.

Tom and I went back inside, finding space in Fannin's office. Our men were using the abandoned barracks, making fires and catching chickens for dinner. Angry gray clouds were threatening another storm.

"Thought they'd stay for the gold, if nothing else," I said.

"What gold?" Tom said.

"The gold in California."

"Ain't no gold in California, Autie. Lest, that's what Bill and I have

24

been whispering around."

"Why would you do that?" I asked. "It was our best hope of recruiting an army."

"And when thousands of men flock to California looking for gold, how do we control them?" Tom answered. "How many prospectors rushed west in 1849? Ten thousand? Twenty thousand? Fifty thousand?"

"They don't know where to look," I argued.

"Best we get there first. That's what Bill and I think. And it may be awhile if we're stuck here in Texas fighting Santa Anna and Sam Houston."

"One problem at a time, Tommy. Try not to scare off the rest of our recruits."

Raindrops started falling. Isabella and Morning Star entered the office with hot cups of coffee. Isabella draped a warm blanket over my shoulders. I gave her a quick kiss. In the main room, Slow and Señor Seguin were sitting before the fire hovering over a chessboard. I doubt Slow had ever seen such a game. Señor Seguin was giving him lessons.

"Mr. Fannin has left?" Isabella asked.

"Yeah, and took his army of traitors with him," Tom grumbled, sorry not to have shot him when we had the chance.

"General Urrea has withdrawn, also. Looks like we have La Bahia to ourselves," I said.

"Supper's ready, General," Ben announced from the kitchen door.

"Thank you, Mr. Travane," I answered, smelling a stew.

Ben's cooking skills were no accident. He had served as a steward on Atlantic trade ships, come to Mexico from Washington D.C. with Colonel Almonte, and was supervising Santa Anna's household when we first met in San Antonio. Stout, bald and a little gray, some thought Ben a former slave, but he was born a free man. After the Alamo, I had made Ben a sergeant and put him in charge of my commissary.

I took a seat at the table as John rushed to serve my meal. It was a thick vegetable stew with bits of chicken. The spoon was made of silver, engraved with a silver cross on the handle.

"Did you win the battle?" Morning Star asked, serving Tom herself.

Tom looked up. The long scar on his jaw, from a Confederate

25

bullet at Sailor's Creek, crinkled when he offered a tired grin.

Tom and I had met Morning Star, a charming nineteen-year-old beauty, on a cold Texas plain just after our miraculous transition from 1876 to 1836. Her family was being attacked by marauding buffalo hunters when Tom boldly rode to their rescue. We also saved her grandmother Walking-In-Grass, her cousins Spotted Eagle and Gray Wolf, and her younger brother, Slow. These wandering Sioux had ridden with us ever since. Gray Wolf was killed standing next to me at Cibolo Creek, the victim of a Mexican bullet.

"We didn't lose. Hard to say we won anything. Seems Urrea was just trying to slow us down," Tom said.

"I see Santa Anna's hand in this," Señor Seguin said, coming to sit with us.

Crockett and Autry arrived, sitting together at the end of the table.

"How would that be?" I asked.

"The dictator will regroup at Copano, then move along the coast where his ships can keep him supplied," Seguin explained. "Today was a message. If we continue south, we can be fought at every river crossing. We will grow weaker as he grows stronger."

"'Specially with Fannin's boys runnin' out on us," Autry said.

"Takin' up military science, Miciagh?" Crockett asked.

"Just sayin'," Autry replied, stuffing his mouth with a tortilla.

"Gots to be hard on these Southern boys, findin' fellow 'mericans standin' a'gin 'em," Crockett said.

"What about these other forces? Ward and King?" I asked, for my knowledge of them was vague.

"Defeated, though it seems Fannin hasn't gotten the news yet," Kellogg said, entering from the kitchen with a plate of tortillas. That he wasn't sharing.

Kellogg could be annoying, but his knowledge of Texas history had proven valuable. As a reporter for the *Bismarck Tribune*, and by proxy, the *New York Herald*, he'd had the luxury of studying western lore while I was making it.

"Captured?" Tom asked.

"Mostly. Some executed. Some got away. A few were supposed to be brought here and die with Fannin. Don't know what Urrea will do with them now," Kellogg explained, sitting next to Crockett.

"Your news from Gonzales?" I inquired.

"Far as I know, Houston is still there with about two hundred volunteers. They'd just heard about the Alamo," Kellogg said. "Houston didn't really believe Santa Anna had been defeated, though. Figures it's some kind of trick. They also weren't too happy about you and Crockett nullifying their declaration of independence."

"Too bad for them," Tom said, finding a bottle of wine and several glasses.

"I tried to ask Houston what he was going to do, but they called me a spy. Gave me twenty minutes to clear out. Heard you were headed for Goliad and thought I'd best report in," Kellogg explained.

"Think Houston will move on San Antonio?" I asked.

"Not likely. He's low on supply. Volunteers are untrained," Crockett said.

"My guess is Old Sam will fall back behind the Brazos. Maybe try an' find some artillery," Autry suggested.

"I hope you're right. Just in case, we better send a messenger to Harrington," Tom decided. "Green Jameson and Sergeant Major Sharrow may have less time to fortify Béjar than they know."

After dinner, we settled down in the main room enjoying the warmth of the large fireplace. Isabella sat next to me on a fur rug. Tom and Morning Star nestled in the corner. Señor Seguin and Slow were once again at the chessboard, shadows from the fire dancing off the pieces.

"You grasp this quickly, young man," Erasmo praised, though the two games they played were really no contest.

Slow looked over to me, his brows scrunched as if with a question, but declined to speak. When Señor Seguin turned in, Slow rearranged the chess board and waved me over.

"The old one is wise, but he does not understand war," Slow said, adjusting two rooks.

"He's a very good player. I've only beaten him once," I responded.

"In this chess, there are only two opponents."

"That's the way it's played," I said.

"In war, there are many enemies. Do you not have many enemies?"

"Yes, there are many."

Slow moved several black pieces, then several white pieces, and added half a dozen brown pieces from another set, forming three groups.

27

"If the white attacks the brown, the black will win. If the white attacks the black, the brown will win," he said, pushing pieces back and forth. "It is like the Seventh Cavalry. If you attack one of your enemies, the other enemy will win."

"I don't think it's that simple," I said, staring at the confused board.

"Then you are not thinking," Slow replied.

That night, Crockett and I shared the commandant's office, laying our blankets out near the hearth, for it was cold.

"Guess I should sort of apologize," Crockett said, using a stack of worn blankets as a mattress. The bear hunter's bones were chilled. I hardly had more than a thin fur between me and the slate floor.

"What for, David?" I asked.

"Kinda misjudged Fannin. Believed them letters he wrote us."

"I've got a hunch he's not the only one we'll have trouble with. Your friends in Tennessee may not take kindly to you riding with abolitionists," I said, trying to be gentle, for I'd had many comrades at West Point faced with a similar dilemma. Most had chosen wrong.

"Know'in what's a comin', don't see how it kin be no different," Crockett said. "I wouldn't be no kind of man if I let my country fall into civil war. Have armies marchin' through all over, burnin' farms and killin' folk. Maybe it's you who got the burr?"

"Me?"

"You was right optimistic in San Antone. Thought we'd march through Texas like shit through a goose. Now ya knows it ain't gonna be so easy. Maybe ya gots to think it through a bit?"

"Yeah, a bit," I admitted, rolling over for some sleep. My dreams were troubled, but at least there was no grassy hill.

Like the warriors of the People, the white men often challenge too many enemies and still expect victory. Yet foolishness in war is of little help to the families left behind. Wisdom dictates caution in battle, for is it not our women and children that we fight for? But to be a warrior is a great thing. I could not tell if Yellow Hair's vision of glory exceeded his grasp, for his vision was addled by a Strong Heart's ambition.

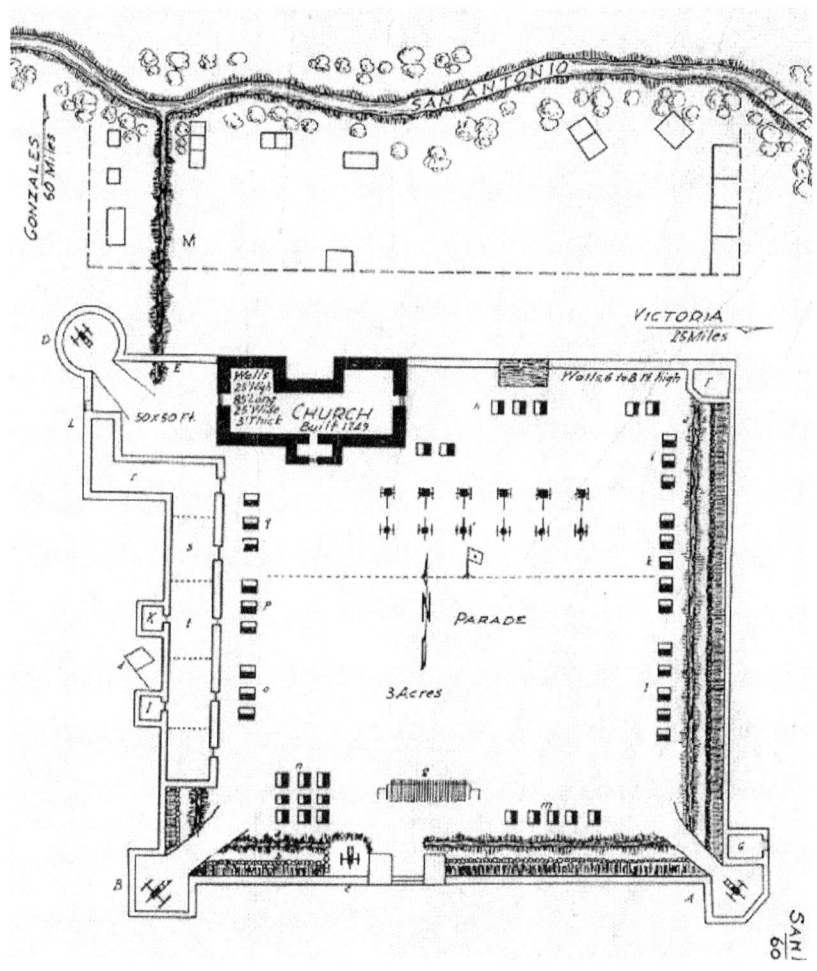

La Bahia, aka Fort Defiance, by Chadwick, 1836

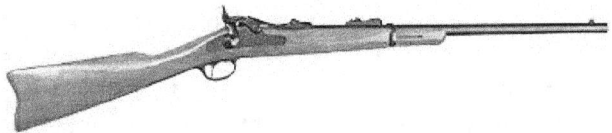

Chapter Two
TOO MANY FLAGS

As was my habit, I made my rounds of the fort just after dawn. Most of the men were still sleeping. Eight guards were on duty, two on each of the four corners. I visited the horses, checked their feed, and woke Sergeant Howell, the regimental saddler, to order Traveller some new tack. While walking back to my headquarters, I encountered another early riser.

"General Custer, may I speak with you for a moment?" Colonel Almonte requested, approaching with another young Mexican officer.

"Of course, Juan. Who is your friend?" I asked.

Though Almonte agreed to ride with us, he had done so with reluctance. Nevertheless, I liked him. And trusted his judgment. He also reminded me a little bit of Tom. And Bill Cooke. And Fresh Smith. They were all similar in age, measured in temperament, and experienced soldiers.

"This is Colonel Jose Enrique de la Peña from Jalisco. He has been keeping a journal of our campaign," Almonte said. "He has an idea that may interest you."

"*Me encantaría escuchar su idea, señor,*" I said, anxious to practice my diction.

"Many in Mexico are unhappy with the dictator," de la Peña responded in English. "I was thinking. I could write letters to newspapers in Mexico City. To important members of Congress. Explain that the Seventh Cavalry is not in league with the American pirates attempting to steal Texas."

The young colonel appeared to be a straightforward, intelligent fellow, with a pleasant continence. I dwelled on his suggestion for a

31

moment before seeing its value. And some broader implications.

"I would find that a worthy service, Señor," I agreed. "Though there must be some requirements."

"Yes, Señor Custer?" de la Peña asked.

"You must tell our friends to the south that these are uncertain times," I said, trying to rapidly organize my thoughts. "Say nothing to embarrass President Santa Anna, for his enmity at this time would be inconvenient. And say nothing of the Seventh Cavalry being ghost riders. Such rumors will spread on their own, but I have no intention of promoting them."

"The dictator's hold on power is weak now that he has been defeated. Enemies will seek his overthrow," de la Peña said.

"Santa Anna still has a large army in the field," I replied. "Until I know his plans, there's no point in provoking him further."

"That is a cautious approach, General," Almonte said with surprise. It surprised me, too.

"Write some letters and show them to Major Cooke. He'll provide you with instructions," I decided. "And thank you again."

As the fort was beginning to stir, I walked across the compound back to my headquarters looking forward to breakfast. Isabella greeted me at the door wearing a lush red woolen coat with a fur collar. It helped to have a wealthy father.

"Good morning, Autie," Isabella said.

I looked into the main room and saw twelve at our board, including Tom, Morning Star and Slow. Ben had whipped up a dish of rice and chicken in a strange red sauce that was simply delicious.

"Good morning, Izzy," I said, taking her in my arms for a passionate kiss.

Everyone was surprised, especially Isabella, for we had kept our relationship free of public display. I no longer felt so constrained. Before the quiet hearth sat the chessboard that Slow had set up the night before, it's message clear. Tom, Crockett, and even the Indian boy had sought to tell me something, but in my desire for a quick victory, I had refused to listen.

"Nice to finally rest up for a few days," Tom said, eating heartily.

Morning Star sat next to him dressed in a long beaded dress made of course blue cloth, probably found in one of the abandoned adobes. I saw a question in her eyes that troubled her.

"Rest day for some, Tom," I replied, taking a seat across from Crockett and Cooke.

"We need to rest the horses," Tom said.

"And the men," Cooke added, his accent more upstate New York than British.

"Don't worry, I have no plans to move out. Not for a week or two. But we have planning to do," I said.

They had been worried that I would order an immediate pursuit of the Mexican army, but I had no such intentions.

"This here presidio is a right more comfortable than that Alamo," Crockett said, dressed casually in a flannel shirt and rawhide trousers. He wore a red scarf similar to my own. "Reckon it would make a good base of operations?"

"Not a bad idea, David, but only for a small detachment," I replied, having reached certain conclusions. "I'm going to take three companies. Tom, you'll have command of C Company. Smith will bring E Company. Bill, Almonte and Kellogg will serve with my headquarters staff. Captain Sepulveda will lead G Company. Everyone else will return to San Antonio."

"Béjar?" Crockett said in surprise.

"Jameson and Sharrow are fortifying the town. You and Keogh will help them. Train recruits and maintain a forward guard here in La Bahia."

"Thirty-two men from Gonzales rode into the Alamo at a time of great need. Now it be thar homes needin' protection. Maybe we kin return the favor?" Crockett suggested.

"Speak with Keogh about it," I agreed.

"We're not marching south?" Cooke asked.

"Not with the army. For now, the Buffalo Flag will hold west Texas and watch for developments. Gather all the wagons, oxen and mules you can find. Fatten them up, they have a long journey ahead," I said.

"What have you got in mind, Autie?" Tom asked.

"California," I answered.

Isabella and Morning Star didn't know what to make of my remark, but the men smiled. Not one of us from the original command had forgotten the bonanza laying in the Sierra Nevada foothills, but other obligations had gotten in our way. Like Crockett, Dickenson, Brister and others, the women had heard stories of California, but no one in dirt poor Texas could imagine the immense riches waiting to be discovered.

"It won't be easy, Autie. There are no established trails to California in 1836," Tom warned. "Mostly mountains, deserts and Apaches. No railroads. No stagecoach lines. Probably not even a wagon trace."

"If Butterfield can cut a road through the wilderness, so can we," I said, hoping it was true.

"Besides, we have the maps," Cooke said.

"Maps?" I inquired.

"Of course. I always carry an atlas in my saddlebags. I'd be a poor adjutant if I didn't," Cooks answered.

It made me wonder what treasures lay in my own saddlebags. Several magazines, including my *Harper's Monthly*, had been delivered by the steamer *Far West* just before we rode up the Rosebud. I'd not even had a chance to read them.

"After the Black Hills and Yellowstone expeditions, I think we've got enough trail blazing experience by now," I said. "I'll give Sergeant Major Sharrow instructions to organize supply wagons. Three or four hundred men should be enough."

"Enough?" Señor Seguin inquired.

"Enough to conquer California. From what I read in Fremont's journals, the province is lightly garrisoned," I remembered.

"Every schoolboy knows of John C. Fremont," Cooke said. "The great expeditions of the 1840s. Kit Carson. Alex Godey. Magnus Coloradas. Even illiterates like Tom know their stories."

"I done my fair share a reading before joining the army, and more while I was there. Pa have tanned my hide otherwise," Tom answered, for he had never formally graduated school while living in New Rumley.

"Now we'll be getting there ten years before Fremont," Cooke said.

"And history will write about us instead," I suddenly realized. "I might even write the history myself. My articles in *Galaxy* have been well received."

The room fell quiet. Crockett and Señor Seguin were looking at us like we were addled. John stood near the door to the kitchen, staring. Ben was there, too, shaking his head. Even the women seemed a bit concerned. But not Slow.

"There is great work to be done beyond the lands of our enemies," Slow said.

Which enemies he meant were anyone's guess, for the Sioux were no more popular among the western tribes than they were among the whites.

"We will go to these lands," Morning Star said, getting up to find us more coffee.

"This will be a hard trek. No place for women," Tom objected.

"Where the Custers ride, Slow and I will ride. We are part of your journey," Morning Star said, and that proved the final word on the subject.

———————

With much to do, everyone was busy, but I did not wish to neglect Isabella or her father. As I expected their quick return to San Antonio, there was little time. I made a point of having lunch with them under an oak tree near La Bahia's village.

"Only a week ago we were at Casa Blanca," Señor Seguin wistfully said.

I knew the prosperous ranch well. On the Goliad Road thirty miles below San Antonio, it was rich in farms, cattle, sheep and horses. It was where I had first met Señor Seguin and his beautiful daughter. The Seguin ranch reminded me of my boyhood in Ohio, before Pa sent me to Monroe to live with my sister. The Custer clan had been farmers as well as blacksmiths. We were also poor, a condition that did not sit well with Judge Bacon when I began to court Libbie

"Will you soon be seeking another victory?" Isabella asked, having seen the men repairing their saddles. We were eating tortillas stuffed with roasted chicken and peppers, a dish I had never tasted in Michigan. The day was pleasantly cool.

"Urrea has retreated to Refugio. That should give us some time," I said.

"José still has a thousand men. Supply and artillery," Isabella said.

"José?" I asked.

"My late husband was a colonel in General Urrea's cavalry," she explained. "Alejandro and I often dined with José and his wife. You will find Urrea to be a capable officer. He is not rash like the dictator."

"We're well arrayed. How fares your task, quartermaster?"

Señor Erasmo Seguin was now fifty-four years old, descended from French immigrants, and born in San Antonio. When Mexico achieved independence from Spain, he was the sole representative from Texas to the constitutional convention that drafted the Constitution of 1824. Though slightly shorter than I, he was thicker with squared shoulders. He had bushy gray hair, a well-trimmed beard, and insightful gray eyes.

"We are moving the munitions works to Béjar," Seguin explained. "It is too dangerous for my craftsmen in Victoria. We have made a press for the brass shell casings and new molds for the bullets."

"Can you produce fifty thousand rounds for the Springfields by May?" I asked.

"Fifty thousand? George, refined powder is scarce. Perhaps ten thousand. Maybe not even that," Seguin said.

"I am sorry, Erasmo. Sometimes I forget where we are," I said.

"And when?" he smiled, for he was the first person we had told of our amazing journey.

"Yes, you wouldn't think forty years would make such a great difference," I said.

"My son, forty years ago Tejas was part of Spain," Seguin replied. "This land was ruled by the Comanche. There were not more than a few hundred Mexican families between Copano and the Red River. I know what forty years can mean."

"The next forty will be important, too," I said. "And not just for Tejanos."

"*Sí*, I understand. I am sorry now that I helped my good *amigo* Stephen Austin bring slaves into his colonies," Seguin said, for he had been instrumental in Austin's venture to bring American families to east Texas.

"That can't be helped, but we can still make slavery unprofitable," I said.

"And how would that be?" Isabella asked.

"By hanging their owners," I replied.

After a pleasant lunch, Isabella returned to the fort while Señor Seguin and I walked down to the river for cigars. I normally did not smoke, nor drink for that matter, but had modified my strict rules since riding into the past.

Señor Seguin and I sat down for an hour reviewing our plans. He had been postmaster of Texas since 1807, so there was little he didn't know about the towns and roads we would encounter. Once we had driven our enemies back across the Rio Grande and the Sabine, we would need to build a new country. Farms, factories, lumber yards and railroads. I had strong ideas on what needed to be done, and Seguin had the connections. And, of course, profit would be involved.

Later that evening, after a fine meal and several songs before the fireplace, everyone started drifting off to bed. As they had before, Tom and Morning Star spent a little time on the porch, not far from where Isabella and I were sitting. They were making plans, but I did not overhear them.

Crockett did not appear in our quarters that night, possibly bunking with those New Orleans Greys who had not deserted, but I did not sleep alone. After the halls grew quiet, Isabella slipped into my room, crawling into bed.

There was no dishonor. She was a widow, entitled to make her own decisions. And she knew my interest in her was not casual. Beautiful, wealthy, intelligent, and high-spirited, Isabella was just the sort of woman I wanted when it came time to remarry. And her family ties to the West Texas Tejano community would give me status similar to what the late Jim Bowie had enjoyed. Nevertheless, we were discreet.

"Have I mentioned I'm going with you?" Isabella whispered.

"Izzy, that's not a good idea," I objected.

"Your Libbie went everywhere with you. During your war. On the plains. Even a journey here to Texas. She must have endured many hardships."

"So many hardships that she could have written a book about them," I said.

"I am not afraid of hardships. If Morning Star can ride with the Seventh Cavalry, so can I," she insisted.

After a week of rest and refitting, our army divided. Juan Seguin agreed to remain in Goliad as commandant. It was a vital point of contact with the port towns to the south and colonies to the east. With his troop of Tejanos ranging the area, the local population would not feel like an occupied people as they had under Fannin. Such considerations would become increasingly important, reminding me of my days after the Rebellion. Texas and Kentucky rarely appreciated the presence of Union soldiers.

The bulk of our force that had so jauntily marched from San Antonio now headed back with much to do. Cos had failed to hold Béjar against the Texan rebels the previous December, and Travis had failed to hold the town against Santa Anna in February. It was Keogh's job to make sure such failures were not repeated. I was going to miss Crockett.

"I can ride with you," Crockett had said.

"No, David. You need to organize a government. Write a declaration that will offer an alternative to Burnet and his band of land grabbers," I encouraged.

"I don't know nothin' 'bout organizing no gover'met. I was a congressman, not a lawyer."

"Plenty of lawyers running around," I said. "Your friend Autry. Green Jameson. Erasmo Seguin has some experience. But none of them are the famous Davy Crockett. David, there are thousands of colonists in Texas who have no stake in slavery. They just need an honest man to rally around. They need you. And so do I."

"I'll do my best, George," he said, shaking my hand. "Where ya runnin' off to?"

"Heading for the coast. We'll be back in a few weeks."

"Well, don't go gettin' ambushed like Johnson and Ward," Crockett warned.

"Good advice," I agreed, knowing from personal experience.

———————

"San Antonio is an important post, but I'd rather be riding east," Keogh objected when I gave him his orders.

The burly Irishman was sitting on his sorrel, Comanche, as we rode along the wooded river road. I wanted a private talk before sending my highest ranking subordinate on an independent assignment. I gave Traveller a scratch behind the ears.

"Myles, I need someone I can depend on in Béjar. Who better than you?" I said.

"Guess that's true enough," Keogh agreed. "But before I go, I'd like to know what you really think of all this."

"All of what?" I asked.

"How we got here. Years before we're even born," Keogh said.

"Don't know that it matters, does it? Can't do anything about it."

"Come on, George, don't say you haven't thought on it," Keogh persisted. "We're forty years in the past. We fought side by side with Davy Crockett. You met Jim Bowie. Seems to me we should be a little curious."

"I've heard a few theories," I said, fixing my white campaign hat as I squinted at a dismal winter sun. "Morning Star says we came here by magic. Fresh says it must have been one of Edison's new inventions. And Queen's Own says that a French fantasy writer has got us caught up in one of his fantastical novels."

"Algernon didn't say Edison sent us, only that it could have been an experiment gone wrong," Keogh protested, though I couldn't tell if he was serious. "And Cooke didn't blame Jules Verne, only one of his machines."

As a former member of the Vatican guard in Rome, the Company of St. Patrick, Keogh knew his way around Europe. He was no fan of the French.

"And what would the Pope say about magic?" I asked. "As the Vicar of Christ, only he could send the Seventh Cavalry back to Texas right in the middle of their revolution. Isn't that right? Any reason why the Pope would want to do that?"

"Pope don't move people back in time. No sir. Especially not two sassy bone-head brothers leadin' an army of misfits," Keogh said.

"So what is the answer?" I pressed.

"Maybe we should ask Slow," Keogh replied.

"I have asked Slow. More than once. He says the Great Spirit will not speak of it. But he did say the Alamo was only the beginning."

"What about . . .?" Keogh started.

"Myles, no more hocus pocus. It only makes the men nervous. We've got an army and a cause worth fighting for. That's enough for any soldier."

As Keogh went to organize the ride back to San Antonio, Mitch Bouyer finally caught up to me outside the main gate. I had been avoiding his complaints all afternoon, but he finally had me cornered.

"We don't got 'nough Injuns," the crusty half-breed said, riding up on a spirited paint mustang.

The horse was white with black spots and gray legs. Probably raised by Comanche, though I didn't ask Bouyer where he got it. The horses we'd brought with us from Montana were played out, ready for several weeks of rest that we didn't have time to give them.

"Mr. Bouyer, you are chief of scouts. I expect you to find your own Indians," I responded.

"Gen'ral, we had two fine Injuns, and you kilt 'em both," Bouyer said.

I remembered seeing Gray Wolf fall at my side during the Battle of Cibolo Creek. While negotiating a truce with Mexican Lancers, the brave Indian lad had joined me in the meadow and died when the shooting started. We never did find out who fired first.

"Spotted Eagle is not dead," I complained, for the other young cousin was doing quite well. "Since we evacuated the Alamo, he's been tended under my own roof."

"Can't scout for me, neither, can he? Not shot through the side by a musket ball. Ah need a baker's dozen a good scouts an' ain't got a one," Bouyer said.

"Mitch, you've got Juan Seguin and his Tejanos. They live here. They know the land better than anybody," I answered, trying not to sound impatient.

Though I *was* impatient. In my twelve years as a senior officer, I had never needed to do so much explaining. And cajoling. And occasional threatening. But this was no longer 1876, we were no longer the United States Army, and the Texas revolution we had stumbled into was growing ever more complicated.

"Tejanos ain't good Injuns, sir. Just ain't," Bouyer insisted. For no good reason.

"You want some Karankawa Indians, don't you?" I said, finally catching on.

"Jus a few, sir. Jus a few. Got 'em picked out," the rascal confessed.

"Hire them on, but don't offer more than our teamsters are getting. I'm not funding a charity."

Bouyer rode off, happy as a lark. I didn't tell him we weren't actually funding anything. The stash of gold Ben Travane had found in Santa Anna's hacienda was just enough to buy food and ammunition for a few months. After criticizing government my entire life for its spendthrift ways, it was strange to discover that I was now the government.

Keogh and Crockett were not the only ones returning to San

Antonio. Though technically a prisoner-of-war riding with my army, General Manuel Fernández Castrillón had proven himself a gentleman. Deserted by Santa Anna with a starving army in the fields north of the Alamo, he had surrendered his infantry on honorable terms. Now I needed him returned to Béjar, pending a formal exchange.

"I do not like keeping you prisoner, but I do not see how it can be helped," I said, speaking with him on the broad plain outside La Bahia's main gate.

"We must be practical about such things," Castrillón replied.

Born in Cuba, Castrillón was a proud man in his mid-fifties, tall, lean, and always immaculately dressed in a blue and red uniform trimmed with gold lace.

"Some describe me with terms that are unflattering, but I'm a soldier, and a soldier makes difficult decisions. A good commander isn't necessarily loved."

"A general's life looks better than it is lived, Señor Custer," Castrillón agreed.

"Perhaps you can call me George?"

"All right, youngster. You may call me General Castrillón."

"I understand you are Santa Anna's best friend."

"To the extent Antonio has such friends."

"I would like you to write him," I said. "No military information, in keeping with your honor. See if there's a way to arrange a truce."

"You defeated our rear guard at the Rio Grande. And our cavalry at Cibolo Creek. And the president himself in Béjar. I should think you are not afraid of battle."

"Not afraid, sir. Not afraid at all. But I'd rather not turn Texas over to the Brazos Convention with their recruits flooding into the eastern colonies. They will take over the country if we continue this war."

"It is a great problem. I will write my friend, but he is unpredictable," Castrillón warned.

"So am I."

I returned to the fort, leaving Traveller with Corporal Fuentes, my orderly for the day. Crockett had been gone much of the afternoon and there was work to do. I finally asked Tom if he knew the bear hunter's whereabouts.

"He's in the church," Tom said, as if everyone knew.

41

Presidio La Bahia did not boast much of a church, the cathedral was cramped and dark. Nothing like the Methodist churches I knew so well in Monroe. I remembered my old comrade Georgie Yates, whose wedding had been such a joy. He was dead now, killed in a pointless skirmish during our march to Cibolo Creek. My Libbie and Annie Yates had been best friends.

Slow and Crockett were near the altar looking at the candles while an old priest in gold vestments mumbled a Latin verse. Crockett noticed me and we went outside into a grassy courtyard.

"Is Slow having another vision? Did he find us some buffalo?" I asked.

"The birds ain't talkin'," Crockett said.

"Seems we've got as much supply as we're going to get. I think it's time I leave for Galveston."

"Reckon that be true," he agreed, scratching a day-old beard.

One thing history was right about, Davy Crockett did not disappoint. The former congressman, army scout, and frontier legend stood six feet tall, broad-shouldered, and was trim as the trails he'd spent a lifetime traveling.

"Why Texas, David?" I asked. "After failing to get reelected, you could have done other things. Maybe written another book?"

"When I objected to Andy Jackson's Indian polices, and how his land agent friends was stealin' folks' homesteads, ole Andy up and wrecked my career. I told the voters they could go to hell, and I would go to Texas. So 'ere I am."

"What newspapers are you familiar with back east? The New York Tribune?" I asked.

"Know a few. Went on a tour of the Yankee states jus' two year ago. Saw Philadelphia, New York, Boston. Met lots of right friendly folks," he replied.

"We've got to write some letters."

"Letters?"

"Southerners are flooding into east Texas. Several thousand now, more later. Many are bringing slaves with them, in defiance of Mexican law. The northern states will raise objections if it looks like a plot of the plantation owners."

"George, no one hates plantation owners more 'an me, but I don't think this is no plot. Jus' folks lookin' for good land," Crockett said.

"They will need to find good land somewhere else. If we can discourage immigration, Burnet and his gang of horse thieves will be forced to flee."

"Flee who? Thought the Mexicans is headed south."

"Doesn't matter. Let's sit down and write some of those newspapers. Explain the Seventh Cavalry is upholding the laws against slavery in Texas. It should rile up Washington, and maybe win us a few recruits."

"You takin' up politics, George?"

"Don't know that I have a choice," I replied.

Slow and Morning Star emerged from the church. I don't think Slow was planning on taking up Christianity, but he continued to be impressed with the ceremonies. Morning Star, not so much. She had spent two years at a Catholic girls' school in St. Louis. Slow was bundled up in a heavy fur coat, for he was not fond of the cold wind. Morning Star was less sensitive, wearing a lovely beaded leather dress, high rawhide boots, and a blue cavalry cape.

"We must go east," Slow said, the black eyes shining like they still had candle light in them.

"Yes, I know," I said, for it was no secret.

"I have heard the Gulf of Mexico has much water. I will see this thing for myself," Slow said, walking toward our headquarters.

"Morning Star, I'm thinking it's best the women stay behind when we begin our march. Harrington and Jameson will be rebuilding the town, and there are a hundred wounded men to care for. Including Spotted Eagle," I said.

She smiled in a condescending way. Beautiful, but condescending. It was no surprise Tom was smitten with her.

———

I wasn't optimistic as we rode southeast along the river. With volunteers pouring in from the slave states, the Brazos army could swell into the thousands. And they'd be well-armed, though likely low on food. And the Mexican army was far from defeated.

"What's wrong?" Tom asked.

"If I commanded a thousand operational troops, I'd launch another campaign within the week," I explained.

"Will Santa Anna be so bold?" Cooke asked. "Half of his army was

43

captured or killed at the Alamo."

"He wasn't bold at Churubusco," I said. "In his memoirs, General Scott wrote that Santa Anna often hesitated when confronted with the unexpected."

"Hesitation has never been one of your faults," Tom said.

I rode to the head of the column, finding Slow riding with Voss. The boy seemed to sense my uneasiness, but he could hardly grasp the complexities.

"Which enemies will you kill first?" Slow inquired as we rode together.

"That is a good question. What do the birds say?" I asked.

"The birds will not speak of the future. There are many clouds."

"Then I will attack the clouds, that the birds might speak," I replied.

"Even Custer may not attack a cloud," he said, irritated by my teasing.

"I have ridden in the clouds," I boasted. "As a young lieutenant in Virginia, I rode in a gas filled balloon a thousand feet above the ground. I flew higher than the birds."

"How many clouds did you slay while flying among the birds?"

"I was a general. Then a ghost. And now I am a general again. One day I will be the Great Custer, compared to Caesar, Charlemagne, and Bonaparte. If I choose to slay a cloud, what cloud may resist my onslaught?"

I gave Traveller a kick, riding toward the head of the column. It had rained that morning, but only lightly, giving us a good trail. Without wagons, we maintained a rapid pace. Bouyer and Kellogg were at the front, an unusual duo, for they normally didn't care for each other's company. Bouyer spoke little, and when he did, it was of the landscape, the weather, and available game. Kellogg cared for none of these things, but would not shut up about everything else.

"Gen'ral, why we headed for Galveston? Ain't no gold there," Bouyer said, dressed in frontier leathers and a straw hat shading the emerging sun.

"It's the largest seaport in Texas. It needs to fly the Buffalo Flag," I answered.

"Ah don't give a damn 'bout none of these Texians, and you shouldn't, neither. 'Specially after that Fannin," Bouyer complained.

"Mr. Fannin was a disappointment, and he won't be the last, but there is a method to my madness. Can you bear with me for a few weeks?"

"Care to explain this madness?" Kellogg asked, wearing a thick maroon coat and tall fur cap against the cold.

"And what has our representative from the fourth estate so irritable? Still sore about your clay-footed hero?" I said.

"Not pleased Houston called me an abolitionist spy after refusing a meeting, but this march is a little more worrisome," Kellogg said. "I agree with Mitch. This seems a foolhardy adventure. And not your first."

"Mark, if you'd come with me to the Alamo, you'd have had the noblest war story since Leonidas bled Xerxes at Thermopylae. You dashed off instead. When we get to Galveston, you can take ship back to the states and spend the rest of your life writing dime novels."

"Now who's irritated?" Kellogg said.

"We've got some difficult days ahead, and I can't read the future," I replied. "Even the damn birds aren't talking."

I spotted a small group of hunters in the trees off to my right, recognizing Tom, Morning Star and Fresh. With no interest in debating Kellogg or listening to Bouyer complain, I broke off at a gentle trot.

"What you got?" I asked, pulling my Remington hunting rifle from the sheath. I only had a few rounds left until Señor Seguin could make more, but spending a cartridge would be worth a good kill.

"Herd of elk," Tom said.

Instead of his Winchester, Tom was holding a borrowed Springfield for its greater range.

"Mind if I join?" I said.

"Don't hog the biggest buck, Autie," Tom said, glancing at Smith.

I took out the Austrian field glasses stolen from Lt. DeRudio above the Little Big Horn, taking a look. The herd was about forty strong, moving slowly up a broad valley away from the river toward a stand of timber. They hadn't smelled us yet, but that could change with a shift in the wind.

"Not elk. Mule deer," I said, being an expert on all the western species.

"Don't have to eat them if you don't want to, George," Smith said.

I saw Fresh had borrowed Butler's .50 Sharps, the heavy weapon

45

lying across his lap.

"We'll see who eats what," I replied.

We rode down the broad valley slowly before spreading out. I had the far left, then Tom and Morning Star. Smith was near the trees well to the right. I glanced back toward the road where the command was riding in column of twos. Captain Sepulveda and Sergeant Francisco Sanchez stopped to watch the hunt, both riding noble stallions. Sepulveda's horse had previously belonged to Fannin.

We closed within a hundred yards of the herd, a healthy and alert group of beasts. I spied a buck that would make a good kill. Smith dismounted and moved along the edge of the trees. Tom and Morning Star stopped in the middle of the meadow. I saw Morning Star was holding Tom's Winchester. I started to go around the herd near the tree line when they suddenly spooked, and I quickly saw why. There were half a dozen Comanche on the far side of the clearing.

Unlike the Plains Indians of my experience, who often dressed colorfully and wore paint appropriate for the occasion, be it hunting or war, the Comanche appeared drab. Their leather outfits were worn and dirty, lacking in decoration. They seemed like poor cousins of the more famous tribes, but they were not to be underestimated. These warriors had a fierce reputation, were bold in battle, and determined once they'd set their minds to something.

No words were spoken. I waved to Tom, who nodded to Morning Star and motioned to Smith. The three of them withdrew slowly. Once they were headed back, I rode Traveller out into the meadow and raised my hand, a sign that I wanted to parley. An arrow was loosed at me instead and a dozen warriors burst from the woods, riding hard on spotted mustangs. I wheeled about and rode for my life in the other direction, just as I had when a hundred Sioux had chased me near the Tongue River in 1873. Tom had been there that day, too, with twenty troopers to hold off the charging horde.

This time we had the odds. Sepulveda deployed G Company just as I had trained him, every fourth man holding the horses while his command formed a skirmish line. Armed with Baker rifles, they would make short work of the Comanche if they came within range.

Morning Star reached safety first, quickly followed by Tom and Fresh. I stopped twenty yards short of the road and turned, the Remington lying across my knees. Traveller danced beneath me, excited by the sprint. I held up the rifle in warning to my would-be enemies, for I did not want a war. The small band of savages wisely halted, debated for a moment, and then skulked back into the forest. The mule deer had gotten away.

We left the San Antonio River behind us, turning east through low foothills. I was not very familiar with west Texas, but I knew east Texas fairly well. After the war ended, I had spent six months headquartered in Austin with the 2nd Cavalry. Diligent in my duties, I had earned the respect of the Texans, but not the riffraff assigned to my command. Desertion and insubordination had been vexing problems. So unlike the loyal soldiers of the 5th Michigan I nobly led during the Rebellion.

"We should be there in a few days," Isabella said, riding at my side.

"Have you used this trail before?" I asked.

"Many times. It is the quickest route from Casa Blanca to Galveston, where my father often had business when I was young," she said. "It was from Galveston that I left for Cuba."

"I did not realize you are so well traveled," I said in admiration, for she was not only a handsome woman, but well-spoken.

"My father sent me to the Sisters of Mercy in Mexico City for an education, and later to finishing school in Havana," she recalled. "My best friend was Anna, the daughter of Sir Lawrence Mulberry. Sir Lawrence was the British consul. Anna and I once wintered in New Orleans. It is a beautiful city."

"I've been to New Orleans, too. Back in 1865."

"You mean *up* in 1865," she corrected. "If you are to be a ghost rider, you must remember these details."

"I did not set out to be a ghost rider. None of us did. We were sent to corral the Sioux tribes and return them to the reservations, but things didn't turn out as we expected."

"You were killed in this battle? Truly?"

"That's one of the strange things. I don't remember being killed. I remember riding down into a draw toward the village, and then a fog rose up. There was gunfire, and hollering. The pounding of hooves. I've had dreams of standing on a weed-covered hill waiting for my regiment to regroup, surrounded by hostiles. And then I was in Texas, forty years in the past. It makes no possible sense."

"My father thinks it is a miracle of God," she said.

"I don't know about that. I've been lucky all my life, not but enough to attract God's attention. Besides, Tom and I aren't the only beneficiaries of this miracle. Morning Star and her cousin Spotted Eagle are ghost riders, too."

"What about Slow?" she asked.

"No, not Slow. Weird, isn't it?"

"I should think there is significance there."

"He's an unusual boy, no doubt about that," I said. "What was New Orleans like when you visited? And Havana? Large garrisons? Trade? What sort of ships are people using in 1836? How often do you see an American flag?"

"You ask many questions, Autie," she said with a charming smile.

"We have many days on the trail, Izzy. There is time."

––––––––––

It was a late June day, stifling hot, the air choked with dust. The hazy sun hung in the great Montana sky, possibly for the last time. I had divided the command to prevent the hostiles from escaping, unaware that the non-treaty tribes had gathered in unprecedented numbers. But even then, I sensed a chance of victory. A chance that proved illusionary.

"Tom! Any sign of Benteen?" I asked, turning in my saddle. Vic was tired but still game, having served me well for many years.

"Nothing, Autie," my worried brother answered, sitting astride his prized thoroughbred, Athena.

The command was spread along a grassy ridge. Below us was the Little Big Horn River, and beyond that, the biggest village I had ever seen. Most of the warriors were gone, having ridden south to oppose Major Reno's charge.

"I don't see the women and children," I said, studying the village through Lt. DeRudio's Austrian field glasses.

"Maybe run off, Gen'ral," Mitch Bouyer said, an experienced scout I had borrowed from General Terry.

"We've got to find them. If we capture the non-combatants, the warriors will return to the reservations without a fight," I said, glancing to the north. For that's where I suspected they had gone.

"Thought you wanted a fight, General," Mark Kellogg said, a reporter from the Bismarck Tribune. He was riding a mule, but a sturdy one.

I looked at the village again. Large enough to house thousands. Perhaps thousands upon thousands.

"I will settle for a victory, Mr. Kellogg," I replied. "Sergeant Butler, order Lt. Calhoun to hold the southern end of this ridge until Benteen comes up. Captain Keogh will stand in reserve. Lieutenant Smith, you will hold this hill and watch for developments. Captain Custer, you're with me."

Tom and I rode down the gently sloping hill overlooking the river. Bouyer and Kellogg followed. Close by was Sergeant Bobby Hughes, my guidon bearer, and Corporal Henry Voss, the regimental trumpeter. Companies E and F casually followed, sharing what remained of the water and checking their weapons. Our portion of the battlefield was surprisingly quiet.

"Sir, there they are," Voss said, pointing to thick woods around a sharp bend in the river.

We stopped on a bluff, looking down at hundreds of women, children, and a few old men. They had taken what food they could, but most possessions had been left behind in the village in the panic of their flight. There were a few horses and dozens of barking dogs.

"Rounding them all up will take more men than we have," Tom said.

"We need Keogh and Benteen. Let's reunite the command," I decided.

A shot rang out. I glanced at Tom, then Voss. Both were startled.

"General?" Kellogg said.

The reporter had a stricken look, his mouth hanging open.

Several more shots whistled by, and then a group of mounted Cheyenne were riding toward us, hell bent for murder. We wheeled around and headed back up the hill, belatedly realizing Kellogg was no longer with us.

The command did not make directly for Galveston. I knew the town to be located on a barrier island in Galveston Bay. Crossing the wide waterway would require a ferryboat. Probably many ferryboats. Getting a hundred and twenty-five troopers across the water in time to seize the town by surprise seemed a remote possibility.

We rode south instead, down a marshy peninsula where Seguin said we would find a ferry station. The village there was recently abandoned but not looted. We found several large flatboats and some fishing boats, enough to move the command across the straight to the western tip of Galveston Island. The operation took the entire day, the waters off San Luis Pass being treacherous.

Finally back on firm ground, we had the Gulf of Mexico on our right as we moved east along a long spur of land only forty yards wide and filled with reeds.

"I've had enough of these swamps," Tom said.

"Better than rowing across the bay in broad daylight. This whole end of the island is unguarded," I replied, walking cautiously with Traveller trailing behind me.

"Glad when we find a campsite. It's starting to get dark," Cooke said, the sun low on the horizon behind us.

"Slow?" I asked.

The boy was up ahead on Vic, the only one of us riding.

"There is a hill," Slow tiredly said.

"The birds tell you that?" Tom asked.

"I can see it," Slow answered.

The narrow strip of swamp land gradually widened into a meadow filled with scraggily trees. We fed the horses and pitched our tents, some of the men searching for firewood. Everyone was looking forward to supper and a hot cup of coffee.

Though Tom and Morning Star often shared a tent on the trail, respectfully, Morning Star and Isabella had been tent mates on this journey. I would risk no question of Isabella's virtue.

"We're about five miles from the town," Cooke said, having drawn a map based on his atlas. "I'm guessing flat terrain most of the way."

"Port city. Could be a lot of ships. Sailors, too," Tom said, for we had both visited the harbor before taking ship for New Orleans.

"Small fort. Only a few cannon," I said. "We'll ride in with guns ready. If we're lucky, no one will need to fire a shot."

"I'd call that pretty optimistic," Almonte said, lingering in the shadows of our campfire with Smith.

Sepulveda, Bouyer and Kellogg came to join us. Along with Hughes, Butler and Voss, they compromised the majority of my immediate staff.

"We're going to reorganize a little," I announced.

I stood up, standing near the fire, casting a long shadow, and waited until everyone was paying attention. Enjoying the suspense. General Sheridan had used similar methods, and it was standard practice in the theatres I loved so well. I sincerely hoped to see Shakespeare again, perhaps in New York at the Winter Garden. Though the Bard would never be performed so well as my good friend Lawrence Barrett had done. I had attended forty of his performances as Cassius at Booth's Theatre on 6th Street, learning every word of *Julius Caesar* by heart.

"We aren't dividing the command again, are we?" Tom asked.

"No, little brother, but we are changing the order of march," I said, clasping my hands behind my back and pacing. "We don't know if Houston or the Mexicans hold the town. We won't know until we see what flag they're flying. Colonel Smith, E Company will wear their winter jackets and fur hats. Baker rifles only. If the town is flying a Brazos flag, you'll ride in first. Put the garrison at ease. You'll be followed by C Company in cavalry blouses and take control."

I strolled over to Captain Sepulveda and Sergeant Sanchez. Colonel Almonte was sitting with them.

"Mario, G Company will come last, but ready to move up. If the town is held by Santa Anna's troops, your Zacatecan will be the first to enter, pretending to be Tampico lancers, followed by E Company and Tom's men arriving last," I said.

"The men from Coahuila, too, General," Sergeant Sanchez interrupted, for their province had also been decimated when the dictator sought to crush their revolt.

"Yes, Francisco, the heroes of Coahuila, also," I acknowledged. "Once we capture the town, I want G Company to occupy the docks where the ships can see you. I want them to think the Mexican army has occupied the port. We'll run up one of our Mexican flags to throw them off."

"Why all the fuss, Autie?" Tom asked. "Why not run up the Buffalo Flag?"

"Galveston is visited from ships from all over the world. Including American ships," I explained. "If the Brazos army knows our small force has captured the port, they may try to retake it. And the

American ships might help. But if they think the Mexican army is here, the American ships will be reluctant to interfere. If the Mexicans see their own flag flying over the town, they'll assume it's in good hands and continue chasing Houston. This is my answer to your riddle, Slow."

"My riddle?" the boy asked, his eyebrows bent.

"On the chessboard, you asked what happens to the third army that is caught between the white and black pieces. My solution is to not let them know we're here until we've accomplished our objective."

"So you will not fly your flag?" Isabella said, wondering if such a thing was proper.

"Oh, we may fly it just before we leave," I answered. "Just to show our opponents that the Seventh Cavalry is a force to be reckoned with."

"You are very clever, General," Morning Star complimented. "Such a plan is worthy of Chief Lone Man himself."

We started out early, intending to reach Galveston by midday. Spirits were high, the mounts enjoyed firmer footing, and the men sang a few of the traditional songs. I rode at the head of the column with the two women and Kellogg, Slow just behind us with my sergeants.

Bouyer and three Karankawa scouts were blazing our trail. I had never heard of this tribe, though they apparently migrated seasonally between the mainland and the barrier islands. No one in my command knew their language, but they spoke enough Spanish to communicate. I gathered the name Karakawa meant dog lovers.

"You've been quiet, Mark," I said, hoping to provoke him.

"We're approaching an unexpected challenge," he said.

I'd only known Kellogg for a few months. His editor at the *Bismarck Tribune*, Clement Lounsberry, was supposed to accompany my regiment to Montana, but had backed out at the last minute. Like Cooke, Kellogg was a Canadian. He had roamed the Midwest working for various newspapers and occasionally running for public office. Unsuccessfully.

"I've been to Galveston before," I said.

"That's not the challenge I mean, though you've got a bit of a surprise coming," he said. "When this started, we knew the history.

The Alamo fell to Santa Anna on March 6th. Coming up from Matamoros, General Urrea defeated Johnson at San Patricio, then won battles at Agua Dolce and Refugio. At the Battle of Coleto, Fannin's entire army was taken prisoner and later executed. Houston fled east on the Runaway Scrape, only to turn and fight at San Jacinto on April 21st. Santa Anna was captured, ending the war."

"We defeated Santa Anna. And there will be no Goliad Massacre. Fannin's army is retreating," I said, thinking it a good thing.

"That's what I mean," Kellogg replied. "History has been changed. Houston is not fleeing east, that we know of. Santa Anna is free to continue the war. We really don't know what to expect anymore."

"Mark, I never knew what to expect the first time. And it doesn't matter. We'll deal with each new situation as it comes," I said. "We'll make our own history now."

Though hardly more than a narrow sandbar on the western end, Galveston Island grew wider as we rode northeast. I noticed a beach of crushed seashells that Libbie and I had enjoyed. It hadn't changed since my last visit. But even at the broadest point, I doubt the island is more than three miles across. The terrain tended to undulate, sometimes thick with growth, at other times nearly barren. A few farmers, all of them Mexicans, stopped to watch as we passed, but none seemed alarmed. Nor particularly interested. Their concern was the land, not the soldiers riding over it.

When an estuary appeared on our left, I knew we were getting close. A low dune rose up ahead from which we could view the east end of the island. Bouyer, Cooke and Slow were already there. I dismounted and walked the final few yards, taking out my binoculars to survey the town's defenses.

"Where's Galveston?" I sputtered in surprise.

"Thar, Gen'ral. Down by the water," Bouyer said, pointing toward my left.

"All I see is the harbor," I replied.

"Told you there'd be a surprise, General. Galveston hasn't been built yet," Kellogg said.

It was true. The broad, flat plain was barren except for a few small farms. Several miles closer, on the north side of the island, was a long pier and two short docks. In 1865, this had been a bustling port, filled with merchants, sailors, German immigrants and freed slaves. The

53

Galveston of 1836 was thirty or so wood frame buildings, a sagging warehouse, assorted adobe shacks, and a walled customs house built in the Spanish style.

"Well, this is a hell of a thing," I sputtered, for I had thought to charge a small city, not a shabby hamlet.

"Custer will find no glory here," Slow said.

"Take 'bout ten minutes to kill 'em all Gen'ral," Bouyer suggested. In jest, I assume.

"The ferry dock is empty," I said. "I see a schooner tied to the pier, probably a New Orleans trader. Three ships in the harbor, none look heavily armed."

"There's a flag flying from the customs house. A half-naked lady liberty on a white background," Tom reported.

"What's the plan, General?" Cooke asked.

"Go with Sepulveda down to the pier. Seize the schooner in the name of Mexico," I said, studying the scene carefully through the binoculars.

"Mexico?" Kellogg said.

"Don't worry, Mark, we'll seize it back," I answered. "Bouyer, tell Smith to swing to the right, across that mud flat that might be Galveston someday. He'll approach the port from the south. C Company will ride straight into that plaza, guidons flying, Colts at the ready. I want the garrison to know we can kill them all if provoked."

"Yes, sir," Bouyer said, riding back to the waiting troops.

"Mark, hang back with Almonte and the women. Keep an eye on the pack animals. We'll call you forward when it's safe," I said.

"I can shoot, and I'm not afraid," Kellogg protested.

"Follow orders," I insisted,

Sepulveda took G Company to the left, riding down to the beach for a direct assault on the docks. Tom came forward with C Company, the men anxious for a good fight.

"Ready, Autie," Tom reported, Butler and Hughes at his side.

"We will advance at a steady gait, then at a gallop when the town realizes we are bearing down on them. Voss, be ready to sound the *Charge*," I instructed, excited by the prospect of imminent action.

"Just give the signal, sir. I'll do the rest," Voss said.

"Okay. Company, advance!" I ordered.

We crossed over the low ridge in column of fours and down a

mossy slope. Beyond a partially plowed field were several buildings, a couple of wagons, and a corral. I expected to see riflemen appear on a roof or sortie out, but all remained quiet. A trap? Another ambush like Goliad? If so, they would pay in blood.

I drew the fine Spanish cavalry saber found on the body of a Mexican major and almost gave Voss the order. But we were yet to see an enemy.

Forty strong, the command pushed forward from a trot to a gallop. I was out in front for a few moments, but Traveller was no speedster, and others quickly moved ahead. One of them was Slow, urging Vic on as he waved a feathered hatchet, his black eyes filled with the thrill of battle. Vic was no less excited, my old war horse striving to hold the lead, froth splattering from his bit as his hooves churned up the damp soil. But none could match Tom on Athena, the thoroughbred outdistancing us all.

We skirted the first few houses, entered a wide dirt road, and passed half a dozen mercantile shops on our way to the town square. I saw a crowd of people up ahead, perhaps fifty or sixty, mostly well dressed. There were banners hanging from second floor balconies. I heard a band playing, but it suddenly stopped as the Seventh Cavalry bore down on them.

"What the bloody hell?" a surprised man shouted.

The crowd formed into a circle, a number of woman and children in the center. A squad of militia dressed much like the New Orleans Greys started to raise their Kentucky long rifles, then thought better of it. A bugle sounded to my right where Smith and E Company were entering the town from the other direction, forty more troopers against the score of frontiersmen in the plaza. They were wise to lower their guns.

"I am General George Custer, commander of the Seventh Cavalry. I claim this town in the name of the Buffalo Flag," I announced. "Surrender your weapons. No one will be harmed."

"Sir, this is most irregular," a distinguished man in a brown frock coat declared. He wore a tall beaver hat and high black boots. A man of some wealth.

"Butler, make a sweep of the outer buildings," I ordered. "Hughes, see how Cooke and Sepulveda are doing. Tom, secure these prisoners."

I dismounted and approached the man in the frock coat. I saw now they were engaged in some sort of presentation ceremony. Two brand new bronze cannon were decorated with ribbons.

"My name is Dr. Charles Rice, new to Texas," the man said, accompanied by two young girls in frilly gingham dresses. "These are my daughters, Elizabeth and Eleanor. You are white men. Why have you launched this unprovoked attack?"

"Have you brought slaves to Texas?" I asked.

"I own no slaves, sir. But even if I did, there is nothing illegal about it," Rice answered.

I inspected the cannon mounted on new gun carriages. Fine six-pounders.

"The people of Ohio have donated these field pieces in the name of Texas liberty," Rice said.

"Now they belong to the Seventh Cavalry," I announced.

At the end of the street was the customs house, both a fort and an administration center. The two-story stone building was surrounded by an eight foot tall adobe wall enclosing a courtyard. An old pirate cannon was posted on a bastion overlooking the bay. Hughes pushed the heavy oak gate open and waved that all was clear. Butler soon had two men standing guard outside the weather-beaten warehouse. I walked to a point where there was a good view of the harbor. The ferryboat had returned from the mainland, bumping into a short dock. It was a large flat boat, capable of carrying horses and cargo.

"What are ya gonna do with us?" the militia captain asked with an Alabama drawl. I guessed him to be a Red Rover. His men looked nervous. Perhaps rumors had spread of the executions at Refugio after Urrea captured some of Ward's men.

"Colonel Custer, escort these gentlemen to the ferry. Minus their weapons," I instructed. "Townspeople, any who wish to leave may do so now. Those who stay will be under martial law. Violators will be summarily shot."

The militia members gathered their haversacks and hurried down to the ferry, followed by a dozen civilians. Those who remained were mostly farmers and merchants. It would take an hour to evacuate the refugees. I put Sergeant French in charge.

"Fresh," I summoned. "Take down that rebel flag. Run up the Mexican flag we captured in Béjar."

"Right away, sir," Smith said, seeing to it himself.

"You follow many flags," Slow said, now holding my personal silk guidon usually carried by Hughes.

"It's best if our enemies stay confused," I explained.

"Is it not you who is confused?" he asked, giving me the stare.

"What does that mean?"

"The slave keepers have declared their land free of the Mexicans, but you have made no such declaration. Yet you claim to govern this land in the name of the Buffalo. What flag truly rules this land?"

"Youngster, when we know who wins this war, you can ask me that question again."

———————

On the whole, the Port of Galveston was disappointing. The streets were dried mud with no sidewalks. Most of the buildings were single story, though a few around the plaza were taller, all built on pylons to rise above the sagging soil. It was said the village had been founded by the pirate Jean Lafitte, but I didn't think the structures that old.

Few of the dwellings offered the comforts of civilization, the floors being plank board with a few rushes. The furniture was crude, probably castoffs from unsuccessful plantations. The saloons were tolerable, though they weren't called saloons, hiding their identities under various *nom de plumes*. I liked the Customs House for its offices and barracks, but chose the King's Arms for my headquarters, a two-story hotel near the waterfront. Ships had been arriving from the States with donations for the revolution, providing medical supplies, guns and ammunition. Had we arrived only a few days later, the bounty would have been on its way up the Brazos River to Houston's new camp at San Felipe.

In the late afternoon, my officers and I sat on a wide balcony looking at the harbor. With us were Kellogg and Slow, though the youngster spent most of his attention on the motley fleet of anchored ships. A full-bodied Mexican waitress named Maria served fish, rice and red wine. On my suggestion, Isabella and Morning Star were dining with the harbor's womenfolk, learning everything they could of recent events.

"So what do we do now?" Tom asked. "We can't go west to fight Urrea with Houston behind us. If we strike toward San Felipe, there will be no one to check Urrea."

"The sooner we get out of here, the better," Cooke said.

"I've never learned how to retreat," I said, somewhat falsely.

"Not saying we should run, only find a better position," Cooke said. "If you haven't noticed, we're trapped on an island with our backs to the sea."

"It sounds like running to me," I replied.

"No one will follow our flag if we get our asses kicked," Tom said.

"That won't happen," I insisted.

"It wasn't supposed to happen at the Little Big Horn, either," Tom said.

"Damn you, Tommy. One mistake! One mistake in a fifteen-year career," I protested.

"And it was a pip," Cooke said.

Tom laughed. I turned to look at Smith, who wisely remained quiet, before walking to the balcony railing. It had a fresh coat of whitewash. Galveston Bay was calm, the wind having died down. I counted several ships floating at anchor in the blue harbor.

"Remember McClellan?" I said.

"You knew him better than we did," Cooke said, for he had not joined the 24th New York Cavalry until 1863, long after Lincoln removed McClellan from command.

Tom had not known McClellan, either. Having served honorably in the 21st Ohio Volunteers, Tom didn't become my aide-de-camp with the 6th Michigan until late 1864, the year McClellan was running for president.

"I was appointed to Little Mac's staff during the Peninsula Campaign. Promoted to captain from a green second lieutenant. He built the best trained, best equipped army in the history of the world."

"And then he wouldn't let it fight," Tom said, echoing President Lincoln's complaints. Complaints I had heatedly disagreed with, until my service under Sheridan had shown how a vigorous commander wins wars.

"McClellan may have been reluctant to commit his army, but he still deserves credit for its creation," I said. "The Army of the Potomac held together after Burnside failed at Fredericksburg. Survived Hooker's bungling at Chancellorsville. Held Cemetery Ridge for Meade. When Grant came east, he inherited a fighting force second to none."

"President Grant had an army of a hundred thousand men. We barely have six hundred," Cooke said.

"Grant wasn't president in '64," I corrected.

"So what are you saying, George? Should we still plan on attacking Santa Anna before taking on the Southerners?" Smith asked.

"No, Fresh, I'm not saying that at all. Slow showed me it won't work. But we can't look like we're running. We've got to make our mark. Present an obstacle that requires respect," I answered.

"And how do we do that?" Kellogg asked.

"Hell, Mark, think I'd be pacing this deck if I knew the all the answers?" I said.

"We captured Galveston easily enough, but we can't hold it," Cooke remarked. "And getting out could be tough if an enemy force arrives to block our retreat."

"Someone is coming," Slow suddenly said, otherwise disinterested in the conversation.

"And who is that?" Smith asked.

"One known to the general. It will bring change," Slow said.

"Good or bad?" Tom asked.

"It will be good," I quickly said. "Custer's luck."

"Haven't seen much of that lately," Cooke said.

"Then you're not paying attention, Queen's Own. Not paying attention at all," I replied, suddenly feeling better for no reason.

"General! Enemy approaching!" Voss shouted from the Customs House across the plaza.

"What enemy, Henry?" Smith called out.

"Sir, it's the whole goddamn Mexican army!" Voss replied.

I smiled, looked over at Slow, and clapped my hands together.

"Excellent," I said.

Before any of my surprised officers could react, I charged down the stairs to the plaza. What had been a half-baked idea a week before now appeared possible.

"Sepulveda, organize your lancers, full dress uniforms. Parade them to the dock," I ordered. "Tom, Smith, draw your men into the buildings around the plaza. Butler, sharpshooters on the roof of the warehouse. Heads down, not a peep out of anyone. Bouyer? Bouyer? Where the hell are you, you half-breed?"

"No reason ta git insultin', Gen'ral," Bouyer said, emerging from a tavern with a tankard in one hand and a barmaid in the other.

"Take Kellogg. Go down to the pier and keep watch on the harbor. Take a Mexican flag with you and wave it when you hear the bugle," I demanded.

Bouyer made no response, loping off with his head down. Dressed as civilians, neither would look suspicious if seen from the opposite shore.

"Colonel Almonte, I would not compromise your honor in this. Please stay with our horses in the meadow," I advised.

"I swore to serve your staff, General. I will not break my word," he replied.

"I would still feel better if you watched the mounts. We only have a few hired boys. I don't want them getting nervous," I gently said, for I had no desire to offend him.

"It will be as you say, sir," Almonte said, departing for the damp meadow that would one day be a city.

"Isabella, Morning Star. Gather some of the women. Find fish baskets and a vegetable cart. Follow Sepulveda down to the dock ready for market day," I said.

"We will sell fish to the enemy?" Isabella asked.

"Be friendly, Izzy. Just be friendly," I said.

As everyone rushed off to follow my instructions, I climbed up on the bastion of the Customs House, taking out my binoculars. Above me flapped the Mexican flag that we'd hoisted that afternoon. I saw Sepulveda take G Company down toward the water smartly dressed in the captured Tampico Lancer uniforms, forming his ranks well. He needed no explanation from me on what to do, being a clever man. Soon Isabella and Morning Star joined them with a dozen Tejano women, all excitedly carrying products to sell. After setting C Company behind the corrals surrounding the plaza, Tom joined me on the wall. Voss followed a moment later, his bugle ready.

"What is it, Autie?" Tom said, out of breath.

"It's not the whole damn Mexican army, but there are about two hundred cavalry," I said, watching through a British spyglass we'd found in the harbor master's locker. "Dust to the west. Possibly infantry. It's hard to tell."

"Shouldn't we consider withdrawing?" Tom asked.

"I don't think that will be necessary," I said, hunkering down.

On the other side of Galveston Bay several miles away, on a strip of beach I had known as Virginia Point, the cavalry were unsaddling their horses. The ferry landing did not offer many amenities, just a stable and a few sparse buildings for quarters. Most of the land was marshy and undeveloped, used for ranching.

I watched an officer in a red jacket, possibly a colonel, come down to the waterfront looking at the harbor with field glasses. Sepulveda's company remained in formation on the dock, the captured banner flapping in a light wind. Half a dozen Mexican officers were soon being rowed across the bay by a crew of enlisted men in a commandeered ferryboat.

"Looks like someone's in a hurry for warm food and a comfortable bed," I whispered.

"Someone you know?" Tom asked.

"Yes, Tommy. An old friend," I replied. "It's General Antonio López de Santa Anna."

The white men of the east and the brown men of the south are not the same tribe, yet they both seek glory in conquest. While riding to the place of many ships, I saw lands far from those of the Sioux and our cousins, the Cheyenne. There were many animals. The buffalo, elk, deer, and bear. Birds filled the trees. Beaver damned the streams. Crops were grown in great abundance, easing the want of winter. And those who did not hunt or farm traded the white man's goods. I realized such riches could tempt my people from our traditions, for life on the plains is hard. But Custer had proven that warriors will always be needed, for the more a people have, the more others will come to take it away.

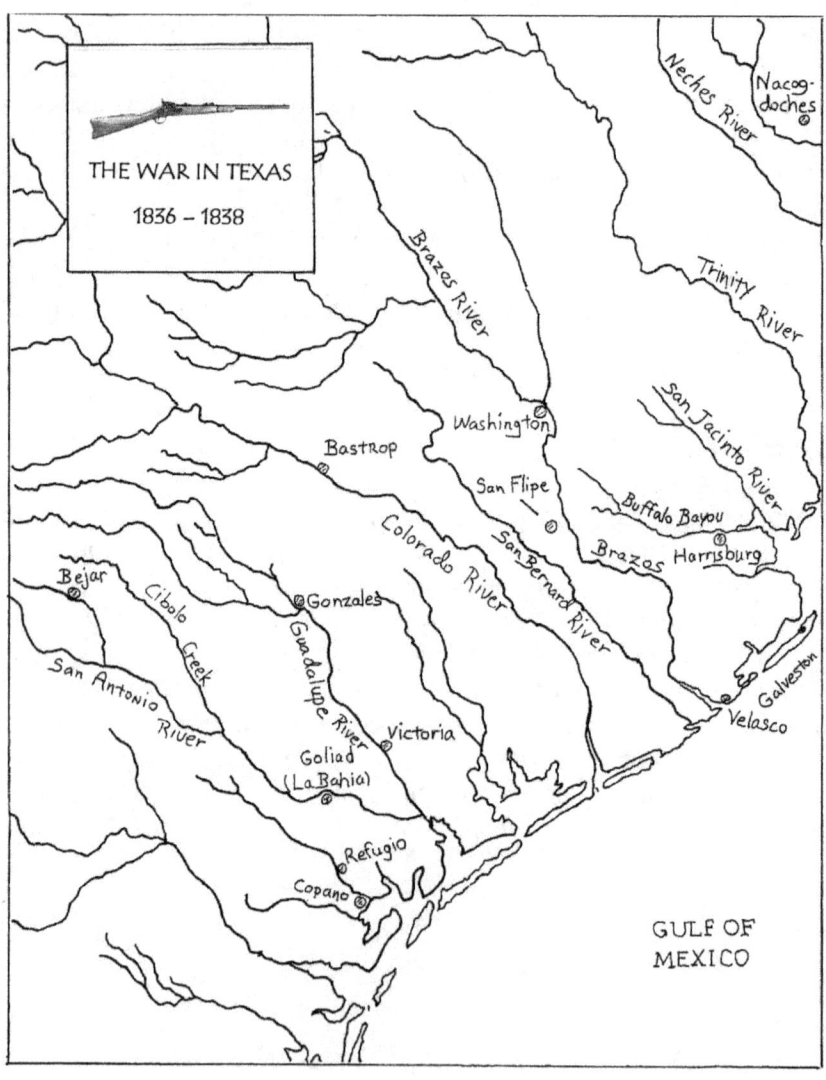

THE WAR IN TEXAS

1836 – 1838

Neches River

Nacog-
doches

Trinity River

San Jacinto River

Brazos River

Washington

San Flipe

Buffalo Bayou

Brazos

Harrisburg

Bastrop

Colorado River

San Bernard River

Bejar

Cibolo Creek

Gonzales

Guadalupe River

San Antonio River

Victoria

Galveston

Velasco

Goliad
(La Bahia)

Refugio

Copano

GULF OF
MEXICO

Chapter Three
CHEROKEE MORASS

As word spread of the dictator's approach, the command burst into excitement. I motioned for Butler to keep the men calm, then signaled Cooke and Smith.

"No firing unless I give the word," I ordered, going into the Customs House courtyard. Hughes was there waiting with his Henry repeating rifle, Voss with a Springfield.

"Stand just inside the gate. Follow a few paces behind when I make my move," I instructed.

"Are we going to shoot another general, sir?" Hughes asked.

"That remains to be seen," I replied.

Thanks to Maria, my uniform was clean, the wide collars straight, and my red silk scarf neatly tied. My blue blouse had a few wrinkles, and the knees of my gray pants were stained, but the noble sword hanging from my belt still marked me as an officer and a gentleman. I adjusted my campaign hat against the setting sun.

The ferry finished the long channel crossing and was quickly tied to a rough wooden dock. Santa Anna was helped from the boat by a corporal, dusty but well-dressed in a fine blue uniform. His tall cocked hat made him look like an admiral. He was accompanied by a colonel, a major, and two lieutenants, all appropriately attired for the president's staff. Fifteen privates and a sergeant, tired from rowing, came last. They were armed with carbine muskets. The rough bay had probably dampened their gun powder.

Logs imbedded in the mud formed a staircase up from the dock, necessary on the otherwise slick ground. Now that the sun had set, the dock and plaza were lit by torches. Sergeant Fuentes guided the party, Sepulveda hanging back with his lancers. Fuentes seemed to be doing the talking, for Sepulveda bore a great hatred toward Santa Anna, whose troops had sacked Zacatecas.

They reached the plaza surrounded by women offering fresh bread and tortillas. Santa Anna waved his hand casually and the privates came forward to accept the baskets, one of the lieutenants distributing pesos. Isabella glanced over at the Customs House and saw me in the doorway. I nodded and the women began to back away.

"*Nos quedamos en el hotel,*" Santa Anna said, pointing to my headquarters.

"*Lo siento mucho, Señor Presidente. Las habitaciones están ocupadas,*" I said, walking into the plaza with my pistols holstered. Santa Anna recognized me. I grinned.

"Señor Custer?" he said, hand clutching his sword.

"I'm afraid so," I replied, giving the signal.

At once, companies C and E rose from their positions, rifles aimed. G Company rushed up from the dock, lances nearly poking the Mexican troopers in the ribs, many of whom dropped their baskets. Hughes, Voss, and even Slow, rushed to my side.

"A Mexican flag flies from this town," Santa Anna indignantly said.

"And it will, as long as I have anything to say about it," was my response.

Santa Anna and his officers looked around for a solution, but there was none.

"Señor President, you invited me to dinner in Béjar. I would like to return the compliment. Will you dine with me?" I invited.

Santa Anna was no fool. The son of a minor official, he had clawed his way to power in Mexico City and tenaciously held it despite betrayals and revolt.

"My pleasure, General Custer," he replied.

I had met Santa Anna once before, at a fine supper in San Antonio cooked by Ben Travane. Crockett and I sought to avoid a fight at the Alamo, but the dictator could not be dissuaded. He was about forty years old, stood 5'10", and well proportioned, with black hair and large dark eyes. He looked Caucasian rather than Mexican, being of

Spanish heritage. Yet it was his charisma that set him aside from ordinary mortals. As Crockett might say, he could charm the hide off a polecat.

Private Gutiérrez, the dictator's middle-aged orderly, was allowed to stay. As was Colonel José María Romero, commander of the elite Matamoros Battalion that had attempted to storm the south wall of the Alamo. I had met Romero in Béjar and didn't particularly like him, but he was my age and without doubt a courageous soldier. All of the others were rowed back across the bay with the incredible story that their president had been captured by the impertinent General Custer.

"You have a port. And a navy," Santa Anna said, sipping wine on my hotel balcony. He wore a thick shawl for protection from the cold. I wore my fringed buckskin coat and red silk scarf around my neck.

"Only a port. The schooner is the *Pennsylvania*, American register. We will have to give it back or risk war with the United States," I said.

I was also sipping wine, though watered.

With us was Isabella, Tom, Juan Almonte, Colonel Romero and Slow. Kellogg wanted to attend but I kept him waiting in the next room. Drinking bourbon, no doubt. Butler was guarding the door.

"We?" Santa Anna said.

"I seized the ship in the name of Mexico," I reported.

"You are very bold," Santa Anna remarked.

"The other two ships in the bay are also American merchants. They've been ordered not to leave, and believing our cannon capable of stopping them, they have complied. I'm negotiating for their cargo," I said.

"They are pirates. And the servants of pirates," Romero declared.

"Yes, they are pirates," I agreed. "They have come to steal our land."

"*Our* land?" Santa Anna said, leaning forward.

"The Buffalo Flag represents the people of Texas," I said. "But that does not mean our Mexican neighbors are excluded. Once this rebellion is suppressed, you and I can sit down and decide the best way to rule this province."

"You presume much, General," Santa Anna said.

"More, now that you are my guest," I replied, raising my glass to him.

"It must be said, you are a man of no uncommon destiny, to outwit the Napoleon of the West," Santa Anna responded. "What is it you really want?"

"I want a land grant."

"You appear to have Texas. Is that not enough?" Santa Anna asked.

"No, I have another province in mind," I answered.

"Would this province require you to leave Texas?"

"Yes, it would. Possibly for several years."

"The province is yours. Let us sign the documents," he said.

Santa Anna was joking. He had no intention of giving away any part of Mexico without a fight. But he was intrigued by the prospect of getting rid of me, and not above a ruse to accomplish it. We had found common ground.

"Señora Velázquez, it is a pleasure to see you again," Santa Anna said, changing the subject. Isabella seemed briefly miffed, but quickly regained a pleasant demeanor.

"It has been two years, Antonio. Since the night you sent Alejandro to his death at Monclova," she replied, elegantly sipping her soup while fussing with a napkin.

"A commander must order men into danger when the country is threatened, even brave officers such as your husband," Santa Anna said. "Would you not agree, General Custer? Have you not ordered many to their deaths?"

"A leader is forced to make such decisions," I said. "Though a wise leader does not make such orders unnecessarily. Like you did at the Alamo."

"Or you did, on the Little Big Horn," Santa Anna said.

"I see someone has been speaking out of school. But certainly a man of your sophistication does not believe such fantastical tales?" I said, glancing suspiciously at Almonte. But Juan appeared clueless, nor would I think him a spy.

"I will believe anything that helps protect the people of Mexico," Santa Anna responded. A politician's answer.

Maria returned from the kitchen with a big platter of sizzling beef steaks. I was surprised to see her followed by a middle-aged Negro woman, her hair wrapped in a bun with white silk. She reminded me of Mary, Libbie's loyal colored servant during our years in Kansas. John was with them, bringing more wine.

"You are keeping slaves?" Romero asked.

"They are free," Tom said. "Free and well paid."

"They *will* be well paid," I corrected. "The Seventh Cavalry is a little short of funds at the moment. Much as you are."

"Money is always a problem for any army," Santa Anna agreed.

Whether Santa Anna knew I had possession of his abandoned war chest, I didn't know. Nor did I volunteer the information. Most of the funds had been given to Erasmo Seguin to buy munitions.

"How much of your army survives, *presidente*?" Almonte asked.

"Enough to defeat our enemies, Juan. Are you ready to return to my service?" Santa Anna asked.

"When General Castrillón was left with eight hundred starving soldiers on the San Antonio plains, I was offered in trade for mercy. My word is pledged," Almonte answered with mixed emotions.

"Promises given under duress are not binding," Santa Anna said. The same fatal advice he had given his brother-in-law, General Cos, who had broken his parole and returned to Texas with an army. Cos died on the north wall of the Alamo only a few feet from Travis.

"My word is pledged," Almonte repeated.

"Unless your new master releases you from his service?" Santa Anna urged.

"It is not Custer's decision to make," Slow suddenly said.

"I see you still travel with the mysterious medicine boy," Santa Anna said, feigning amusement. But I remembered the dictator's threats during our dinner in Béjar, and how his umbrage nearly caused a duel. Slow had belittled Santa Anna for his lack of vision, and Santa Anna had little patience for precocious children. I suggested that Santa Anna and I settle the future of Texas man to man, but he would have none of it.

"The Almonte has a great destiny," Slow said, unimpressed with the president of Mexico. Or anyone, for that matter, except Butler, Voss and Hughes, who he admired.

"Juan Almonte is a junior officer who has betrayed his general, and for that there will be consequences," Santa Anna said, just as unimpressed.

I was enjoying myself.

"More wine, sir?" I asked, taking the bottle from John and pouring it myself.

"You have mentioned my old friend, Manuel Castrillón. How does he fare?" Santa Anna asked, tasting the wine without insulting its vintage.

"The general fares well. He will be returned to your service when I return to San Antonio," I said.

"Oh, you expect to ride so far?" Romero asked.

"Sir, the Seventh Cavalry can ride wherever it wants," I said.

"I am in no position to stop you," Santa Anna agreed. "What may I expect of my captivity?"

"Better than you gave the Georgia Battalion at Refugio," Tom said, having heard of the executions.

"That is a relief," Santa Anna said. "Perhaps it is best I turn in. This has been a long day."

"Your room is next to mine," I said, motioning for Butler to provide escort.

The president set his napkin on the crude table, straightened his long black jacket, and strolled from the room as if leaving a meeting of Congress. Colonel Romero and the orderly followed.

"Tom, make sure our friend is well guarded. And have a patrol keep watch on the shoreline, just in case the Mexicans try a rescue," I said.

Tom took Voss with him, quick to implement my orders. If he hadn't already given the order without telling me. I lingered with Isabella, anticipating dessert.

The next morning I toured the harbor in good humor, congratulating G Company on a job well done. With captured funds intended for Houston, I had Cooke pay the troops, for which they were grateful. The tavern whores would have a busy night.

The Mexican army across the bay had grown to six hundred, but I wasn't worried. There weren't enough boats to transport them in strength, and our Springfields would kill the crews long before their own guns could get within range. Our two captured cannon, nicknamed the Twin Sisters, were stationed on the benchland overlooking the bay.

The American schooner *Pennsylvania* was an interesting ship. Captain Jack Delaure had chosen to remain aboard with his sailors, mostly Frenchmen from New Orleans, with a few free Negros and a Cuban cook. I guessed the ship at ninety feet in length, with two tall masts and a good-sized cargo hold. She carried two six-pounders for protection, the cannon placed forward on either side of the bow. My teamsters had assisted unloading vital supplies.

"I understand the Mexicans have confiscated your ship for piracy," I said, having boarded the sturdy vessel to stand at the wheel.

"The only Mexicans I've seen were rowed back yesterday, except for the tyrant, who you should hang," DeLaure said, a robust man in his early fifties with curly gray hair and hazel eyes. He walked the deck with bowed legs, and had a beard bristly enough to scrub the deck with.

"Well, Captain, there are Santa Anna's Mexicans, and there are my Mexicans. And there is your ship. I suppose we could let you sail back to the United States, though it seems like a waste," I said.

"You've already stolen my cargo. What more do you want?"

"Stolen? Sir! I understand the government at San Felipe guaranteed compensation for your voyage. If I've stolen from anyone, I've stolen from them. And as I don't recognize their misbegotten rabble of a government, it can't honestly be said I've stolen from anyone. Now apologize."

"Sir, I shall do no such thing. I am an American citizen, protected by international law," DeLaure protested. "The moment I return to New Orleans, you may expect my superiors will hear of your conduct."

I heard footsteps on the plank. Tom and Butler were coming with several troopers to secure the ship. Tom sensed the tension between the captain and myself.

"What's the problem, Autie?" Tom asked.

"Captain DeLaure claims we are violating international law and stealing his cargo," I said. Butler frowned and cocked his Sharps rifle.

"Let me understand this," Tom said, scratching the long scar on his chin. "This ship is bringing arms and ammunition to a Mexican port, where the weapons are being sold to rebels fighting the Mexican government, and he is accusing *us* of violating international law?"

"Yes, I suppose that's the brunt of it," I said. "Captain, have we overlooked anything?"

DeLaure stood with arms crossed, daring us to call him a pirate. Though he was.

"I say we hang the son of a bitch, sir," Butler said, looking for a rope.

"Sad, but I guess there's nothing else to be done. Better scuttle the ship, too. Don't want it falling into enemy hands," I said, beginning to walk away.

"The *Pennsylvania* is a merchant ship, sir. My company is contracted to move cargo. The sellers and buyers are none of our concern," DeLaure explained, unsure of our intentions.

"Your ship is for hire?" Tom asked.

"Yes, that's our business," DeLaure said.

Tom and I exchanged a glance. It was important for DeLaure to make the point clear on his own, otherwise we might be guilty of theft.

"In that case, we will hire your ship," I said. "You have one week to get ready."

"Hire? A week? But sir, there are papers to arrange. Agreements and rates to set. I don't have the authority," DeLaure stalled.

"You will come to my lodging tonight. Contracts will be signed, and approvals made," I said.

"Approved by who?"

"General Antonio López de Santa Anna, President of Mexico," I said. "And Captain, if you refuse, I can promise that Santa Anna *will* hang you."

I heard DeLaure gulp, for there was no doubt of my resolve.

"Where is the *Pennsylvania* going?" he asked.

"It will be a long voyage," I replied.

Toward mid-morning, Isabella and I walked up from the harbor to the pasture where a herd of cattle lingered along a shallow creek. Our horses were grazing among a grove of trees getting much needed rest.

"There will be a big city here someday. We should consider buying parcels," I said, holding her hand.

Isabella wore a high-collared jacket, for the early April weather was damp.

"You must feel strange, to expect a town where there is only grass," she said.

"There's no way to explain it," I answered. "The future is so different than the world we know now, and yet the same in so many ways."

"Tom and Bill. And Algernon. They all expect to have a better world than the one you knew. One without the blood of a civil war. My father thinks the Texas you saw, where my people are robbed and reduced to peasants, may now be avoided. Are such things possible?"

The meadow was peaceful, bushy trees surrounding us in a great circle. Some young girls passed by with a goat. A German youngster and his collie were driving a flock of sheep toward town. Recent rains had turned everything green.

"Slow believes there may be a new path for his people, too. One where their land is not stolen by Washington politicians," I said. "Izzy, I don't know if such things are possible. I'm just a soldier. I'm well-read, but not especially clever. I nearly failed philosophy at West Point."

"I think you underestimate yourself, Autie. There is a reason God selected you to repair the world," she said, standing on her toes to give me a kiss.

"If that's true, then there's a reason I found you," I said, clutching her tightly.

––––––––

Our first few days on Galveston Island were routine for an undermanned force constantly in danger of being attacked, but in time, we discovered our foes shared the same fears. The remaining locals quickly adapted to our presence. Part of the Mexican Army across the bay gradually moved north in search of food. I allowed Santa Anna to continue issuing orders, maintaining the fiction that he was my guest. As for Houston, he continued gathering volunteers in San Felipe, lacking sufficient supplies for an offense. Overall, I was very pleased. The Buffalo Flag had become a thorn in everyone's side.

Just before sunrise one spring morning, a party approached me from the King's Arms. Butler, French and Private Engle were escorting Santa Anna. The dictator appeared nervous, for if we had decided to shoot him, dawn was the perfect time. Nevertheless, he held himself with dignity.

"Mr. President," I greeted.

"General Custer. Señora Velázquez," he replied, looking around.

We stood at the edge of town near the south road. A few stars still twinkled in the dark sky. There had been a waning moon, but it was gone now.

"Sergeant French, I see you've brought the weapons I requested," I said.

"Yes, sir," French said, handing me a shotgun recently purchased from the general store. Engle held a shotgun as well.

"May I inquire as to the meaning of this?" Santa Anna said, straightening to full height, his narrow jaw jutting out.

I allowed for a dramatic pause, a technique Santa Anna was well schooled in. Then, to his astonishment, I handed him my shotgun and took the other from Engle.

"It's a pleasant morning, sir," I finally replied. "We are going duck hunting. I understand you are quite the sportsman."

The president sighed with relief and checked the gun, finding it loaded.

"How can you be sure I will not shoot you?" he asked.

"We are both gentlemen," I replied.

It was doubtful Santa Anna and I would ever be friends, but I suspected we might discover mutual interests. We spent the rest of the morning on the south shore, discussing the politics of Mexico City, strategies that might be useful against the Brazos rebels, and how to keep the United States out of the war. He laughed when I told him of the letters we'd been writing to the Eastern newspapers. We bagged four mallards.

That night, I surprised my guest again. As we prepared for a fine meal in the dining room of the King's Arms, three Mexican officers were escorted from the ferry. I had not previously met Generals José de Urrea or Joaquín Ramírez y Sesma. Colonel Juan Morales, who I had met in Béjar, accompanied them. I greeted them warmly, offering wine and seats at our table. They were suspicious at first.

"You are brave to accept my invitation, gentlemen," I said, sitting at the head of the table. We ate from colorfully styled Spanish china, drinking an excellent vintage from crystal cups.

"We are here under flag of truce," General Sesma said, taking the chair next to Santa Anna.

Sesma was about Tom's age with straight black hair and a long goatee. He had led the Mexican advance into San Antonio more than a month before and commanded the cavalry when they retreated south two weeks later. Next to him was Genera Urrea, a stocky man about my age with a fiery temperament. I was surprised to learn he had been born in Tucson.

"You fought well at Goliad, General Sesma. Sad you could not take Fort Defiance when you had the chance," I said.

"Defeating you was a pleasure," Sesma said. "And many of the rebels did not get far. We caught their rearguard at Guadalupe y Victoria."

This was news to me. Sesma smiled.

"Fannin?" I asked.

"Most of the rebel leaders escaped, but we shot a hundred of their minions before marching east," Morales said. "Fannin we will hang, when we catch him."

I glanced at Santa Anna, who showed mixed emotions. He had certainly issued the execution orders and felt no sympathy for the rebels, but had to wonder if the massacre would now lead to his own demise. General Urrea did not seem comfortable with the outcome, either. Perhaps he had opposed the decision.

Sitting near me was Tom, Cooke, and Kellogg. Slow sat on a tall stool by the fireplace. None of the women had been invited, while Smith and Sepulveda were watching the beach for treachery.

"It is sad when courageous men die for an unholy cause," I said, raising my glass. "Gentlemen, a toast to the fallen, may their souls find rest in a better world."

None rejected my toast. As soldiers, we all knew that one day we may be one of the fallen. Santa Anna let out a relieved breath, his anxiety unnoticed except by me.

Ben cooked the meal, John and Maria serving. Young Jimmy Allen of C Company was acting as my orderly. Santa Anna's own orderly assisted, for he had proven a reliable servant. By the time our second course arrived, succulent roast duck, the atmosphere began to relax. Two large fireplaces kept out the chill. Rain still threatened while candles flickered from the occasional draught.

"It's too bad General Filisola could not attend," Cooke said.

"Vicente waits at Victoria with a thousand men," Urrea said, unafraid to reveal military information. "When the Army of Operations reunites, we will outnumber the rebels three to one."

"Americans are pouring over the Sabine in the hundreds. By summer, they will overrun all of east Texas," Tom said, for Kellogg had briefed us on the numbers.

"We are not afraid of such rabble. Nor are we afraid of the troops your President Jackson has stationed on our border," Sesma said.

"He's not *our* President Jackson," Tom said. "The Seventh Cavalry is dedicated to freedom. We owe no allegiance to Jackson or any of his plantation owners."

"But you are Americans?" Urrea said.

"General Filisola is Italian, yet he serves your cause," Cooke said.

"And whose cause does General Custer serve?" Urrea asked.

All eyes turned toward me as the table fell silent. I reflected on many things. My riotous youth at West Point. The daring charge of the Michigan Brigade at Gettysburg. Riding off with the spool-turned table upon which Grant had written Lee's terms of surrender at Appomattox. My court-martial in 1867. The Washita. The Yellowstone Expedition. The Black Hills. The final moments on the weed-covered ridge.

I got up and went to the fire, standing near Slow. The flames danced in his dark eyes.

"Whose cause do I serve?" I asked him.

"You serve the Great Spirit," Slow answered without hesitation.

Several of the Mexican officers laughed. My officers did not. Nor did Santa Anna.

Cooke came to the center of the table and unrolled a map we had prepared. It was a better depiction of Texas than was available in 1836, based on our own maps printed in 1874. The Mexican officers were impressed.

"President Santa Anna and I have discussed the situation here in Texas," I said, directing their attention to an area north of Galveston. "Though we have not reached any decisions, we agree the Brazos government as constituted on March 2nd is illegal and must be opposed. David Crockett and myself have organized an army under the Buffalo Flag to protect Texas from these rebels, with or without help from the government in Mexico. We have not declared for an independent country, nor have we dismissed the possibility. To be perfectly frank, we don't believe Mexico has the strength to hold this territory."

"You are arrogant to think we cannot preserve our nation," Sesma disagreed.

"Mexico cannot even protect itself from France," Kellogg said.

"During the Pastry War, you'll discover . . ."

"Mark, perhaps this isn't the time," I said, offering a cold stare.

"General, they should know that France . . ." he tried to continue.

"Corporal Allen, please escort Mr. Kellogg from the room," I ordered.

The youngster rushed forward, took Kellogg by the jacket, and hustled him outside. Needless to say, this inspired great curiosity among the visitors.

"Let me apologize, gentlemen. Mr. Kellogg is a story writer," I explained as the sound of their footsteps faded on the wooden steps.

"Ghost riders," Santa Anna whispered, studying the expressions of Tom and Cooke, for both knew of the French interventions that would lead to the conquest of Mexico by Napoleon III.

"We are proposing a truce," Tom said, standing over the map. "We occupy San Antonio. We hold Goliad. By now, General Keogh has taken Gonzales. We want a peaceful corridor to the sea, preferably Corpus Christi."

"Corpus Christi?" Urrea asked.

"Copano," Cooke said, for in 1836 Corpus Christi did not yet exist.

"You ask much for interlopers. After brushing aside these Texian vermin, we will sweep north and—" Urrea started to say.

Santa Anna stood up, raising a hand for attention. His expression was imperious, and grim.

"As my good *amigo* José says, you ask much. What do you offer?" Santa Anna asked.

"The Buffalo Flag will hold west Texas as an ally to the Army of Operations," I said, cautiously feeling my way. For I had not expected such a question so soon. "General Castrillón will be released. We will protect Mexican citizens from marauding Indians, and from the outlaws infesting the country. And we will use our influence in the United States to force the American government to remain neutral."

"You have such influence?" Sesma asked.

"We will," Tom answered.

Our guests looked at each other, wondering what to make of the proposal.

"There is something else," I added. "Tomorrow morning, after a pleasant breakfast, your president will be returning to his army, without conditions."

75

Tom turned in surprise, but said nothing. I had not warned him of my decision. Cooke scratched at his long sideburns.

"We have made no agreements," Urrea warned.

"Either have I. You know my expectations," I concluded, very happy with myself. "Gentlemen, another toast. To friends and foes, whoever they may be."

After dinner, the women were invited back. We played music and emptied several bottles of wine. I would not say there was no tension, for we remained adversaries, but we grew to understand each other.

The next morning was cold and shrouded with fog. Before he boarded the ferry, I made Santa Anna a final gesture.

"Your Excellency, a gift from the Seventh Cavalry," I said, presenting him with a sword we'd found on the *Pennsylvania*.

"It is a fine blade," Santa Anna said, the ornate weapon shining with a gold-plated hilt.

"A South Carolina planter intended it for Sam Houston," I explained.

"I have something for you," the president of Mexico replied, reaching into his heavy coat. He withdrew rolled parchments tied with red ribbon. I gripped the documents firmly and shook his hand.

"Good luck, Antonio," I said.

"And to you, George," he replied.

The flat boat was loaded with officers, crew, and forty sacks of cornmeal that we were donating to our potential allies. The bay was fairly calm for early April. Santa Anna stood on the stern near the tiller, looking at me until the fog swallowed them.

"What the hell, Autie?" Tom said. "First you let that son of a bitch go, and then give him that fancy sword?"

"Tommy, you should listen to your own advice," I said. "Santa Anna isn't going to be bound by any agreements we make. He's a dictator. And a politician. We're better off making friends than provoking enemies."

"What's on the scroll?" Tom asked.

"A worthy exchange for a stolen sword, brother."

In the days that followed, I kept Tom, Cooke, Smith, and even

Kellogg busy with constant projects. At first they were mystified by my inquiries, but the lists I gave them soon made my plan clear. We would take everything from Galveston we could carry. And what we couldn't carry, I would ship to California on our hired schooner.

"Really, General? A printing press?" Kellogg asked, watching as the equipment was being crated. In addition to the press, an old-fashioned cylinder model made in Boston, we had gathered type, paper, cleansers and ink.

"Until a few weeks ago, it was the *Brazoria Gazette*. The publisher shipped it here for safety," I said, appreciating the irony.

"And what will you do with your own newspaper? Glorify the adventures of George Armstrong Custer?" Kellogg said.

"Yes, that's exactly what I'm going to. Along with handbills, advertisements, and proclamations. Anything *Harper's Weekly* can do, we can do."

"*Harper's Weekly* isn't even published yet," Kellogg said. "Won't be for another twenty years."

"Good, that makes us innovators. Haven't you ever wanted to publish a newspaper? You helped establish the *Bismarck Tribune*, didn't you?"

"You know I did," he said.

"We'll need a newspaper when we reach California. One that will tell people what they need to know."

"What you want them to know."

"Mark, we fought a Civil War where newspaper correspondents from all over the world reported every battle. They watched Congress. Quoted Lincoln. Wrote editorials. Men like Greely and Raymond shaped opinion. Now we'll do the same."

"Was this your idea, George?" Kellogg asked.

"No, it was Bill Cooke's idea, but it's still a good one."

"I'll make sure they use plenty of straw in the packing," Kellogg said, going to help.

The printing press wasn't the only booty we were confiscating. Galveston had a blacksmith, a gunsmith, barrel makers, leather shop and feed store. If we didn't take advantage, the Mexican army or the rebels would.

"No twinge of conscience, Autie?" Tom asked, for several craftsmen were now out of work.

"We're issuing notes in lieu of payment. What more can we do?" I answered.

"Worthless script, isn't it?" Tom said.

"It worked for Sherman's army when he marched to the sea. Would you rather go without? California in 1836 is a wilderness. We're not going to find any of these tools there."

"Someday we'll make the notes good," Tom swore.

During the night, one of the American merchant ships in the harbor slipped away, no doubt warned by Captain DeLaure that they were sure to be shanghaied. The second ship ran aground on Pelican Island. I sent French and Voss with twenty men to see what supplies they could salvage. A ship of the Texas navy, the *Invincible*, flirted with an anchorage, but withdrew into Galveston Bay. Another ship was not so fainthearted, gliding toward the harbor through a light morning mist.

"Sir, look at that," Butler said, standing with me on the bastion of the Customs House. "I haven't seen anything like that since Hampton Roads. What is it?"

"It's a British man-of-war, Jimmy. I knew they patrol Caribbean waters, but didn't expect to see them here," I said, watching through the long spyglass. Butler had my binoculars.

The ship was a beauty. Three tall masts with billowing sails. There were a dozen cannon on the upper deck and closed hatches on the lower deck for a dozen more. Seamen were tying down unneeded sheeting. A large British flag flew from the stern while smaller flags flapped from the top mast. Hundreds of people on both sides of the bay rushed toward the beaches to watch.

"What does it mean, sir?" Butler asked.

"I don't know, but that ship is much too large to dock at our pier. They'll need to anchor in the channel and use their rowboats. Have Sepulveda take a detachment down to greet them."

"Hell, sir, are we going to capture the limey ship now, too?" Butler inquired.

I looked at Butler in wonderment, and a bit of pride that he thought me so daring.

"No, Jimmy, I'm not declaring war on the British Empire," I replied.

Butler rushed off to issue my orders, though it would take the warship at least two more hours to find a good anchorage. I left

Cooke in command of the Customs House and returned to the plaza, wondering how to deal with our new guests, but was soon interrupted by a passel of German immigrants.

"Voss, what is this?" I asked as six large wagons with thirty hardy men entered the town, followed by a dozen women and just as many children.

"Sir, Mr. Johann Friedrich Ernst from Oldenburg," Voss explained with great excitement. Born in Germany himself, he clearly enjoyed finding these fellow expatriates. "They were forced to flee their ranches when the Mexicans came."

The tall German whispered to Voss, shaking an angry finger as his cheeks turned red. He was about forty years old, stoutly built, and dressed better than average for this part of the country.

"Mr. Ernst says it was General Burleson's men who stole his cattle and burned their colony, which old Steve Austin gave them," Voss continued. "Says he didn't survive Napoleon just to have his land ravaged by outlaws."

"What are they doing here? Looking for a ship home?" I asked.

"Been camping down near Pelican Island, sir," Voss said. "Helped us offload some of the supplies from that wrecked ship. Don't think they want back to Germany."

I went to inspect the wagons, impressed by their quality. Back in New Rumley, my father had repaired such wagons in his blacksmith shop, though not quite so good as these.

"Mr. Ernst appears to be a master of his craft," I remarked.

Ernst spoke again in rapid sentences. My own family has German roots, originally being the Küster clan from the Rhineland. But that was a hundred and forty years before I was born. I had never learned to speak my ancestral language, nor the Irish of my mother.

"Their town was called Industry, sir," Voss explained. "Says they made everything they needed, and sold the rest to colonists around Mill Creek. He hoped more immigrants would follow them here, until the war broke out."

The wagons not only had sacks of coffee and sugar from the beached merchant ship, but Voss had salvaged crates of French wine, rolls of silk, and a chest of fine china. For a country at war, the Texans were sure importing some strange cargo. I took Voss aside.

"Henry, a colony with such skills can be very valuable," I

whispered. "Can you convince them to join us in California?"

"Sir?" Voss said in surprise.

"Invite Mr. Ernst to dinner. We'll talk more," I eagerly said. "The ship that ran aground. Can it still sail?"

"Hell, sir, I don't know," Voss said.

I smiled before running toward the hotel, seeking my best uniform. And wondering if acquiring a fleet would make me an admiral.

Just before noon, the British warship dropped anchor in the channel with a great splash. The sound of a crisp whistle echoed over the water, assembling the crew. I ordered our Mexican flag taken down and the Buffalo Flag raised in its place, for I did not wish the English captain to feel tricked. They lowered a long boat and smoothly rowed toward our small dock, the craft carrying twenty men.

Slow and I watched from the pier, where they would need to dock opposite the *Pennsylvania*. Isabella and Morning Star joined us, straw baskets filled with fresh picked oranges, plums and cherries. On the embankment to my right was Smith with E Company. To the left was Sepulveda and G Company. Tom had C Company in the plaza, the Twin Sisters pulled back to avoid misunderstandings.

When they docked, the Royal Marines came first, a dozen brightly red clad soldiers armed with single shot muskets, bayonets hanging from their thick white belts. The marines lined up on the pier in column of twos led by their sergeant. Two officers followed.

"Captain William Bush of His Majesty's Ship *Lydia*," the younger officer introduced, tall and thin with clear perceptive eyes. His straight brown hair was cut short, and he had recently shaved, smelling of lilac water. "Accompanying me is Sir Thomas Cochrane, 10th Earl of Dundonald, Rear Admiral of the Blue."

The admiral was smartly dressed in a black frock coat and gray trousers. Brass buckles adorned his shoes, worn over long white stockings. His cocked hat was carried under his left arm. I would put him at sixty years old, likely Scottish. Gray stubble ran along the edge of his broad chin.

"Not *Sir* Thomas," Cochrane said with a trace of bitterness. "Whom do I address?"

"General George Custer, commanding the Seventh Cavalry," I said. "This is Isabella Seguin, daughter of Erasmo Seguin, quartermaster of

Texas. And Morning Star of the Great Sioux Nation with her brother, Slow."

"Yesterday your town flew a Mexican flag. Last week, it flew a Texian flag. Now it flies a buffalo. May we inquire as to the meaning?" Captain Bush asked.

His accent was common for an Englishman, possibly not an aristocrat. Unlike Cochrane, who reeked of nobility.

"Most certainly, but first the ceremony," I said, giving Voss the signal.

My troops came to attention, presenting arms, and the band began playing "God Save the King." When they were done, the men stood down and returned to their duties.

"We have organized a demonstration for you," I said. "The Seventh Cavalry carries weapons you've never seen before. You will find them interesting. And the women of Galveston have goods for sale. After the festivities, I've arranged a fine meal for you at the King's Arms. Your sailors may have the liberty of the town."

Captain Bush looked to Cochrane for instructions. The admiral acquiesced.

The sun had set by the time we finished our tour. Twelve years before, I had met a British admiral while in Washington, just before the Grand Review. Times change, but admirals don't. Cochrane was proud, stuffy, and easily offended, though I did not sense his anger was directed at me.

"We have long standing obligations in this sea," Bush said, drinking rum. "The Admiral led the Chilean Navy to victory over Spain. And the Brazilian Navy, too. His counsel on local conditions is much sought after."

"But he has no command of his own?" Tom asked.

"My knighthood was stolen from me by the Prince Regent. I will not accept a command until my honor is restored," Cochrane said, sipping our best vintage wine.

"But they made you an admiral?" Tom pressed.

"I *earned* my flag, youngster," Cochrane replied.

We were a small dinner group. The two British officers, Tom, myself, and the ladies. Even Slow had found excitement elsewhere.

"Does your government intend to take sides in the revolution?" I asked, for that is what I most wished to learn.

During the Civil War, the threat of British recognition of the Confederacy had been a constant worry, for France and Spain would quickly follow. Our blockade of Southern ports would have been disrupted. Only the issue of slavery, unpopular in England, had kept the British Navy out of the war.

"No. We are watching, but no more," Captain Bush said.

"Placing any bets?" I asked.

"Sir?" Bush replied.

"The Earl may have won independence for Chile and Brazil, but he didn't do so well in Greece, did he?" I said.

"What would you know of my war against Ottoman tyranny?" Cochrane asked, eyes wide and chin out.

"I read your autobiography while at West Point, sir. Even got demerits for being late to drill. Liked it so much, I sent a copy to Tom. Cooke has read it, too. Your adventures read like a novel," I said.

"Sir, I have not yet published my memoirs. Have not even finished them," Cochrane insisted, his ruddy cheeks blushing.

Tom and I laughed, though we should have shown more restraint. Cochrane was the stuff of legend, like John Paul Jones or Horatio Nelson. Just meeting him was an unexpected honor.

"Your knighthood will be restored," Tom said. "Though it's sad you must spend so many years idle. It's a bustling world, your Highness."

"I am a lord, not a highness, and I doubt you can read the King's mind on matters of state," Cochrane said. "But it is indeed a bustling world."

"Your rapid fire weapons are impressive, and there are strange stories about," Bush said. "But we have traveled the world. We hear many strange stories."

"If a new nation were to appear, one stretching from the Gulf of Mexico to the Pacific Ocean, what position might your government take?" I abruptly asked. "Such a nation might not wish to ally with the United States. Or with Mexico. Such a nation might seek allies elsewhere."

"You ask where I place my bets?" Bush answered. "Not on a small mercenary force with no support among the population. Mexico has a government. The Texians have a rudimentary government. All you have is a flag."

A rocket lit the sky over the bay. I dabbed my chin with a napkin and walked out on the balcony. The night had cleared, the stars twinkling off the dark water.

"A flag and a navy," I casually remarked.

The others came to the railing with me, watching as another rocket streaked overhead.

"Major Cooke has just captured the *Invincible*," I said, taking out my binoculars. "Schooner class, eight cannon, 125 tons. Formally registered to the Provisional Government of Texas. A fine escort for my fleet."

"How?" Bush asked, taking the binoculars from me without asking.

"A bit of a ruse, I'm afraid. Cooke borrowed your long boat and went out under a British flag. Cooke is Canadian. He can speak with a Welsh accent when he wants to. Those rockets mean C Company now has command of the ship."

"Piracy! It's piracy under His Majesty's colors!" Bush said, not at all pleased.

Admiral Cochrane laughed, his gray eyes squinting with delight. He returned to the table and filled his wine glass to the brim. We had a long evening ahead with much to discuss.

Seven days after *HMS Lydia* dropped anchor, the warship had taken on fresh water and departed for parts unknown. My ships left the next morning. Escorted by the *Invincible*, the schooners *Pennsylvania* and *Santiago* were on their way to California. Cooke had been given the assignment, taking Sepulveda and G Company with him, along with Frederic Ernst and his colonists, ready to begin a new life in a richer land.

Admiral Thomas Cochrane had joined Cooke as well, as an unofficial adviser. At least, that's how the log books read. He had really taken command of the fleet, promising them a safe voyage around the cape. The old man seemed anxious for one last adventure, and I had promised him one for the history books.

When the ships sailed from Galveston Bay, they carried cargo more precious than cannons, tools and Germans. Isabella had decided to visit Mexico City, meet with old friends, and speak discreetly to members of the Mexican congress. I asked her not to become a spy. We didn't need another Belle Boyd, but Isabella said the Seguin family name could do much for our cause. And she was quite determined. I gave her the red silk scarf that had saved my life at the Alamo, kissing her farewell. And I dispatched Juan Almonte to keep her out of danger.

On Thursday, April 21th, 1836, the remaining troopers of the Seventh Cavalry crossed Galveston Bay and rode out for Goliad, led by Smith. He took the heavy freight wagons and a train of pack animals. Mules, burrows, oxen, and every horse we could find. It was either take them or shoot the poor beasts, and I'd had enough of that at the Washita.

Only a few of us stayed behind, for we still had a special mission to accomplish. That afternoon, I formed my party aboard the steamboat *Yellowstone*, contracted to carry us up the Trinity River. There were ten of us, our horses, and enough supplies for two weeks. It would not be the swift moving battalion I wanted, for we dragged along six mules and the weather was still poor. Nor was I pleased that Morning Star had decided to join us.

"She is necessary," Slow declared.

"It's also dangerous," I said. "We cover two hundred miles of enemy infested country before reaching the Cherokee villages."

"The *Tsalagiyi Nvdagi* need to know your treaty is not another trick of the white man. As they have been tricked by this Houston," Slow said.

"I don't know that Houston has tricked them, only that he's made promises he can't keep," I said, wanting to be fair.

"Is that not the way of the white man? To say he cannot keep his promises?" Slow challenged, annoying and quite correct.

"If you feel that way, what makes my word any better?" I asked.

Slow stared at me with those big black eyes, gazed toward the trees for a moment as if hearing something no one else could, and then nodded. But he didn't answer my question.

Morning Star looked beautiful, having acquired a red British marine uniform, complete with a short blue cape. The leather boots were knee length, and she wore a black cockade hat. She laughed when I gaped at her in amazement, for she was a vision not to be dismissed.

The *Yellowstone* pushed off from the dock, leaving Galveston to whichever army occupied it first. Captain John Ross joined me on the main deck, a brusque old river rat smoking a corncob pipe. His sailor's cap was faded, the sleeves of his flannel coat frayed. His shaggy gray beard hung down over a yellow scarf.

"Sure ye won't rather go up the Brazos? Get ya lots closer to Gonzales," Ross recommended.

"We're headed for Fort Worth," Tom said, standing on the bow with Morning Star and Slow.

Morning Star had seen many steamboats during her school years in St. Louis, but this was a first for Slow. And a disappointing one. The *Yellowstone* was an old Mississippi cotton barge, patched up just enough to stay afloat, and there were bullet holes in her smokestacks.

"Don't know no Fort Worth," Ross said. "Ain't no forts upriver a 'tall, though there's been talk of buildin' one. Had some good fightin' below Groce's Landin' when Houston moved his men 'cross. Cannon, even. But they's all moved on by now."

"Just get us as far as you can. We're on our way to visit Chief Bowles," I said, looking back to see how the horses were doing. Vic and Athena had been on boats before, but Traveller and some of the new mounts looked a little skittish. Butler and Voss were keeping them calm. Poor Jimmy Allen was on shovel duty.

"Cherokee? What in Sam Hill for?" Ross asked, spitting over the wooden rail. "Kill 'em all, sir. Kill 'em all. Nothing but hell-born heathen scum."

"What do you think, Slow? Should we kill them all?" I asked.

"No, Yellow Hair," the boy said in all seriousness. "They are Cherokee, not Crows."

"There you have it, Captain. The Cherokee are not Crows," I said.

Captain Ross walked away, convinced we were crazy.

"This shouldn't be hard, Autie," Tom said. "We'll be riding straight north until reaching the Neches. From there the Cherokee won't be hard to find."

It took several days to work our way up the Trinity River. Most of the countryside was wilderness, though there were occasional plantations and small outposts. We learned Fannin had fallen back from the Colorado River and General Filísola was quick on his trail. With Santa Anna and Urrea slowly approaching from the south, the rebel army would soon find itself pressed on two flanks.

The river grew narrow, the water shallow. The *Yellowstone* could give us another twenty miles or so. From there we would need to find our own way. The only maps we'd found for this part of Texas weren't helpful.

Life aboard the *Yellowstone* was not bad. It reminded me of the *Far West*, the steamboat General Terry had used for his headquarters during our march into the Dakotas. Our cramped cabins were bearable, and we had use of a latrine rather than buckets. We had brought meats and vegetables with us, not trusting the riverboat's cuisine, and there was plenty of jerky for the trail. John insisted on serving us, just as he had insisted on joining our party rather than return to San Antonio. I promised myself to give him a raise when funds permitted.

Finally grounded, we disembarked to make camp, needing a full day to organize our march. Captain Ross accepted the hundred dollars in gold I gave him, and a note for a hundred more. Kellogg told me the *Yellowstone* would disappear somewhere in the Buffalo Bayou in 1837, presumably sunk in the swamps. I offered no warning, for making such predictions gathered more scorn than appreciation.

"Suppose ya knows all Texas is talkin' 'bout you," Ross said, shaking hands at the foot of the gangplank.

"And what could they be saying? Not that ghost rider nonsense," I replied.

"Nah, no God-fearin' man believe that," he said. "Canadian rangers, workin' for the British. Even saw ya on their ship."

"You've found us out, Captain. I hope you'll be discreet and not say anything," I urged.

"Ain't none of my affair," the man lied.

Then the gangplank was drawn back and the riverboat edged off the shore, returning to Galveston with a tale to tell.

The Cherokee town had been alerted to our approach, the tribe emerging from their teepees and roughhewn cabins. The land sloped from the low foothills down to the Neches River, the rolling acres filled with spring farms. On a gentle wooded plain up ahead was a log stockade.

"Jus' as I said, Gen'ral," Bouyer boasted, riding lead.

"The Cherokee are one of the Five Civilized Tribes. We shouldn't have any trouble," I said, though we were prepared.

Tom and I both carried Winchesters in our saddle sheaths. Butler had his .50 Sharps. French had possession of my Remington Rolling Block. Hughes had his .44-40 Henry while Voss and John were armed with Springfield carbines. And everyone had their Colts. Bouyer liked his old buffalo gun. It kicked like a sassy mule but was still a formidable weapon. Slow still had the Colt that Tom had given him at Béjar. Most remarkable of all, Morning Star now owned a pair of Harkom dueling pistols tucked in her wide black leather belt. I never asked where she got them, but assumed she had charmed one of the naval officers aboard *HMS Lydia*.

"Hughes, unfurl my guidon. French, raise the Buffalo Flag," I ordered. "Butler, pull out our instruments."

"Instruments, sir?" Butler said.

"Get to it, Jimmy," I said, straightening my saddle. "Slow, ride at my side with Morning Star."

Butler and Voss jumped to obey, breaking out the trumpet and drum I'd cleverly thought to bring with us. The road before us was dried mud, lined with rail fences. We were causing great interest, hundreds of Cherokee crowding forward. There were many children among the crowd, most dressed in sewn buckskin and checkered cloth.

Suddenly, I could not help bursting out in song, my high-pitched voice shattering the silence and nearly spooking the horses.

> "Hark! I hear the foe advancing,
> Barbed steeds are proudly prancing,
> Helmets in the sunbeams glancing
> Glitter through the trees!"

The veterans of the Seventh needed no extra prodding, for "Men of Harlech" had been a popular ballad in the final years of the Civil War, quickly joining in;

> "Men of Harlech, lie ye dreaming?
> See ye not their falchions gleaming,
> While their pennons gaily steaming
> Flutter in the breeze?"

87

The mounts began to pick up the pace, bouncing with new energy. My red and blue silk guidon waved in a gentle breeze. Needless to say, our Cherokee audience was astonished.

> "From the rock rebounding,
> Let the war cry sounding
> Summon all at Cambria's call,
> The haughty foe surrounding."

And then came my favorite part;

> "Men of Harlech on to glory!
> See your banner famed in story
> Waves these burning words before ye
> Union scorns to yield!"

We let out a cheer, slowing our pace to a walk as we reached the settlement. There were many smiling faces awaiting us, though whether it was our reputation preceding us or love of song was difficult to tell.

"I am General George Custer of the Seventh Cavalry," I boldly announced. "I am come to speak with the Cherokee people."

"I am Di'wali, called Colonel Bowles, leader of the *Tsalagiyi Nvdagi*. We welcome the brave Seventh Cavalry to our village," an elderly chief said.

Colonel Bowles was a tall man, or had been in his youth, with sharp brown eyes and flowing gray hair. I jumped from Traveller to shake hands, finding a firm grip. This gentleman knew the white man's ways.

"We have come far to meet your people. May we have sustenance for our horses?" I asked.

"You are welcome," Chief Bowles said, waving us through the gate of their enclosure.

Like many towns on the plains, this village was guarded by a tall wooden tower, and they even had an old Spanish cannon in the courtyard. Indians or not, even the Cherokee were sometimes attacked by roving bands of Comanche.

The command dismounted and led our horses to a corral were water and hay awaited. As always, the first order of business was making sure the mounts were well cared for, and I left Hughes to oversee the duty. Slow and Morning Star walked with me toward a large meeting house made of wicker and timber, Butler and Voss a few steps behind watching our backs.

"You have ridden from the Great Sea," Bowles remarked.

"You are well informed," I responded.

"These are troubled times. Those who have been our enemies now wish to be our friends," Bowles said.

"Those who claim to be your friends are still your enemies," I said.

"This we have seen before," Bowles agreed, for the man was no fool. He had led his people across the Mississippi River twenty-seven years before, looking for a home in Arkansas before moving on to Texas.

We entered the lodge to find a warm fire and a dozen grim chiefs sharing an afternoon meal served by squaws. The walls were hung with spears, hide shields and buffalo skins. Elaborate bead work showed on many of their dress coats. But one of the chiefs was not an Indian.

"Hell, General, that's Sam Houston," Butler whispered, standing at my elbow.

It sure as hell was.

When I was growing up, every school boy in America knew the story of Sam Houston. He had been a hero in the War of 1812 fighting with General Andy Jackson before being wounded at the Battle of Horseshoe Bend. Elected governor of Tennessee at thirty-four, he resigned under mysterious circumstances just eighteen months later. There were rumors of a marital scandal.

Houston quit white civilization and went to live with the Cherokee, who gave him the name Big Drunk. After an infamous trial by the House of Representatives in 1832 for caning a congressman, in which he was represented by Francis Scott Key, Sam left for Texas. After the fall of the Alamo and the Runaway Scrape, he won the Battle of San Jacinto and went on to a long career as President of Texas, U.S. Senator, and governor of Texas. When the South seceded in 1861, the old patriot refused to swear an oath to the Confederacy and was removed from office, dying in disgrace two years later.

My father admired Sam Houston more than any other public figure. When the 2nd Division reached Texas in August of 1865, my father traveled with Tom and I as a civilian forager. We talked about Houston constantly, visited his grave in Huntsville, and heard endless stories from those who knew him. And now here he was, still in his early forties, famous but not yet a national hero. Something told me we wouldn't be friends.

"A war council?" I asked.

"We hope not. The Raven urges us to join with the Texians," Bowles said.

"How can he be a raven? Does he speak with the birds?" Slow said.

"Do you speak with the birds, my young brave?" Bowles asked.

"Better than a white man," Slow answered.

I turned to Butler, asked him to wait outside with Tom and Morning Star, and looked to Chief Bowles. He offered Slow and I seats on the south side of their circle, sitting cross-legged on thick buffalo furs. Houston sat in the corner whittling a small block of wood with a short knife. No introductions were made. A fermented beverage was provided by a toothless old squaw in a red shawl.

"Allying with the Brazos Convention would be a mistake," I said once everyone was settled.

"Why is that, General Custer?" Bowles asked.

"The white men will take your land," Slow said. "You are few. They are many."

"The Texians want our help. They offer a treaty," Bowles replied, the other chiefs nodding.

Houston sat quietly, rotating the block of wood in his hand. It looked like he was carving a whistle.

A chief leaned over, speaking firmly to Bowles. Had he spoken Crow, Arikara or Cheyenne, I may have known a few words, but I knew nothing of Cherokee. Slow followed their conversion with keen interest.

"We have asked the Mexican government to confirm our land grant for many years, but our petitions are always denied," Bowles said, repeating the chief's remarks. "With the Texians, we will finally have our land."

"Within the next few years, these so-called Texians will turn on Cherokee. Your people will be driven north to the Indian Territory," I said.

"The Cherokee are strong. Many wish to be our friends," a chief said from the far end of the circle, a middle-aged warrior with high cheekbones.

"The Brazos rebels need your help now. Their army is smaller than the Mexicans. They are low on supply," I said. "When the Mexicans are defeated, and thousands of Americans come to Texas for free land, it is your land they will take. Just like they took your land before."

"Only a fool believes the word of a white man," Slow added.

"It is not a white man who brings us these promises, it is our brother," another chief said, older though perhaps no wiser.

"I know much of General Houston. All of my people do," I said. "He is high with honor. A good man and a good friend. But he makes promises he cannot keep."

"We have known this man for many years. You are strangers," the chief argued.

"The Buffalo Flag is forming a government to the west," I explained. "The rights of the Tejanos are respected, and many have joined us. The slavery of the black man will be ended. We have had words of peace with the Comanche. If the Cherokee join us, we will be your friends."

"If we join the Texians, will you be our enemy?" a chief asked, daring me.

I looked over to Slow, wondering at his thoughts. The boy's eyebrows were scrunched, the mouth tight. His hands lay in his lap.

"You have enough enemies," Slow said.

"These are difficult thoughts. What wisdom would *Colonneh* share?" Bowles asked.

Houston stood up, standing gravely in the firelight. He was more than tall, his head nearly scraping the hide roof. He held the half-carved whistle in one hand, the pocketknife in the other. He looked like he'd been drinking, having a haggard appearance, and hadn't shaved in a week. The beaded coat and headband marked him for Cherokee, the wool trousers and brown leather boots speaking of New Orleans.

"Do not be fooled by these ghost riders," he said. "They are foreign mercenaries in the pay of the British. Or the French. Maybe even

Santa Anna himself. They are sent to sow discord among natural allies. They come with tall tales and a boy mystic, like the carnivals of the east. My friends, my brothers, do not listen to their lies."

Needless to say, I was astonished. Almost admirably so, for Sam Houston was a legend for such bold pronouncements, however false they may be, and he spoke with an undeniable authority. The chiefs in the circle were nodding their heads in agreement. Houston was family, we were strangers. I could not fault them, but I refused to pity them.

"We are going west," I said, abruptly standing up. "This is not a time for promises. I have come here out of courtesy. I will not tell you to disbelieve *Colonneh*. He is a great man, and an honest man. But even a great man can be wrong."

I bowed my head and left the lodge. Nothing could be gained by further debate, for only a fool would debate Sam Houston.

"You are right to leave," Slow said.

"Wasn't it you who said we should come here?" I asked.

"And we have," Slow answered.

Tom and Morning Star were standing near a cooking fire, a plump squaw offering hot broth. Sergeant Hughes approached from the corral where our horses were munching hay.

"What's the plan, sir?" Hughes asked.

"Let the horses eat their fill. Purchase what supplies you can. We'll camp near the river and be on the road in the morning."

"Guess the meetin' didn't go so well?" Hughes suggested.

"Bobby, I'm not even sure how this meeting was supposed to go," I replied.

Houston emerged from the council lodge, accompanied by Bowles and two other chiefs. Tom and Morning Star came forward, wondering why the meeting had ended so soon.

"See here, brothers, who this false prophet travels with," Houston said, pointing at Morning Star and Slow.

"What's that supposed to mean?" Tom asked.

"Are they not Sioux? Blood cousins to the Cheyenne? Nothing but murderous savages. They give a bad name to every decent Indian," Houston said.

Knowing what I did of the Sioux, I could not entirely disagree, but I stepped forward to protest. Tom pushed me back, unbuckled his sword belt, and then his gun belt, dropping both to the ground. His lip was curled in a snarl, the scar along his jaw burning red. And then he charged.

At first glance, this looked like David and Goliath. Houston stood at least 6'4" and was well over two hundred pounds. Tom was 5'8", barely weighing a hundred and fifty in his boots. The Cherokee expected Houston to swat Tom aside like a fly. Butler and Hughes ran up, but I put out my arm to stop them. This was a personal fight.

"Stay back," Houston demanded.

Tom closed fast and smacked the tall man in the mouth with a round-house right. The next punch almost bloodied his nose.

Houston was not slow to respond, bracing his feet while blocking a punch and throwing a powerful left hook at Tom's head. Tom ducked the haymaker, but was struck on the chin by a strong right, knocking him down.

Cherokee began to crowd around, wondering if the fight was over. They didn't know Tom Custer.

In an instant Tom was up again, pushing Houston back against the council lodge with his left hand pressed on the tall man's chest. Then Tom hammered a hard right into Houston's kidney. Houston pretended a dismissing smile, but grunted on the second blow. His eyes bulged on the third, and suddenly desperate, Houston grabbed Tom by the forelock and tried to pound his head into a pylon. Tom was dragged forward but came in with a knee flying high, kicking Houston full in the gut.

Several spectators murmured with satisfaction, all of them enjoying the fight. Bowles and his chiefs stood aside, not interfering. Two youngsters squeezed in front of me so they could see better.

Houston shoved Tom back and swung, but Tommy ducked, closing in again with another kidney blow. Houston came down with his elbows on Tom's head, but Tom slid aside, countering with an overhand right that smacked Houston in the eye. Houston delivered a punch to the face. Tom gave two back.

"Damn you cussed son of a bitch," Houston grunted.

Tom paused, straightened up, and then suddenly threw a left jab at Houston's nose, this time splattering blood. Houston grabbed Tom by the jacket with both hands, lifted him off the ground, and threw him a good ten feet into the cooking fire, scattering coal and ashes.

As people jumped out of the way, I saw Tom jump up and shake off the soot, kicking burning embers back into the fire. Then he turned toward Houston, who was now armed with a long steel hunting knife.

"Thomas!" Slow shouted, running to his side.

Slow reached under his jacket and pulled out a Bowie knife. It was the same knife he'd taken from Bowie's room the night he died. Tom drew the blade from the decorated leather sheath, holding the famous weapon up for all to see. Houston's eyes went wide, for he instantly recognized it.

"General, shouldn't we do something?" Butler asked.

"Cover me," I whispered, walking out between the combatants.

"Stay out of this, Autie," Tom warned.

"Ain't none of your affair," Houston agreed.

"It's my fault this has gone so far. Let the blame be mine," I said, standing closer to Houston than Tom.

The big man had blood running from his nose and lip, not that it bothered him any. Tom had a nice bruise on the forehead. I took out a handkerchief, poured a bit of water from my canteen, and dabbed Houston's wounded eye.

"Sir, I beg you to reconsider," I quietly said. "My brother spent four years fighting the most vicious war in our country's history. Spent ten years on the plains fighting Indians. He's spilled blood in every saloon from Boston to Béjar. Forgive me, General, but you're just a lawyer. He will gut you like a fish."

"It's a matter of honor," Houston said between labored breaths.

"Then you shouldn't have insulted his wife," I replied.

"His wife?"

Houston looked over at Morning Star, fear in her expression. But not for herself.

"I had an Indian wife once," Houston said.

"I know."

Houston put the knife back in his belt and straightened to full height.

"Sir, my words were poorly chosen. I apologize," he announced in a clear voice.

And then the savior of Texas ducked back into the lodge followed by the two lesser chiefs. Bowles stood at the entrance watching, the black eyes studying our small but determined group. Then he went back inside, too.

"Proud of yourself?" I asked Tom.

"Damn right, Autie," the rascal said. "I just licked the tar out of old Sam Houston."

San Antonio was busy, as expected. Spring planting had started with confidence that the Seventh Cavalry would keep the peace. Young Henry Harrington and Green Jameson had enhanced the presidio with several strong gun emplacements. Smith had returned with his detachment in good order, while Keogh reported success in Gonzales. In truth, I had come to believe our position stronger than anticipated.

At the edge of town, I encountered Don José Navarro and Francisco Ruiz, who had attended the Brazos Convention and signed the declaration of independence. These distinguished gentlemen stood high in Béjar's Tejano community.

"Good day, señors," I said, doffing my campaign hat. "Have you reconsidered your allegiance?"

"My good friend Erasmo urges us to follow the Buffalo Flag, though his reasons are vague," Señor Navarro said.

"We all oppose the dictator. Should that not be enough?" Ruiz asked.

"No, good sirs, it is not enough," I replied. "But we have time to speak of it. In time, I believe you will see the justice of our cause."

"Honorable men may disagree," Ruiz said.

"And I know you to be honorable men," I replied, tipping my hat again.

Honorable disagreement or not, I could not afford to have such prominent citizens opposing me in the capital of our new country, but I could not hang them, either. They were as godfathers to Isabella.

As I rode up to the Governor's Palace, John dismounted first to take my horse. My staff would be inside, mapping our next move, along with Crockett and Erasmo Seguin. I was anxious to join them. To my ire, I discovered Mark Kellogg sitting on the front porch, his feet up on a table and a glass of tequila in his hand. He squinted with an annoying grin.

"Glad you finally made it, George," he said. "Lots of important decisions being made without you. Where have you been?"

"Visiting the Cherokee," I said. "We met Sam Houston. And Chief Bowles."

"The Bowl? Really? Gosh, what an honor," Kellogg said, making me wonder if he wasn't part Cherokee. "Too bad about what happens."

"What do you mean?" I asked.

"After Houston finishes his first term as president, Mirabeau Buonaparte Lamar, the second president of Texas, will lead a militia force to attack the Cherokee towns. The Bowl will fight them and be murdered on the battlefield. They cut up his body for souvenirs."

I put up my hand and turned away. It should not have surprised me. After what I'd seen in the Civil War and on the plains, no barbarity should surprise me. But the thought of that brave old man sliced to pieces by a gleeful mob was a bit too much.

I did not see how the path to a better life for my people could lead through Texas. The Tsalagiyi Nvdagi believed in a raven who did not know the spirits. Custer's white men fought the brown men, and the rebel white men, who also fought the brown men. And there were stories of the Comanche seeking plunder, even from those who would be their friends. And now Thomas said we would ride west to find more gold in one river than was in all of the Black Hills. I would have thought his words false had I not seen him defeat a giant.

Gregory Urbach

Chapter Four
THE GILA TRAIL

Two months and ten days after the Battle of the Alamo, the Seventh Cavalry was ready to march. We formed up on The Alameda, stretching from the top of Powder House Hill all the way down to the new wagon bridge crossing the San Antonio River. Tall trees and pastures were to our left. As were the shanties and saloons of La Villita. Farmers once again worked the land.

The Alamo lay to our right, the chapel and south gate still battered from the bombardment. The Long Barracks was still being used by Mexican wounded, General Filisola having sent a doctor for their care. The corrals were used for plow horses. A Buffalo Flag flew from its highest point, this version sewn with more care than our earlier attempts.

The west wall of our noble fortress, and most of the north wall, was rubble. The locals were carrying the battered adobe bricks away for building materials. Of the eighteen cannon, only five were left, two in the empty courtyard, two in the apse at the back of the church, and one on the southwest bastion. One day we would erect a monument to Bowie, Travis, and the other fallen heroes. Perhaps even one to General Cos.

On the hill behind us was a vast new cemetery. The Catholic portion held nearly a thousand of Santa Anna's soldiers. On the adjoining acre were the graves of seventy-six defenders of the Alamo. In my time, there had been a Masonic cemetery, but that would need to wait.

"It's not like the Black Hills Expedition, Autie," Tom said, astride

Athena.

"No, five hundred men is not the same as sixteen hundred. Twenty wagons instead of three hundred," I agreed. "No photographers this time. No geologists. No botanists. Only one annoying reporter."

"And no politicians looking over your shoulder," Tom said.

"We'll see if that's a good thing," I replied, for a desire to impress my superiors had always been a source of my motivation. Now I acknowledged no superiors, and no equals, except for Crockett.

I gave the signal, Voss blew his bugle for the *Advance*, and we crossed the bridge into town. Butler and Hughes went first carrying our flags, followed by Tom and Morning Star, then the regimental band playing "Garry Owen." We proceeded down the main boulevard, now lined with excited townspeople, until reaching the central plaza. I rode to the church and dismounted, standing next to Crockett, Erasmo Seguin and a dozen of Béjar's leading citizens, including Navarro and Ruiz.

The procession halted as two more bands joined in, playing a variety of Mexican folk tunes and old camping songs. Then each cannon in the city sounded, sixteen in all. A formidable display of firepower, for San Antonio was now the strongest fortification between New Orleans and Mexico City. And with Keogh as the military governor, it would not betray the weakness it had under General Cos and William Travis.

"Good luck, Myles," I said, shaking his hand.

"Make us rich, George," Keogh replied with an Irish grin.

"One for all, and all for one," I agreed, for there was no other way to keep the army loyal than by promising a generous division of the spoils.

The last song played was "The Girl I Left Behind Me" as the Seventh Cavalry rode out on the west road. We had six companies of soldiers, most of my original troopers now supplemented with American adventurers, Mexican volunteers, Tejano rangers, and even a handful of ambitious Comanche scouts. Supporting us were two hundred teamsters, cattle drivers, cooks, and camp followers. Fifty were recently freed Negros who found Texas an unsafe place to live, preferring unknown lands to the west. I could not blame them. The provisional government of David G. Burnet had recently declared that all escaped slaves would be hanged if recaptured.

Bouyer's scouts had started an hour before dawn, their job to watch for enemies and secure the best campsites. Water would be a priority, for even in spring, west Texas can be dry. Nearly as important was grassland for the stock.

"Thanks for lettin' me come, George," Crockett said, riding to my side on a spirited mare he'd named Mable Ann.

I was riding with K Company on a clear day. Despite incessant late April rains, the road had dried out, allowing us to make good time. I looked back before asking my question.

"Who is commanding your troop, Colonel Crockett?"

"That green lieutenant Micajah Autry, but your Sergeant French is keepin' an eye on him," Crockett said.

"French is your sergeant now, and you should be riding with your company unless you hear Voss blow *Officer's Call*," I instructed.

"I knows servin' in the Secon' Rega'ment of Volunteer Mounted Riflemen ain't exactly like being in a real army," Crockett said, making light of my order. "Just kick me now an' then. I'll catch on."

Crockett pulled his horse from the line and waited for A Company to catch up.

"You stay at the front of your soldiers," Morning Star said, riding a tall gray gelding that Tom had found for her. She was dressed head to toe in brown fringed buckskin, except for a blue kepi and bright yellow sash.

"I've learned from long experience that when traveling with several hundred horses, it's best to ride at the head of the column," I replied. "Morning Star, where do you get so many outfits? Even Libbie never owned so many."

"It is my duty, so I trade materials and make my own. Mrs. Dickenson has been very helpful," she replied, adjusting the cap.

"Your duty?" I asked.

"General Custer, do you think me ignorant?" she said, though not in an annoyed way. "You often have me riding with you when we enter new towns. The people like to see a beautiful woman on a brave horse. It puts them at ease, and enhances your reputation. Did I not greet Santa Anna? Was I not first into the Cherokee village?"

"I have not done so deliberately," I replied, though she was completely correct about the rest.

"If I can help, and make our journey safer for Thomas, then it is my

101

duty," she said. "And as I learned in St. Louis, colorful clothing attracts attention."

"It certainly does, young lady," I agreed.

We pushed hard, making better than fifteen miles the first day and stopping at Leon Creek. Crockett finally got his officer's call.

"Soon this road will turn into a trail, and after that is anyone's guess," Smith said, looking at his map.

"Thar ain't no good maps, only lots a 'pinions," Crockett complained, for his famous travels had not taken him this far west.

"We have copies from Cooke's atlas, and every officer has a compass," Tom said. "Besides, this road should be good all the way to Del Rio. From there we move up the Pecos to Horse Head Crossing, cross over to the Rio Grande, and make a beeline for El Paso."

A Catholic priest's fine skill had drawn a map for each company commander. I had personally added the most important notes.

"You make it sound easy, lad," Captain Blazeby said, his English accent strange among so many Southerners and Midwesterners. At least he was my age instead of being one of the kids, tall, stout, and getting a little gray in the whiskers.

"Can't say it will be easy, Billy. But we know what to look for," Smith said.

"We is jus' gonna follar the old Wells Fargo trail," Bouyer added, chewing black tobacco and spitting in our campfire. I considered ordering him not to, but he'd had a long day.

"A trail that doesn't exist yet," I said, playing devil's advocate.

"Trail's a trail. Be there before. Be there still," Bouyer said.

We moved on to Del Rio, arriving a week later. As I expected, the small trading post near San Felipe Springs was not well defended. The locals had built a church with a few surrounding walls to discourage roving bands of Comanche, but the score of crude wooden buildings were vulnerable to attack. Like many west Texas towns, cattle was the primary industry, though the springs were feeding a growing farming community.

The weather was good. The Seventh Cavalry stayed in Del Rio several days building a supply depot and corrals for horses. I ordered the construction of a watch tower and prepared a redoubt on the highest ground, though it would be several months before cannon could be sent from San Antonio. Above the redoubt was mounted a tall flag pole, so none would doubt that Del Rio now belonged to the Buffalo Flag. When I rode out of town at the head of my troops, the townspeople cheered their new hero.

Not all of my army was securing our western base of operations. Tom had been sent forward with C Company, the scouts, and fifty laborers to turn the northern trail into a wagon road. They would fill in ruts with clay and stones, erect bridges over creeks, and build cisterns at waterholes.

"Tom, I realize not everyone is happy about my vision of the future," I told him, catching up at the Devil's River crossing.

"The men are anxious, Autie," Tom said, without actually complaining. "With a hard ride, we could be in California in thirty days."

"And then what?" I asked.

"And then what? We make for the gold fields," he said.

"Maybe Bill is right, you should have finished school," I said.

"At least I wouldn't have been last in my class," Tom remarked.

"Smart ass."

"Autie, I understand we need a road. Do we need such a good road?" he asked.

"This is the Custer Road, Tommy. By this time next year, it will be moving cargo and stagecoaches. Forts will protect travelers. One day it will support a railroad."

"Which Custer are we talking about? Seems like I'm doing all the work."

"If there's anything Rome taught us, it's that you can't have an empire without roads," I insisted.

Tom looked at me in the strangest way, then shrugged his shoulders and walked back to our camp along the creek. Freshly slaughtered beef was roasting on big fires. The women were serving cornbread and laughing at the soldiers' jokes, though most knew no English. Perhaps the men were restless, but I didn't share Tom's concern.

We were on the move at dawn, crossing the new bridge on our trek north. When we reached the Pecos Crossing, we stopped to build a fortified trading post. I named it Fort Yates, after my good friend who died at the Cibolo.

Eventually we left the Pecos River behind at Horsehead Crossing, turning west over the Guadalupe Mountains and back down into the Rio Grande Valley. We were now nearing the home of the Chiricahua Apaches, who lived along the headwaters of the Mimbres River, so we needed to be careful. Most of our Comanche scouts left us, declining to challenge the Apaches in their own land. They were well rewarded, for I had determined the Seventh Cavalry had enough challenges without provoking the savages.

"The Apaches will be near the river," I said, halting on a brushy hill within sight of the Rio Grande. Thick growths of trees and glistening water could be seen even from several miles away.

"Still gots lots a men back in them hills," Bouyer warned, for my work crews were busy widening the trail all the way to the pass.

"Order your scouts to watch our flanks, I'll have Crockett bring his men up to supplement Brister," I decided.

"Takin' greenhorns into the valley of death?" Bouyer remarked.

"I'll be in command," I answered.

Crockett arrived a few minutes later. After the companies led by Tom and Smith, I thought Crockett's the best.

"Finally makin' it back to the Rio," Crockett said with a tired smile. "Beginnin' to wonder if we'd e'er see it a'gin. Pretty sick of them damn hairless mountains."

"Apache country now, David, so careful what you say about going hairless," I warned. "The Mexican government has offered a bounty on every Apache scalp, and the Apache are all too willing to return the favor."

"Plenty a In'gins tried for my scalp. None gots it so fer," Crockett answered.

"Have A Company blaze a trail down to the river and find us a campsite. B Company will ride in support. Tell Dickenson I want the artillery down there before sunset."

"No small order there, General," Crockett said, for bringing the guns over the pass had proven difficult.

"If we build a fort here, we can call it Fort Crockett," I suggested.

"Hell, George, if I kin get me a hot meal and a shave, ya kin call if Fort Diablo fer all I care," he said, riding back to his troop.

Slow arrived, riding with Morning Star. They looked tired, too.

"Well, boy, what are your thoughts?" I asked.

"The Great Spirit does not inhabit this land," Slow gravely said.

"You've spent many hours with Catholic priests on this journey. Though their ideology is tainted by Popery, even their Bible teaches us that Jesus inhabits all lands. And all hearts."

"And this is your belief?" Slow asked.

"It is."

"Then you are a fool," he said.

"You are not the first to think that," I answered. "I've been driving the men hard to build this road. They are tired. What wisdom may the Great Spirit offer?"

"The Great Spirit's wisdom is not for the white man. I have seen the Seventh Cavalry ride with honor, but this is because of Tom. And Algernon. You, and Bill Cooke. Without such leaders, many peoples would suffer."

"Slow, the leaders you speak of were given a gift. Not all white men have seen what we have seen. Not all have become ghost riders. Now we must teach our brothers the meaning of this gift."

"With a road? With gold?" he asked.

"I'm doing the best I can. West Point taught me to be a soldier. It didn't teach me how to remake the world."

"And yet that is the mission given you by the Great Spirit," Slow said. He gazed at me as if able to sense the future. Or a possible future.

"If the Great Spirit wanted a new world, he should have picked Mr. Lincoln," I said. "Or General Sheridan. Or Mark Twain."

"I fear you speak the truth," Slow remarked, getting up and wandering off into the darkness. Maybe the birds would have something to say.

———

Once again in the Rio Grande Valley, we found a good road moving northwest. Wagon tracks were visible in the dried mud. We had seen several small ranch houses, now abandoned, but proof of civilization. The El Paso of 1836 was unlikely to resemble the bustling city of 1876, where ranching, mining and the railroad had made such a difference. The issue of *Frank Leslie's Illustrated* that Private Engle had shown me was vague on details regarding the Territory of New Mexico, focusing more on California, but many of us had heard stories.

And I still remembered the adventures I'd read of Kit Carson. Only fourteen-years-old in 1853, I was an avid reader of *Harper's Monthly*, a journal filled with illustrations of a world much larger than Monroe. There were tales of Saint Paul in Damascus, Napoleon, Charles Dickens, and even Tahitian cannibals. That July, they published *A Ride with Kit Carson*. I must have read Brewerton's journey a dozen times.

I had never been to El Paso. In fact, none of the men had. Only a few had ever been to California, and those by ship or the Oregon Trail, so we were in new territory, led only by maps made forty years in the future. But first we had an unexpected encounter.

"Who are they?" Butler said, pointing to group of Indians camped near the Rio Grande just short of a village called San Elizario.

"Apache. I guess 'bout fifty or so. Men, women and kids," Bouyer said, spitting tobacco. "Reckon we should attack?"

"I reckon we should talk with them first," I said, waving for E Company to halt.

"Let me come, too," Tom requested.

"I'm leaving you in command. We can't both go," I said.

"Then take Slow. They won't try anything with Slow there," Tom said.

"You think they'll be afraid of an eight-year-old?"

"You know the answer to that better than anyone," Tom replied.

I waved Slow forward and we rode toward a rock ledge where the small camp had been set up, four hide teepees and one straw wikiup. At the last minute, Hughes and Butler appeared at my side, my personal guidon and the Buffalo Flag unfurled. I let the insubordination pass. In my experience, Indians are always impressed by flags.

We reached the base of the rocks and dismounted, Butler holding the horses while Slow and I went forward. Half a dozen Indians came down to meet us, armed with bows and arrows except for one old Spanish musket. One heathen in particular was impressive, tall and square shouldered with a face to make the ladies swoon.

"I am General George Custer, Commander of the Seventh Cavalry," I introduced, offering my hand.

"I am called Mangas Coloradas of the Mimbreños," the tall Indian replied in Spanish, accepting the gesture.

"George Custer has heard of Red Sleeves. Why are his people

camped so near the Mexican village?" I asked.

"The Mexicans are bitter enemies of the Mimbreños. When their soldiers went south, we came to discover why," Coloradas said.

"Has San Elizario offended the great Apache?" I asked.

"They have harbored scalp hunters who slay our women and children," he said.

"Perhaps the Mexicans have a grievance against your people? There is much violence in the Gila River country," I suggested.

Coloradas looked behind me as B Company came up, dismounting in skirmish formation. A dust cloud showed more troops were on the way.

"You have many soldiers," Coloradas observed.

"Yes," I replied. "We are making a road from the east to the west. A road my people must travel in safety."

"This road must not be through our hunting grounds," Coloradas warned.

"It will not be," Slow said.

"And if we capture scalp hunters, they will be hanged," I promised.

"Come to my camp, General Custer. We will talk," Coloradas said.

A few days later, Tom, Bouyer and I went up a nearby hill to view our objective only half a mile away. We took turns with the binoculars. The landscape was dry and mountainous, though I understood there was a pass that led to Santa Fe.

"I expected a large trading center, not another dismal village," I said. "Looks like most of El Paso is on the south bank. Barely a hundred people on the north side."

"No sign of Fort Bliss, though I see an adobe tower. Could be armed with a small cannon," Tom observed.

"Kinda thin walls to protect from Indian attacks," Bouyer said, spitting tobacco. "North side's only gots hedges of mesquite brush."

"The mission is their main fortress. That's a big church. The biggest I've seen since leaving Philadelphia. And the walls surrounding it are thick," I said.

"Alamo had thick walls, too, for all the good they did," Tom said.

"Alamo weren't attacked by no In'dins," Bouyer said, spitting again.

"We're dealing with Apache now," I said, annoyed by Bouyer's bad habit. "And it's not just a church. There's a military plaza behind it, just like San Antonio. Customs House, too. We may encounter a hundred or more Mexican soldiers when we ride in."

"We outnumber them, Autie," Tom said.

"I don't want to start a war in New Mexico, little brother. Not until my other objectives are achieved," I insisted.

"Thought you wanted to conquer the whole damn world, like Napoleon?" he answered.

"El Paso isn't the world, it's just a flyspeck on the Rio Grande," I replied.

We rejoined the command that was now ready to move. Our approach could not be a secret after lingering so long in San Elizario, but so far, no force had sallied out against us.

"I'll take the lead with my staff," I decided. "Sharrow, watch our left flank. Brister, keep an eye on the right. Crockett, you will stay close. Flags and banners, gentlemen. Let's show the locals what a real fighting force looks like."

I didn't wait for reactions, turning Traveller toward town with a kick of my heels. Slow was quickly at my side, ready for adventure. Bouyer and Morning Star were close behind. Hughes, Butler and Voss formed up on my flanks, flags unfurled. Voss had his bugle ready to relay orders.

We had barely gone a quarter mile when a group of twenty men on mules began riding in our direction. They looked like a rough lot, possibly mountain men by their dirty leathers and brushy fur caps decorated with feathers. Leading the riders was a young man with long blond hair, not tall but stout, with an expression of great confidence. I recognized him instantly.

"General, isn't that...?" Butler started to say.

"Sure is, Bobby," I said. "That there is Kit Carson."

Carson had seen us, too, raising his hand in greeting.

"Gen'ral Custer, I presume?" Carson said.

"Has my fame preceded me?" I asked, dismounting.

"Kan't take 'an army in dese parts 'out folks a knowin'," he replied, jumping down and offering to shake hands.

Though Carson couldn't have known it, we had met before in Washington during one of his visits from the west. He'd been in his early '50s then, already gray and growing thin from hard years on the trail. The Kit Carson of 1836 was short but strong boned, with clear blue eyes and tousled sandy hair. He had just turned thirty, about Tom's age. He was not yet a legend, the man whose daring adventures would thrill every school boy of my generation. He wore the stiffened deerskin that I'd read so much about.

"I need a guide to California. Are you available?" I asked.

"That's a what we come fer," Carson said. "But we're a wantin' real pay, no dreams a gold mines."

"No interest in gold?" I said.

"Folks been diggin' gold out of them hills for years. Ne'ar found 'nough ta trouble with," he replied.

And I knew it to be true. Prior to the gold rush in 1849, small amounts of gold had been found near Los Angeles, but not enough to spark attention.

"Take us where we need to go. You'll be paid in coin," I promised.

I didn't actually have much in the way of hard currency, but expected to start my own mint once we had the right equipment. Both Tom and I had spent enough time in my father's blacksmith shop to get a smelter going. I might even put my face on the first twenty dollar gold piece.

"Gots good boys here, Gen'ral. We'll get ya thar," Carson said.

Carson waved to his scruffy mountain man army and they whooped up a cheer. Most were trappers, but beaver pelts for men's hats had gone out of fashion, and the beaver themselves were quickly disappearing. The rough-and-tumble pioneers of the early West were finding themselves unemployed.

I breathed a secret sigh of relief. The maps I had scavenged from Cooke showed roads into California, but most of the trails did not exist until the late 1840s. Having an experienced scout would make a great difference.

I waved the command forward and we rode into El Paso in fine fashion, the band playing "Garry Owen". Sheep herders and farmers greeted us coolly as we approached the old wooden bridge. I saw evidence of extensive irrigation ditches.

Though the north bank only held a few houses of substance, the town on the south bank was bigger than Galveston. I guessed the population at a thousand.

"The garrison?" I asked Carson, stopping at the river's edge.

"Pulled out a few days 'go. Some ta Santa Fe, most headin' back to Mexico," he said. "Town folk glad to see ya. 'fraid of In'dins with their soldier boys gone."

I hadn't thought to garrison El Paso myself, but now realized the necessity. And I'd need to guard my road. The Apache weren't likely to respect the Seventh Cavalry if we didn't maintain a presence.

By midday, all but E Company had crossed the bridge into town, finding lunch in the plaza. I had appropriated the former commandant's quarters in the presidio, Tom and Morning Star were in the fanciest hotel. Crockett's men took over the largest cantina, promising not to tear it apart. Slow had chosen a small room in the Franciscan Mission, called Our Lady of Guadalupe, but I doubted he planned to become a monk. I saw Carson's men were impressed, not just by the organization of a real army, but by the strange weapons we carried. Even the best muskets of the former garrison were ancient by comparison.

"I believe the Mexican army is withdrawing from New Mexico," I announced as my officers took stools underneath a splendid elm tree.

There were fourteen of us, along with a few trusted sergeants and scouts. The sky was clear with a fresh breeze bringing the scent of wild flowers off the prairie. The adobe town was old, having been founded almost two hundred years before, but was maintained with pride. The marketplace was robust, the houses decorated with colorful paints, and the merchants were busy. My first impression of El Paso as a dreary settlement had been wrong.

"It's good we have a treaty with the Apache," Smith said.

Bouyer laughed under his breath and looked for a place to spit. I ordered him away from the table with a frown.

"We have a treaty with the Mimbreño," I pointed out.

"And there are plenty of Apache who don't give a damn about that. The locals are without protection now," Tom said, reading the situation well.

"I need an officer to garrison El Paso and order patrols from here to Del Rio, and from here to our next post at Yuma," I said. "No offense to you, Mr. Brister, or to you, Mr. Blazeby, but it has to be someone who understands chain of command. And most important, someone who understands supply."

Immediately, all eyes turned to Captain William Sharrow, former sergeant major of the Seventh Cavalry. He'd been born in England and packed a lifetime of experience into his thirty-three years, having served in the 2nd Cavalry at the end of the Civil War before joining the Seventh. My height, lean, strong and broad-shouldered, he had never failed me.

"Leaving me in the wilderness, sir?" Sharrow asked, staring at me with questioning blue eyes. He ran a hand through his shaggy brown hair, as he often did when perplexed.

"Temporarily, for now. Governor Sharrow," I said.

"Governor?" he said.

My other officers stirred, wondering at my thoughts.

"I need to leave a man of authority in charge. Until someone more suitable is available, you are now the military governor of New Mexico," I answered.

Now some of the men were jealous, wilderness or not. And El Paso was filled with enough pretty senoritas that the duty would not prove tiresome. I would miss Sharrow on the trail, but I now saw El Paso as the key to uniting Texas and California into a continental empire. It was a post for a thorough organizer, not an ambitious adventurer.

By early July my advance scout was on the road west toward the Yuma crossing of the Colorado River. Carson showed us the short route to the Gila River Trail, and from there we rode through a parched landscape toward a setting sun.

Tom was not with me. To insure our claim to New Mexico, I sent C Company to secure Santa Fe, the largest municipality in the territory. Tom would raise the Buffalo Flag in the plaza and then rejoin us. My little brother smiled as he rode off, looking forward to an independent command.

Riding with Tom was K Company under its new captain, Juan Antonio Badillo. Though tall for a cavalry trooper, Badillo had proved a good junior officer, efficient in his duties and popular with the men. As a Tejano recruit for Jim Bowie at the Alamo, he had a reputation for loyalty. I had initially offered the posting to Almaron Dickenson, but Susanna was with child again and they decided to stay with Sharrow in El Paso. Dickenson would prove a good adjutant.

"Some of the boys are unhappy 'bout that," Crockett hinted to me after the announcement.

"Badillo?" I asked.

"Promotin' a Tejano o'er a white man," Crockett warned. "Don't git me wrong. Don't got no objection myself. Jus' sayin'."

"David, this is largely Mexican territory," I said. "As we ride through, I don't want the people thinking of the Seventh Cavalry as an occupying army of Anglo-Saxon mercenaries. When in Rome."

"Rome?" he said.

"When in Rome, do as the Romans do. A saying of Saint Ambrose," I explained.

"George, I think you read too many books," Crockett remarked.

The trail west was mostly flat, the vast landscape filled with cactus and sagebrush. Much of our path was an old wagon road that made the ride easier. Rather than the green hills of east Texas, or the brown hills of west Texas, we now saw towering formations of red rock, limestone, sandstone, and piles of gigantic boulders. I could remember nothing in my previous experience to match such scenery, with the possible exception of the Dakota Badlands.

"Left lots of your boys behind," Carson grunted, riding next to me on a thick mustang named Apache.

"I'm not worried," I said, glad to be on the move again. The sun had barely risen behind us, and already the day was warm.

Carson's concern was that I'd left Crockett, Smith and Brister to repair Fort El Paso, but I still had Blazeby's company. Forty well-armed men, not counting Carson's frontiersmen, half a dozen Tejano scouts, and my regimental staff. More than enough firepower to turn back a band of nomadic marauders. We also rode with two women, for Morning Star and Carson's squaw, Singing Grass, had insisted on joining us. Slow rode at my side.

"Crockett will follow with the main body in a few days, and Colonel Custer will catch up in a week," I said with confidence. "We only need to blaze the trail."

"Gots unfriendly In'dins out 'ere," Carson warned, looking back over our line of march. I had left the wagons behind, for I wanted to move fast. A string of mules carried our supplies, nearly forty in all.

Morning Star arrived wearing her fringed tan leather outfit and a black broad brim hat. As the mounts kicked up a good deal of dust, Morning Star was pleased to be riding at the head of the column.

Singing Grass went down toward the Gila River with Slow, looking for rare plants.

"Is the story about how you won Singing Grass true, Mr. Carson?" Voss asked.

"Name is Kit, and didn't 'xactly won 'er," Carson said.

Carson was a hard man to draw comments from. Not unfriendly, but taciturn. He had heard tales of the ghost riders and largely dismissed them, not realizing what a hero he was to the men he was now guiding.

"Heard you won her, sir. In a duel," Voss persisted.

We all looked toward the river. Singing Grass was seventeen-years-old, an Arapaho, and said to be the daughter of a chief. Between her and Morning Star, it would be difficult to say who was more beautiful. She sat her white mustang like one born to the saddle. When she noticed our stares, she and Slow rode up the embankment to join us.

"Met Waanibe at the rendezvous," Carson reluctantly explained. "Prettiest girl west of Saint Louie, bar none. Well, ya gots ta know, these gatherings are momentous. Lots a drinkin', gamblin', dancin', shootin' and whorin'. For them that take to such. And sure, we trade pelts, powder and swap stories. Most of 'em lies, each taller than the last.

"Third day of the rendezvous, a French bully named Joe Chouinard was botherin' Waanibe plenty, and I set out ta put a stoppin' to it. Mounted our horses and charged each other, exchangin' shots. Got my hair singed by a musket ball, but done him worse. Ya always gots to do your enemy worse, so they knows not ta comes back at ya. Me and Waanibe took up a likin' an' been 'gether e'er since."

"I've heard much of these rendezvouses," I said.

"Had a big 'in on the Green River just a year 'go," Carson boasted.

"It's true then?" Voss asked. "Hundreds of mountain men from all over the Rockies? Drinking and trading. Indians, too?"

"Still do," Carson said.

"Not much longer," Slow said, showing interest.

"Ain't 'nough civilization ta stop us," Carson said.

"Not enough beaver, either," Slow replied. "Soon the beaver will be gone. Wiped out by the white man. Then you will kill the deer and the buffalo, leaving the People to starve."

"You kan't know that, boy," Carson said.

"It has already happened," Slow answered, giving Vic a kick and riding forward to catch Bouyer.

"Ah try ta like kids. Hope to have some, but don't know 'bout that boy," Carson said with a frown.

"Slow is right about the beaver," I felt compelled to say. "A few years from now, the rivers and streams will be played out. The mountain men will move on to new professions, like scouting for the army."

"You a mystic, too?" Carson asked.

"No, not a mystic, Kit," I said.

On a moonlit night just a day short of the Colorado River, we made camp on the Gila's north bank near a stretch of low foothills. The horses were hobbled in a meadow while the men pitched their small canvas tents along a babbling creek. There was plenty of scrub wood for fires.

Morning Star and Singing Grass had quickly become close friends, as women do when on the trail. I could not recall the relations between the Sioux and Arapaho in my own time, and Slow offered no opinions on them. Maybe he was trying to be polite. Nevertheless, it was nice to have the women around camp. They helped John with the cooking, fetched water, and provided pleasant company. Just before sunset, dispatch riders caught up to us, their horses tired.

"Sir, Colonel Custer's compliments," Sergeant Allen said, handing me a packet of roughly scrawled letters.

Mark Kellogg and Micajah Autry were with him. Each had an extra horse in tow, allowing them to switch mounts and keep them fresh. Kellogg was brimming with news, which annoyed me. I had not seen him since leaving San Antonio and hoped not to see him again before returning.

"Colonel Crockett's compliments, General," Autry reported with a salute. "David says he's a doin' good on da damn presidio an 'ill be along shortly."

"Thank you, Micajah. Get some grub. You, too, Jimmy. We'll be on the road at sunrise," I said, letting Kellogg wait his turn.

"Not curious at all, General?" Kellogg asked.

The trail was beginning to show on him. Now nearing his mid-forties, standing at my height though a bit thicker in the waist, his curly brown hair was ragged, and his scraggily beard was half gray. He should have been carrying his 1868 Spencer rifle in such dangerous country, but the heavy weapon was secure in its saddle sheath.

"News from Béjar. Hardly more than three weeks old," Kellogg said, following me to my campaign tent under a drooping cottonwood. John had already set up my table and chairs, made my cot, and started a cooking fire. The ladies were preparing food.

"News from you or General Keogh?" I asked.

"It's from the *San Antonio Gazette*, that I was proud to establish just before riding out," Kellogg said. He had always wanted his own newspaper.

I found a log to sit on outside the tent, forcing Kellogg to take a blanket on the ground. Morning Star quickly had stew for both of us, giving Mark a warm smile. Slow came to join us, also happy to see Kellogg's arrival.

"Santa Anna finally caught up to Houston at a little town called Egypt on the Colorado River," Kellogg said, swabbing gravy with a corn tortilla. "The Mexicans held the field when it was all over, but they got hurt. Santa Anna is falling back on Victoria. Houston tried to take the dictator by surprise with an afternoon attack, but the plan failed."

"Glad to hear Antonio took my advice," I remarked.

"You warned him? Warned that dictator?" Kellogg said.

"Now Houston will need help from the United States, and if those letters we wrote to the Eastern press have any effect, it will be hard for Jackson to intervene," I explained.

I opened Tom's report and saw that events in Santa Fe had been tense but successful. With such a small garrison, and a thousand miles from Mexico City, the alcalde had seen no reason to fight. Tom's battalion was already on the move.

Suddenly there was a commotion on the edge of camp. Shouting followed by several gunshots. We jumped to our feet and started running, drawing our sidearms. Clouds had covered the new moon but the glow of our campfires was enough to guide our way. From a low hill above the river, I sensed chaos among our mounts.

"Butler! Hughes!" I shouted, searching the dark landscape.

Voss reached me first, followed by Autry and Kellogg, all out of breath.

"Indians stealing our horses," I said. "Voss, sound *Boots and Saddles.* Autry, with me."

Autry and I charged down the hill, skirting the mule herd on our right. I struck a cactus with my thigh and cursed, but drove on. We reached a bluff overlooking the river, almost falling off before stopping ourselves. White splashes of water and grunts from the mounts proved a force crossing in the dark below us, probably Apache seeking booty from the Seventh.

"Micajah, take aim," I ordered, seeing Autry armed with a Colt. My Bulldog was already drawn.

"General, don't shoot!" Butler yelled, lumbering up the dirt slope in front of us.

"What is it, Jimmy?" I asked.

"Those are Carson's boys down there. They're chasing the Indians who took our horses," Butler said.

"Damn redskins," Autry muttered, still clutching his sidearm.

I agreed, and in a more reckless time, would have said so. But I was the commander-in-chief now, like George Washington, and with heathen allies to consider. Not to mention the insult my brother's future wife would feel at such an unseemly comment. Finally, after all these years, the many times Libbie had lectured me on careless remarks began to make sense. She was always the better politician, having learned from her craft from Judge Bacon.

"These are not the Mimbreños," I said. "Could be Chiricahua, or Navajo. Organize the command to sweep the ground south of here. We'll get our horses back."

"If Carson don't beat you to it," Butler said.

The threat of a raid was nothing new, though this time the thieves had been particularly crafty. Much like Mosby's Rangers in the Shenandoah. We built up our campfires, lit torches, and secured our supplies before riding out in two companies of fifteen, leaving our teamsters and John behind to guard the camp. We should have had more.

"Slow, too?" I said in surprise.

"The boy was with Carson when the Indians attacked," Hughes reported. "They wounded a guard. Carson and half a dozen others are on their trail."

"Seven men against an unknown number of In'dins?" Autry asked.

"Didn't seem to bother Carson none," Butler said.

We rushed to find horses that remained on the picket line and were mounted within minutes. I found a black sorrel. Kellogg found his trusty old mule named Sarah, who John had brought along to carry our commissary.

"We're going south?" Kellogg asked, riding at my side with the Spencer ready.

"Can't tell for sure," I said, able to hear more than I could see.

Bouyer appeared in the gloom ahead of us.

"This way, Gen'ral. Headed toward the rocks," Bouyer said.

I gave the sorrel a poke with my spurs, the reluctant animal spooked by the commotion. I spotted the churned path between partings of the clouds, the moon suddenly illuminating the prairie. The raiders were moving fast, but would need to control the stolen mounts. They would not outride a determined force for long. We trotted steadily for a mile.

"To the left. The land falls toward a valley," Bouyer said, pointing the direction.

"Scouts to the flanks," I ordered.

It should have been Captain Blazeby who gave the command, on my instructions, but I'd grown excited. Blazeby seemed not to notice the slight, or pretended not to.

I gave the scouts time to probe the flanks before pushing forward. The sound of sporadic musket fire was heard echoing through the shallow hills. And then screaming. And wailing.

"Voss, sound the *Charge!*" I shouted, spurring forward.

The bugle call was like thunder on the desert, crisp and clear in the dry night air. A well-worn trail went through a gap in the hills, leading to a village. I rode at the head of the column, though several soon passed me.

When we came to a clearing, I quickly reined in. The scene before us confusing. Carson and his small band of frontiersmen were besieged in the center of a village, hiding behind a burning wikiup. Half a dozen women and children lay dead or wounded. Seven or eight half-naked savages were attempting to rescue the noncombatants. Another twenty or thirty warriors were firing arrows, and the occasional musket, from the surrounding darkness.

Several of Carson's men were bleeding, but they were putting up a great fight against long odds. Without thinking, I rode into the middle of the fray, a hand up for attention.

"Cease fire!" I shouted in English, following with, *"Cese del fuego. Cese del fuego!"*

The firing continued. One bullet tore the hat off my head. Another clipped the ear of my horse. It sounded like bees all around me.

F Company formed a half circle along the north edge of the clearing, some armed with Springfields, others with Baker rifles. There was no shouting. No desperate oaths. Blazeby ordered volley fire into the air, which sounded like cannon, and both sides suddenly stopped shooting.

I dismounted, slapped my horse's rump to chase him away, and stood there in the firelight with a sword in one hand and a Bulldog in the other. I should have taken cover, but the idea never occurred to me. I stomped about the clearing, waving at Carson's men to stand down and daring the Indians to shoot me. No doubt they thought me crazy, and as a rule, Indians are reluctant to kill the mentally disturbed.

Before long, my troops were encroaching on the enemy flanks and the Apaches withdrew. I was glad to see Slow emerge from the shadows safely, his face smudged with powder. I was not happy to see two dead squaws.

"Mister Carson, what has happened here?" I demanded.

"Found ya horses, Gener'ral, but theys put up a fight," Carson said, covered in soot but otherwise unharmed. Two of his men had painful wounds, but I saw nothing serious.

"You had no orders to attack this village," I said, for I feared it might compromise my agreement with Mangas Coloradas.

"Kan't wait fer no orders, Gener'ral. Not in this country," Carson defended. "Kill or be kilt. I rather do the killin'."

An Indian walked from the darkness. He held a long bow but was pointing his flint-tipped arrow down. He was an older man with shaggy white hair wearing a colorful blue silk shirt and yellow headband. I glanced back, seeing a dozen of the women and children had failed to escape in the confusion. It was the Washita all over again.

"I am General Custer, commander of the Seventh Cavalry," I said to the old Indian, walking over to face him directly. "Your people have stolen horses from my army."

"The Chiricahua stole no horses. It was the Ben-et-dine," the old man said in Spanish. "They came south to raid the Mexicans. When you attacked, they ran away and left the horses."

"They are cowards," a young Apache in red leathers said, standing next to the old man. This brave was six feet tall and straight shouldered, a defiant gaze in his dark brown eyes. Probably in his late twenties or early thirties. I guessed him at a hundred and seventy pounds. A man to be reckoned with.

"The Ben-et-dine are crazy," the old man stated.

"Gener'ral—" Carson started to interrupt.

"Mister Carson, you will hold your counsel until asked," I required.

I did not object to fighting Indians, especially Apache, for their cruelty is well known. But this was not the time or place.

"My army did not know the Benit Din stole the horses. If you wish battle, there will be battle. If you wish peace, there will be peace. So speaks General Custer."

"Our cousin has spoken of you as a friend. What compensation is offered?" the old chief asked.

I had to admire his nerve, though he wasn't the first Indian I'd known to ask for gifts after committing a crime. I looked again at the dead squaws, one old and the other aging. Other women were returning to the camp without being told. They sensed the fighting was over. Children were taken into the wikiups for treatment and rest.

"My adjutant will cut out two horses for you. Not the best. Not the worst. And then we will be friends," I decided.

There was no further bargaining. Two horses was a fair price for a supposed misunderstanding. The cagey old chief and I shook hands.

We stayed near the village until dawn, camping on the outskirts. I did not want to take the recovered horses back in the dark, and I wanted the Chiricahua to see the weapons carried by my soldiers. It would make them think twice about attacking us. Or it could induce them to attack, in an effort to steal our guns. With Indians, you never know.

"Gener'ral, we should talk," Carson said, coming to my fire.

I had been angry with him earlier, especially while being shot at, but managed to cool my temper. I needed Carson to get me to California.

Carson sat down next to Slow, who was strangely quiet. The boy usually had something enigmatic to say after a fight.

"I gots yer horses back," Carson said.

"Do you think the Seventh Cavalry doesn't know how to get our horses back?" I said. "We've fought the Cheyenne, the Sioux, the Kiowa, the Arapaho, the Comanche, and every other kind of damn Indian there is. When Crazy Horse stole our horses, my brother threw his damn butt in jail. We know our business."

"And Apache 'as like fought 'em, too," Carson said. "They ain't 'fraid of nothin'. If you show any weakness, they'll take ya fer a fool."

"That will be their mistake, but for now, I don't need another war," I answered. "I've got one in Texas. I'm about to start another in California. And I have a road to protect. You're not to shoot any more Apaches without orders. Is that understood?"

"This 'ere ain't a good idea, Gener'ral. Not good a'tall," Carson warned.

"Will you obey orders?" I asked.

"Yes, sir. No one 'ere accused Kit Carson of disobeyin' orders," he said, going off to find some sleep.

"What about you, Slow? Are you going to attack Apaches again?"

"No, General Custer. But you should have killed them," Slow said.

"Maybe someday I will," I answered.

———

At dawn, I sent the men back to the Gila River camp with orders to start west. I wanted to be on the Colorado without further delay. But Slow and I stayed behind for a final talk with the Apache.

We likely made a strange pair, walking into their camp dressed in traveling leathers, wide brim hats and modern pistols on our belts. Slow had become adept with a Colt .45 at close range, and I was an expert with my Webley Bulldogs. I doubted we would need to draw our weapons. Coming as we did was a sign of respect, and most Indians are known to extend hospitality on such occasions.

In the daylight, I saw this was a temporary camp. Wikiups made of grass and tumbleweeds. A few teepees. A hide lean-to among the rocks where their dead had been placed. Slow and I sat at the central fire with three of the older men and the tall younger Apache we'd seen the night before.

"Are we enemies?" I asked in Spanish, for none of them seemed familiar with English.

"We are not," the oldest chief said.

"Are you afraid of the white man?" Slow asked.

"We are Chiricahua. We know no fear," another chief said, trying not to sound annoyed.

"Why have you come here?" the younger Apache asked.

"Cheis, you are invited to sit. Not to speak," the old chief rebuked.

Almost Tom's age, it seemed to me the young man was old enough to have a seat in counsel, but it wasn't my place to judge.

"It is a fair question," I said. "I represent the Buffalo Flag, a league of nations in Texas. My army is now traveling to the great western ocean, there to establish more nations. We are building a road that travelers may go in safety from the east to the west and back again. Mangas Coloradas has agreed to let my people travel freely. I would have the Chiricahua agree also."

"Our war is with the Mexicans. We care nothing about your road," the second chief said.

"I care about my road. If my people cannot travel in safety, then I will be forced to make enemies. I have enough enemies. I do not want more enemies," I said.

"You are not afraid of making enemies," the oldest chief observed.

"*Custer es un jinete fantasma*," Slow said.

All four Apache looked at each other with a similar thought, part curiosity and part dread. I was going to say something, but held back. Slow's statement, and his grim expression, were making an impression. He glanced up, spotted a large black crow, and pointed. The bird appeared to be watching us.

"We have heard much of these ghost riders," the second chief said.

"A meeting will be called for the next moon," the oldest chief announced. "We will leave the white man's road in peace, but our hunting lands must not be walked upon. The Mexicans take too much already."

"I will tell my people that we are at peace with the Chiricahua. Your lands will be your own," I promised, hoping it was a promise I could keep. "There are men in the east, and in the west, who value hides and silver rocks. Travelers on my road will want food and shelter. If the Chiricahua wish to trade, they would bring blankets and medicines."

"And weapons?" Cheis asked.

"I have told Mangas Coloradas if his people wish to join the Nations, he can trade for weapons. I offer this to the Chiricahua also," I said, believing it would be many years before such a trade need be established.

"You know much of our cousin," the second chief said.

"We are friends," I exaggerated.

"I hope to marry his daughter," Cheis said.

"I have met Dostehseh. She is young and spirited. She will make a good wife," I said, tapping the ground for emphasis.

Offering the daughter's name made a good impression on my audience. Libbie had taught me to give attention to the families of friends and opponents, for you never know when a bit of intimate knowledge might prove useful.

I stood up, having finished my business, and walked to Traveller without looking back. Slow spoke privately with the old chief before following.

––––––––––

The command reached the Colorado River the following afternoon, camping along a broad beach under thick groves of sycamore trees. We found tribes of peaceful Mohave Indians nearby growing crops and gathering mesquite beans. It looked like the Spanish had once attempted to establish a settlement there. We found a broken down presidio on the east bank of the river, and the foundation of a church that was never completed.

"The town of Yuma doesn't exist yet, General," Kellogg said, standing next to me where the river suddenly narrowed. "Going to call it Custer's Crossing?"

"Tempting, but Yuma works just as well," I said. "We'll build a fort here and run lines to maintain a ferry. That prominence across the river will make a good observation post."

"You've never been here before, how do you know the lay of the land?" Kellogg asked.

"I read about Yuma in *Harper's Weekly*. So has Tom, Smith, and half of the Seventh's enlisted men," I said. "We're soldiers, Mark. We spend months in barracks, especially during the winter. The men like to read, when they aren't getting drunk."

"Are we getting drunk?" Tom asked, walking up with Morning Star and Slow.

By riding hard, C Company had caught up with us just short of the river. Had I not hustled, Tom would have gotten there first and claimed the credit.

"Heard you tied one on in Santa Fe," I said.

"Hell, Autie, we conquered New Mexico. Isn't that worth a night of celebration?" Tom said, a twinkle in his blue eyes.

Morning Star hugged his arm. Slow approved, for Tom had gained quite the reputation as a warrior. A better reputation than mine.

"And how big was the enemy garrison?" I inquired.

"Twenty-four, fully armed and ready to fight to the death," he said.

"They sound fearsome. How many did you kill?" I said, already knowing the answer.

"Well, when they saw they were outnumbered three to one, they kinda decided not to fight," Tom admitted. "They hadn't been paid in six months, you see, and they were getting' kinda irritated with the government in Mexico City."

"So what happened?"

"Twenty-two of them work for us now," Tom said.

In time, I would need a more permanent administration, but for now Santa Fe was one less problem to worry about. And absorbing the locals into my plans was beginning to look like a good idea, for my forces were stretched thin.

"How long until the stragglers are up?" I asked.

"Crockett should be here in two days," Tom reported.

"We'll start work on the fort in the morning. We need corrals for the horses, store rooms and a good place to position the artillery," I said.

"Our guns? The horses?" Tom said.

"It's mostly desert from Yuma to Los Angeles. Poor trails, no water. From here on, we only take the mules," I said. "The horses and cannon will stay."

"Autie, that's crazy," Tom protested.

"Ask Carson how crazy it is," I replied.

Crockett's men rode in two days later. David was wearing his coonskin cap, smiling and waving to all. Everyone was bursting with excitement. How I envied the Old Bear Killer's ability to set a crowd on fire.

For the first time in several weeks, I held an officer's call. Getting all three hundred of us across the desert at the same time, with only a hundred and fifty mules, did not seem practical. And Carson laughed when I suggested it.

"Ya ain't leavin' me 'hind again," Crockett warned. "Always wanted to see Californee. Ain't bein' denied."

"Me either," Tom said. "You shouldn't be hogging all the glory, Autie."

"Didn't you just conquer New Mexico?" I said.

"California is bigger. It has an ocean," Tom replied.

No one wanted to be left behind, and I couldn't blame them. Fort Yuma was greener than any of us expected, but it didn't have the lure of a Sierra Nevada river or the brothels of San Francisco.

"I'm taking half the command," I announced, seeing Carson shake his head out of the corner of my eye. "The Seventh has crossed barren plains in Kansas and the Dakotas. We'll strip the units down to the bare essentials, carry our own water, and find what we need on the other side of the desert."

"What about the rest of us?" Brister said, already guessing he wasn't one of the lucky few.

"We'll mark a wagon road, and once across, send back supplies and guides to bring you in," I said.

"Think it can be done?" Blazeby asked.

"William, when I was in charge of the Black Hills expedition, I organized hundreds cavalry and infantry, thousands of horses and mules. I had Bloody Knife and Lean Bear leading my Indian scouts. Fresh Smith was my quartermaster. Tom commanded Company L. It went so well, I even had time to shoot a grizzly bear."

"Ain't no grizzlies in the desert, Gener'ral," Carson complained.

"Maybe I'll catch enough rattlesnakes to make a pair of boots?" I said.

———

We traveled light on supply, except for ammunition and water.

Each mule carried two canvas water bags lined with buffalo stomach. Three wagons, one for each company, held camp supplies. We brought twenty-five horses, but none were allowed to be ridden in the desert.

We were better armed than Kearny's expedition had been in 1846. Every veteran of the Seventh, a third of the battalion, was armed with a Springfield and a Colt. The rest were armed with Baker rifles. Tom and Smith had their Winchesters, Butler his Sharps, and Kellogg his Spencer. And Erasmo Seguin had manufactured a hundred rounds for my Remington, the most accurate weapon in the regiment. Hell, this was 1836. It was the most accurate rifle in the world.

The desert was just as dreary as promised. Fuentes and a few of the Mexican teamsters kept an eye on the horses, all carrying lightweight packs and given more water than the mules. Or the men. We stopped in the middle of the day for a siesta, and continued well after dark, when the ground finally began to cool.

Carson proved a good scout, knowing what I wanted and having an instinct for how to get there. Besides, we were just traveling in the wake of the Mormon Battalion, whose travails were well known. Though now we had stolen their glory. I made notes in a journal each night, expecting to one day publish my adventures.

My distrust of Kit Carson was not shared. He was popular in camp, singing songs with Crockett, playing cards with Tom and Fresh, holding hands with Singing Grass, and telling the occasional tall tale about his journey with Ewing Young to California seven years before. I did my best to set aside my prejudice, letting him share my fire and food. When Carson slipped off in the night to scout the area for hostiles, he would often take Slow with him.

It was a hundred and ten miles from Yuma to Vallecito Springs, four days of hard marching. Several times I considered abandoning the wagons, but my commanders were loath to give up their transport, so I relented.

The trail went west, then turned northwest to several shallow but welcome rivers. The water was brown and murky, and our food low, but spirits were high as we made the final distance to the famous springs.

In my own time, Vallecito had been an important stop for the Butterfield Stage and the overland mail routes. What had once been loosely called the Jackass Trail. No facilities existed in 1836, though there was evidence that roaming Indians occasionally used it. The waters of the oasis were slightly sulphurous but drinkable, within easy walk of our camp. We marked a dozen springs were the water squeezed out of the ground, flowed down to a little stream, and then disappeared into swampy soil. It took hours, but we refilled every water bag in the battalion.

"San Diego or Los Angeles?" Tom asked. "Or shall we divide the command and capture both?"

"Getting ambitious, little brother?" I said.

"Not thinking of renaming the towns after myself, though Tom Custerville does have a nice sound," the scamp said.

"Anything named Custer is named after me," I insisted.

"I like Tom Custerville," Butler said, poking his elbow at Hughes.

"So do I," Hughes agreed.

My sergeants were having more fun than they were entitled to.

"Okay, the first town we find with brothels can be Tom Custerville," I relented.

"And if we find a town filled with iron butts, we'll name it for you," Tom said.

Butler and Hughes laughed so loud I was forced to dismiss them from my campfire. Louts.

We lingered in Vallecito for three days, resting the animals, repairing the wagons, and erecting an adobe way station for future visitors. The sign of the buffalo was carved above the door. Carson did some scouting and returned on the third day with a small herd of cattle.

"Buy them or steal them?" I asked.

"Ranch in the next valley is owned by one of the missions. Mission San Luis Rey, I think they calls it," Carson said. "Not too good a ranch. Two old vaqueros sold the stock fer a dollar each, if they gits to keep the hides."

"What did you pay them with?" I inquired.

"Your promise, Gener'ral," Carson replied.

"Then we'll need to visit," I agreed. "But first we need to carve out the pass for the wagons. Steep one, too, as I recall."

"Now how in hell did ya know that?" Carson said.

I smiled knowing the Mormon Battalion had widened two passes.

We had already chiseled our way through Box Canyon, so only the final range remained. But I didn't bother to explain myself.

The desert was behind us now, a heavy oak forest ahead. We crossed a final summit into Valle de San José and followed a creek called Cañada Buena Vista, intending for the famous Warner Ranch. Though in this time, there was no Warner Ranch, just an old adobe manned by the elderly vaqueros. I gave them twenty dollars in silver pesos stolen from Santa Anna, paying my debt and buying more cattle. I had an army to feed.

"San Diego is still an option, Autie," Tom said, once again riding Athena.

"Could have gone San Diego from Vallecito if I'd wanted to," I answered. "Los Angeles is the better option. Like Texas in 1836, California is in turmoil. I want to take advantage of that."

"What sort of turmoil?" Crockett asked.

"I don't exactly remember, and for once, even Kellogg seems stumped," I said. "He just knows there was some sort of revolt that must have failed."

"The Bear Flag Revolt?" Tom asked.

"Maybe. Guess we'll find out soon enough," I answered.

The road to Los Angeles was well trod, but we continued to post markers along the way so there would be no misunderstandings. Most of us who grew up reading about the gold rush knew all about San Francisco, Sacramento, the American River, and Sutter's Fort. Few knew very much about the southern part of the state that was largely insignificant.

September was warm and dry. The dirt road looked twenty or thirty years old, wide enough for wagons and cattle herds. There were many small farms, the farmers keeping a discreet distance. A few of the women came out offering jugs of water or fresh bread. Younger women came out waving their handkerchiefs and offering flowers. I sensed some distrust of such a large armed force, but no animosity.

After several days, we came in sight of the San Gabriel Mission, a sprawling complex of corrals, workshops, fruit trees and wineries. An Indian village nearby was partially deserted, and the mission itself was falling into disrepair. Several of the padres came out to meet us.

127

They looked thin, their brown robes frayed.

"Greetings, General Custer of the Seventh Cavalry. I am Father Tomás of the Franciscan Order," the tallest of the group said. He was bald and eagle-nosed, with large hands good for planting.

"Good day to you, friar," I replied. "Does the garrison in Los Angeles know of our approach?"

"They do, but we know naught of their intentions," Father Tomás said.

With me was Tom, Crockett, Smith, and Kellogg. Carson and Bouyer were scouting our flanks, should someone be planning an ambush.

"Pueblo de Los Angeles lays through a pass only a few hours away," I said to Tom. "We can be there by dusk."

"Better to fight them in the morning. The mounts will be rested," Tom suggested.

"Give them Mex'cans time ta worry, too," Crockett said. "They kan't have all that many soldiers."

"We should scout the ground," Smith added.

I wanted to attack immediately, for I had few concerns about victory. Nothing I'd read of El Pueblo de los Ángeles warned me of formidable defenses.

"Gentlemen, I will abide by your advice," I decided, much to their surprise. "Let's make the most of this wonderful mission, but post a strong guard."

After three weeks of low rations, tarps for tents, and sagebrush for bedding, the men were glad to have a roof again, for the mission had many rooms. We also gathered tents for the trail and loaded the wagons with fresh supplies, for the friars were generous. Though I had John set up my campaign tent on a grassy knoll with a good view of the valley, I accepted the invitation of Friar Tomás to supper. He was filled with information, and complaints.

"When the criminals in Mexico City secularized the missions, they gave away our land," the priest said, presiding over the mission's dining hall.

There were eight tables seating forty of my men, five friars, and a dozen Indians. Our plates were filled with grilled beef and peas, the squaws from the village doing the serving. Wine flowed freely. For a poor land, this was quite a feast, so I knew they wanted something from me. I whispered to Slow, who sat next to me, that he might understand the ways of civilization.

"We could no longer feed our supplicants, who are now made servants of the rancheros," Father Tomás continued. "Many of our tools were stolen. Our stock was sold for pesos, for we lacked feed. Once our missions ran the length of California, sheltering Indians and travelers, tanning leather, growing crops, raising cattle. Now every mission suffers under cruel abuse."

"Who's running the territory? Mariano Chino?" Tom asked.

Santa Anna had spoken of Chino while we were in Galveston, but had little good to say of him.

"No, Colonel Nicolás Gutiérrez was governor last year, but replaced by Chino in April. Chino could not rule," Father Tomás said. "He is a tyrant and a fool. Now Chino has returned to Mexico City seeking troops and Gutiérrez rules once more. Gutiérrez is also a tyrant and a fool, but a good soldier."

"He has support in the south, especially San Diego, but is weak in the north," another padre said. "There are rumors of revolt."

I looked at Kellogg, wondering what he knew of a revolution in 1836, but he seemed unsure. The history of California we knew began in 1846, at the beginning of the Mexican War.

"What of this revolt? Gonna git the In'dins back their land?" Crockett asked, taking a sympathetic look at our hostess.

The elderly squaw was one of a score still living at the mission, dressed in dyed cotton and looking a bit heavy. Her smile was charming.

"Can't say that," Father Tomás said. "It's mostly the Californios. They say this territory is neglected. The *Diputación* has demanded statehood, but they are ignored."

"Californios?" Smith asked.

"Native born citizens of Spanish descent," Father Tomás explained. "They have benefited greatly from the secularization, gathering millions of acres."

"Maybe there's something the Seventh Cavalry can do?" I said.

"Helping the people would be a blessing," Father Tomás said, believing his flattery had been successful.

The evening was not all business. We sang songs, played cards, a few troopers got drunk, and the noise attracted a few señoritas, who danced with the boys. The padres played musical instruments and were very good.

The next morning, Voss sounded *Boots & Saddles*. We were off to conquer Los Angeles.

Never a real city, the pueblo was said to house eight hundred residents. But the village I attacked on the Little Big Horn was said to be eight hundred also, and Governor Gutiérrez was known to be raising an army, so Bouyer and Carson joined me on an advance scout. We found a nice little hill overlooking the entire floodplain.

The distance from the San Gabriel Mission to the town was about eleven miles, all excellent roads. I was amazed by the large tracts of sycamores, walnut trees, and oaks. Extensive irrigation ditches fed hundreds of small farms and ranches. Plots of grapes were growing on the rolling hills, particularly near the meandering river. I had thought to find a semi-desert, but this country looked more like Ohio.

"Typical Spanish fort," Carson said, having been here on previous visits.

"Hardly a fort, Mr. Carson," I said. "It's much like San Antonio. A central plaza, church with a few walls, a barracks and a stable. There's activity on the open ground just south of the town. Mostly cavalry. Maybe some artillery."

"Orders, Gen'ral?" Bouyer asked, having seen all he needed to.

"We will attack," I said.

I rode down the steep hill anxious to proceed. The command was drawn up behind the ridge, flags unfurled and the mounts pawing the soft earth. The new horses we had acquired in the San Gabriel Valley were broken for riding but would likely spook in a battle. I had the sergeants keeping a close eye on them. Not sure how Traveller would react in a fight, I took Vic back from Slow.

"Colonel Custer, Company C will sweep south of town. Keep the enemy occupied. They may have some artillery. Flank them if you can. Colonel Crockett, Company A will proceed down the main road. Dismount within rifle range and engage their infantry. Colonel Smith, you are the hammer. Swing Company E to the north and threaten the enemy rear. We'll give the garrison a chance to expend their ammunition, then advance along our entire front. Questions, gentlemen?"

"What if they surrender, sir?" Lieutenant Autry asked.

"We don't want more blood than necessary, Micajah. But what blood is spilled should be theirs," I answered, my voice growing a bit high-pitched, as it sometimes did in moments of excitement.

"They might retreat?" Tom said.

"There's a road to the west that turns north along the ocean. If they withdraw without their supply train, let them go," I decided. "I want the town, their food, their wagons, and their ammunition. We don't need prisoners."

"Ya mean shoot the prisoners?" Crockett asked with a frown.

"No, Colonel, I did not say shoot the prisoners," I responded. "Please do not read more into my orders than intended. That happened at the Washita, bringing criticism to the regiment. There will be none of that today."

"Where will you be, Autie?" Tom asked.

"The regimental staff will take the scouts to Company A's right flank," I said. "There's a blind spot on their northeast corner I wish to probe. More questions? Very good. Keep your trumpeters close at hand."

131

Once around the edge of the hill, our army formed up on the wide wagon road. Smith was in the lead, followed by Tom. Crockett and I brought up the rear. Our wagons came last with spare ammunition and medical supplies. Dr. Lord and Sergeant Major Williamson commanded this reserve. Our mules had been left at the mission where they were needed for the trek back to Yuma.

The enemy stirred, guards on top of the tall stone church sounding the alarm with a brass bell. There seemed to be about forty or fifty buildings, most low slung mud and adobe brick with thatched roofs. The best structures were situated around the plaza, some of them two stories tall. I did not see a presidio, but there was a fortified hacienda, likely the commandant's headquarters. The streets had been barricaded with bundles of wood. Only three cannon were visible, all small bore. Two faced east and one south.

Smith separated from the command first, having the longest ride. Moving at a right oblique, forty troopers crossed over the end of a long green ridge and down toward the river where it snaked around a shallow plateau. A mile farther on, Tom broke off to the left through a late summer wheat field. Crockett and I slowed during the last thousand yards, stopping short of the town.

"Now, Mr. Crockett," I said, for it was Crockett's duty to lead his company.

"Dismount," Crockett calmly said to his trumpeter, who quickly blew the signal.

"Skirmish line, horse holders to the rear," Crockett ordered, his voice clear in the late morning air.

The troops spread out at fifteen foot intervals, thirty men on the line, three sergeants giving direction, and ten men standing back holding the horses. Crockett and Autry remained mounted, riding up and down the line to maintain order. They had learned their lessons well.

The first cannon shot burst from the east wall, falling twenty yards short. It looked like a 3-pounder, solid shot. Not likely to be very effective except for the poor soldier it accidently hit.

"Good luck, David," I said, saluting before riding off to the right.

Butler and Hughes rode with me at point followed by Voss, Howell, Allen, Fuentes and Espalier. Bouyer stayed on our right flank, joined by Carson's men and nineteen Shoshone Indians who hated the Californios. I told Carson that his men were not required to join in, not having been hired as soldiers, but they were staying close, looking for some action.

"Good ground," Butler approved, the Sharps lying across his lap.

I had my Remington in the sheath, my Bulldogs in the black leather holsters. Hughes held his Henry. The rest of my men were armed with Springfields. Carson had gathered some Baker rifles cut down to carbine length. Most of the Indians had antique muskets, though a few carried bows and arrows.

"Company E is almost in position, sir," Hughes reported.

I halted the men, searching the landscape with my binoculars. Smith had skirted the plateau in good order, swinging north of town. Crockett's men were waiting for the advance, holding their fire. Tom had dismounted his force to the south and was slowly pressing the walled church. They were met by sporadic musket fire. I saw Tom counting their guns.

"Follow me," I said, leading the way down a draw into a swampy irrigation channel.

The path allowed us to ride toward a pair of two-story buildings connected by a wicker enclosure, probably a chicken coop. I lost sight of the position while splashing along the ditch, but caught sight again as we emerged into a bean field. The enemy was too busy on their other flanks to see us. We were only a hundred yards away.

Far to my left, Tom's trumpeter sounded *Commence Firing*. Only six shots rang out. I assumed he had advanced his sharpshooters and was picking off the gun crews. A single shot came closer from my left. I looked toward Company A and saw Crockett out in front of his men with his Springfield. At a distance of four-hundred yards, Crockett could threaten his targets and still be out of the enemy's range.

A Mexican lookout toppled from the top of the church, and then one fell from the east wall. They could hardly have understood they were up against weapons far superior to their own. Suddenly their small cannon didn't seem so formidable.

"There go the noncombatants, General," Butler said, pointing west.

From the rear of the town, hundreds of old men, women and children were scattering into the fields, some along the road, other dashing into the yellow wheat.

"Shall we round them up, sir?" Hughes asked.

"Don't be a smart ass," I replied. "Voss, sound the *Charge!*"

I drew my Bulldog and gave Vic a kick, galloping toward the wicker pen. On my right, I saw Smith charging the barriers blocking the main street. Behind me, Carson and his boys were rushing to catch up, caught by surprise. I could not see Crockett but heard his bugler sounding *Forward*. Up ahead, Mexican lancers in the plaza were mounting their horses. I could not tell if they forming up or getting ready to retreat. The streets looked clogged with women and children. Smoke from the muskets began to linger over the town like a gray haze.

Vic reached the wicker pen first and jumped over, landing among a flock a squawking chickens. Butler and Voss were quickly at my side. We charged into the plaza ready for battle, but there were only a handful of soldiers making a fight. One raised his musket at me but I shot first. Two more turned to shoot. Voss and Butler cut them down. Within minutes eight or nine *soldados* lay wounded. At least five were dead. The lancers disappeared down the west road at a gallop.

"Voss, sound *Rally*," I ordered.

My command formed around me, pistols ready should there be treachery. Among the surrendering soldiers were at least a hundred Angeleno peasants, frightened but refusing to abandon their homes. I also noticed several merchants standing in front of their shops. One of them, a well-dressed man in his mid-fifties, came forward with his hands held out.

"Sir, I am Jean-Louis Vignes, master of El Aliso," the distinguished gentleman introduced. "In the absence of Colonel Gutiérrez, I am given authority for our pueblo. I urge mercy."

The Pacific Ocean is an endless prairie of water. It is told that the White Man came across such an ocean to steal the land of the People, but not from across this western sea. The brown men of Hawaii and yellow men of China come from the west, though not as conquerors. They are servants of the White Man, as the White Man would have the People be their servants. This will never be, but I finally understood the power of such great distances. After the battle of the adobe town, Custer and Thomas rode down to the beach, walking into the waves and splashing. I did not understand what made them crazy, but followed them into the surf, feeling the buffeting about my legs. The White Men say they will someday own all of the land between the great oceans. Will they drown all who live in-between?

Custer and Crockett

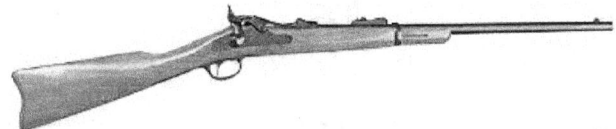

Chapter Five
THE BATTLE OF MONTEREY

Los Angeles had fallen in a battle lasting twenty minutes. We had a few wounded but none killed. The Mexican commander had escaped with the bulk of his force, leaving behind his artillery and wagons. It was a glorious victory, though a minor one. During the Rebellion, it would hardly have gotten mention on page two of the *New York Tribune*.

"Autie, what the hell?" Tom shouted, riding into the plaza with his men.

Closer to the action, Crockett's men were approaching on foot. Smith had taken Company E partway down the west road to make sure the enemy was in full retreat, but according to orders, offered no pursuit.

"Jealous I got here first?" I boasted.

"The Mexicans were retreating. There was no reason to charge at all," Tom scolded.

I dismounted, handing Vic's reins to Corporal Fuentes. Señor Vignes was still waiting, and I didn't wish to be rude.

"Have no fear, sir. The citizens of Los Angeles are safe under the protection of the Seventh Cavalry," I said, shaking hands.

The gentleman relaxed and waved to his people. They emerged from the surrounding buildings, quickly starting to clean up the streets and take down the barricades.

Once Smith returned, I gathered the command before the fortified hacienda. Voss blew his bugle as the Mexican flag was lowered and the Buffalo Flag raised. Six men fired a salute, and that was it. No speeches. No brass band. My musical instruments were still in Yuma.

That night, as the troopers celebrated good food, good wine and dancing señoritas, I met with the town fathers in the former commandant's office. They were surprisingly well informed. With me were Tom, Crockett and Kellogg, also well informed, for they had been speaking with the locals. Not all of whom thought highly of their leaders.

"Your conquest of Texas failed, and now you come to Alta California?" Señor Vignes inquired.

"And who are you? Mercenaries? Filibusters?" old Señor Rodriquez inquired, owner of the town's largest mercantile.

"The liberation of Texas is proceeding as planned," I exaggerated. "The Buffalo Flag represents whites who oppose slavery, Mexican Federalists, Indian tribes, and patriots seeking a better life in a free land. The government in Mexico City cannot protect California. We will do better."

"So you have ridden two thousand miles to protect us poor ranchers?" Juan Bandini asked, a visiting emissary from San Diego. Near middle-age, he was lean and sharp-eyed, as most frontier settlers tend to be. "My Rancho Tecate is under pressure by bands of renegades, as are my neighbors. Will a handful of horsemen drive the plunderers back into the deserts?"

"California—" I said.

"Alta California," Father Tomás insisted. I failed to value the distinction.

"Alta California needs an honest government and an army to protect the citizens," I explained. "This will be provided in time, but first the Seventh Cavalry must establish order. You gentlemen must help maintain this order."

"And if we don't?" Bandini asked.

"Then I will find men who will, and reward them accordingly," I promised.

"What of the missions? The Indians?" Father Tomás said.

"Some of the land must be returned to the missions," Crockett said. "They was doin' a good job. Good to be helpin' folks."

"The land belongs to us now," Señor Vignes insisted.

"It belongs to the people," Tom said, frowning.

"And you Buffalo Flags? Are you the people?" Vignes inquired.

"We have the most guns," Tom answered.

"Gentlemen, please, there will be a fair distribution," Kellogg intervened, for he now considered himself quite the expert on California land issues. In truth, he'd given the problem more thought than I had.

"Mr. Kellogg is right," I agreed. "Give us time. This country is about to change in ways you can't imagine. Patience is called for."

Ironic, coming from me.

Seven days later, the Seventh Cavalry was moving up the old Camino Real, a road built by the Spanish missionaries to connect their twenty some odd missions between San Diego and San Francisco. It was well-marked with many ranches and springs along the way, good forage for the horses, and remarkable weather. I wanted a secure base before the snows started.

Carson and his boys were no longer with me, having been sent back to Yuma. I wanted the rest of the command brought up quickly. Orders were also issued to finish the Custer Road. When the time came for our return to Texas, I wanted nothing to slow us down. One day, I would build a railroad, telegraph lines, and trading posts, but for now watering holes and bridges would suffice.

Our first stop was the Mission San Fernando Rey de España, established forty years before. Like San Luis Rey, the mission was still the center of spiritual life for Indians and farmers, but slowly falling into disrepair. Hearing of our advance, many people came out to see the Seventh Cavalry, so I encouraged the men to make a good impression. Unlike my travels through Virginia during the Rebellion, where spectators were sullen and often holding pitchforks, the settlers of Alta California greeted us with hope. They had felt protected when the land was ruled by the King of Spain, but ignored under the rule of Mexico.

"Don't like this none at all," Crockett said as we dismounted in the mission courtyard.

"How's that, David?" I asked.

"Seems this 'ere Figueroa fella was stealin' land from the poor an' givin' it to the rich," Crockett complained. "If I'd a wanted that, I could'a stayed in Tennessee."

"José Figueroa is dead. There isn't much we can do about him now," Kellogg said.

"But what he done was wrong, and we *kin* do somethin' 'bout that," Crockett replied.

"What do you have in mind?" I asked.

"Let's undo this 'ere secularation," Crockett said.

David had the word wrong, but I knew what he meant. Everywhere we went, the secularization of the missions seemed to be the most divisive issue. I looked to Tom, who was nodding agreement with Crockett. As the sons of farmers and blacksmiths, we were inclined to sympathize with the little folk. But I also knew the big ranchers would not yield their land grants willingly.

Our pattern in the next few weeks became set. The Seventh Cavalry would ride into each new settlement with flags flying and our new band playing "Garry Owen". At meetings with local leaders, Crockett would advocate for the missions while I urged caution, leaving both the Franciscans and the ranchers hopeful of a decision in their favor. And as a result, the army never lacked for supplies.

––––––––––

We reached the outskirts of Monterey in early November. Though the former governor, Pio Pico, had tried to make Los Angeles the capital of the territory, all of the administrative work remained in this northern port. It was here that Commodore John Sloat had raised the American flag on July 7th, 1846, claiming all of Alta California for the United States. But now history had been changed, no one would ever hear of John Sloat, and it would be George Armstrong Custer who raised the flag of liberty over this green land.

"Country is in revolt," a well-dressed merchant said, coming into my camp just before dark.

He was an American in his mid-thirties named Isaac Graham, a former mountain man who claimed to know Kit Carson. He wore a brown broadcloth jacket and carried a Pennsylvania rifle. His fluffy red beard grew down over a blue cravat.

Graham rode in on a fine Spanish stallion with two grizzly fur trappers, three ambitious shop keepers, and a burly gunsmith, all new immigrants to California. Graham himself was a brewer.

"The roads we've traveled have been peaceful," I remarked.

"South is better at complainin' than fightin'," Graham said. "Up here, folks get more riled up."

"The Seventh Cavalry will reach Monterey by noon tomorrow. Are you offering assistance?" I asked.

"Depends on what ya want," Graham answered. "Most of us are lookin' for independence, like the Texans. The Californios ain't so sure, but we all agree that Gutiérrez has got ta go. He's only governor in name. Chico went to Mexico City for more troops. Might be back any day."

"That's not very likely," I said. "Tom, make our guests comfortable. Mr. Graham and I will have a talk."

Our camp was next to a wide creek under tall oaks, the horses grazing on a lush hillside. Cooking fires were roasting fresh meats. Several kegs had been opened, but Crockett was watching to make sure there was no drunkenness. There were enough tents for everyone, and we had even attracted a small but loyal train of camp followers, some Indian and some Mexican. The peons chopped wood and groomed horses while the women prepared food and washed our clothes. And a few provided other services, which I turned a blind eye to.

I led Graham to my campaign tent near the wagon park. A small pot belly stove kept my headquarters warm. A buffalo hide was used for a rug. John had even arranged for a curtained latrine, making my accommodations quite luxurious. Tom had wanted Morning Star to stay with him, but that I wouldn't allow, keeping her and Slow with me. Singing Grass was my guest, too, for Carson had decided to leave her with the Seventh. Graham found the arrangement curious.

"How many men can you count on?" I asked, offering Graham a seat at my table.

"Twenty-five. All good men," he said, finding a folding chair.

"I have more teamsters than that."

Morning Star was kind enough to serve us lamb and beans while John poured a cup of brown ale. Slow sat in silence, merely observing, while Singing Grass sat at Graham's feet. As a girl of fourteen, she had met him at the Pierre's Hole Rendezvous, along with Jim Bridger and Joe Meek. There had even been a battle, of sorts, though Singing Grass was reluctant to speak of it.

"This can be a great nation, but not with the Mexicans runnin' it," Graham said. "They don't like immigrants, and those they accept gots to convert. Me, well, I don't care 'bout that, but some folks got a delicate conscience. The good folks we need to come here, they won't swap their religion for land."

I tried to show no reaction to his observation, though I knew it to be true. In recent months, I'd been giving much thought to Isabella and the Seguin family. If I wanted to take a place in their community, as Jim Bowie had, I would need to become a Catholic. If Pa was still my pa, and not a man several years younger than myself in far off Ohio, he'd whip me good for such a thought. The Custers were Methodists and everybody in New Rumley knew it.

"Gots other problems, too," Graham continued. "We get taxed but got no garrisons for protection. Land is given and then taken away. Can't run a store or a shop without officials wantin' bribes. The Franciscans once ran the whole territory, and they could git greedy, too. But now a handful of rich Spaniards are takin' it all."

"What of Señor Juan Alvarado? Does he have an army nearby?" I asked.

"Can't call if much of an army, but Gutiérrez don't got much, neither," Graham said. "Juan was goin' ta take Monterey two weeks ago, but held off when he heard cavalry was marching up the Camino Real. At first he thought you was Chico."

"Who does he intend to fight?"

"Gutiérrez, I assume."

"Tell Señor Alvarado to withdraw his rebels and meet me in San Francisco," I decided.

"You mean Presidio de San Francisco?" Graham asked. "Juan's boys are holding the old Spanish fort. May not be willing to give it up."

"Yerba Buena," I corrected, remembering that the bayside port wouldn't be called San Francisco for another eleven years. "Juan won't resent me taking the city, will he?"

"Ain't never heard folks call Yerba Buena a city before," Graham said.

"I will try to cooperate with Señor Alvarado and his patriots, but we may discover ourselves at cross purposes," I said. "Should that happen, where will Isaac Graham stand?"

"I'm an American, sir. Would like ta see California be free. If not, then part of the United States," he answered.

"Mr. Graham, your support is welcome. But I can't promise you'll like the changes I'm going to make," I warned.

"Fair enough," he said, getting up to leave. "By the way, General, I heard you fellas come here lookin' for gold. Got bad new fer ya, sir. There ain't no gold in California. Not enough to bother with."

"Thank you for the advice," I said, shaking his hand.

Late in the evening, after *Taps*, I slipped off to a grassy ravine downriver from the camp. We had a first quarter moon for light and a sea of stars on a cloudless night. With me were Tom, Smith, Crockett, Kellogg, and Slow. Morning Star brought two bottles of a very fine wine found at Mission San Carlos del río Carmelo. John started a campfire for us, for there was a cool breeze coming from the ocean only a few miles away.

"Gentlemen, tomorrow we occupy Monterey, the capital of California. The key to holding this territory. By tomorrow night, we will be the government, but until then we must be careful," I explained.

"Is this a prank, Autie? Since when are you careful?" Tom snickered.

"Gutiérrez won't put up much of a fight. History says Alvarado fired one cannon shot at him and the entire garrison surrendered," Kellogg said.

"That's what we must avoid," I said.

"Okey, now ya got us confused," Crockett said, drinking the wine but preferring whiskey.

"When we confront Gutiérrez, he must still be governor of Alta California. It's vital to my plans," I said.

"Could it be vital to *our* plans?" Tom asked.

"Split hairs if you must, little brother, but I have business to conduct with the governor. There can be no surrender or resignations until that business is concluded," I insisted.

"Ya still ain't makin' no sense, George," Crockett said, scratching his gray whiskers.

"It is the piece of paper," Slow said, gifted with a half cup of wine.

"Wedding certificate for George and Isabella?" Smith asked, though he knew better.

"No. It is more," Slow said.

"And what do you know of pieces of paper, youngster?" I asked.

143

"The white man gives and takes with paper. So do the Mexicans. Paper is powerful in your world," Slow explained.

"The boy is right," I said, reaching into my jacket for a rolled parchment. "When I was in Galveston with Santa Anna, we had many a long talk. He finally came to see my side of things."

I unrolled the parchment. It was a land grant, signed and sealed by the dictator himself. I let Smith see it first, for he had attended Hamilton College and was well acquainted with such documents.

"What do you think, Fresh?" I asked.

"My Spanish isn't real good, but this looks like you own most of northern California," Smith said.

"From the American River to the Rockies," I clarified. "But only after the current governor acknowledges Santa Anna's signature."

"Are *we* going to own any of this land?" Kellogg asked.

"John?" I summoned.

John rushed up with my leather bag used for maps and reports. I took out a hefty sheaf of papers filled with scribbling.

"As you know, Ben Travane spent many years aboard merchant ships," I said.

"Travane? Your Negro slave?" Kellogg asked.

"Mr. Travane is not my slave. He was born a free man," I objected, for if Kellogg had such an impression, others would, too. "Ben came to San Antonio with Santa Anna to manage his commissary. After the battle, Ben found the dictator's strongbox and turned it over to me. He's good with numbers, so he's become my clerk."

"So what do sailors gots do with the land?" Crockett asked.

"Some of the crews used articles of agreement to divvy up their profits. Particularly pirate crews, which we may fine somewhat fitting. We'll need a few good lawyers on this, but everything I've gotten from Santa Anna, and whatever else we can take, will be subject to these articles."

"An' ya thought of this way back in Galveston?" Crockett asked, looking at the fine lettering of the land grant.

"Antonio actually suggested it," I confessed.

"Antonio?" Smith said.

"When Santa Anna and I went duck hunting, I bragged that I could conquer California before New Year's Day. He said conquering and possessing are two different things."

"So Antonio López de Santa Anna is now a friend of yours?" Tom said.

"A friend? I wouldn't say that. But he is a partner."

We were on the road just after dawn, keeping good order with Bouyer's scouts in the lead. I rode with Slow and Kellogg, watchful but not worried. Our trail was often lined with observers; farmers, vaqueros, tradesmen and Indians. A well populated area. Reaching the end of the valley, we entered a pass and emerged overlooking a wooded peninsula. In the distance was the Pacific Ocean, and just to the north, a large bay protecting a sprawling port.

The town of Monterey rose back from the waterfront on gentle hills. A wide road ran along the edge of the harbor, lined with taverns and warehouses. Two main avenues turned off at a left angle, with businesses, stables, and a few fancy haciendas. Above the town, I saw a long ridge topped with a thick forest.

Closer to us, on a small plateau, was the presidio attached to an old walled church. The presidio did not offer a serious threat, having only a tower and corral for defense, but there was a more pressing concern a mile farther on. Using my binoculars, I spied a ramshackle fort on the hill beyond the town, with artillery guarding the entrance to the harbor.

"They call it El Castillo," Tom said, using his binoculars to study the fortifications.

"More like a mud latrine," I said. "But it's got eight cannon, probably six-pounders. I also see a shack and a stable. The *soldados* are scrambling, about five dozen in all."

"El Castillo may threaten ships, but it's not well placed to repel a ground attack," Smith observed.

"We need to take that redoubt," I said. "Smith, E Company will maneuver west around the edge of the hill and come up on them from behind. Do not attack until you hear the bugle. Voss, stay close to me. Colonel Custer, occupy the wooded heights above the town. Be prepared to charge through the village."

"We can take those streets in five minutes," Tom said.

Below the Presidio, along the coast road, I counted forty adobe buildings, most single story with thatched roofs. A few were two

145

stories with balconies and courtyards. Probably hotels, saloons, and perhaps a merchant's guild. The sandy shore had two piers jutting out into the water next to a newly built customs house. A dozen ships lay at anchor, none of them warships. Two I suspected to be whalers, some were small barks, and one was a New England schooner. At least one cargo vessel was flying a Spanish flag.

"Crockett, we are going down toward those white dunes, then make a left oblique to the main road," I said. "Have the band play the usual songs. Weapons will remain holstered. My regimental staff will have the lead. When we reach the town, take Company A to the Customs House and await further orders."

"Jus' the eight of you gonna take on Gutiérrez?" Crockett asked.

"I'm not going to take on anyone, David. I'm going to file my land grant," I said.

We rode on for another hour at a slow gait. It would take Tom and Smith time to get in position. Meanwhile, we were being watched by Monterey's garrison, though I sensed no panic. One way or another, they were not expecting a bloody encounter. I was just as complacent.

The dirt road divided. The docks were off to the right, the Presidio about a quarter mile up the grass-covered hill. The military headquarters had no walls to speak of, but the fifteen-foot adobe tower overlooked the northwest corner of the compound. The belfry of the old Spanish church behind the Presidio could also be used for observation. A corral made of split wood fencing was large enough for twenty horses, but the enclosure was empty.

"To your station, Mr. Crockett," I ordered, sending David to the Customs House near the longest pier. "And detain anyone you find there. Hughes, Butler, you're with me."

I turned Traveller up the hill, parts of the road filled with gravel to prevent erosion. The sleepy town of Monterey lay several hundred yards to our right, strung out along a few narrow avenues. There was a quaintness to it, like the Mexican version of a New England fishing village. The sloping ground to my left was used for grazing, mostly sheep and a few goats.

"General, I should go, too," Kellogg said, hanging back with Morning Star and John. Slow did not wait, riding Vic up to my side.

"Permission granted, Mr. Kellogg," I said.

146

Voss rode with us, along with Sergeant Fuentes, Corporal Espalier and Corporal Hannum. Sergeant Howell, who I had stolen from C Company, would stay behind with Crockett. As my regimental saddler, George had more important duties than carrying a rifle.

"Stay here at the foot of the hill with the scouts," I told Howell. "Bring Crockett forward if there's trouble. Alert the rest of the command if necessary."

"Yes, sir," Howell said, returning to Crockett and keeping a trumpeter at his side.

The rest of us rode halfway up the hill, then dismounted and led our horses the rest of the way. The corral gate was open for our mounts. Two guards in blue cotton uniforms and black sombreros guarded the headquarters door armed with Brown Bess muskets.

The Presidio was larger than I'd thought, contained on two sides with a barracks, kitchen, repair shops, and a commandant's office. A gate farther back led to the church gardens and presumably the stables. Three small iron cannon ringed the flag pole, the carriages in such poor condition that I doubted the guns could be fired.

"Expected better," Butler whispered, for San Antonio appeared cosmopolitan by comparison.

"You should have seen Fort Lincoln when Libbie and I first arrived," I said, for frontier life is often primitive.

A middle-aged man approached wearing a black frock coat, a rain-stained slouch hat, and store-bought spectacles.

"*He venido a ver al gobernador,*" I greeted the clerk.

"*Su excelencia lo espera,*" the clerk said, a mild-mannered Spaniard with a humble posture. "Though, if you wish, I speak English, General Custer."

"Very well, señor," I replied.

While Espalier and Hannum took our horses to the corral, I entered the headquarters with Kellogg and Slow. It was a long rectangular building with a central corridor and windows for each room, much like the governor's palace in Béjar. Fuentes, acting as my orderly, followed with my leather bag of documents. Hughes and Butler lingered just inside the front door, their strange weapons attracting attention from the guards.

Waiting for us was a man of medium height with reddish hair tinting gray, somewhat round, and lighter skinned than many in this part of the country. He had a genial expression, though an odd cast in his right eye that had given him the nickname *El Tuerto*.

"Governor Gutiérrez, I presume?" I said, reaching to shake hands.

"I am Lt. Colonel Nicolás Gutiérrez, military commandant and acting governor of Alta California," he said with a strong Spanish accent.

The reception hall was hung with flags and banners. The floor was polished blue paving stones. Several statues of Catholic saints adorned the alcoves. I could see the church garden through glass windows in the rear door.

"Pleased to meet you, sir," I replied.

"So the mystery riders arrive at last," the One-Eyed said. "Have you business in Monterey?"

"We do, sir. Important business," I said.

He waved me toward his office at the rear of the building. I took Kellogg and my orderly with me, leaving the sergeants and Voss in the hall. Slow arrived a minute later, looking wary. Gutiérrez's office had an impressive maple wood desk, several elaborately carved chairs, and a Mexican flag hanging on the wall. His clerk stood nearby.

"Señor Armand, offer our guests hospitality," the governor said, walking to the back of the room.

"May we offer tea?" the clerk asked.

"We're not Englishmen," Kellogg said, hoping for something stronger.

"Perhaps coffee?" Armand suggested.

"Maybe later," I said, reaching into my valise. "I have here a land grant to be certified, along with our travel papers. They are signed by El Presidente Antonio López de Santa Anna. And here is a letter of introduction."

Armand took the papers, glanced them over, and handed them to Gutiérrez with a nod. Gutiérrez acknowledged them with a frown.

"This grant would make you a very rich land owner, General Custer, if you were not a pirate," Gutiérrez said, the genial smile fading.

"I am no pirate, Señor," I protested.

"A ship arrived last week from Mexico City with reinforcements for my garrison," the frowning man said. "I had hoped to ambush Alvarado and his rebels, but the messenger gave me notice of strange

Americans coming to overthrow our government, so I have been forced to wait."

"That is a genuine deed, Governor," I said, taking a step back.

"It would be, if Santa Anna were still president of Mexico, but he has been removed by Congress," Gutiérrez explained. "And the new Congress has ordered me to eliminate this threat to our province."

Suddenly four lancers emerged from a side room armed with muskets. Gutiérrez drew a pistol from his desk.

"Does this mean you will not ratify my land grant?" I brazenly asked, for my mind needed time to discover options.

"You will not live long enough to enjoy it," Gutiérrez said.

A shot rang out in the reception area, followed by two more, and then a rapid series of shots that could only be Sergeant Hughes' Henry. I kicked the desk backward, throwing Gutiérrez off his balance, and drew a Bulldog. Fuentes drew his Colt. Kellogg fumbled for the small caliber Smith & Wesson in his coat pocket. Slow pulled out Jim Bowie's famous knife. The lancers opened fire.

The loud reports were followed by clouds of billowing smoke that quickly blackened the room. I fired at the lancer nearest me, shooting him through the jaw. The soldier next to him was shot in the throat, probably by Fuentes. Gutiérrez had fallen against the wall, but rose to aim at my chest. Kellogg pushed me out of the way and was hit. The lancer on the end, unable to reload, stepped forward using his musket as a club. Slow slashed at his thigh, cutting deeply, but was struck over the head and fell senseless to the floor.

I shot the lancer who clubbed Slow, then the last one, turning to point at Gutiérrez, the only enemy still on his feet. I wasn't sure if my Bulldog had any bullets left, so I drew the other one. The governor was astounded. Apparently no one had told him of the ghost rider's magic weapons. Señor Armand was cowering in the corner.

There was a noise behind me. I wheeled around, ready to fire, but recognized my own men. Butler was shot through the right hand, now cradling his Sharps. Hughes and Voss were out of breath but unharmed.

"Thirty Mexicans in the courtyard, sir," Hughes said, guarding the door.

I looked around. Fuentes was dead, shot through the heart. Kellogg lay against a toppled bench, bleeding from the neck. It looked serious.

"Bandage that hand, Jimmy," I said, taking a gold-knit handkerchief from the sideboard and throwing it to him.

I knelt next to Slow, who was coming around. There was a large bruise on his forehead. His breathing was good. I put him on a couch and went to Kellogg.

"Thanks, Mark," I said, seeking to stop the flow of blood.

The ball had entered above the shoulder and exited near the spine. I tried to straighten him up, but he was in too much pain.

"Sure wanted to start that newspaper," Kellogg whispered. "The *San Francisco Examiner*. Best journal west of New York."

"You still will. Dr. Lord can patch this up," I encouraged, pulling a pillow for him off the bench.

"Got us trapped, don't they?" he said.

"I've gotten out of worse."

"Were you hit?" Kellogg asked.

"Not a scratch."

"Custer's Luck," the reporter said.

And then he wasn't breathing anymore. I closed his eyes, wiping a tear from my own. He'd been an ass, but I admired him.

I stood up and went back to the desk. Gutiérrez and Armand were standing together, several pistols pointed at them. I found my land grant and slapped it down on the desk.

"Register my grant. Now. And date it," I demanded, my voice low and cold.

Gutiérrez hesitated, but Armand didn't, taking out a large book, making the appropriate notations, and holding out a quill pen for the governor's signature.

"I am only doing my duty," Gutiérrez said.

"Then do your duty and sign the damn book," I said.

Gutiérrez took the quill, and with the greatest reluctance, authorized my document.

"I will file a protest in Mexico City," Gutiérrez said.

"Not likely," I replied.

I raised the second Bulldog and shot Gutiérrez in the chest, then shot him two more times as he spun around, smearing the plaster wall with blood as he sank to the floor.

"I am just a civil servant, General Custer," Armand cried, holding his hands before his face.

"Put the seal on my grant," I said, watching as he applied a stamp at the bottom of the document and fixed the date. Then he looked up, waiting to be shot.

"A civil servant? That's all?" I asked.

"*Sí, sí Señor,*" he said.

"Then you work for me now. Bolt the door after we leave and take care of the boy. If anything happens to him, I'll feed you to the hogs. Understand?"

"Yes, sir," Armand agreed.

"Everybody ready?" I asked, going to the door.

"Ready, General," Butler said, drawing a Colt with his good hand. Voss now carried the Sharps. Hughes cocked the Henry. I reloaded the Bulldogs, carrying one in each hand.

"Think any of our boys got out?" Voss asked.

"Not sure about Hannum and Espalier. Howell will have alerted Crockett by now," I replied, though I wasn't sure what Crockett would do. None of his officers were Seventh Cavalry, though Sergeant French could offer valuable advice.

"Henry, we need to get you on a roof or a tower," I decided. "Signal Colonel Custer and Smith to attack."

"I can get out the back door, sir. Go up in the church with the bells," Voss said, a smart lad.

"Jimmy, you go with him," I ordered. "Don't let anyone get in your way. Bobby, you and I are going out the front. Are you with me?"

"I was the last time, sir," Hughes said.

There had been a lull in the fighting. As I opened the heavy door, the halls were ghostly quiet. I took the lead, followed by Hughes. Voss and Butler soon disappeared out the rear door. I moved calmly and steadily, burning with anger. Hughes held his rifle at his waist, ready to work the lever to maximum advantage.

"What should we do, sir?" he asked.

"Kill 'em all," I answered.

Hughes and I paused at a broken window to scout our opposition.

"Least a score in the courtyard, all on foot. Most got muskets," Hughes said.

I saw one officer carrying a sword next to the guard tower. His sergeant looked confused. Near the corral, two lancers were mounted holding long spears. There was no precision to the enemy formations.

"I'll go left, Bobby. You've got the right flank. Tear into them," I whispered.

And then I stepped out the door, opening fire. Two *soldados* went down fast, and when the third was hit, the enemy realized I didn't need to reload after each shot. I aimed the second Bulldog, firing twice more. At such a range, it was hard to miss. Hughes fired eight rapid rounds at the lancers in the corral.

In a matter of seconds, half of the *soldados* were on the ground, wounded or dead. Six lancers were stout enough to return our fire, but their aim was rushed. One was a tall sergeant whose bravery was rewarded with a bullet through the forehead. With no time to reload, the survivors starting running. The three that didn't were gunned down where they stood.

We found Corporal Hannum next to the horses, shot several times. He had bled out quickly, his Colt still in the holster. Espalier was shot in the leg and shoulder, but was still holding Traveller's reins. His pistol was empty, and having only one good arm, could not reload. He started to get up, but I waved him back down rather than let him get in the way. I took Hannum's pistol, for the Bulldogs were expended.

Hughes stayed near the corral, watching for a counterattack. I searched the kitchen and barracks, looking for hidden foes. I found a group of women and children, and one unarmed lancer who instantly surrendered. It was all I could do not to shoot him outright.

The adobe tower had a lower room and upper observation platform. Leaving the women to care for Corporal Espalier, I summoned Hughes to the second floor. There was skirmishing along the docks, and then a cannon fired from El Castillo to the north, striking a warehouse where some of Crockett's men were positioned. I could not see Crockett. Below us, half a dozen lancers were retreating on foot to the northeast, heading for the open road. I shot one in the leg, watched him roll over, and then get back on his feet. He limped away as fast as he could go. The rest were out of range, so I let them escape.

"Targets, Bobby?" I asked, for the ground between us and the docks was crowded with scurrying sheep herders and panicked flocks.

A bugle sounded from the church behind us, loud and clear in the afternoon air, the urgent notes ringing off the hills. If there was any doubt among my officers before, there would be none now. The call was answered from my left as I saw Company C charge down the long mountain slopes into the village.

There was no call from Smith, Company E merely rode up from the ocean and over the hill into the rough wooden redoubt overlooking the bay, swords waving and Colts blazing. There was one more cannon shot, fired in a direction that would do the garrison no good, and then they were overrun. From the tower, all I could see were banners, dust, and puffs of smoke, but the firing was not heavy.

"Let's give Crockett a hand," I said, climbing down the ladder and mounting Vic.

Hughes opened the corral gate, but I was out before he found his horse, galloping down the hill and through the lower end of town. Old men and young children ran to get out of my way.

A small group of lancers, two with muskets, were kneeling behind a stone wall taking shots at the Customs House. I pulled Vic around and shot one in the back. Another jumped up and charged at me with his lance, seeking to skewer me from the saddle. He was a courageous man. I shot him in the face. The remaining lancers dropped their weapons and held up their hands.

"*Carrera! Carrera!*" I shouted.

They ran like jackrabbits.

Company A's horses had been taken to the beach for protection, every fourth man holding their reins. Another dozen, commanded by Lieutenant Autry, were stationed behind a seawall in support of the Customs House. Crockett had stormed the house with the rest of his men and apparently captured it. I recognized privates Steiner and González on the roof.

The lancers fleeing the town turned north toward El Castillo just as the redoubt survivors were coming down to the main road. Company E's guidon flew from a livery stable near the cannon. The first members of Company C were appearing behind me, having charged through the town. Some of Crockett's men emerged from the Customs House, roughed up but in good spirits. I noticed a score of Mexican soldiers gathered on the road ahead still armed, and without much thought, galloped forward firing my borrowed Colt.

The lancers were not organized for resistance. Most were bewildered by gunfire coming from several directions, and they seemed to lack officers. A sergeant tried to rally them without success, and then their flag bearer went down, the banner fluttering into the dirt. I continued to shoot, and so did Crockett's men, who were rushing to keep up with me. Several lancers went down. I would have kept shooting had a bugle not sounded the *Cease Fire*.

"Think that's 'nough, George," Crockett said, riding to my side on a borrowed mule. "No point in a massacre."

It was not a massacre yet, but might be if we didn't stop the indiscriminate killing. I holstered my weapon and dismounted, giving Vic's reins to Sergeant French.

"I need a bugler," I shouted, for the battlefield was chaos.

"Here, sir," Jimmy Allen said, holding a trumpet.

"Sound *Recall*," I ordered.

Jimmy blew the call. Crockett and I moved forward, waving to the men. It took several minutes to establish order, for mounted units were chasing the broken enemy into the hills.

"Gather our wounded in the Customs House. Dr. Lord can treat them. The doctor is alive, isn't he?" I asked French.

"Kept him on the beach with the horses," Howell confirmed.

Butler and Voss came down from the Presidio with two old men carrying Slow on a stretcher. The boy kept trying to sit up, but they wouldn't let him.

"We'll requisition these haciendas for the next few days," I decided, not interested in what the owners might think. "Bring up the wagons, and let's raise the Buffalo Flag above the plaza."

The panic in town slowed when the last of the shooting stopped. I guessed half the population had fled into the trees, and other half stayed to protect their shops and livestock. There were stray chickens everywhere. I sent Autry to find the village elders, and requested a priest, for there were going to be a lot of funerals.

"Autie! What happened?" Tom asked, reining in next to me on Athena.

Company C was spread through the lower end of town holding a broad skirmish line. I sensed there were no causalities, for there had been no fighting in the streets. Tom seemed more confused than angry.

"It was a trap," I confessed. "Santa Anna has been removed from power. Gutiérrez had orders to ambush us. Kellogg is dead. So are my orderlies."

"Gutiérrez?" Tom asked.

"I shot the son of a bitch," I answered.

"Where is Mark?"

"Still in the Presidio," I said, pointing up the hill.

Tom rounded up a few men and dashed off. If Armand was still in the office, I hoped Tom wouldn't shoot him. Smith rode up.

"Forty prisoners, sir. What should we do with them?" he asked, out of breath from the battle.

"Secure them in the church," I said. "If any try to escape, shoot them."

"General, we've been letting prisoners escape since the Alamo," Smith said.

"They made this one personal, Fresh," I replied.

By early evening the town had quieted. My troops were billeted in the adobe houses along the coast road, those not on duty were either in the taverns or tending the wounded. The day had not gone well. What should have been a simple occupation had cost me six men. And fifty-five of the enemy. I took up quarters in the Presidio, confiscating the large feather bed that had once belonged to Governor Gutiérrez. Peons were hired to wash blood from the office.

John took command of the Presidio kitchens and made a fine meal for my staff, but I brooded.

"What's wrong, Autie? Tired of victories?" Tom asked, his charge through town with sabers flashing being spoken of everywhere. Even though it had no effect on the battle's outcome.

"Kellogg was a good man, George," Crockett said. "Died fightin' fer what he believed in. Kin't ask fer more 'n that."

"Monterey must stand for more than a shallow victory," I said, reaching for my wine glass. "We need to send a message, like the Emancipation Proclamation after Antietam, or Lincoln's speech at Gettysburg."

"No offense, Autie, but you're no Lincoln," Smith said.

"Wouldn't try, but I do have a proclamation," I said. "Tom, did you leave a copy of the Kearny Code in Santa Fe?"

"Left a copy with the commandant," Tom answered.

"Send messengers to Los Angeles and Yuma. Send messengers all the way to San Antonio. Tell them to issue the proclamation, and call it the Kellogg Code," I said.

"Generous of you," Tom said under a bent brow.

"Mark earned it."

"Ya keep talkin' of this 'ere code. Jus' what is it?" Crockett asked.

"When the Army of the West invaded New Mexico in 1846, General Stephen Watts Kearny proclaimed the Kearny Code in Santa Fe," I said.

"What is a code?" Slow asked.

The boy had a cloth bandage wrapped around his head and appeared a little weak, but his eyes were sharp as ever. Morning Star was feeding him soup near the fireplace.

"Among civilized nations, a code is established for the rule of law," I explained.

"Now we need a code for the people of California. And New Mexico. For everyone living under the Buffalo Flag," Tom urged.

"Does this code give all the land to the white man?" Slow inquired.

"No, this code will make everyone equal under the law," I said, hiding my doubts, for good intentions often fail.

"You realize we're going to spend the next twenty years fighting to enforce it, don't you?" Tom said.

"More than that," I guessed.

"Why would you do this?" Slow asked, for the code held little importance for him.

"Because a great man proved it's our duty," Smith said. "He proved it with courage and persistence."

"And blood," Tom added.

At noon the following day, the citizens of Monterey assembled in the town plaza, unsure what to expect. On Crockett's suggestion, food and drink was served. I instructed the band to play "Yellow Rose of Texas", "Bonnie Blue Flag", and just for fun, "Marching Through Georgia", smiling at my little joke. The townspeople played a few of their traditional Mexican songs. By the time I rose to speak, the sense of gloom had eased. My Spanish was still a little shaky, but getting better.

"On this day, the 5th of November, 1836, by my authority as Lt. General of the Buffalo Flag Nations, I do proclaim this, the Kellogg

Code, for all our peoples," I announced, trying to stay calm so my voice would not sound squeaky. "This code is a bill of rights, based on the rights of the United States. This code will apply to all people, white or Mexican, Indian or foreigner. Free and former slave. There will be no slavery in our blessed country. All will have the right of free speech, freedom of religion, freedom for life, liberty, and the pursuit of happiness. All will be equal under the law."

"Here, here!" Tom and Smith shouted, followed by dozens of my men.

The people in the plaza showed little reaction. It wasn't that they didn't understand, they seemed not to care. In time, maybe they would.

"In the spring, leaders from all over Alta California will gather to ratify a constitution," I continued. "Until that day, all decrees of the provisional government must be obeyed."

I rolled up the notes I'd been reading and climbed down from my soapbox, returning to the Presidio with Slow. Tom and Morning Star stayed to mingle with our new subjects. Crockett found a fiddle, playing clever tunes while wearing a coonskin cap. Autry found a keg. Only Butler and Hughes followed me up the hill.

We were not alone for very long. Ranchers from all over the area were coming in, asking if their lands were being given back to the missions. Missionaries wanted to know the same thing. Merchants wished to know if the Buffalo Flag was friendly to their commerce. A Mexican lieutenant entered begging mercy for Monterey's former garrison, still under guard in the church. The whole time, Slow sat in the corner, watching but rarely commenting.

"What do you think, lad?" I finally asked, curious about his silence.

"They have many questions. You give them few answers," Slow observed.

"I have no answers. If I make harsh demands, they'll resist me as a dictator," I said. "If I'm too meek, they'll ignore my commands. Tom or Crockett may have a better idea how to answer them."

"You are the leader," Slow said.

"Among the Lakota, a chief may be a leader. But what if the people don't want to follow him?"

"Then he is no longer chief."

"Can he shoot the warriors who won't follow him?"

157

"That would not be wise," Slow said.

"Wisdom has never been my strong suit, boy. I'm decisive. A risk taker. A good judge of character. But wisdom? That's for smarter men than me."

Just before dusk, after a long day of interviews, Autry came up the hill with another unhappy petitioner. The November day was cooling off fast as a brisk wind blew in from the sea. The office windows were closed and the hearth lighted.

"General, this 'ere is Captain Francis Gaston of the *Don Quijote*. That big boat out in the harbor," Autry said. "He wants ta' sail out. With all 'is cargo."

It took me a moment to realize what Autry was suggesting.

"Piracy, Micajah?" I inquired.

"Ain't piracy, sir. Not if we give 'em letters of credit," the lawyer said.

This was indeed a promising idea, for the ships in the harbor probably carried all kinds of valuable supplies. And despite the friends we had made, the Seventh Cavalry was still two thousand miles away from our base of operations.

"Tell Tom and Fresh to seize the ships," I ordered.

"Kinda late for that," Autry said. "Tom recruited those captured Mexicans in the church. That lieutenant? Lucius Fernandez? He agreed to man the guns in Fort Castillo. They aren't letting any of our sailor friends leave Monterey without permission."

"Tom released the prisoners?" I asked.

"Said if you was gonna sit on yer butt all day, he may as well git somethin' done," Autry reported.

"Very well, lieutenant. Carry on," I said, offering a salute.

"Sir, I must protest," Captain Gaston said, a portly man with a French accent.

"Yes, I'm sure you do," I answered.

———————

The funerals weren't until the next day, a Sunday. Because Mark Kellogg and our other lost comrades were to be buried in the cemetery of the San Carlos Mission with full military honors, we needed time to organize the ceremony and mend our uniforms. We had a Catholic priest from the mission and an Anglican minister from the English schooner *Wisp*. I paid a mason for engraved headstones.

Toward the end of the day, a light rain began falling, but it wasn't the frosty November so familiar in Ohio. Father Joaquin warned me not to expect much in the way of snow.

By Monday night it began to rain in earnest, keeping the troops indoors except those needed for guard duty. I was particularly pleased that I had conquered Monterey before the wet weather arrived and used the time wisely, writing notices to every town along the coast. Unlike Virginia, the roads did not turn to intractable mud.

"Good writin', George, but none gots my name on them," Crockett said, visiting my office often.

"You're president of Texas, David, not Alta California," I said, the subject coming up for the first time.

"And who be president out this 'way?" he asked.

"I haven't decided yet. Possibly Alvarado, if he cooperates," I answered. "He's just a kid, though, and possibly loyal to Mexico."

"Tommy would be good," Crockett suggested.

"Tom's also a kid, and I need him with me."

"How 'bout Slow?"

"How about Autry?"

"I need Micajah. I gets lonely for Tennessee," Crockett said. "Besides, ain't gonna be no democracy 'ere anytime soon. Reckon army rule fer least a couple a years."

"The first California gold rush saw thousands of migrants rush in. Fifty-thousand in the first year alone. Couple hundred thousand, all told," I said. "I don't expect that many in 1836. Communications are poor, shipping is primitive, and Indians block most of the western trails. But there will still be a lot."

"And they's gonna bring trouble," Crockett realized. "How ya gonna keep control with jus' a few glory seekers and ghost riders?"

"That is a fine question, Congressman. Any ideas?"

"When land jumpers were a takin' homesteads from farmers back home, and stealin' land from the Cherokee, I thought we should hang 'em."

"We're going to need plenty of rope," I replied.

Late in the afternoon of Thursday, December 1st, three more companies of Seventh Cavalry rode into Monterey pulling eighteen wagons and a fine 8-pounder artillery piece discovered in Santa

Barbara. I assembled them in the plaza, letting Hughes and French find quarters for the men.

"Carson?" I asked.

"Sharrow paid 'em off. Sent back to Santa Fe," Bouyer reported.

"Just as well," I said. "Having a guide into the Sierra Nevadas would be good, but we don't need an Indian war."

"Kit weren't so bad," Bouyer said. "We met a raidin' party of Apache on the way back an' he giv 'em a good talkin' to. Weren't no fightin'."

I decided not to inquire further. Tom, Smith and Crockett rushed into my office. With the Seventh Cavalry reunited, we had two-hundred and fifty soldiers in addition to a hundred and forty scouts, teamsters and camp followers. A formidable force in such a sparsely populated country.

"Any news from Texas?" I asked.

Bouyer handed me a large pouch of dispatches. Letters from Keogh, Sharrow, Erasmo Seguin, and a dozen others. And newspapers, too, from Baltimore, Philadelphia, Charleston and New Orleans. I yearned for a New York newspaper, maybe the *New York Herald*, but wasn't that lucky.

"Only thirty-two days old," I said, checking the date on Keogh's report. "Not bad for a first run. Wells Fargo did better, though."

"Wells Fargo had stations every forty miles. We don't," Tom said.

"Not yet," Smith replied.

There was a day of celebration, welcoming the new arrivals with a fiesta, speeches, and tours of Monterey. We cooked plenty of beef, enjoyed the local wines, and had music all day long. Stories were swapped about crossing the desert, visiting the missions, and the temperate weather. It was good to see the men enjoying such comradery, for we would need it in the months ahead.

"You are busy, chieftain," Slow said, wandering into my office at the end of a hectic afternoon.

"I've been meeting with more Californios," I said. "They are ambitious men, seeking land to become rich. This is a trade I am intimately familiar with."

"I did not know you owned so much land," Slow said.

"I've never owned any land. The largest home I've ever owned was an ambulance wagon converted for Libbie's use. But I did live in the

Gilded Age, as Mark Twain called it. A time of vast expansion. An era of robber barons. Railroads. Newspapers. Mining companies. Though my own investments performed poorly, I knew dozens who made fortunes. Now such men are coming to me, seeking favors."

"This is a common problem for a chief," Slow said, dismissing my concern. "Are they solved by bonfires and ale?"

"I need the men to form a special bond, like the Michigan brigade did during the Rebellion," I explained, glancing over my shoulder to make sure we were not being overheard. "After our civil war, the Seventh Cavalry was spread all over the county. Suppressing the Ku Klux Klan. Protecting travelers on the western trails. Exploring unknown lands. Now we are going to be spread thin again, from Sacramento to San Francisco. Yuma to San Antonio. How will I keep everyone loyal?"

"Gold. The white man craves gold," Slow answered.

"No. No, lad, I'm afraid you're wrong. Crockett has shown me that," I said. "Gold is a motivator, but we'll need more than that to succeed. I just don't know what that is."

"Thomas knows. And Señor Seguin. And the Crockett," Slow said, unconcerned. "You need only be Custer. Let the wiser chiefs weigh such problems."

Like all casual observers, Slow saw a general as a man on a white horse, issuing commands and free of responsibility. Few realize most generals are glorified clerks. And I still had plenty of paperwork to do.

On a foggy December day, the Seventh Cavalry rode out to complete our conquest of California. I left Smith behind with orders for Monterey to continue business as usual, only under the Buffalo Flag.

"Damn it, Autie, C Company has earned the privilege," Tom protested, for I had given Brister the lead position.

"Ya earned second place, Tommy. Was my boys that won the battle," Crockett said.

With five companies riding north, everybody wanted the place of honor.

"Gentlemen, while your men were winning glory, Brister, Blazeby and Badillo were bringing up the rear. Finishing the road. Insuring our supplies," I said. "Now it's their turn to win some glory."

"But Autie—" Tom started.

"Tommy, the Custer Clan cannot keep all the laurels for ourselves," I said. "We're not on the plains anymore. We're not working for Phil Sheridan. *We* are the army now, and if we want loyalty, we need to give loyalty."

"I hate it when you're right," Tom conceded.

"Don't happen often," Crockett chimed in.

"Very amusing. Now for this march, I have duties for each of you," I said.

"Ain't cleanin' no stables," Crockett joked.

"Not far wrong, David," I said. "I need you to organize the teamsters, hire Indians, bribe Mexicans, and gather every wagon you can. Then buy up all the timber you can find."

"Sacramento?" Tom asked.

"Sutter hasn't built a fort there yet. We'll need to do it ourselves," I replied.

"Fort Custer?" Crockett asked.

"Has a nice sound to it," I said.

"Fort Crockett sounds better," Crockett said.

"I suppose. But the town should still be called Sacramento. Build it on the high ground for when the floods come," I recommended.

When the army reached San Jose, Brister took the bay road up the peninsula to Yerba Linda, which would soon be rechristened San Francisco, while Blazeby went up the Pacific Ocean coastal route. Tom was sent to establish Oakland on the east bay. With Señor Luis Maria Peralta's help, we would be building a dock for the new ferry. Badillo and I rode with Company K toward San Francisco's presidio, where Juan Alvarado was said to be flying the Mexican flag.

"That's a town?" Butler asked as we passed the settlement.

We stopped on a hill overlooking Yerba Linda, a mud-flat fishing village of two hundred people with docks for the occasional trading vessel. San Francisco Bay was popular with whalers for its safe anchorage. The Presidio was another three miles farther out, on the edge of the peninsula where cannon might dominate the bay's mile wide entrance. The townspeople turned out to see Company B riding by. Brister waved his hat in triumph.

K Company had just passed Mission Dolores when a cannon shot rang out from the north. I had Voss blow the *Forward* and we trotted up a wooded trail and over a ridge until we could see Presidio de San Francisco half a mile distant. It had been a large fort at one time, with barracks, stables, a parade ground, and several bastions for cannon, but that seemed long ago. Now only a portion of the installation was being used, and the adobe walls were in desperate need of repair. I paused the command on the hill.

"Raise our colors. I want them to know we're here," I ordered.

A moment later, I saw Isaac Graham leave the fort, walking up the hill under a flag of truce. There were several other Americans with him, but no Californios.

"What is the meaning of this, Mr. Graham?" I asked, sitting on Traveller. Slow was next to me on Vic with Captain Badillo riding nearby.

"Juan don't want ta surrender," Graham said. "Says they is loyal to Mexico."

"How many men?" Smith asked.

"'bout eighty," Graham said. "Four working cannon. Supplies for a month."

"What of you, Graham? And your men?" I inquired.

"Reckon we're with you, sir," he wisely replied.

I was surprised by Alvarado's resistance, and could not let it stand. Opposition at this late date could inspire Californios all along the Camino Real to rebel. I had two companies in close proximity and a third only minutes away.

"Corporal Sanchez, my compliments to Major Brister. I want Company B up here on the double, and he should bring the 8-pounder," I said. "Sergeant Espalier, my compliments to Captain Blazeby. Company F is to flank the Presidio on the west side and prepare to advance. Captain Badillo, form Company K in skirmish formation along the base of this hill."

The messengers rode off to deliver my orders. It was late on a gray day, a cold wind blowing in from the ocean, and I was not in a good mood. I paused, wondering what else should be done.

"What's that hill over there?" I asked, pointing to my right.

"Goat Hill," Graham said. "But the Spaniards call it Alta Loma."

"We're calling it Telegraph Hill," Hughes said, having studied the maps.

"It has an observation tower. Sergeant Hughes, I want you to place a red flag atop that tower where the Presidio can see it," I decided, remembering Santa Anna's gesture at the Alamo.

While waiting for Brister and Blazeby to get in position, Crockett arrived with A Company, their mounts winded from a gallop up the steep trail.

"What are you thinking, George?" Crockett asked, reining in next to me.

"I was looking forward to warm quarters, a thick steak, and a conversation with Alvarado about the future of this country," I replied. "Now I'm going to kill the son of a bitch."

"Let me have a talk with him," Crockett requested.

"I'll go, too, sir. My Spanish is pretty good," Allen offered.

I remembered my unfortunate meeting with Gutiérrez, and Mark Kellogg lying dead on the stone floor.

"There will be no negotiations," I decided.

A civilian rode up from town on a mule, well-dressed in a fine blue frock coat and beaver top hat. Two Mexican servants rode with him. He tipped his hat and dismounted.

"Sir, my name is William Richardson," he said with an English accent. "I own that fine house down near the anchorage. I beg you to avoid violence. Francisco de Haro, the alcalde, is coming with ten men. We will secure the Presidio for you."

Letting the locals deal with the problem was tempting. Major Brister arrived with the 8-pounder mounted on a new carriage, the limber pulled by four study horses. The gun chief quickly had the cannon loaded with solid shot.

"Ready, sir," Sergeant Ogden announced.

"Mr. Ogden, please fire a round over the fort into the bay," I instructed.

The 8-pounder, nicknamed Ginny, roared with defiance, smoke engulfing the hill as the shot flew downrange into the bay. It was well done, making me glad I'd spent time in Monterey to train the gun crew. Four of them were new recruits from Monterey's garrison, who at Tom's urging, I had reluctantly forgiven. They were reliable young men, excited to be part of a real army.

"Excuse me, Mr. Richardson. You were saying?" I inquired, taking the pioneer with me to the edge of the hill.

Morning Star came up with the supply train. Somehow, John had managed to make hot coffee.

"Alvarado and Castro are well-meaning. They had plans to overthrow the government's tyranny and represent the people," Richardson explained. "You've taken them a bit off-guard, but they'll come around."

"I'll give them an hour," I said, taking out my new silver watch. "After that, there will be no quarter."

"Sir, this is Yerba Buena, not Béjar," Richardson bravely protested.

It seemed he had read of Santa Anna's red flag in Texas, and not with approval. A moment later, the alcalde raced up from town on a fast stallion followed by half a score of militia outfitted in blue wool uniforms. The middle-aged man spoke so rapidly to Richardson that I could barely make out the details, and then he rode down to the Presidio past Company K's skirmishers.

By now my officers had drawn up the entire command, a hundred and twenty troopers, twenty armed scouts, and nearly fifty friendly Indians. Alvarado must have been impressed, for a few minutes later, he walked out of the gate with de Haro at his side. Just before sunset, we ran up the Buffalo Flag in front of the Yerba Buena Customs House overlooking the harbor. I had captured San Francisco with one shot.

———————

Two days later, I appointed Algernon Smith acting governor of California, in cooperation with Mariano Vallejo of Sonoma, one of the largest land owners in the north. The next day, I crossed the bay to Oakland with my regimental staff, bringing the best horses with us. Laborers were busy building store houses.

Having some engineering experience, Blazeby was assigned Fort Peralta as his regular post. The same skills he'd employed as adjutant of the Alamo would now be used in laying out roads and rounding up supplies for the winter. Like all of the New Orleans Greys, the Englishman's efforts were energetic. I considered him for a promotion, and in the meantime, appointed him alcalde of the new town.

With Crockett and Brister in the lead, we rode north to the Sacramento River and then northeast, crossing a vast green flood plain filled with deer, elk and wild horses. It would be hard to explain to Easterners how rich the land was. How abundant. Even a spare description would brand us as liars.

It took several days to reach the confluence of the Sacramento and American rivers. Tom rode ahead to stake out Crockett's Fort on the east bank, a hundred Indian workers making bricks from mud and straw, while vaqueros were constructing cattle pens. Our teamsters had acquired dozens of wagons bringing extra tools and timber.

"Good of you to make it, Autie," Tom said, emerging from my campaign tent with his sleeves rolled up. He was sweating despite the cold weather, never one for shirking physical labor when there was work to do.

Morning Star rode up on her gray mare and jumped from the saddle, rushing into Tom's arms. I saw that Slow was not entirely pleased, but resigned to the situation. At least Slow respected Tom, which could not be said for most white men he met.

"Gone east yet?" I asked.

"Waiting for you," Tom said.

He pointed to a dozen canvas covered wagons filled with supplies, including picks and shovels. Eighty of the best mules were being groomed for service. I hadn't realized Tom's organizational skills had gotten so good.

There was already a rough dirt road heading east, and as a reward, I let Company C take the lead. As we moved out at dawn the next morning, we found small ranches and Indian villages along our route. The people were friendly, offering water for the mounts and looking for trade. Little could they imagine how everything was about to change.

About fifty miles out, as we moved though foothills into pine-filled mountains, we came across a Nisenan village nestled among tall trees. Good logging country. A creek was feeding their small farms, and they had a few of civilization's benefits, including iron pots and two muskets. I knew we must be close to the south fork of the American River, but could not be sure how close. Our trail had taken us up along a series of brush covered ridges. Slow stood with me as I spoke to the Nisenan chief.

"Coloma. Coloma," I asked.

"*Cullumah?*" the old chief said.

Slow made a gesture, possibly asking about our destination, though I couldn't be sure. The chief offered a toothless smile and waved us on. We walked down a hill, strolled along a deer trail, and emerged into a grassy pasture surrounded by tall trees. A vigorous river lay before me, the sound of rushing water music to my ears. Tom, Crockett, and Brister were only a few paces behind. Hughes, Butler and Voss were carrying shovels. A hundred other men were following with more tools.

The gold was not just lying in the river like sparkling trout. During the Black Hills Expedition of 1874, every man in the command had spent time panning for the precious mineral, including Tom and I. We knew to dig down below the gravel, for gold is heavier than sand and shale.

Were we near the spot where James Marshall had found nuggets while deepening the tailrace of Sutter's Mill? Maybe. The area looked right from the numerous descriptions I'd read, but it didn't really matter. We had been patient in our quest long enough, and like madmen, we charged into the river, splashing along the shallows.

I discovered Slow beside me, knee deep in the cold rushing water, a tin plate in his hands filled with sandy river bottom. How he learned gold panning was a mystery, though he'd likely picked it up from Tom. I worked that much harder, competing for the privilege of discovery. We were both disappointed.

"Eureka!" someone shouted, standing only a few feet away. It was Voss, his German accent strong, his eyes lit with joy. Everyone crowded around to see the gold flakes in his pan. It was December 30th, 1836.

"Ya did it, George," Crockett said, shaking my hand.

"We did it, David," I replied.

The white's man thirst for gold was so great that many would die for the soft metal, but for others, the gold became a tool. I found this most curious, for in the Black Hills, the gold seekers were only interested in discovery. It had rarely occurred to me what the prospectors did with their small bags of dust. Many said that Custer was not so smart as other white men, and in some ways, this was true. But Custer understood gold, and in the months that followed our trip to the mountain river, no lesson was more valuable.

167

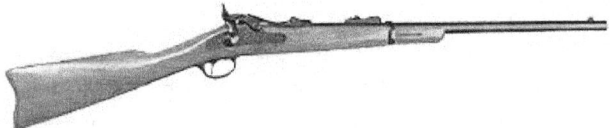

Chapter Six
CROCKETT'S FORT

By May of 1837, the Seventh Cavalry was making good progress. El Presidio de San Francisco now had a new barracks under construction next to the parade ground while I was building an office on the north wall. The town had grown from a sleepy village of two hundred to nearly a thousand, and mountains to the south that had once boasted thick forests were being cleared for lumber, replaced by grapes from the mission. A 4-pounder fired a signal shot from the Presidio's east bastion.

"Another ship arriving, General," Captain Autry said, now serving as my aide-de-camp.

Buried in legal documents, I found it necessary to surround myself with lawyers instead of cavalrymen, and accountants like Ben Travane, newly arrived from San Antonio. My temporary office in the old commandant's quarters was cramped and draughty. On dry days, I preferred my tent near the gate.

"Admiral Cochrane?" I asked.

"Not yet, but the *Invincible* is due any time now," Autry said, checking the calendar tacked on our freshly plastered wall. "Looks like a schooner. Maybe up from Mexico."

"Make sure they register properly," I ordered.

The Buffalo Flag had been registering every visitor to our new country, and making sure they understood the rules: taking gold from our land without a prospecting permit was grounds for hanging, no different than robbing a bank or stealing a horse.

"I'll see to it," Autry said, departing with a salute.

I climbed the stairs to the parapet overseeing the bay where a dozen ships lay at anchor, including my newly arrived cargo schooners *Pennsylvania* and *Santiago,* with the captured booty from Galveston. Thanks to Admiral Cochrane, San Francisco now had a foundry and an engraving press for minting coins.

"Any word from Major Cooke?" I asked when Autry rejoined me.

Bill Cooke and William Richardson had gone up the coast to Fort Ross, a failing Russian fur colony, to buy their tool shops. Come summer, we would dismantle the buildings and move them south. I was looking forward to glazed windows.

"Sure the Russians will sell?" Autry said.

"They sold to John Sutter. No reason they shouldn't sell to me," I replied. "At least I'll pay them. That's more than Sutter ever did."

"You speak of this John Sutter often. Was he such a legend?" Autry asked.

"A legend? No, Micajah, not a legend. He came to California in 1839 and built his famous fort. He hired Indians to plow the land. Had workshops that cured hides, made furniture, and even repaired guns. The equipment he bought from Fort Ross produced pots, hinges and iron tools. But when gold was discovered in 1848, his land was overrun. The cattle stolen. His workers quit. Everything he built was destroyed."

"A lesson to be learned," Autry realized.

"A lesson I won't forget," I agreed.

I'd had enough paperwork for one day, closing the books and looking for my winter coat. There is only so much a man can read about customs duties, petty theft complaints, latrine placement, equipment shortages and payrolls. The administrative work I'd done at Fort Lincoln had not prepared me for such a deluge. And I no longer had Libbie to help me.

"You have the duty, Lieutenant Allen," I said, leaving the Presidio for my quarters in town.

Young Jimmy waved from the watch tower. Life at the edge of the peninsula was quiet enough that only a dozen guards were needed, mostly to keep watch on the occasional ships sailing into the bay.

Vic waited for me in his hay-filled stall just inside the fort's main gate. Sergeant Travane quickly caught up to me, a ledger in his hand as always.

"Twenty more escaped slaves from Texas, sir," Travane report. "Makes eighty-three this month. Lots of angry masters back there."

"The alcalde in Los Angeles says nineteen Texans have arrived, too, hoping for gold," I said. "Tom is due back today with the latest news."

"He's already back, sir. Got in a couple of hours ago," Travane said.

"The hell you say? Where is he?"

"Usual place, General. Usual place."

"Thanks, Ben. Give the newcomers their assignments. We still need dock workers in Oakland, carpenters in Sacramento, and bridges on the Coloma Trail."

"Some wants to look for gold," Travane said.

"Then tell them the rules. Four weeks of gold hunting for every four months of service—white, black, Mexican or Chinese. No service, no gold," I insisted, for our country needed laborers more than we needed immigrants stealing our precious minerals. And we offered fair wages, though it was still in green script.

"Yes, sir. Yes, sir, I do that now," Travane said, slipping into his sham slave accent.

I tried not to frown. My middle-aged bookkeeper had gotten an education in New Orleans, sailed three of the seven seas, lived in Washington and managed Juan Almonte's household. If he hadn't been a Negro, I'd have made him an officer.

As Travane returned to his office, I rode along the waterfront toward town where *La Sirena* was located. The northern end of the peninsula was still unencumbered, having only a few fisheries along the beach. The mountains were steep, good for grazing but not for building. The road had gotten bad during the winter rains, but was drying up.

Vic spied an apple tree and I stopped, giving his neck a good scratch. After months of deprivation, my old friend was once again eating grain instead of grass and getting plenty of rest. He shook his head in gratitude, but I was the one who owed thanks.

I reached the edge of town after turning south at Clark's Point. The former Yerba Buena was growing fast. The cove, where the shore turned inward from the choppy bay, was a natural harbor. The coastal avenue, that locals called the Embarcadero, was filling with taverns, hotels and warehouses. Fancy homes were appearing on the hillsides. A long oak pier had been built where ferry boats crossed the bay several times a day.

Up from the harbor, just past Portsmouth Square, was a new tavern. A month before, *La Sirena* had been a Spanish bark run aground on the gravel beach without a crew, for they had all decided to seek their fortunes in California. Led by Tom, a hundred men had hauled the large boat three hundred yards up from the water with ropes and pulleys, then cut a hole in the hull and turned it into a saloon. Tom, Smith and Cooke were all owners, and I heard Crockett cut himself in for a share.

The ramp up to the door had been improved since my last visit. I hoped Tom wasn't stealing workers who had more important tasks. Several windows had also been cut in the hull, looking like pirate gun ports. A half-naked mermaid had been painted over the entrance. The hulk still smelled of barnacles.

Tom's private table was up a flight of steps where the captain's cabin had once been, the interior walls now removed for more space. There was a large crowd, for it was the first time since we'd left Texas that all of the company commanders were gathered, except for Keogh and Harrington, who were still in San Antonio. I could tell the ale was flowing freely.

"Colonel Custer, should I assume your mission to Los Angeles was a success? Is that why you haven't bothered to report?" I inquired from the ground floor.

The room grew quiet, but only for a moment. Tom came to the railing, looking down with flushed cheeks and a week-old beard. Light danced in his blue eyes from the whale oil lamps.

"Los Angeles is on the verge of revolt, Autie. So is San Diego," he replied for all to hear. "And once we celebrate Crockett's arrival, the Seventh Cavalry is going to ride those bastards down!"

The men shouted, pounding their tin cups on the pine tables. Fresh Smith and Dr. George Lord joined Tom, offering a toast. And I noticed Bill Cooke was back from Fort Ross. Apparently none of my officers felt a need to report.

Most of *La Sirena's* patrons were my troopers, the townspeople preferring the hotels along the waterfront. Which was good for me, I owned one of those hotels and was getting ready to add a new wing. I glanced at the Seventh Cavalry guidons hanging from the walls, the bent swords on display, and the Mexican flag we captured at Los

Angeles holding a place of honor. All very appropriate.

"Is this a general revolt, or just more complaining?" I asked, going up the stairs to take a seat at their sturdy oak pirate table.

It was then that I saw Slow sitting in the corner, holding a small glass of wine. He was not much of a drinker, but liked to join in. And he was not the skinny little boy I had found on the Texas prairie a year before, growing fast and filling out.

"The Californios resent giving some of their land back to the missions," Tom explained more seriously. "They don't like that the Indians who were tending their farms are now working for us, and they think cattle prices are too low. At what point do complaints become revolt?"

"Have they a leader?" I asked.

"Alvarado and Castro, mostly," Smith said. "Rumor says Mexico is sending a new governor to rally behind."

"No army?" I wondered.

"Autie, what army Mexico has is still trying to hold Texas. Houston is giving them a bad time," Tom said.

Holding the northwest from Goliad to Yuma, I knew Keogh had largely stayed out of the Texas Revolution, letting our enemies wear themselves down. But if Mexico gave up the fight, Brazos Convention forces could turn on the Buffalo Flag in a matter of weeks. They had already declared the loss of their runaway slaves a provocation.

A cheer went up, and I didn't have to ask who it was. Davy Crockett burst through the door in a fringed buckskin jacket and coonskin cap, a violin ticked under his arm. He shook hands, grinned like a mountain lion, and yelled to our barkeep for a jug. It was good to see David again. He had spent the last two months in Sacramento supervising the gold country.

After making the rounds and back-slapping, Crockett worked his way up the stairs to Tom's clubhouse.

"Bill! Good ta see ya, boy," Crockett said, heartily shaking hands. "Any 'citement on that voyage? Heard roundin' that cape is a bitch."

"A once in a lifetime experience, David," Cooke said, his Canadian accent stronger after several months on a British ship. "And I mean once. George, how long will it take to build that railroad?"

"Ask David," I said.

"Are we rich yet?" Cooke asked.

"Depends how ya define rich," Crockett said. "But we's gots lots a gold comin' outa those hills. Hell more than I 'xpected. About fifty thousand worth of ore waitin' right now ta follow me down river."

"Under guard, I hope," Tom said, for he was doing double duty as district marshal.

"Nat Brister's in Coloma. His rangers ride regular outa Crockett's Fort," Crockett replied.

"You mean Sacramento," I corrected.

"Same place, but Crockett's Fort sounds better," Crockett said.

"Who's guarding the Indians?" Cooke asked.

"The Nisenan ain't bothered no prospectors yet," Crockett reported. "And we're trying to keep poachers off their hunting grounds. Besides, me and Chief Maidu is best friends, 'specially since I giv 'em blankets and old muskets. Some of the other tribes, they may gettin' a bit irritated with us, but they ain't willin' ta cause no trouble 'lessin they git provoked."

"A few whites got greedy. They stole food instead of earning it," Smith mentioned. "Their trial is next week."

"Bill brought in the goods we stole from Galveston," Tom said. "Several tons of..."

"We didn't steal anything," I protested. "We gave script on every purchase."

"Autie, most of the shops were deserted. All we did was tack up notes on their doors," Tom said. He completely failed to understand the legal technicalities.

"It may take a few years, but we'll make good on those notes," I said.

"There is no need," Slow said, moving forward to take a seat next to Crockett.

"Why is that, Slow?" Cooke asked.

"The Galveston is a stronghold of your enemies. A warrior takes from his enemies. He does not pay them," Slow said.

"Lad, we can't do that," I said. "In civilization, we must—"

"Hold on thar, George, I think the boy is on ta somethin'," Crockett interrupted. "What do ya say, boys? Ain't Slow right on this?"

"I think he is," Smith agreed.

"No rewarding enemies. Isn't that where you always say Caesar went wrong? Pardoned his enemies just so they could knife him in the back?" Cooke asked, exploiting my love for the Bard.

"None of those notes have my signature on them," Tom said with a shrug. "But I suppose Autie can reimburse them out of his share, if he wants to."

"Smart ass," I murmured. "Now that Slow is minister of finance, what else should we do?"

Everyone looked at Slow, which was not an unusual experience for him.

"If many people are to live as one tribe, they must be cousins, as the Sioux and Cheyenne are cousins," Slow said. "Cousins should have patience."

"Got some truth there," Tom agreed.

"Any word on what Washington thinks of us takin' California?" Crockett asked, for the *San Francisco Examiner* was still in the planning stages. "Ya know, March 4th was the last day of Andy Jackson being president. That skunk Van Buren is president now."

"Van Buren is no friend to slavery, and he doesn't support Texas becoming a state, either," I said, for it was common talk among my father and uncles when I was a child. "He was a Free-Soiler in 1848."

"We should write him a letter," Cooke decided, for it was the diplomatic thing to do.

"And say what?" Tom asked. "We're glad you supported President Lincoln during the Civil War?"

"I wish Mark was here. He'd know what to say," Smith said.

"To Mark Kellogg, and other lost friends," Tom said, raising his cup. Even I drank to that one.

The signal gun rang out from the Presidio. I looked out the stern window to see a large ship with tall sails rounding the headland. Had it been a British or French man-of-war, three shots would have been fired, but we were still on alert. The United States was not the only country with imperial ambitions. We rushed up to *La Sirena's* stern deck for a better view.

"Twenty-gun frigate, sir," Voss reported, studying the ship through a long spyglass. "Flying a Spanish flag and Cuban pennants. More ships coming around the point. Four or five, at least."

"This could be an invasion," I speculated, a hand on my sidearm.

"We should have been warned," Tom said, holding his binoculars.

As the ships grew closer, I saw the frigate was an old warship.

There were also two schooners and a bark, probably merchants.

"It's not an invasion. None of the guns are rolled out. No marines on deck," Cooke said, knowledgeable of such tactics.

Then I saw why only one signal gun was fired. Herding the flotilla into port was the armed schooner *Invincible*. Admiral Cochrane was on the foredeck holding his cocked hat under his arm, his long gray hair blowing in the brisk wind.

"Glad to see him," Cooke said with relief.

"Let's get down to the harbor," I urged, reaching the stairs first.

The *Santa Victoria*, dropped anchor twenty yards off the end of the pier. One of the merchant ships halted close by, the other two headed across the bay to Oakland. The *Invincible* continued straight into the northern end of the bay until making a broad turn around a rocky island famous for its noisy bird population. I supposed Cochrane had VIP guests aboard who wanted some sight-seeing before docking.

The captain of the Spanish galleon appeared above a jolly boat being lowered into the water. He was just as ancient as his ship, with a flowing white beard and tall cocked hat. He remained on board as several passengers descended a ramp to the rowboat, all huddled against the cold. It wasn't until they had almost reached the pier that I recognized one of them.

"I'll be a son of a bitch," I said, breaking into a grin.

I ran down to the Embarcadero as a man, three women, and a young Negro boy reached the landing. The rowboat docked and they disembarked, looking tired from a long voyage.

"Antonio!" I shouted, gripping his hand.

General Antonio López de Santa Anna, former president of Mexico, seemed surprised by my warm greeting but was quick to return it.

"George, let me introduce my wife, Inés, and my daughters, María de Guadalupe and María del Carmen," Santa Anna said. He did not introduce the boy, who was struggling with their luggage.

"Welcome to San Francisco, ladies," I said, gallantly sweeping the hat from my head. "Please be my guests at The Appomattox, the finest hotel in town. You'll find a warm bath, hot food and feather beds."

"That is very generous," Santa Anna said.

His wife's black hood fell back and I saw she was quite lovely, with pale skin, dark brown eyes, and reddish brown hair. Her daughters were of like coloring. I guessed them at ages ten and seven, but was no expert on such things.

"My staff is still aboard the *Santa Victoria*. May they come ashore?" Santa Anna requested. He pointed to about thirty officers and aides, now exiles from their country, and almost as many women. They looked anxious.

"There's a new hotel on Kearny Street. The top floor isn't finished yet, but the lower rooms don't leak. I'll have Sergeant Travane find your people quarters," I replied.

I signaled for Corporal Espalier to help with the ladies' bags and led the party toward Portsmouth Square, past the startled stares of my officers.

"We've heard things have not gone well in Mexico City," I said.

"My enemies used the Texas problem to undermine me, but they are fools. Their government will soon fall," Santa Anna said. "When it does, I will be ready."

"Until then, I hope you will enjoy the benefits of California. Perhaps share your wisdom on some thorny problems?" I asked.

"Mexico still does not recognize the Republic of Texas. Or your Buffalo Flag," he warned.

"They will, in time," I replied, expecting it to be true. "And in the meantime, you may share in the fruits of our labors."

"I heard you found gold," Santa Anna said, his tone cautious.

"Of which you will receive a rightful share. As we agreed in Galveston."

The fallen politician relaxed his shoulders in relief.

"What do you need of me?" he asked.

"I would like you to help govern California," I answered.

The wily politician smiled and nodded his head.

The Appomattox might not have been the largest of the new hotels in San Francisco, but it was becoming an oasis of civilization, as I intended. William Richardson's wife, Maria Martinez, had taken over management, and she was an exacting woman. The eldest daughter of Ygnacio Martinez, the former commandant of the Presidio, she was also the most influential woman in town. Maria had not much cared for me on early acquaintance, but after I introduced her to Santa Anna's charming wife, my stock went up. Her sons worked for me as well, one supervising my carpenters, the other as harbor master.

They were fluent in Spanish, unlike their father, who retained a strong English accent.

I ordered a fine meal for us on the second floor veranda just as the sun was dipping behind the mountain. We ate thick beef steaks, boiled green beans, and baked potatoes grown by an Irishman in San Jose. As we neared dessert, I saw the *Invincible* drop anchor near the *Santa Victoria* and row its passengers to shore. Even from a distance, one of the passengers was unmistakable.

"Excuse me," I said, nearly jumping down the stairs with a pounding heart.

Isabella was walking up from the dock with Admiral Cochrane carrying her bags when she saw me. She pulled back her cowl with a lovely smile and rushed into my embrace. Only decorum stopped us from kissing in front of everyone.

"I'm so glad you're safe," I said.

"*Y usted, mi dulce*," she whispered. "Congratulations on your great achievement."

"*Nuestro gran logro*," I said with uncharacteristic modesty.

"I see Yerba Linda has houses. I was expecting mud huts," she said as we strolled arm-in-arm up Washington Street.

One of my first acts had been to rename the town plaza Portsmouth Square, but I did not explain why, much to William Richardson's confusion. The honor guard was just taking down our flag. A cannon fired from the Presidio three miles away as Voss played *Retreat* on his bugle. Tom and Morning Star emerged from their bungalow, happy to see Isabella looking so well.

"Santa Anna is here," I said.

"Yes, we met in San Diego," Isabella said. "Antonio was very gracious. The people of San Diego were not. They do not appreciate your activities."

"So Tom has said," I replied, unworried about a sleepy fishing village five hundred miles away.

I offered Isabella a chance to clean up, but she was hungry, so the four of us returned to The Appomattox. I would have invited Admiral Cochrane as well, but he had gone to the Boar's Head, Isaac Graham's new tavern at Clark's Point. Decorated with a Union Jack and a portrait of King William IV, it was a popular bit of England for our British friends.

"*Inés, su viaje ha ido bien?*" Isabella asked, taking a seat between Santa Anna's two young daughters.

"*El barco no se hundió,*" Mrs. Santa Anna said, her accent cultured. Isabella laughed, possibly in agreement. I could sympathize, for ocean voyages were not to my liking, either.

"No pirates?" I asked.

"Everyone says the pirates are in California," Santa Anna remarked.

"Sixteen years ago, California was a province of the Spanish Empire," Tom said. "Was California stolen from Spain by pirates?"

"Ferdinand VII is dead, and so is his empire," Santa Anna said, an important figure in those tumultuous times.

"America became free because the British could not defeat us," I said. "Mexico became free by throwing off the chains of Spain. California will be free as well, if we are strong, and if we are vigilant."

"*Hablas como un hombre de destino, General Custer,*" Mrs. Santa Anna said.

"A man of destiny?" I replied. "I don't know about that, but there is a job to do."

"George *is* a man of destiny, in the opinion of my father," Isabella said. "And I know of an Indian boy who says the same thing. Where is Slow?"

"Slow is huddling with Butler, Hughes, French and Voss," Tom said. "They're planning some sort of enterprise."

"Is that legal?" I asked.

"No law against making money in California, Autie," Tom said. "And if you really want a revolt, try making one."

After dinner, Isabella and I strolled several blocks down toward the beach. Yerba Linda had maintained a gravel road along the shore for wagons, but as new buildings were erected, we had started to build rough wooden sidewalks along the streets to keep our shoes out of the mud. The boards creaked beneath our feet.

"This will be Clay Street," I said. "Señora Richardson's husband and Francisco de Haro are laying out the town. I'm calling that peak to the north Nob Hill. We'll build a house on it."

"Don't you think Béjar is a better place for a family?" she asked.

"San Francisco will be a big city someday. Prosperous. Cultured. It will have opera houses."

"And mud. And fog. And sailors."

"A few years from now, Sacramento will look like Béjar. We have a town square, and the Franciscans have promised to build us a church," I suggested.

"Alta California is a long way from home, Autie," Isabella softly protested.

"We have time for these decisions. I haven't even asked Erasmo for your hand yet."

"You had best do that before making too many plans. My father liked Jim Bowie, but he thinks Americans are crazy."

"He's right about that," I said, taking her in my arms.

———

I cannot say operations in California over the next few months went smoothly. Controlled chaos would be a better description, but I had trained under General George B. McClellan, and Little Mac was the best organizer in the history of the United States Army. I don't know that anyone could have done better.

"General Custer, I hear you are going to Sacramento," Sergeant Voss said, having made an appointment at my office in the Presidio.

"Yes, Henry. Colonel Crockett has invited Isabella and I to the grand opening of Crockett's Fort. Going to be quite a party," I said, rushing to wrap up my paperwork for the day. A much smaller stack since the appointment of Governor Santa Anna.

"I have a ship going up river. Me and Slow," Voss said.

This caught my interest. So many ships had been abandoned in the harbor that they had been put up for auction. Containing nails, hinges, rope, sails, barrels, pots, tar, and hundreds of other scarce items, the auctions were well attended and often vigorous. On the morrow, four of the auctioned ships were being towed upriver to Sacramento where the hulks were destined for building materials.

"What's this about you and Slow? Going into business?" I asked.

"Harpoons," Voss said.

"Harpoons?"

"Slow's idea. We're going to be rich," Voss said, abruptly leaving.

Ben Travane walked in with another batch of dispatches. None were from Texas, so I set them aside.

"Ben, what's this about Slow and Voss?" I asked.

"Don't know 'bout that, but everyone is getting' into some enterprise," Ben said. "I gots a piece of Mister Graham's new brewery on Market Street, and there's a brickwork startin' up in San Leandro. Lots a people wantin' bricks."

"Is everyone going to be rich except me?" I wondered.

"According to Colonel Custer, you never was much good with money," Ben replied.

"Maybe you can manage my investments for me?" I said, trying to make a joke.

"Only for a fee, sir. Only for a fee," Ben demurred.

The next morning, our newly acquired riverboat, the *Sacramento Queen*, started the seventy-five-mile trip upriver pulling the four old boats. Progress was slow where the currents were heavy, but gradually grew faster. Along the way, we saw numerous animals in the marshy flatlands including black-tailed deer, beaver, muskrats, eagles, and more ducks than a man could count. Tom and Morning Star joined Isabella and I on the main deck.

Morning Star was wearing an attractive homespun dress made for her by Mrs. Richardson in the popular fashion. Tom was wearing the buckskin jacket he'd taken into the battle at the Little Big Horn. The white broad-brimmed hat was new, purchased at a recently established millinery shop on Second Street. I wore a blue dress jacket like General Sherman favored, made for me by an Austrian tailor. The gold-colored buttons were from a sea captain's blouse.

"Word from Keogh?" Tom asked, for he'd had no recent news, having just returned from Fort Ross.

"Just a little about the spring campaign. Filisola is moving east along the coast supported by the Mexican navy," I said, though it was nothing that hadn't already been printed in the New Orleans newspapers. "They expect to retake Galveston and cut off Houston's line of supply. Burnet's government is still in Washington-on-the-Brazos waiting for reinforcements."

"Béjar?" Tom inquired.

"Ignored, for the time being. Whoever wins will eventually turn toward San Antonio, but neither can take the chance right now. Myles is strengthening the fortifications. Señor Seguin has ten men making new Springfields and ammunition."

"How is Juan doing? Still holding Goliad?" Tom asked.

"It's been quiet since he came to terms with la Graza," I said.

"We should get back there soon. Late fall," Tom said.

"Why?" I asked in surprise.

"Autie, we can't let Burnet's government take control of Texas," he said. "They're building their army with money from the big plantations. If Filisola is defeated, thousands of colonists will pour in with their slaves."

"I see no reason to hurry," I argued. "Myles can hold Béjar until hell freezes over. For now, we have a lot of work to do right here."

"Myles only has four companies and a few Tejano volunteers. Two hundred men won't hold off an army," Tom complained.

"It's been done before," I said.

Sacramento was a bustling place. When I had last visited in late March, it was a cold encampment of gray tents and pinewood sheds. Now log cabins with stone foundations lined the main road. New warehouses rose on the dock. Several decommissioned ships were anchored in an estuary, some used for barracks, others for storage. A Miwok Indian village had appeared near the American River. Back from the plaza on a low hill stood Crockett's Fort, built on the sketches Cooke had provided of Fort Sutter. It was a close copy, with eighteen foot walls, four corner towers, and a large compound.

North of the fort, in a sheltered green valley, was a quaint German village. Johann Ernst, formally of Oldenburg, had chosen Sacramento to reestablish his colony. These industrious immigrants were now making wagons, forging tools, crafting furniture, and creating a new standard of prosperity. Their services were in such high demand that they had hired dozens of Indian apprentices.

"Good day, Isabella. Morning Star. Glad you ladies could make it," Crockett said, hustling down from his headquarters to the docks.

He was not Davy Crockett on this morning, wearing a brown frock coat and top hat. I noticed he was freshly shaven. The graying hair that hung halfway down to his shoulders had been washed. I smelled lilac water. And there was a ledger book under his arm. For all of Crockett's pretense at being illiterate, he kept good accounts and could write a clear report when he wanted to.

"*Hola, David, es un placer verla de Nuevo,*" Isabella said.

"*El placer es mío,*" Crockett said, kissing her hand.

Crockett took the women by the arms and led us to the plaza

where I caught the succulent aroma of roasting beef. A keg of ale was being shared by a dozen guests. Indian women were making tortillas and fried beans. I nodded to our old comrade, Sergeant French. He was wearing a Buffalo Flag coin as a medallion around his neck.

Recently promoted Major John Forsyth arrived. Having served with me at the Alamo, he was now Crockett's aide-de-camp in charge of Coloma. A good post for a cavalry officer. Forsyth was my age, and a New Yorker. He also wore one of the gold medallions. I considered having one made for myself.

"Good to see you, John," I said, shaking hands rather than saluting due to the informal circumstances. "Would you be related to Van Buren's new Secretary of State? He's John Forsyth, too."

"Sorry, General. My family don't rate so high. Just simple folk from Livingston," Forsyth explained.

"How is your son? Any word from home?"

"Edmond's almost fourteen now," he said. "Once everything settles down, I'd like to send for him. Ed's still back on my father's farm."

"Lots of the recruits have family back east, Autie. Maybe we can make some arrangements for them?" Tom suggested.

"With the Apaches quiet, Governor Sharrow thinks the trail out of St. Louis is safe," I said. "If anyone wants to organize a wagon train, the Department of New Mexico could assign protection."

"That would be fine, sir. I'll write my father and ask what he thinks," Forsyth said, running off to write the letter. I hoped it wasn't premature.

"I gots youngins back home, too," Crockett said. "Six of 'em, by last count. Oldest is John. Gonna turn thirty next month. Little Matilda should be 'bout sixteen now. I even got a wife, come to think of it."

"Would you rather bring them to California, or wait until the war in Texas is over?" Tom asked.

"That could take some thinkin' on, Tommy," Crockett replied. "What would you do?"

"Most of my family hasn't been born yet," Tom answered.

There was a commotion down at the dock. Several hundred Indians had suddenly formed into mob, shouting and waving their fists. I put a hand on my sidearm without drawing it and rushed down the hill with Tom on my heels.

"Wait your turns! *Esperar tu turno!*" Voss shouted from the

183

gangplank of the ship he and Slow had purchased.

Slow and three hirelings were on the deck holding iron spears. No, not spears. Harpoons. I finally recognized the ship, it was the *Northampton*, a Boston sloop which had provided supplies to New England whalers in the Pacific before the crew abandoned her in Oakland.

The mob settled down a little, but only a little. Indians are not famous for their patience. Crockett caught up to me.

"Don't worry, George, they have a license," Crockett said, out of breath.

I thought of objecting, but didn't know what to object to. The mob looked ready to riot, but there was no actual violence, only a lot of shouting and hand waving. I couldn't hear most of what Voss was saying, being too far back.

After a few minutes, part of the crowd cleared and an Indian emerged holding a harpoon. It was a young Patwin, well dressed and exuberant with his new prize. He whooped with excitement, holding the harpoon above his head for all to see.

"Harpoons? Where are these Indians going to find whales?" I asked.

"They's pretty fancy weapons in these parts, that's fer sure," Crockett said.

Soon other young Indian men were leaving the scene clutching the iron spears as if they were the most valuable of prizes. Squaws came up to them, stroking the smooth iron shafts and showing interest in the manly owners. One young woman was so attractive it made me want to buy a harpoon.

When the spectacle was finally over, I saw Voss and Slow on *Northampton's* deck looking very pleased with themselves.

"What the hell is this?" I asked, stomping up the gangplank. "Why are you giving harpoons to Indians?"

"We are not giving the people spears, we are trading," Slow said, ignoring my anger.

"Trading for what?" I demanded.

"Gold, General," Voss said, holding up scores of small pouches. "One hundred dollars each, in gold."

"A hundred dollars? For that junk?" I said. "You must have sold seventy or eighty of them."

"One hundred and five," Voss said. "Slow and I just took in ten thousand dollars."

"I don't understand," I said.

Crockett came up the gangplank wearing a grin. He shook Voss' hand, then Slow's. He handed them a document.

"Don't forget, boys, the gold belongs to the mint," Crockett said. "Here is half pay in script. You kin have the other half in land grants or cattle vouchers."

"Cattle," Slow said. "The white men who seek gold need food."

"Señor Peralta has a herd coming up next week. Three hundred head, and we get first crack at them," Voss said, slapping Slow on the back.

I found a barrel to sit on. Others were coming onboard congratulating the successful businessmen. Everyone seemed to know more about it than I did.

"George, this 'ere ain't nothin' ta git 'xcited 'bout," Crockett said, sitting next to me. "We gots hundreds of prospectors and thousands of In'dins fetchin' gold fer us. It's needed. In returns, we is tradin' 'bout anythin' we kin. Ain't no other way. In'dins are happy with their trinkets. Cavalry is keepin' the peace. What more do ya want?"

"I'd like to think I'm more enterprising than an eight-year-old," I said, jealously looking at Slow. The lad was surrounded by well-wishers, for the idea of making harpoons a popular product among the heathens was apparently his doing.

"I weren't always so successful," Crockett said. "Back 'n Tennessee, I owned a gristmill. Owned a distillery. Even had a powder mill. All got wiped out when Shoal Creek flooded an' left me bankrupt. Didn't do so well in politics, neither."

"You are a legend in your own time," I said.

"That don't put food on the table fer my children," Crockett answered. "But now I got a second chance. We all do."

Crockett was right, of course. I got up, pushed my way through the admiring crowd, and shook Slow's hand. Then I offered Voss a salute.

Our visit to Sacramento was not all frivolity. We had important business to conduct, and not all of it pleasant. The orderlies were getting our horses ready.

"You may wish to stay here at Crockett's Fort, humming bird," I warned Isabella.

She was dressed in red riding leathers with a broad brim trail hat, as was Morning Star. Neither woman would be dissuaded from joining us.

"Do you think I've never seen a hanging, George?" Isabella said.

"I look forward to the white man's justice," Morning Star added.

"It's everybody's justice, young lady. I will thank you to remember that," I said, still sensitive of criticism by a few malcontents.

———————

On the third day of our journey we reached Placerville, a growing settlement where the search for gold was becoming industrialized. One day it might become the county seat. The next morning, we rode through thick woods back down toward the American River nine miles away, where we found Coloma near the site of our first discovery.

Coloma had grown from a sleepy Nisenan village to a town of twelve hundred prospectors, merchants, Indians, a Chinese laundry, and home to Company B of the Seventh Calvary. Major Nat Brister greeted us at Fort Necessity, which looked more like a big corral than a fort. A blockhouse and the company headquarters sat on a knoll overlooking the town square. The river was only a few hundred yards away.

"Good to see you, General," Brister said, my age, thick in the chest, and looking hardy. I had liked his cool presence at the Alamo, and the bushy auburn hair gave him a striking appearance.

"No trouble about the prisoners?" I asked.

"None the boys can't handle," Brister said.

"We'll hold the trials in the morning," I announced.

"Yes, sir," Brister said with a salute, going to make the arrangements.

There was a swagger in Brister's step that told me morale was high.

The troopers milling about the plaza looked satisfied with their duties, unlike most frontier posts, where danger or drudgery eventually saps the spirit. Officers like myself could find excitement in Chicago or New York while on leave, but the rank and file could afford no such holiday.

With an hour left before sunset, Isabella, Tom, Morning Star and I walked through the new town, which reminded me of Dodge City. The outskirts was mostly tents and wood shacks. The main road running parallel to the river was still dirt except for two sidewalks. Gravel had been added in places to fill in mud holes. But the plaza was a little better, beginning to show evidence of civilization.

"Colonel Crockett has done well here," Morning Star observed, for most of the buildings were made of sturdy wood framing with solid stone foundations. I admired the broad porches, suitable for lounging on a summer evening.

The town center was laid out in typical Spanish style, with a customs house and hotel. Two more hotels were under construction. There were also five taverns and, behind them, a house for what we in the army often call fancy women. Such commerce was not encouraged, but I would not provoke a riot by preventing it.

"Are the Franciscans building a church?" Isabella asked, pointing to a new foundation being laid beyond the plaza.

"They have souls to save," I said.

"A lot of souls, and not just the Indians," Tom said.

"The church will give comfort to the community," Isabella said. "George and I will make a generous donation."

"We will?" I said with surprise.

"Yes, George," Isabella replied, giving my elbow a tug.

As the daughter of a prominent family, Isabella well understood how to show status in a community. Libbie had helped my army career in a similar fashion.

Many greeted us in the plaza, among them prospectors, merchants, and some of my own troopers. There were also scores of Indians, mostly Nisenan, but also Patwin and Washo. We required no extra attention, for everyone was busy, and gradually worked our way down to the river. The blue current was vigorous here, flowing among heavy growths of trees. I noticed a hand-painted sign on a wooden post indicating the spot where Voss had found the first nuggets. A sign I'd wanted my name on.

"It's beautiful, George," Isabella said.

"Prettier before hundreds of miners started dredging," I said, for the riverbank was now filled with sluice boxes, timber mills, flour mills and breakwaters. "And this is only the beginning. As more immigrants arrive, we'll expand operations. Within the year, we'll have engineers following the richest veins deep into the mountain sides."

"You have such vision," Isabella said, staring at me with awe.

"No, hummingbird. Every schoolboy of my generation grew up reading about the California Gold Rush," I admitted. "When I look at these diggings, I don't see the future. I see the past."

"Autie's just being dramatic," Tom said. "We've been working our goddamn butts off around here. The reason we haven't had the same problems as 1849 is because we've learned from their mistakes."

"What do you mean, Thomas?" Morning Star asked.

"First time around, this was a lawless country," Tom explained. "Gold seekers came in without any scruples. They stole horses and cattle. Trampled crops. Robbed travelers. Outlaws stole from honest prospectors, and they killed the Indians, forcing the Indians to fight back. Vigilante justice was unable to keep order."

"And this time you've done better?" Morning Star said.

"The Indians seem peaceful. Most of the time," I replied. "Few of the vaqueros complain about rustling. Those who think they can break the law are proven wrong."

"That's why we're here today," Tom said.

We had nice rooms on the top floor of the new Park Avenue Hotel, with a long patio overlooking the river. We could hear the rushing water beyond the trees, observe birds high in the branches, and smell the green forest. Few places I knew were as beautiful.

I invited Major Brister to dinner, along with the mayor, Giovanni Raffetto. I learned Raffetto was a merchant from St. Louis, typical of the sturdy frontier type, with shaggy brown hair, trimmed beard, and prone to wearing flannel shirts. As an administrator, he had proved reasonably honest.

Joining us was Dr. Amos Pollard on his first trip to the high country. Pollard was a well-spoken physician who had come a long way from his native Massachusetts, or the medical practice he once held in Manhattan before losing his wife. Thirty-three years old, tall, thin and bald, Pollard was more interested in building hospitals than filling them. His courage treating the wounded at the Alamo had impressed me.

Our official host was Chief Maidu. The chief brought his oldest son, Konkow, who was Slow's age, and the boys sat together at a small card table deep in talk. To keep the flies away, a delicately woven netting had been hung around the edge of the patio. The netting, made by Nisenan squaws, was in high demand. I promised to buy one for Isabella after hearing Tom had bought one for Morning Star.

"*Qué opinas jefe?*" I asked the forty-year-old chief, a distinguished leader with his long black hair tied in the back. His narrow eyes could be fierce, but more often than not, he was genial.

"My opinion may change after the judgment," Maidu replied, his accent rough but intelligible.

"We brought a reporter from the *San Francisco Examiner*. Marcus will send the story to New Orleans, New York and London," I said, though I doubted a village chieftain could grasp the implications. "Notices will be posted in Sacramento, Oakland, Monterey, and on the Embarcadero."

"We know the meaning," Maidu said, unimpressed with my litany. "Many chiefs and their sons have come from far tribes to see the white man's justice. All will know."

"Nat, good work on the town," Tom said, thinking it time to change subject. "It's bigger than Deadwood and looks better."

"Never heard of Deadwood, Tommy, but I can't take all the credit," Brister replied. "Colonel Crockett is up here every few weeks telling stories and kicking butt. There's not a man in Coloma who won't walk into hell for him."

"Let's hope it doesn't come to that," Pollard said, having walked there once already on a cold March morning.

"There should be a good market, tomorrow. Morning Star and I will need our coins ready," Isabella remarked.

"That's true," Brister said, offering the ladies a smile.

"Market?" Tom asked.

"People come from all over for a hanging," Isabella explained. "There will be vendors of fresh fruit, pies, scarfs, and leather. The taverns will run dry."

"Nathaniel?" I asked, making a point by using his first name. Which I rarely did.

"Don't worry, General. The taverns won't run dry," Brister replied. He turned to Tom and they laughed, tapping the table with their spoons.

"I don't want a drunken mob tomorrow," I protested.

189

"Beer's kinda weak. Need to drink a lot to get drunk," Brister added.

"Drunk Indians are nothing to laugh about," I insisted.

"General Custer, there is no reason for concern," Raffetto promised, raising his hands for attention. "The constables are on duty. As Major Brister and Colonel Custer well know. I believe they are teasing you."

Raffetto took out his hand-carved pipe and gave it a light, leaning back in his comfortable Birchwood chair. Tom and Pollard lit cigars.

"The General worries too much," Morning Star said.

"Young lady, a general who doesn't worry too much isn't fit to wear his stars," I replied.

The next morning dawned clear except for a mist rising off the river. We had a nice breakfast of eggs rolled in tortillas, bits of ham, and strong coffee. There was no wine, by the gentlemen or the ladies. There would be no drinking until after the day's business.

"Ya lookin' good, sir," John said, helping me dress.

"Thank you, Mr. Armstrong," I replied. "I know I don't say it often, but I'm glad to have you in my service."

"Ain't no need, sir. No need at all," John said. "Still be Mr. Chenoweth's slave if not for you. Still be living in a shed, eatin' scraps off the master's table. Being yo man is my privilege."

I looked John in the eye and shook his hand. In another life, I'd taken much for granted from those who cooked my food, mended my clothes, set up my tent, and polished my boots. It was time to learn from those mistakes.

I walked down the creaking plank stairs and out on the broad patio where several hundred people had already gathered. It was a conglomeration of California, all types in all ages and genders. I was wearing my best dress uniform, a dark blue jacket, gray trousers, gold buttons and a red scarf. John had polished my old black boots to a shine. My hair, growing long again, was thoroughly combed, my bushy mustache trimmed. I gazed steadily, knowing my steel blue eyes could be seen from anyplace in the crowd.

"Let the proceedings begin," I announced.

A high pinewood bench had been erected on the south side of the plaza with three tall stools. The center of the plaza was kept clear by Raffetto's constables, half of whom were uniformed Indians. A clever move on his part. Company C was formed in skirmish formation to the west, but their weapons were holstered. They were there to protect, not intimidate. Company B loitered to the north of the plaza, mixed in with the spectators. Joining me on the judge's bench were Chief Maidu and Mayor Raffetto, representing civilian authority.

"Bring out the prisoners," Raffetto said, his native Italian accent sounding almost Southern.

Six men were brought out of the adobe headquarters, three whites and three Indians. Their clothes were disheveled, their hands tied behind their backs. All appeared of the rougher sort.

"These are of my tribe," Chief Maidu said, standing up and pointing at the Indians. The chief was immaculate in white leather and an elaborate feather headdress, more reminiscent of the Sioux than the Nisenan. I wondered if Slow had sold it to him. "They killed four gold hunters, then stole their guns and clothes. They boasted of their deed. They are to face justice."

"Witnesses?" I summoned.

For thirty minutes, a small list of Indians and tradesmen gave testimony to the foul deed. There was no doubt of their guilt. After consulting with my fellow judges, I pronounced sentence.

"Death by hanging," I said.

The crowd stirred but remained quiet. I believed the judgment popular, but there was no cheering. This was only the first act.

"These white men have been charged with killing Mésto of the Nisenan tribe and raping his wife," Raffetto said. "They are Tom Miller, Bull Backstend and Ronald Wynton."

"There ain't no witnesses agin' us!" Miller shouted, struggling against his bonds.

"That we shall see," Raffetto answered. "Bring the witnesses forward."

Eight witnesses came forward, five squaws and three Indian boys. The boys were dressed well for the occasion in flannel shirts and fine buckskin jackets. I had a hunch Raffetto paid for the outfits. Father Sanchez, the new town friar, stepped up with a Bible to swear them in.

"Wait! Wait," Miller yelled. "Them is Indians. No Indian can testify agin' a white man. No place, no never."

"Welcome to the Buffalo Flag, Mr. Miller," I said, pounding a mallet on the podium. "Let the witnesses proceed."

191

The women gave their testimony in Maiduan, translated by a mixed blood carpenter named José. The Indian boys spoke English and a little Spanish. They were convincing, explaining how the drunken white men had invaded their camp, then robbed, raped and murdered. Not discreet about their deeds, the villains had been tracked to a Placerville saloon by the young boys and reported to the constable. Several law officers had been injured in the arrest.

"Have you a defense?" Raffetto asked.

"We weren't even thar," Backstend denied, a bearish man with a black beard. "Ask Rumford. Ask Skinny Sam."

There was a shuffle in the back of the crowd and two men came forward. Maxwell Rumford owned one of the general stores. The heavyset merchant was from Alabama and known to resent my lenient Indian policies, but his work ethic had made him prosperous. The second was a sometime prospector called Skinny Sam, a fitting nickname, typically found doing menial labor around Buckhorn's Tavern. When he wasn't lying in an alley dead drunk.

"They was with us," Skinny Sam said, speaking loud enough for all to hear. "We played cards. Played the whole day. I won five dollars. They could not been up in creek country."

"Yes, they were in town," Rumford said a bit more hesitantly. "They ordered supplies. Bought shovels and coffee."

There was a murmuring through the crowd. The whites chose to believe the story, while the Indians didn't. I glanced at Raffetto and saw he didn't believe the alibi, either. I waited for the crowd to quiet down.

"May we see the invoices?" I requested.

"The what?" Rumford said.

"I've been in your store, sir. You make receipts for everything," I pointed out. "I would like to see your books for the supplies these men purchased."

"I don't know, sir. They may be hard to find," Rumford stalled.

"Sir, if you cannot produce the invoices, you may be hanged as an accomplice," I warned.

There was silence. Rumford looked at the defendants, wondering what he should do. Everyone in the crowd leaned forward to hear his response.

"There are no invoices," Rumford conceded.

I nodded for Raffetto to proceed.

"Is there additional testimony?" Raffetto requested.

No one stepped forward. There had never been any doubt about their guilt, so reaching a verdict didn't take long. I stood up, removed my hat, and took a dramatic pause. The hundred times I had watched my old friend Lawrence Barrett perform were not wasted.

"The defendants are pronounced guilty. The sentence is death by hanging," I declared.

The spectators were stunned at first, then the Indians showed approval. Reaction among the white townspeople was mixed.

"Death? Fer killin' In'dins? Is you out of yo' mind?" Wynton said, so angry he was spitting.

"Friar Sanchez, the condemned have half an hour to make their peace. Constable Jacobs, make ready the gallows," I instructed, pounding my mallet with authority.

I thanked Raffetto and Chief Maidu before walking back toward my hotel. Behind me, a clerk was busy making out the death warrants. Slow and Morning Star met me on the porch.

"What do you think, lad?" I asked, quite pleased with myself.

"What of the Eighth Commandment? Those who bear false witness?" Slow asked.

"By god, boy, you are the smart one," I answered.

I rushed back to the high bench, straightened my jacket, and pounded the mallet for attention.

"Ladies and gentlemen, a last piece of business," I shouted, my voice a bit too high-pitched. "In the opinion of this court, Mr. Rumford and Skinny Sam have borne false witness. Perjury is a serious crime. I sentence both to confiscation of their goods and exile from California."

"Confiscate? General Custer, no. I meant no harm," Rumford apologized. "I only sought to help friends."

"And to free three murderers, sir," I rejoined.

The man was thinking of his business, probably worth ten thousand dollars. Sam said nothing, not bright enough to think up a new lie.

"I'm sorry. I'm sorry," Rumford pleaded.

"You will be sorry. That is a promise," I said.

As Rumford and Skinny Sam were led away by the constables, I turned to Raffetto.

"The storekeeper will ask you to intercede on his behalf," I whispered. "Is he of value to your community?"

"Max is a trifle outspoken, but reliable," Raffetto replied.

"Take up his cause. On your recommendation, I will remit the sentence. In exchange for a fine, of course."

"Of course, sir," Raffetto said, happy with the arrangement. The appearance of such influence would enhance his status among the other merchants. "What about Skinny Sam?"

"He has thirty days to leave California or I'll hang him," I answered, for saloon trash only cause trouble.

This time I returned to the hotel ready for a glass of apple juice. The street fair that Isabella predicted would not begin until after the hangings, but I expected there to be good food.

"General, pardon, sir," Captain Forsyth said, following on my heels. "Not to be disrespectful, but are you really going to hang white men for killing Indians? I like these Indians well enough. Most of them. But they're only heathens."

"Will you say that to Morning Star?" I asked, for she was standing next to me on the porch. Morning Star gave the man a gentle stare. It was hard to read her thoughts.

"Sorry, mam. Really, but it's the way of things," Forsyth said.

"Captain Forsyth, I'm not in a habit of explaining myself," I said, taking the man aside and speaking softly. "This one time, I'll make an exception."

Like all New Yorkers, Forsyth was handled best by a straightforward manner.

"It's just not usual, sir. Not usual at all. And that reporter wrote everything down. He'll probably print it in the newspaper," Forsyth said.

"He *will* print it in the newspaper. That's why I brought him," I replied.

Slow joined us, a knowing look in his black eyes. He was finding the day filled with interesting events.

"John, I don't want a war with the Indians," I said, using my hands to make the point clear. "The Seventh Cavalry is spread thin. Thinner than most realize. If we fight the Indians, the Californios might rebel. Mexico might invade. The English might land troops in San Francisco.

Wars are costly and unpredictable. If the Indians believe they will receive justice, as they did here today, maybe there won't be any fighting. Isn't that true, Slow?"

"For a time," Slow agreed.

"Time is what I need, and if it means hanging three worthless bummers, or three hundred, that's what I'll do. Do you understand?"

"Yes, sir. It makes sense," Forsyth said.

"That's good, John. You should know I have big plans for you. Plans that don't include questioning my decisions."

Before we made our way back to Crockett's Fort, I said goodbye to a friend. For the time being.

"Be back in the spring, Gen'ral," Bouyer said.

"Nevada can wait, Mitch. What's the hurry?" I asked again.

"Everythin' 'ere's gettin' discovered. Want my name on somethin'. Somethin' good," he replied.

"You wanted the gold more than anyone. I kept my promise," I insisted, for I did not want to lose my most reliable scout.

"Gots me a gold claim. Now I want silver, too," Bouyer said. "Comstock Lode is just out there a waitin'. A bonanza fer the takin'."

"You'll be a regular George Hearst," I said.

"Who?" Bouyer asked.

"Hearst is a famous prospector," I replied. "He discovered silver outside Virginia City. Packed forty tons of high-grade ore over the Sierras in the dead of winter for smelting in San Francisco. Made him rich."

"And when did Mr. Hearst do all this magic?" Bouyer inquired, wondering if I was spinning tall tales.

"1859, as I recall."

"Well, it ain't 1859 yet, Gen'ral. An' I am to get me a piece of history," Bouyer swore.

"Will you cut me in for a share? It is on my land," I hinted.

"Have to think on that," he said, offering a rare salute.

Many believe the Missouri River country of my birth was a peaceful land before the white man came. This is not true. The People have always struggled against many enemies. The Crow and Pawnee are treacherous, knowing no honor. Our hunting lands were often encroached upon, even by our cousins, the Cheyenne. And life in the village could be troubled. Crazy Horse was shot in the face by No Water for trying to steal Black Buffalo Woman. But throughout it all, the Sioux stood tall as a great nation. We needed no writing on paper to do this. The white men are not so strong.

Chapter Seven
BUFFALO FLAG NATIONS

"We have news from Texas," Tom said, entering my Presidio office wrapped in a thick bearskin coat. The cut was good, the collar made of rabbit fur. I guessed Morning Star had been busy, for her furrier shop on Montgomery Street was always crowded. It was turning into a cold winter, and everyone in town knew Morning Star traded for the best hides.

November 4th, 1837, had dawned cold and clear. Knowing the regional leaders would want to be back home in time for the Christmas holidays, I had summoned them for an important occasion. Many were friends, and many were not.

"It will need to wait, Tom. The delegates are arriving about now," I said.

"Autie, this is important," Tom persisted.

"Texas is nine weeks away. It can't be that important," I replied.

"After the meeting. No later," Tom said, departing as quickly as he'd arrived.

"The *Pennsylvania* has docked with the delegates from San Diego," Sergeant Travane said, entering my office with Slow. "I've asked Señora Richardson to start making coffee."

My office was comfortably warm and decorated with numerous keepsakes, but not lavishly. Not like some of the new houses appearing on the hillsides above San Francisco, with their covered porches and gilded window frames.

"Are those my accounts?" I inquired, pointing to the ledger Ben was carrying close to his chest.

"Yes, sir. Got the final tally," Travane said.

"So where do I stand?"

"You ain't poor, sir. Least, not land poor. Ya just ain't got much money."

"Maybe Slow can loan me some?" I asked, only half in jest.

"Interest rates are high, General," Slow said.

Some would think an Indian boy dressed in a fine gray wool suit, black boots and a stringy black tie would look ridiculous, but not Slow. He carried the appropriate gravity and was growing fast, with straight shoulders and a proud demeanor. He wore his hair at half-length, like Crockett, and enjoyed his growing fame.

"Gentlemen, leaders are coming from all over Alta California to vote the new government," I said. "And not just California. John Jones, the American consul in Hawaii, is joining us along with the British consul, Sir Richard Charlton. Faxon Atherton is bringing a delegation of merchants with ties to the Chinese trade. While I have been promoting our new country, everyone else has been getting rich."

"Not everyone, sir," Travane said.

"Name one of our group who isn't?" I asked.

They avoided my gaze.

"You have large land grants in Sonoma," Travane pointed out. "A few in the south, too. That valley north of Los Angeles."

"I get little revenue from any of them, thanks to the Gang of Three," I complained.

"Is that what you call them now?" Cooke asked, entering our conversation without permission. He took a place by the fire, shaking out his heavy blue navy jacket.

"Alvarado, Castro and Vallejo oppose me at every turn," I explained. "All of the Californios do, and I'm tired of it."

"You have bad partners," Slow agreed.

"That's easy for you to say, youngster," I replied. "You have Voss, Butler, Hughes and French. Williamson and Howell. Nearly all the non-commissioned officers that regulations forbid me from doing business with. You own horses, cattle, stables, freight companies, barrel makers, and your own riverboat. You even own your own towns."

"They are not towns. Henry Voss calls them stagecoach depots," Slow corrected.

"Depots with hotels, corrals, and even saloons."

"The white men must have food. They like to drink," Slow said. "The tribes want guns. Their women want pots and knives. It is good to give people what they want."

"And make a fortune doing it."

"That is what Butler and Hughes often say."

"Ben, can't you find me enough cash to look respectable?" I pleaded.

"You gots cattle on your ranches. Come spring we can round 'em up," Travane suggested.

"And how do I do that? I spend my time managing soldiers, not vaqueros," I replied.

"I will speak with Father Mendez. Perhaps he can loan you some workers from the mission," Slow offered, his influence with the Catholics much greater than mine.

"You know, I've returned a million acres of land to the missions, and made enemies doing it. You think they'd be more grateful," I complained.

"Least you're not going to hell, George. They light candles for you," Cooke said.

I went to the window, looking over the north wall. The entrance to San Francisco Bay lay to my left, the harbor around the point to my right. Barges were moving up the Sacramento River delivering trade goods and coming down with gold, timber and furs. Ships were arriving from all over the world with engineers, carpenters, drovers, tanners, blacksmiths, and every other trade. Most thought they would rush to the gold fields, not realizing they would need to establish residency first.

"Let's get going, gentlemen," I said.

The meeting was being held at *La Sirena*. I told Tom to clean up the vomit and chase out the whores, which he did. Boasting a fresh coat of paint, the old hulk was large enough for the fifty delegates I was expecting. John waited for me outside my office, ready to drive my fine black carriage into town. A few months before, the large wheeled coach had belonged to an opinionated merchant in San Diego who didn't want the Buffalo Flag flying over his town. Two

199

companies of Seventh Cavalry had convinced him otherwise. And now his imported Spanish coach belonged to me.

John was better dressed than I was, wearing a gray wool suit with a fox fur collar and high leather boots. I looked like General Grant, my uniform worn and streaked with mud from my morning ride on Vic. I would change in the coach on the way to town, but there was little time to clean up.

The gravel road from the Presidio wound around Telegraph Hill along the waterfront. Where there had been several ranches interspaced with forest, there were now quaint houses, workshops, livery stables and fisheries. I owned a smokehouse near Clark Point, but was still trying to pay off the construction cost.

We turned south along the Embarcadero and then west up Washington Street to Portsmouth Square. Laid out with stone and brick, the wide plaza had become a popular gathering place. Our flag waved proudly from a tall pole, the painted buffalo on a white field with its underlying green stripe.

I disembarked in front of the new municipal building, walking up the slate steps through heavy oak doors into the lobby. Every newcomer to California, immigrant, merchant or visitor, needed to register with the administration office or face arrest.

"*Hola Manuel. Está el Gobernador Santa Anna?*" I asked the clerk on duty.

Corporal Contreras sat behind a high desk lit by oil lamps. Six men in traveling clothes waited for his attention.

"*Mis saludos, General Custer. Su Excelencia está en su oficina,*" Contreras answered, pointing up the stairs to the second floor.

I knocked on the former dictator's door and let myself in. Santa Anna stood at his massive oak desk, a gift from Admiral Cochrane before he had departed for the Atlantic. He was magnificently dressed in a blue uniform, black tunic, gold epaulets, and high leather boots. He looked like Napoleon, only taller.

"Almost time, George. Are you ready?" Santa Anna asked.

"Are you sure this will work?" I asked.

"If you or I tried this alone, probably not. But together? How can they stop us?"

"Antonio, I need to thank you again," I said, reaching to shake hands. "Leading an army is quite different from running a country."

200

"Then it is good I have done both," Santa Anna said.

We walked across the square to *La Sirena* perched on its low rise. The nearby stables were filled with horses. Morning Star's Garden, planted with fruit trees and flowers, was crowded with arriving delegates. Including the Gang of Three, who I barely managed to acknowledge with a tip of my hat.

"Everyone's here, General. Even got reporters," Cooke said.

I noticed Marcus of the *Examiner*, who worked for me, along with Samuel Jeffers from the *New York Tribune* and Argon López, who wrote dispatches for several Mexican newspapers. They were harder to handle, as many still sought to cast the Buffalo Flag as mere freebooters occupying conquered lands. I made a point of shaking the British ambassador's hand right in front of them.

La Sirena quickly filled up. Having been impressed by the drawings in *Harper's Weekly* and *Leslie's Illustrated*, I had contracted a sketch artist to immortalize the scene and wondered if cameras had been invented yet.

The long wooden tables had been turned to face the stern. Most of the delegates sat on benches, though there were a few chairs for the older men. Slow was sitting with Señor Peralta and Friar Mendez among the delegates. Sitting on the second deck was Isabella, Señora Santa Anna, Señora Richardson, and many of the territory's most prominent women. Outside, my band was playing our favorite songs until the meeting was called to order. It was quite the gathering.

"Gentlemen, thank you for coming," I said, standing nervously before the assembly. "In the year since the Buffalo Flag sought our destiny in California, there have been many changes. Good changes. Our land is prosperous, and will grow more prosperous. The administration of Governor Santa Anna, and the efforts of the Seventh Cavalry, have kept the peace. We enjoy the benefits of the Kellogg Code, and we are obligated to no foreign power. Now it is time to formalize our new country."

I gave way to Santa Anna, who was especially charismatic on this occasion. He was not popular with the immigrants, for he restricted their activities, but he was widely respected. And obeyed.

"*Saludos mis amigos. Bienvenido a San Francisco,*" he said. "Let me congratulate General Custer, Colonel Crockett, and all who have forged an empire from this wilderness. When the history of the world is written, they will stand tall in its annuals."

The convention applauded, even the Gang of Three. A neglected province whose primary trade had once been cow hides was now a source of pride.

"You have all read the Articles of Confederation," Santa Anna continued. "These statues will apply to Alta California, New Mexico, and in time, the nation of Texas. The Buffalo Flag will wave from the Pacific Ocean to the Caribbean Sea. Roads have been built for trade, treaties signed with the Indians."

"We is makin' a new world fer our kids," Crockett said, suddenly standing up in the middle of the hall. "I've sent word fer my family, as have many others. This here is a free land, and by our vote today, we be a keepin' her free forever!"

I heard another cheer, mostly by the white immigrants, but also some of our Indian friends. The Californios were less convinced, but applauded politely. Santa Anna stepped forward again as Crockett sat down. I almost expected Slow to make one of his mysterious pronouncements, and was thankful he didn't.

"Friends, it is time for a motion," Santa Anna said, using a gavel.

"I move we accept the Articles of Confederation," Isaac Richardson shouted.

"I second the motion," Father Mendez said.

"Is there any debate?" Santa Anna asked.

A dozen hands went up, nearly all of them Californios.

"Seeing no opposition, the question is called," Santa Anna said, ignoring the dissenters. "All in favor?"

"Aye!" the greater majority of the hall shouted.

"All opposed?" Santa Anna inquired.

The tavern grew quiet. Alvarado stood up but said nothing. He was joined by Castro and Señor Félix of Los Angeles. Two of the San Diego delegates joined them. One white representative, Orrin Welch of Santa Barbara, slowly got up. I waited to see if there were more.

"With forty-four voting in the affirmative and six opposed, the motion is passed," Santa Anna declared.

"Let's hear it for the Buffalo Flag Nations," Crockett said.

There was more cheering, followed many handshakes, before we moved outside. Tables had been set up in the park filled with hot food and strong beverages, the señoritas wearing their most colorful dresses. The band began to play again and dancing broke out.

"Time for some business?" Tom asked.

He was joined by Cooke, Smith and Almonte. I should have called them the Gang of Four.

"This is a day to celebrate," I said.

"General Urrea has recaptured Harrisburg," Tom said, his expression grim.

"And there has been a massacre in San Patricio," Cooke added. "Sesma's troops murdered eighty of Burleson's men after they surrendered."

"Word spread to New Orleans, then to Alabama and the Carolinas. Southerners are outraged. They are gathering militia groups to seek revenge," Smith said, holding out a New Orleans newspaper for me to see.

"By spring Sam Houston will have three or four thousand troops. Filisola barely has two-thirds that number," Tom said. "Mexico is broke. They can't raise another army."

Santa Anna walked up. General José María Tornel, recently arrived from Mexico, was with him serving as aide-de-camp. They were old friends, the forty-three-year-old Tornel having been Santa Anna's Secretary of War. He was a tall, distinguished fellow, with long gray sideburns. Like myself, he was the son of humble origins. His father had been a shopkeeper.

"It is true, George," Santa Anna said, relaxed in our company. "José says the government is pleased with Filisola's progress, but they worry he may overextend."

"*General Filisola tiene la intención de recapturar Galveston y suministro por mar,*" Tornel said. "*Escuchamos los norteamericanos se ajustan a una flota pirata a detenerlos.*"

"If Filisola does not abandon Galveston, and the Brazos forces commandeer a fleet strong enough to hold the harbor, the Mexican army will be cut off," Tom said, suddenly thinking himself a general. Or an admiral.

"We stole half the rebel navy. I doubt they can raise another," I said.

"What if Van Buren sends the U.S. Navy under false colors?" Cooke asked. "We already know they have cavalry on the Sabine River waiting for a chance to invade."

"Gentlemen, the letters we've sent to the Eastern press have Van Buren in a bind," I said, starting to get riled up. "He can't afford to support slavery in Texas— the entire North would turn on him. And Filisola is a professional soldier. I'm sure he won't get himself in such a fix."

I looked to Santa Anna for support, but he didn't seem so sure. After defeat at the Alamo and stalemates the rest of the year, the Mexican generals were under pressure for action. As General McClellan had been by the Lincoln administration before the Peninsula Campaign.

"*Filisola no es un gran estratega*," Tornel suggested.

"I don't like his strategy either," Tom said. "Autie, Myles has raised another company in Béjar, but it's still not enough. Come spring, if Sesma moves against him, he won't be able to hold the town. And if Houston gets enough recruits, he might try for Béjar, too. We need to get back there."

"Béjar is a backwater, Tommy," I disagreed. "I can write to Erasmo. Have him dismantle the armory and bring it here. Keogh and Harrington can provide escort."

"Abandon Texas?" Smith said.

"We'll get back there, Fresh. Someday. No need to worry about it now," I said. "We have enterprises here to take care of. Indians to pacify. West Texas is nothing but buffalo and Comanche."

"You surprise me, Autie," Cooke said.

Tom and Smith exchanged glances. Apparently I had surprised them, too.

"Autie, we're going back in the spring, and taking our companies with us," Tom said. "Better start making plans."

"Tom...?" I began.

"We're going, and that's that," Tom interrupted.

After the Gang of Four returned to the party, I took Santa Anna aside.

"Antonio, are you thinking of reclaiming power in Mexico City?" I asked. "Filisola's mistakes could create an opportunity for you."

"No, my friend, not at this time," Santa Anna said. "Inés and my daughters like this land. So do I. But I would like to see the Americans in Texas defeated."

———

I rushed up river on the *Sacramento Queen* at the insistence of Crockett's mysterious message. The old bear-hunter didn't always express himself clearly in writing, but this was outright cryptic.

"Trouble?" Dr. Lord asked, reading the poorly scrawled note.

Lord was taking a rare break from his new hospital, built at Clarks Point to take advantage of the fresh breezes. His expertise was already attracting attention from medical societies in New England and Europe, especially the *Société de Médecine de Paris.*

"Can't tell, George," I said. "Just says 'Come on. Be quick.'"

"We couldn't be any quicker, sir," Butler said, standing on the foredeck with his Sharps ready.

The rushing water was choppy, as would be expected in January. Jimmy Allen was looking a bit sick and stayed near the wheelhouse. The wetlands all around us thrived with geese and ducks. An occasional log floated downstream toward our speeding craft, forcing the boatmen to steer them off with long poles. Black smoke from the funnels marked our passage.

When we finally reached the pier following a deep bend in the river, the steamer was tied up quickly and we ran across a wobbly oak plank to the deserted dock.

"What's all the excitement in the plaza?" Dr. Lord asked, looking up the gray winter hill where dozens of timbered buildings stood around Crockett's Fort.

"Some sort of parade," Butler speculated.

We rushed along a wide stone path, not waiting for a carriage, panting as we reached the broad plaza south of the main gate. I saw a long line of animals coming down the Gold Road from the east, hundreds of horses, mules, and even a few oxen. Some pulled freight wagons, others bore heaving bags of what looked like gravel. Guiding the cavalcade were a hundred roughly dressed frontiersmen and Washoe Indians. Some rode slowly at the head of the column while others walked alongside their charges, keeping the packs under control.

Lining the road on either side stood a thousand or more gaily dressed citizens. I recognized merchants, tradesmen, ranchers and teachers. School must have let out for the day. There were at least a hundred children, many riding the shoulders of their fathers. The people cheered. Bright colored ribbons were waved. A brass band led by Sergeant French played "When Johnny Comes Marching Home".

I pushed through the crowd to a reception platform where Crockett was standing, fitted in his best gray woolen suit, a tall beaver hat, and a puffy purple cravat.

"Glad ya could make it, George. 'Fraid ya might 'rive late," Crockett said with a mischievous grin.

"Late for what? What the hell is this?" I asked.

"It ain't Washington's birthday," Crockett replied.

"It's not *my* birthday, either," I snapped.

Another cheer went up. I saw the head of the column turning at the far end of the plaza and coming back toward us. It was Mitch Bouyer in the lead, smiling like I'd never seen. He doffed his fur hat, bent over to flatter the ladies, and finally halted before the greeting committee. I noticed Major Brister, Mayor John Raffetto, and Chief Maidu standing with us. A step down were reporters Jay Phillip Marcus of the *Examiner* and Jedidiah Burns of the *Philadelphia National Gazette*. Miciagh Autry was acting as master of ceremonies. Across the plaza, on an iron balcony overlooking the proceedings, I spied Slow, Morning Star and Voss.

"Well, Gen'ral, I done it. Done jus' like I promised," the grizzly old scout said, dismounting a fine Buckskin stallion with a jaunty bounce.

"And what have ya done?" I asked, descending the platform to meet him in the street.

"I found it. The *Bouyer Bonanza*. Biggest silver strike in the whole world," Bouyer said. "An' no one gots to take my word fer it. Brought back fifty tons of blue ore, over the Sierras, in the winter. Reckon that'll make me a famous man."

"I reckon it will, Mitch," I said, shaking his hand.

The son of a bitch had really done it. Found what would have been the Ophir Mine at the head of Six Mile Canyon and then named the discovery for himself. Mitch Bouyer had become immortal.

"I hope you saved a share for me," I said, only half-joking.

"Just a small one, sir. Just a small one," Bouyer said, gesturing for me to lower my expectations. "Thar's plenty more where this come from. Plenty for all. But first I got to reward my benefactors."

Bouyer turned toward the Drake Hotel across the plaza and waved. Morning Star waved back, blowing him a kiss.

"Benefactors?" I asked.

"Didn't ya know, Gen'ral? Slow and Voss, and the little squaw, they grubstaked my claim," Bouyer answered.

I looked up with a frown, unhappy to once again be outfoxed by a boy and a bugler. Crockett came forward to shake Bouyer's hand. Several of Bouyer's teamsters cut their canvas bags open, letting rich blue-black nuggets pour out for all to see. I retreated from the festivities, walking down the line of animals until reaching a heavy freight wagon. The driver was a burly blond-haired teenager in a checkered shirt who'd I never seen before.

"Where you from, boy?" I asked.

"Missouri, sir. All the way from Franklin County," he respectfully replied. His voice was high-pitched, like mine.

"Do you know who I am?"

"General Custer, sir. Everybody knows who General Custer is."

I was glad to hear that. I climbed up next to him on the creaking wagon seat, taking in the scene from the new perspective. Profitable silver mines in addition to our gold fields would draw thousands to Nevada, causing problems and opportunities. I could already see the headlines in the eastern newspapers.

"How did you join up with Mr. Bouyer?" I asked.

"Sixteen of us was comin' west. I done a little mining while minding Pa's farm, then decided to make my own way," the boy explained.

"Have you studied mining?"

"No, not yet. But I intends to."

"What's your name, lad?" I asked.

"Hearst. George Hearst, sir. My Pa is William Hearst," he answered. "I ain't got much schoolin', but I'm smart. I'm gonna make somethin' of myself."

"I bet you will, son," I said. "George, I know a spot or two that might be worth prospecting. Would you be interested in forming a mining company?"

The Brazos Convention had three armies in the field, all making progress. We received newspaper reports of Mexican setbacks, and the Buffalo Flag's position in Texas was beginning to look tenuous.

"It's a message from San Antonio," Smith said, handing the note to Tom first, then to me.

"Keogh is fortifying the Alamo?" I said.

"Erasmo Seguin moved the armory into the Long Barracks," Tom read. "Put a roof on the chapel for a supply depot."

"What are they thinking?" I wondered.

Smith took the note back, reading all the way to the end.

"Señor Seguin has made three hundred new Springfields," Smith reported.

"Three hundred! That's twice as many as the whole regiment has," Tom said. "Autie, we can't let those guns fall to the enemy."

"Myles has scaled back the size of the fort, and he's mostly building bastions," Smith said. "It's going to look like an Irish castle."

"No, not really?" I said.

"Maybe not exactly," Smith conceded.

I went to my desk, pulled out a stack of blank paper, and found a quill. My orders were written quickly but clearly, unlike so many of the missives I'd been given during the Civil War by careless superior officers.

"Every wagon in Los Angeles and San Diego will leave immediately," I said. "Send a rider to Sharrow, and Carson in Santa Fe. They are to raise their militia. Have an interpreter go to Mangas Coloradas. Tell the chief it's time for him to be my friend."

"Where are these wagons going?" Tom asked.

"San Antonio, where else? They'll pack up the armory and bring it here," I said. "They should bring all the tools, molds, powder and forging equipment."

"Myles can't abandon Béjar," Tom protested. "It would be the end of the Buffalo Flag in Texas."

"We can worry about that later. Right now we must act," I decided.

I handed the orders to Tom, Smith and Cooke, waiting for them to agree. They left my office without comment.

———————

It was February, 1838, and I was in a melancholy mood. I finished

208

for the day and went downstairs, finding my heavy overcoat. Five clerks, two of them women, nodded as I left the building. The day was cold and dreary.

Corporal Espalier had Vic waiting for me at the Presidio gate, the old warhorse looking his age. The marches up and down California, and then back and forth to the gold fields, were taking a toll. I felt it, too, and gave him a hug.

"Gracias, Carlos," I said. *"Encontrar un cuarto caliente."*

"Voy a usar su oficina," Espalier replied.

I didn't really think Carlos would use my office to stay warm, but I wasn't sure. I had once slept in General Sheridan's tent.

Vic and I walked slowly on the gravel road toward town. The fishing boats were returning with the day's catch, and a herd of cows briefly blocked our path. We came to an empty stretch that was largely forested on the right where I spotted a winter apple. Vic enjoyed it.

A rider approached quickly on a spirited mount. A woman in red Spanish leathers, sitting the saddle well. I knew it to be Isabella.

"George, Tom is leaving for Texas," Isabella said, breathlessly jumping from the horse. "So is Bill, and Fresh, and Juan. They're all leaving."

"Yes, I suspected as much, but didn't hear it confirmed until this morning," I replied, resigned to the situation. Tom had defied me at the Alamo, too.

"When do we leave? Why aren't we packing?" Isabella asked.

"We're not. There are enough important duties right here."

"Tom says Texas is in danger. Béjar. My father. We must go. We must fight for our families."

I waved for a young Indian boy to hold our horses, tipped him a copper, and took Isabella's hand, walking down to the rocky beach. Some people actually liked to swim in the cold water, which I found astonishing.

"I've sent orders to Keogh and your father," I explained. "They are to blow up the Alamo and retreat to Yuma. When Tom encounters them on the road, they'll all turn back together."

"No, they won't. My father will not leave Béjar, and neither will Myles. They are too brave. You know that."

"Southerners are enraged by the San Patricio Massacre.

Newspapers from New Orleans to Charleston have everyone stirred up. Thousands of volunteers are pouring into east Texas, and Filisola is getting himself boxed in. When the rebel forces overrun the Mexican army, they'll turn on San Antonio. Especially if they've heard about the new rifles. Myles needs to be smart and withdraw."

"You told me the plantation owners must not be allowed to rule Texas," Isabella replied, looking down at the ground. "Tom, Bill— they all say there will be a terrible war if they do. You cannot let this happen."

"We'll stop them, when we're stronger," I said. "We need gold to fight a war."

"There is already plenty of gold," she flared. "If you aren't going back to Texas with me, then I'll go without you."

"I will not be dictated to. After we're married—"

"We will *not* be married," she said, running for her horse.

Before I could stop her, Isabella was gone. I turned around and went back to the Presidio.

———————

"We're moving out tomorrow," Tom said.

"There's still time to change your mind," I said, clutching a shining California twenty dollar gold piece. "I've recalled Keogh, and asked Crockett to join us here. Damnit, Tom, there's nothing left in Texas but dirt and flies."

"That's not the mission, Autie," Tom patiently disagreed. "We started this to stop slavery like Mr. Lincoln wanted. To prevent the Civil War. Most of us... some of us, anyway, we think this is why we were spared from the Little Big Horn. Slow thinks so, too."

"Sioux gods aren't going to protect you, little brother. They didn't protect Georgie Yates at the Cibolo, or Mark Kellogg from a mangy ambusher. You'll be outnumbered five to one. Maybe ten to one."

"You've faced worse."

"I have Custer's Luck."

"I'm a Custer, too," Tom said, turning to leave the room. "By the way, Autie, I countermanded your order to Keogh. We'll make a stand in Béjar, then drive the rebs back across the Sabine."

I took a deep breath.

"Then you should take these," I said, reaching into my breast pocket.

It was a small snuff box holding two silver stars. I pinned one on each of Tom's shoulders.

"Take care of my army, General Custer," I said, confirming the promotion.

"You always said I should be the general," he replied, tearing up.

"Try not to win all the medals," I urged.

My army, and my girl, were going east whether I liked it or not. On February 23rd, 1838, four veteran companies of cavalry started south on the El Camino Real, first to Los Angeles, then to Yuma, El Paso and San Antonio. They took twenty wagons but no artillery. It was two years to the day since the Mexican army had laid siege to the Alamo.

The White Man can be forgiven for not understanding the ways of the Great Spirit. Even those of us wise in the ways of Wakan Tanka may not always follow a straight path, for there are many clouds. On a day of great victory for The People, I celebrated with a cheerful heart, for hundreds of bluecoats fell before our warriors on the Greasy Grass in brave battle. Proud campfires lit the night. Captured weapons and bloody scalps were raised in triumph. The People shouted, and they laughed, and they cried. The next morning, we prepared to flee. No matter how many white men are killed, there are always more.

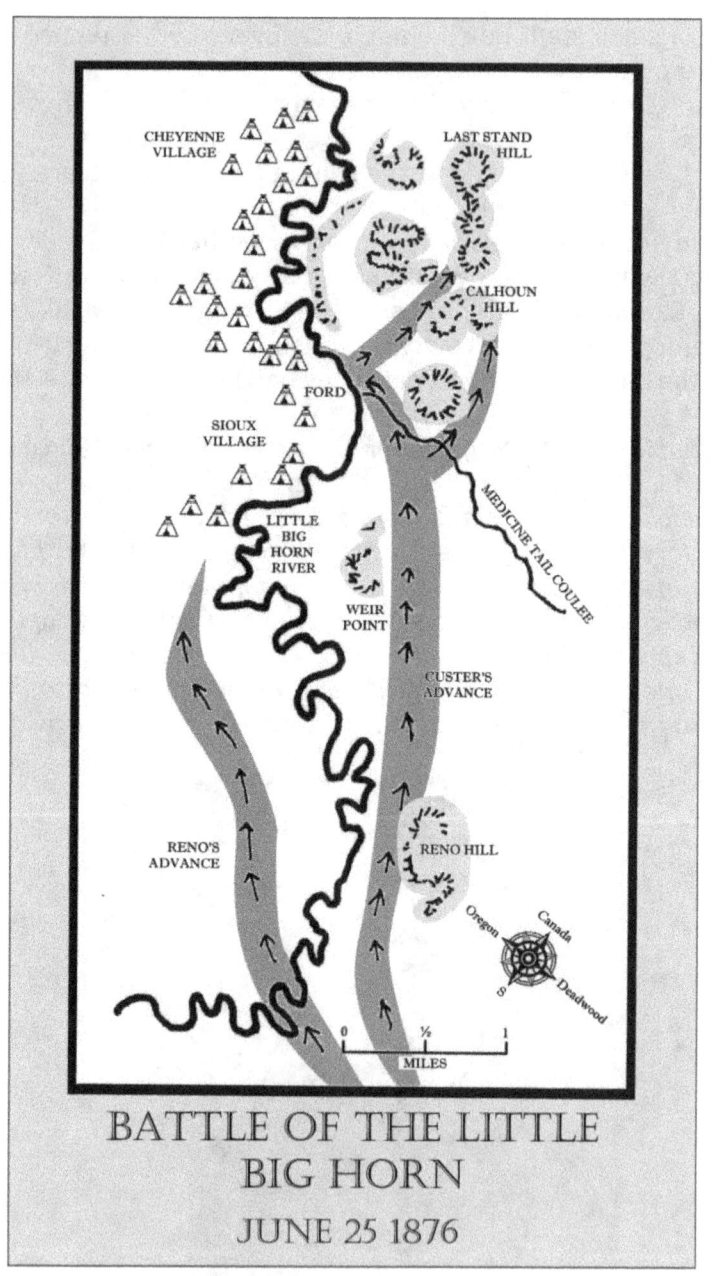

BATTLE OF THE LITTLE BIG HORN
JUNE 25 1876

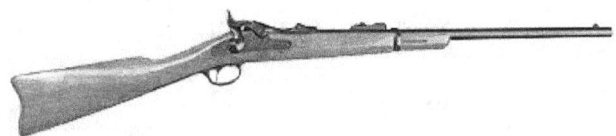

Chapter Eight
VISION QUEST

"History has gone wrong," Slow said, bursting into my office without invitation.

I had just returned from Crockett's Fort, where I'd spent five days adjudicating disputes in the gold fields. The new arrivals pouring into California had slowed during the winter, especially as news of our harsh immigration policy began to spread, but there was still much to keep me busy.

"Don't need a professor to tell you that, lad," I said, glad for the distraction.

"You read more of the white man's newspapers?" Slow asked, taking his usual seat at the edge of my desk.

"The British have recognized our decree of sovereignty," I said, holding up the treaty dripping in blue ribbon and gold seals. "The French are threatening to invade Mexico instead of California. The Russians have abandoned their claims in the north. Even the Indians are building towns instead of waging war."

"Are these things not what you wanted?"

"Our empire grows domestic, and General George Armstrong Custer has become a clerk," I complained.

"We are on an untraveled path. The birds say it is not the correct path," Slow insisted.

"I'm not going back to Texas. Nothing but war and poverty there."

"I do not speak of Tejas," Slow said.

"Then what are you talking about?"

"Our destiny must be served."

"My destiny is doing just fine," I protested, playing with a solid gold paperweight. It looked like a Kentucky thoroughbred and weighed six ounces.

"General, you are not meant to be here," Slow said.

"Boy, I won't even be born until next year. Of course I'm not meant to be here."

"It is more than that," he insisted.

I knew Slow was upset. He was often absorbed and moody, curious and provoking, but rarely emotional. Had he been a normal child, I'd have sent him off to play baseball or clean the stables, but we'd shared too many adventures for that.

"What should we do?" I asked, expecting an enigmatic response. For medicine men, like carnival barkers, are better at attracting attention than providing answers.

"We must go to the mountains. We will perform the Sun Dance," he said. "Wakan Tanka will send a vision."

Civilization knows little of the Sioux sun dance, only that it involves a good deal of superstitious rituals and bloodletting. I have never heard of a sun dance giving any special insight, and judging by the decline of the Indian nations, they would appear to be ineffective. My thoughts were clear to Slow.

"I stood by you at the Alamo," he said, brows bent.

"We'll leave in the morning," I replied.

I'd not ridden Vic in a fortnight, so attached had I become to office chairs. We packed a mule with supplies, found horses for Sergeant Fuentes and Mr. Armstrong, and prepared to find the east trail toward my new winery in the Sierra Nevada foothills. Slow was riding Traveller.

"Where ya goin'?" Crockett asked, coming forward with Old Blaze in tow.

Crockett was in hunting leathers and wearing a coonskin cap. Miciagh was with him, pulling a pack-laden donkey.

"Heard ya goin' on a quest, General," Autry said.

"How did you know?" I asked.

"Youngster ain't so good at keepin' secrets," Crockett said. "Got a favor to ask, George. My history's a might skewed too, ya know.

Didn't die at the Alamo, now I'm president of a Texas that ain't no real country. Don't even know what to write the folks back home. Thought maybe I'd try this 'ere questin'."

"You may not like the answers," I warned, for mystical adventures rarely turn out well.

"That 'ill be for me to decide," Crockett said. "Mind if Miciagh comes along? He's always been a might curious 'bout Sioux ways."

I nodded my consent, for there was little else to say. The six of us made a strong party.

Sacramento was growing fast. My properties, and the government buildings, were on the high ground above the river, for I'd read many stories of flooding. As some of the new settlers found the higher elevations inconvenient, most were establishing businesses closer to the water. I recommended they be put on pylons. Docks, warehouses and saloons were appearing everywhere.

"Ya kin still call it Custer City, if ya wants to," Crockett said, poking fun at me.

"And when it's underwater, what will they call it then?" I answered.

"Don't need to tell me. When the flood washed out my mill on Shoal Creek, darn near put me in the poorhouse," Crockett said.

Now Crockett owned six large lots next to mine, one with an impressive hotel under construction. The Crockett Arms, I supposed.

"San Francisco will soon be the largest city in our empire," I said. "But it remains vulnerable to foreign powers. I think Sacramento should be our capital. Plenty of water, farms, cattle. A good base for military operations."

"A might swampy for me," Crockett disagreed. "Where does Slow plan on this 'ere sun dance?"

"I have no clue what he's thinking."

We traveled for two days, heading toward the gold diggings at first, then veering southeast through lush green valleys. The land was richer than any I'd ever seen. Richer than Ohio, or Pennsylvania. Certainly richer than Texas. Prospectors viewed us with concern, fearing well-deserved punishment if caught cheating on their shares. The vaqueros smiled and waved their lariats. The Indians made us welcome, secure in lands that no white man had time to steal. I doubt Slow knew where he was leading us, though he was not shy about asking the birds.

Crockett and I rode side by side most of the time. We'd left our hunting dogs behind, somewhat to our regret, but kept an eye out for good opportunities.

"Not feelin' guilty, George?" he suddenly asked as we approached.

"Guilty about what, David?"

"Not goin' back to Tejas with the boys."

"Like I told Tom, it's a fool's mission. They'll come crawling back with their tails between their legs."

"Bit harsh, don't ya think?"

"You could have gone with them," I said.

"Promised Tommy to keep an eye on you," he answered. "Sides, I'm an old man. Cavorting 'bout the country is a young man's game."

"A game for young idiots. I should have learned that at Appomattox when I saw Lee riding away on his gray horse, his shoulders slumped by four years of murder. I never was the brightest of the Custers."

"Ya did conquer California."

"And now I'm going to enjoy it," I replied.

Just before dark, Slow settled on a small pasture below a tall steep rock. The area was filled with pines fed by a bubbling creek. John and Fuentes set up the tents while Miciagh and I made a campfire. Crockett went to gather firewood and spotted a young stag, dropping it with a quick shot. I was jealous. By nightfall we had a snug camp with venison cooking for dinner. The coffee smelled great. We still didn't know what Slow was looking for.

"It is time," he announced as a new moon rose over the mountains.

We all stood, but Slow held up his hand.

"Only Custer and Crockett," he said, leading us under a deep overhang beneath the rock facing.

I saw the lad had scribbled markings on the cliff with chalk, images of horses, buffalo, birds, and strange symbols. Possibly tokens of the Sioux gods, though I had never heard of such. Crockett hardly gave the drawings a second thought, for the Cherokee were known to similar practices. Dried droppings indicated the cave was used by bears.

"We will sit," Slow said, sitting cross-legged before a low fire.

The shallow pit contained twisted branches, buffalo chips, and a small amount of coal. Crockett and I sat, forming a triangle. The eerie glow began to bother me, but again, Crockett showed no special reactions. I could see the flames dancing in his cool blue eyes, while Slow's eyes looked like glowing black embers. He took out the Bowie knife he'd carried since finding Jim Bowie dead the night before the Alamo was stormed. Then he cut a piece of flesh from his forearm.

"Hold on! That's enough," I protested, reaching for the knife.

"Wakan Tanka must have his tribute," Slow said.

"Then we will all contribute," I said.

It was a warm early spring night, as California was prone to. My buckskin jacket lay back at camp in my tent. Taking the knife from Slow, I rolled up the sleeve of my blue trail shirt, cut a shallow piece of bloody skin from my arm, and tossed the flesh into the fire. Then I handed the knife to Crockett. The old bear hunter smiled at my discomfort, grinned at Slow, and then made his contribution. He did not hand the knife back to Slow, burying the long blade in the ground next to him.

Slow chanted for a few moments, gazing into the fire, and then drew a leather pouch from his belt. It appeared to be some sort of herb or spice. He tossed a handful into the flames and resumed his chanting. The smell was strong. Stronger than the tobacco used by the Plains Indians in their peace pipes. I grew restless with the endless ritual, beginning to fidget. The air seemed thick. Suddenly I began to experience a strange sensation. I looked at Crockett, who sat quietly with straightened shoulders, his eyes closed. Slow was leaning forward, mumbling. My hands felt numb. I wanted to stretch my legs, but found I couldn't move. The world around me began to fade.

There was a cloud. Or a haze. I couldn't tell. It wasn't like the gray fog that had surrounded me at the Little Big Horn and left me on a cold Texas prairie. This had a ghostly feel.

There was a carpeted hallway, long and shadowed, illuminated by oil lamps. Slow stood at my side, older, grayer. Familiar. Walking before us was a tall man in an old fashioned suit of black cloth with a high white collar and a beaver top hat. The man turned for the briefest moment, looking back, but he saw nothing. It was Crockett, a bit younger, with an angry bounce in his step.

A paneled door opened and Crockett entered a large office,

handing his hat to a waiting Negro servant and stomping toward an oak desk. A grizzled old man sat at the desk. Watchful. He rose slowly. Through the window behind him, I saw the city of Washington. But not the Washington I remembered. The Capitol dome was missing.

"Crockett," the old man greeted with a smug expression. Gray whiskers showed despite an effort to shave. The blue eyes twinkled.

"President Jackson," Crockett replied, refusing to shake hands. "We had an agreement. An agreement ta last the ages."

"Ages don't last forever, David. And our people need room to grow," Jackson said, beginning to frown.

"Don't need to grow on land that don't belong to us. Cherokee made treaties. Good treaties. And they is good neighbors. Fought by our side a'gin the Creeks."

"But they aren't white Christian neighbors," Jackson said.

"That ain't the point," Crockett responded.

"That's exactly the point. This is a big land. A white man's land. Someday it will stretch from the Atlantic to the Pacific. The Cherokee will just have to be happy with new land in the Indian Territory, out of the way of civilization."

"Ya mean 'way from where yar land agents kin carve up their forests and sell 'em to your speculator friends? Just like they keep forcing poor folk off their land in Tennessee and drivin' 'em farther west?"

"The people of Tennessee elected me major general, senator, and president. And even a term in the House," Jackson boasted. "From what I hear, you won't even be a congressman much longer."

"Your paid hirelings are a workin' hard a'gin me, that's fer sure," Crockett said. "But it ain't gonna work, Andy. I'm gonna git reelected, and when your boy Van Buren tries to succeed ya, I'm a gonna win the presidency instead."

Jackson laughed, walked toward the window, and lit a corncob pipe. He puffed several times. The city was primitive compared to the Washington I had known so well during the war. I'm not sure if it even had theaters.

"Those Whigs have just been using you, Davy. Parading you up and down the big cities, giving you fancy rifles, flattering your book. Using you to attack me. But you won't be of use to them much longer. Not much longer at all."

Crockett turned with a fearsome expression, but suddenly we weren't in Andrew Jackson's office anymore. It was a cloudy day, threatening rain, in a shabby pioneer hamlet surrounded by pines and sycamores. A few dozen rough farmers and their wives loitered in the middle of the road while Crockett stood on a cracker barrel, his travelling leathers already stained. Nearby, four men waited on sturdy horses. All were dressed for the trail.

"Well, I kan't help you folks no more," Crockett bitterly spoke. "Ya 'lected me, then un-'lected me, and 'lected me, and now ya done gone an' un-'lected me a'gin. I kan't take none a this no more. Ya all kin go to hell, I'm goin' ta Texas."

I watched Crockett jump down, mount a proud looking stallion, and turn west toward a setting sun. The small group of frontiersmen followed.

Nighttime. There is a party. Banners hang from Spanish balconies. Senoritas dance in colorful dresses. We are in the plaza of San Antonio de Béjar, the cathedral looming in shadows cast by the bonfires. The older vision of Slow is still standing next to me, observing, but no one else can see us. Crockett sits on the back of a wagon playing a fiddle as hundreds dance, drink, shout and fight. I hear someone raise a cup of wine in honor of George Washington's birthday.

Flushed with drink, Crockett sets the fiddle aside and climbs down, stretching his long legs. He's wearing a suit, but not the well-tailored dyed wool he'd worn in Washington. This outfit is older, slightly frayed, and mended with patches.

I watch two quarreling men come up to Crockett. One is Jim Bowie, the other William Travis, both in much better health than when I'd last seen them. They are smartly dressed. Bowie looks drunk. Travis indignant.

"We can't keep sharing command. This drunken barbarian will get us all killed," Travis said.

"Fighting a professional army ain't no job for an amateur," Bowie responded.

"I'm a lieutenant colonel of cavalry, sir," Travis insisted.

"You're nothin' but a goddamn lawyer," Bowie replies.

"Sirs, we must 'ave peace 'til Colonel Neill returns," Crockett said.

219

"Perhaps we gots ta worry more about Santa Anna. Villagers seem ta think he's nearby."

"Santa Anna can't march his army across the desert in the dead of winter," Travis said. "He won't reach Béjar for another two or three weeks."

Bowie nodded agreement and sat down. He looked a little green.

"I leave such things to you all. I'm just a high private in this 'ere army," Crockett said, looking a bit worried.

"Maybe you can do better. Agree to lead the volunteers," Travis urged.

"Like hell he'll lead my volunteers," Bowie said. "Crockett, take command of the regulars until Neill comes back. Send this debtor back to Anahuac."

"I would make you pay for that remark, if you were a gentleman," Travis said, starting to take off his white gloves.

"Why don't we enjoy this fiesta? Talk on it more in da mornin'? When we're all a might fresher," Crockett said with a grin, stepping between the two men.

Suddenly it's the next morning. The town plaza is littered with torn streamers, empty bottles and broken pots. I watch Crockett step from a fancy hacienda across the street that belongs to the former postmaster, though Señor Seguin does not appear to be at home. The street is filled with Tejano men, women and children fleeing the town, their belongings piled in two-wheeled carts. With them are sheep, goats, donkeys and dogs. Church bells begin to ring.

"What's a goin' on?" Crockett asked, still woozy from heavy drinking.

"Mexicans coming, Colonel Crockett," a blond-haired teenager says. I know him. It's Jimmy Allen.

"Ah don't understand," Crockett said, scratching his week-old beard.

"Dr. Sutherland spotted them. Hundreds. Maybe thousands," Allen breathlessly reports. "Colonel Travis has ordered everybody into the Alamo. Sent to Goliad for help."

Allen runs on. Crockett turns and sees the old mission on the other side of the river about three-quarters of a mile away. Most of the whites in Béjar are scrambling toward the old wooden footbridge spanning the San Antonio River, some herding cattle, others searching the small adobe houses for food. It's a chaotic scramble. Crockett dashes back into the hacienda and emerges a moment later carrying his rifle and wearing a coonskin cap.

"Rally to me, boys! Rally to me!" he shouts. "Let's git da guns from the presidio. Grab all the powder we kin carry. We is gonna need it."

A dozen frontiersmen rushed to the arsenal behind the San Fernando cathedral. Others begin to dismantle the blacksmith shop. Crockett is everywhere, encouraging and organizing. Travis rides up on a beautiful gray gelding, a bright red sash tied around his waist. His white broad brim hat is covered in dust.

"Two or three weeks?" Crockett says, looking peeved.

"Hopefully just cavalry," Travis answers. "Fannin will be here in a few days and we'll drive them back to the Rio Grande. Keep the men moving, Crockett."

Travis rides toward the La Villita ford waving an elaborate Spanish sword, yelling at the recruits to hurry.

Bowie walks by, a flintlock pistol in one hand and a bottle of whisky in the other. He looks like he's been dragged under a wagon.

"Get on your horse and ride, Crockett," Bowie said.

"Still have work to do," Crockett replied.

"No, not to the Alamo. Ride back to Tennessee before it's too late. We're all dead men now," Bowie said. "Hundred and fifty volunteers, only a score of good horses. Unless Santa Anna's in a forgiving mood, there won't be no quarter."

"Reckon we'll hold out," Crockett said, gazing at Bowie in wonderment. To see such a hero in such a state must have been a shock. Bowie coughed so hard that blood appeared on his lips.

"See ya in hell, Crockett," Bowie said, staggering toward the bridge.

Crockett just worked that much harder.

I next saw Crockett standing on the Alamo's southwest bastion where the 18-pounder was stationed. It was at least a week after the siege began, judging by the length of his beard and haggard expression. In the town beyond the river were thousands of Mexican troops, flags flying and cannon ready. Captain Baugh came up next to him wearing a damp, heavy overcoat. Both kept their heads low, peering over the wall with caution.

"We can't hold out much longer," Baugh whispered.

The Virginian, barely in his thirties, was worn to the bone. In the muddy courtyard behind him, the garrison was holed up in the barracks and adjoining workshops. Their appearance was generally ragged. Only Green Jameson was active, trying to shore up a barrier in front of the chapel. The fort was a forlorn place, not like the busy stronghold I had commanded after arriving with the Seventh Cavalry.

"Travis still says Fannin is comin'," Crockett said.

"Fannin isn't coming," Baugh said. "No one is coming. Some of the boys think we should break out. Mexican lines are still weak north of Powder House Hill."

"And leave the wounded?" Crockett said.

"A few will stay behind to the end. I will," Baugh answered. "I think you should lead the men out. No point in everyone getting killed."

Crockett gazed at the Mexican lines, creeping closer every day. The artillery would soon be able to batter down the walls.

"'Fraid I gots to stay, too. Davy Crockett kan't be runnin' out like a thief in the night. But if any of the boys want to make a break, they's got my blessin'."

"Thanks, Colonel. Not sure what will happen. Maybe Fannin will make it in time," Baugh said. "How is Bowie?"

"Sicker than before. Might not last another day," Crockett said.

"Bad luck for us. We might have gotten out of this scrape with him in command," Baugh said, trudging back down the long dirt ramp.

From Crockett's expression, he didn't seem to believe it.

Sunday, March 6th, 1836. The pre-dawn hours of the Alamo. Crockett is standing at the wooden palisade connecting the chapel and the low barracks. There is smoke on the cloudy horizon, men are shouting, and the flash of musket fire is everywhere. A cannon booms. Dressed in hunting leathers, Crockett turns, his face smudged with powder. Blood drips from a bullet graze on his forehead. I can feel the desperation.

"Behind us! Behind us!" Crockett shouts, seeing a new danger.

The thick morning darkness is lit by occasional rockets. Several of the outer lying buildings have caught fire, giving off a hellish glow. The north wall, the fort's weakest position, has fallen. A handful of defenders fall back across the courtyard, followed by a horde of bloodthirsty Mexican soldiers.

Crockett fires his long rifle and starts to reload, but sees there is no time. The enemy is on them with such speed that there is little to do but fight or fly. He raises the rifle to swing at an approaching soldier, a captain in full uniform wielding a sword. Some of Crockett's men turn to help. Others jump over the palisade to take their chances on the black prairie. I see Miciagh fall, a lance driven through his back.

Crockett backs up against the Alamo chapel, swinging his rifle. The enemy captain takes a blow and falls, replaced by two privates. The rifle butt breaks off. Crockett throws the broken barrel and draws a knife, but too late. A glistening bayonet flickers from the encircling masses of enemies and stabs him in the chest. Crockett swings the knife at empty air and sinks to the ground, his coonskin cap falling next to him. The cap he only wore for public appearances. Boots trample past his dying body as the soldiers storm into the chapel. Cannon fire from the apse. The screams of frightened women. The grunts of fighting men giving no quarter and asking none.

"No, it didn't happen that way!" Crockett shouted.

We were back at the campfire. In the hills of California. Crockett was sweating, his composure rattled. I had never seen the old woodsman with such an expression.

"Take it easy, David. It's only a hallucination," I assured him.

"I survived the Alamo. We survived it. I didn't die under the boots of a tyrant," Crockett said.

"We're safe and sound," I said, feeling his distress.

But then, Crockett was really just a civilian, attached to the army for a short time as a militia scout twenty years before. He could not be expected to face death with a soldier's resolve.

"That was the other path," Slow said. "The path that led to the destruction of my people.

"Didn't rightly do nothin' fer me, neither," Crockett added, reaching for a jug of corn whisky and taking a swig. He offered the jug to me, but I declined.

"I don't see the point of all this," I said, starting to get up.

"The vision is not over," Slow said.

He was once again a boy, but he looked older. Burdened by the task. He chanted, gazing into the red flames, and threw a handful of the strange herbs into the fire. I caught my breath as a puff of smoke engulfed us.

There was no cloud this time. No fog. None of the niceties

afforded Crockett. I was suddenly riding Vic down a dust-filled coulee, E Company ahead, F Company behind me. It was insufferably hot, the horses exhausted, and my mind was in a haze, for I had barely slept in several days.

"We need a report from Reno," Tom said.

More tired than I, Tom was riding at my side wearing his white broad-brimmed hat and fringed buckskin jacket. Cooke, Hughes, Butler, Voss, and my young nephew, Autie Reed, were all close by. We were in a hurry.

The drainage channel abruptly turned northwest. I halted the command in a grassy swale, five companies of Seventh Cavalry anxious for a fight. Steep ridges rose to our left. To the right, sloping hills and scattered trees. Behind us was the fifteen-mile trail to the Crow's Nest where I'd been unable to see the hostile village. It had taken us three days of forced marches to reach the top of the Wolf Mountains, and most of another to reach the Little Big Horn River.

"Cooke, send another messenger to Benteen. I want him up here on the double with all the ammunition he can carry," I ordered.

Cooke scribbled a message in his notebook, tore out the page, and handed it to a young trumpeter. I looked back along the trail and saw my younger brother, Boston Custer, hightailing towards us on a fresh mount. He had a big smile.

"Reno's giving them hell," Boston said.

"Have you seen Benteen?" Tom asked.

"Just a couple miles behind me," Boston reported with a salute. Though as a civilian forager, he should not have been using military protocols.

"Gen'ral! Gen'ral!" Mitch Bouyer shouted, riding down from one of the tall rocky peaks with a young Crow scout at his side. I think his name was Curley. "Gen'ral, Reno's retreatin' into the woods. Gots a thousand In'dins closing in on him."

"He'll form the anvil. We are the hammer," I said.

"Autie, shouldn't we be falling back?" Tom asked.

Tom was no coward. Far from it. But he wasn't the general, either.

"With the warriors pulled toward Reno, the village is vulnerable. We'll capture the noncombatants," I said, turning to my men and shouting, "Harrah, boys! We've got them. We'll finish them up and go home to our station."

I saw the trumpeter ride out with Cooke's note, a young Italian boy assigned to H Company. Benteen would be along with three more companies in fifteen minutes. Twenty at the most. That would give me a striking force of three hundred and fifty.

"Does this draw lead down to a ford?" I asked Bouyer.

"Yes, sir. In'dins call it Medicine Tail," the crusty scout answered.

Bouyer had been loaned to me by Gibbon, and though a bit insubordinate, had proved reliable.

"Yates, take E and F down to the river. Make some noise to draw the hostiles off Reno. If Benteen's not up in the next few minutes, we'll meet you on the next ridge," I instructed.

As Yates disappeared down the coulee toward a tree-lined ford, I led the remaining three companies up a steep trail to the next ridge. It wasn't the best position, not large enough to maneuver, but I was finally able to get a good view of the river bottom. The village was in chaos, as I hoped, but our angle of attack was poor. With Captain Keogh at my side leading Company I, we crossed a wide gully to the next hill, skirmished with a handful of Indians at a distance, and then moved north again to a good position at the southern end of a long spiny ridge.

"Give Yates a hand," I ordered Lieutenant Jimmy Calhoun, my brother-in-law and commander of Company L.

Calhoun's forty men spread along the edge of the hill in skirmish formation, providing covering fire as Yates' wing moved up a draw to rejoin the command. The fight at the river had been brief.

I paused to study the village through the Austrian binoculars I'd borrowed from Lt. DeRudio that morning. As I expected, the big encampment was beginning to empty, and it *was* big. Bigger than any I'd ever seen. I doubted Deadwood City was so large. The women and children were being herded by the old men away from the teepees, some to the western slopes, but most north toward a heavily wooded bend in the river. There were only a few warriors present, some in the river bottom, a few crossing over into the hills on our left. Not enough to worry about. Once my command was reunited, I quickly issued the necessary orders.

"Keogh, you will hold this hill with companies I, C and L. Keep the trail open for Benteen. Yates, you're with me."

I gave Vic a kick, using no spurs. The poor old warhorse was tired,

225

as we all were, but he'd never let me down. We rode briefly along the top of the ridge, then veered down to the right, riding below the crest so the warriors beyond the river couldn't see us. Though a sharp eye would see the dust kicked up by our passage, most of the Indians were occupied with other problems.

We came around the edge of the hill. The terrain gently sloped down to the river on our left, mostly open space. Like much of the Montana range, the trees grew thickest along the rivers and creeks, the hills being scrub brush and buffalo grass. On the far side of the river, flocks of women and children were fleeing north. Bluffs prevented me from seeing the extent of their flight, but I could hear the dogs barking.

"Forward," I said, pointing toward the big bend in the river.

I rode with F Company, along with Yates, Bouyer, and the reporter, Mark Kellogg, who was riding a feisty mule. Tom rode with his good friend Algernon Smith, who had command of the Gray Horse troop on our left flank.

"Stay close, boys," I said to Boston and Autie, for we might take some fire as we got close to the river. Both were well-armed and restless to prove themselves.

The path down to the Little Big Horn was a cavalryman's dream, steady and unbroken. We reached a good ford, lightly defended, and I tried to count the noncombatants. At the Washita in 1868, there had only been a few score, plus a handful that were killed by skirmishers before I put a stop to it. Now there were hundreds. Maybe even a thousand. I could not capture them with the eighty men close at hand. I needed Keogh, and I needed Benteen.

"That's a lot of Indians," Tom said, cocking his Winchester.

"It's the best way to end this fight," I said. "Remember what I wrote in *My Life on the Plains*?"

"You write lots of things," Tom said.

"The knowledge that the close proximity of their women and children, and their necessary exposure in case of conflict, operates as a powerful argument in favor of peace," I proudly quoted, for my book was a bestseller. Or soon would be.

"They aren't looking very peaceful, Autie," Tom said.

"We need to make the warriors back off, Tommy. There are too many to shoot," I replied.

And that was the truth. The reservation reports had led us to believe that only eight hundred warriors were on the loose, but now I was guessing their numbers at twice that. Not that I was terribly surprised. I knew the Indian agents to be liars and thieves. They were paid by the head for each Indian remaining in their care, and paid nothing for Indians that had left the reservation. Testifying before Congress against those scoundrels had almost cost me my career, for President Grant's brother was one of the crooks.

"Back to the hill," I said, turning Vic around.

There had been some skirmishing at the ford, but not much. A dozen braves would not stop a charge by the Seventh Cavalry.

The long slope back to the ridge was still empty except for a few Indians who retreated eastward. I deployed Company E along the western slope overlooking the river and took Company F to an area near the top where I could keep an eye on the village. The ground was thick with sagebrush and June flowers.

"We've got them, Tom. Got them exactly where I want them," I said with great optimism. "This is when all the training, all the effort pays off. Every newspaper in the country will be singing our praises. And Grant can choke on his own arrogance."

I glanced south. Keogh's wing was at the far end of the ridge, holding the trail open for Benteen. Sporadic carbine fire could be heard, for they were only three-quarters of a mile away. Benteen may even have arrived by now, joining with Keogh and coming forward at a trot. As my command waited on the grassy hillside, the alkaline dust subsided and I took off my rawhide jacket, tying it to Vic's saddlebags. Most of the men were in shirtsleeves, their broad hats protecting their eyes from the glaring sun. It was late afternoon now, about 4 o'clock by the reckoning of my late father-in-law's pocket watch. By nightfall the village would be in hand, the noncombatants secured, and the warriors on their way back to the reservations.

I had Corporal Henry Voss, my regimental bugler, issue *Officer's Call*. Tom and Lieutenant Cooke from by staff were already with me. Captain George Yates, Lieutenant Smith, Dr. Lord, 2nd Lieutenant Thomas Crittenden, and 2nd Lieutenant Harry Harrington arrived within minutes.

"Sturgis?" I asked.

"I think we lost him at the Medicine Tail crossing," Yates belatedly said.

This was not good news. 2nd Lieutenant James Sturgis was the son of Sam Sturgis, the official colonel of the Seventh Cavalry. My immediate superior. Twenty-two years old and fresh out of West Point, this was going to be James' first battle. Apparently it was his last battle. Going home without any Indians, and young Sturgis dead, was not an option if I hoped for another promotion.

"What happened to Kellogg?" Cooke asked, noticing the reporter was missing. As was his mule.

"Haven't seen him since we scouted the ford," Boston said. "Should I go look for him?"

"He'll turn up," I said.

I waited on the hill for nearly twenty minutes, impatient for the moment we could attack. Indians began to approach the fords and wade across. Just a few, at first, and then by the dozens. They seemed to disappear into the tall grass at the foot of the hill.

I ordered Company E back to a line between the hilltop and a deep gully on our left. Smith was a doing a fine job of directing fire, which was slow and controlled. Yates pushed Company F to the left for better contact on Keogh's position, but kept a few to cover our rear. Tom was back and forth all over the field, making sure the ammunition held out and the men were staying calm. No Plains Indians had ever charged a prepared skirmish line over open ground, and the Northern Cheyenne weren't going to do so now.

"We've used half of our .45/70s," Tom reported. "We'll be down to pistol shot in another twenty minutes. Autie, I think we should retreat. There was good ground about four miles back along the ridge."

"That would be surrender, Tom," I protested. "The defeat of the Seventh. Satisfaction for Grant. No, we can still win this."

"Can I shift the wing south?" Tom asked, not really listening.

"Tell Keogh to come up. We'll strike the village with what we have," I decided. "Damn Benteen. Damn that insolent back-stabbing scoundrel."

Tom went to deliver the message himself, riding his Kentucky thoroughbred Athena along the top of the ridge to the cheers of the men. Tom doffed his hat.

"Autie, the damn Indians are encroaching on our rear," Captain

Yates said, sweating from the heat. "They're swinging down around the hill and infiltrating our flank. We need to recall E Company."

I glanced to the top of the hill. Good observation, but exposed from every side. I didn't like it, yet we needed to solidify our defense. I nodded approval to Georgie and he dashed off to reorganize our skirmish line. We had served together since 1863 and he'd never let me down. Annie and the kids would be proud of him.

I heard a sudden explosion of volley fire on the left, down where I knew Jimmy Calhoun's position to be. It must be Benteen, thirty minutes late but finally arriving. It would take ten more minutes for his three companies to cross from the coulee to join Keogh, and another ten minutes to reunite with the command. The valley was filling with Indians. It was going to be close.

"Smith, get the men mounted for a charge," I ordered. "Yates, follow close on Company E to the ford. The moment Keogh and Benteen come up, we will attack."

I got up on Vic, the noblest warhorse in the regiment, and rode to the top of the hill, noticing scores of Indians on the eastern ridges, but all at a respectful distance. More were gathering down to my right at the ford. They would run quick enough with cavalry bearing down on them.

With a few minutes to spare, I reflected on the great events that had brought me to this battlefield. Though last in my class at West Point, I had become the youngest Union general at 23. I had turned back Jeb Stuart at Gettysburg, saving Meade's army from certain defeat, and become a brevet major general by war's end. I had not only captured the first Confederate battle flag at New Bridge, but personally accepted Lee's flag of surrender at Appomattox Courthouse. Or, at least, his offer to parley. After this battle, I would return home to Libbie, rebuild my fortune, and if Grant still delayed my promotion to full colonel, maybe I would run for Congress. It's a wonderful thing to be blessed by Custer's Luck.

"Gen'ral, we got trouble," Bouyer shouted, out of breath. "Keogh. It's Keogh."

I looked back along the ridge where huge dust clouds swirled around the southern end. Then Tom rode up, his face gaunt and filled with desperation. I had never imagined him with such a look.

Tom reined in and slipped from his saddle. I immediately noticed a bullet hole through Athena's side, though the brave horse was still responding to Tom's instructions. The horse loved him as much as he loved her. Then I saw Tom's left leg soaked in blood. He'd been shot through the knee, the bones shattered.

"Tom!" I shouted, rushing to support him.

"It's bad, Autie. Real bad," he said.

"You'll be okay," I said. "Lord! Lord, get over here!"

"It's not about me," Tom said in great pain. "C Company attempted to drive some Sioux back. Got caught in a crossfire. Winchesters and Henrys. When they retreated, the Indians followed. Hundreds. Maybe a thousand. They overran L Company, then fell on Keogh. Jimmy's dead, Autie. So is Myles. They're all dead."

I looked south. A few stragglers were emerging from the dust, protected by Company F's covering fire. Some had horses, most didn't. It was a beaten rabble, not an army.

My God, I thought.

"Form a line around this hill. If any of the horses are wounded, shoot them for cover," I told Yates. "Dr. Lord, get my brother up the hill. We'll hold out until help arrives. Butler! Butler, where are you?"

"Here, General," Sergeant Butler reported.

"Jimmy, you're our last hope. Ride to Reno. Tell him to bring the entire command forward on the double."

"Yes, sir," Butler said, jumping on his horse and riding down the ridge without a second thought. A good man, tough and reliable. I hoped he'd make it through, for his sake if not ours.

For the next ten minutes, I raced around making sure the ammunition packs were taken off the horses, for the horse holders were having trouble controlling them. About twenty men from our south flank finally came in, most from Company C, a few from Company I. I didn't see anyone from Company L.

Commotion on my right. Some Cheyenne had rushed forward waving blankets, scaring Company E's horses. More than a dozen got away, running down the long slope toward the river. One of the gray horses had a helpless soldier bouncing on his back, riding straight into the hands of the enemy. If he had a pistol, he'd best use it on himself before letting the Indians catch him.

I went to kneel by Tom. He was sitting against a dead horse, the Winchester in his hands and four boxes of ammunition lying next to

230

him. Dr. Lord was working on the wound, which looked serious.

"You're not walking anytime soon, Tom," Dr. Lord said.

The doctor, already in poor health, looked very frightened. All around us, soldiers were preparing to fight it out. It didn't seem that we had much choice.

"Boston. Young Autie," Tom said, pointing to our little brother and Maggie's son. What had started for them as a summer lark suddenly wasn't so diverting.

"Smith. Smith, I need Company E," I said.

"Sir, Lieutenant Smith is dead," Sergeant Hughes answered, pointing to the corpse fifteen feet away. An unlucky bullet had struck him through the head.

I looked around and saw several of the men were wounded. Arrows began to fall around us. How had the Indians gotten so close?

"Bouyer! Bouyer!" I shouted.

The scout came running, his trail leathers dirty and tinged with blood. But it wasn't his blood. One hand held a revolver, the other a hatchet.

"Told ya, Gen'ral. I told ya, I told ya, I told ya," he sputtered.

"Yes, you told me. Now I need you to take Company E. Break out to the river," I said. "Company F will cover your charge and then follow. Hurry, there isn't much time."

As Bouyer ran off, I turned to Tom.

"We'll get you on a horse. Lead the charge. Take Boston and Autie with you. The regimental staff will cover you from here."

"There's no riding out for me, brother," Tom answered. "I'm going to die right here where I am now. But I'm not selling my life cheap. You should lead the charge."

Something hit me in the chest. Something hard. It wasn't an arrow. I reached under my shirt and found a bloody hole. Probably a spent shell, but painful. As I could still breathe, I doubted the wound was fatal. It was my judgment that had proven fatal. I sat down next to Tom, keeping upright by leaning on my Remington Sporting rifle.

I could hear the screams of the Indians now. War hoops. Heavy gunfire, some of it captured Springfields. A thousand warriors had surrounded the hill, firing and ducking. Firing and ducking. Elusive targets, and most of my men weren't trained as sharpshooters. Steel-tipped arrows fell around us. I soon ran out of ammunition for my rifle and drew one of the Webley Bulldog pistols. What had happened to Vic? Was he dead? Run off? I would never know.

"Trevilian Station was tough, too," I said to Tom.

"Jumping the Reb lines at Sailor's Creek was no picnic," Tom answered.

He had won his second Medal of Honor at Sailor's Creek, and was shot through the face doing it.

"It's not looking good, Tom," I regretfully reported.

"They've got us this time," he agreed. "Get the boys out, if you can."

It hurt like Hades, but I slowly stood up next to my silk guidon, fired several shots, and turned to my subordinates. Lieutenant Reily was sitting near the top of the hill trying to reload his Colt. He'd been shot in the hand and was bleeding heavily.

"Cooke, Hughes, Voss. Afraid I'll need you to stay with me," I sadly ordered. "Everyone else who can still move, prepare to charge the river. We'll cover you as long as we can. And God help you."

Company E still held the forward position. Company F was near the hilltop. I looked for Georgie Yates but didn't see him. Poor Annie. Poor Libbie.

"Bouyer, get going," I said with a grunt.

To encourage them, Voss blew the *Charge* on his trumpet. Bouyer led about thirty men down the hill, some firing their rifles, most using their Colts. The Indians briefly scattered, giving them a chance.

"Harry, your turn. Charge," I ordered.

Voss blew the trumpet one last time, weakly. He'd taken an arrow to his neck.

With Harrington in the lead, about fifteen men got up and followed Company E toward the big gully. From there they might fight their way through to the river, and the village beyond looked deserted.

"Boston. Autie—get going. That's an order," I insisted.

The young men were scared to death, but it did not take extra motivation to get them moving. There was nothing but doom waiting on the hill. With a final glance back, they rushed to keep up with Company F.

Now I saw hundreds of Indians rising up. They were popping from the grass. Jumping from ravines. Appearing out of nowhere. Some had rifles, some bows and arrows. Many were wearing Seventh Cavalry hats and blouses. Company E battled to the deep gully, their guidon flying, and then disappeared. Company F didn't make it that far, blocked by braves waving tomahawks and clubs. Boston and Young Autie caught up to the faltering skirmish line, firing their pistols. Then they faded from view in the swirling dust.

I fired my Webley, sitting behind a dead horse near Tom. There had been forty or so of us remaining on the hill, but our rate of fire slackened. Cooke fell, fighting gallantly to the last, and then Voss. Riley now had two arrows in him and was still trying to reload his Colt. He should have stayed at the Naval Academy and become an admiral. No Sioux on the high seas.

Tom leaned forward on his dead horse, shouting at the enemy and doing terrible damage with his Winchester. It would be a long time before these heathens forgot such courage.

I should have been as brave, or angry, or frustrated, but I felt nothing. No emotions. No fear. A complete absence of feeling. Until the pain in my chest increased. Perhaps the wound had been more serious than I thought.

I looked for Dr. Lord, but he lay farther up the hill, an arrow in his shoulder. He was trying to treat a private who was already dead.

"Tom," I whispered, starting to feel faint.

I drew my other Webley and fired a round, but doubt I hit anything. My blue and red guidon, the one Libbie had sewn for me, was flapping in a light breeze, held by Hughes as he fought to the end. The sky was blue, streaked with smoke and dust.

"Autie," Tom said, sliding next to me.

Suddenly I was on my back, lying against the dead horse, arms unable to move.

"I'm sorry, Tommy. So sorry," I whispered.

"They're coming up the hill. Nothing we can do will stop them," Tom said. "I won't let them have you. I love you, brother. I love you."

I felt the barrel of a Colt .45 placed against my temple.

The world returned. The real world. Crockett and Slow were staring at me in the glittering firelight. Had they seen what I had seen? The night had turned cold. It was somewhere between midnight and dawn, the full moon drifting over the western horizon. Owls hooted in the woods.

"You okay, George?" Crockett asked.

"I guess so. You?" I said.

"A bit shook. And I thought the Alamo was hellfire," he said.

"You were courageous. And stupid," Slow said with disapproval.

"Yes," I agreed.

Crockett offered me his jug. I took a swig, feeling the jolt. My brow was covered in sweat. My legs felt numb.

"I still don't see the point of these visions," I complained. "Hallucinations prove nothing. Wounded men on morphine see all sorts of strange things, and Bloody Knife often spoke of visions. Nothing ever came of them."

"There was a Sun Dance on the Rosebud after the defeat of the General Crook," Slow said in disagreement. "In this vision, soldiers were seen falling into the camp of the People. The vision was true. We won a great victory on the Greasy Grass."

"Then why are we here? What's all this 'bout a different path?" Crockett asked.

"The vision warned the People not to covet the goods of the white man," Slow explained. "To keep the shirts and trinkets of the white man is to become the white man. The People did not listen."

"You can't blame folks for wanting a better life," I said. "Iron pots are better for cooking than stomach linings. Blankets are valuable in the winter when buffalo hides become scarce. Crops and cattle will feed villages when game is scarce."

"Cherokee learned that. All the Five Nations did. Din't save 'em from losin' thar lands," Crockett said.

"What happened to the Cherokee was a disgrace," I said. "They proved themselves civilized. Can't say that about the Sioux and Cheyenne. They murder homesteaders. Ambush stagecoaches. History proves those who stand in the way of civilization will be pushed aside."

"Not if they fight," Slow said.

"Especially if they fight, not that they don't have good cause," I replied. "If I was an Indian, I would fight for my land. But there comes a time when fighting just makes things worse."

"I will never believe that," Slow insisted.

He reached into his pouch and grabbed another handful of the mystic herbs. I wanted to get away from the fire but reacted too late. There was a puff of smoke, and then a gradual descent into a different reality.

Crockett and I stood as ghosts, observing a pathetic scene. A bleak village of several hundred Indians huddled along a frozen creek, the snow ankle deep. Tall pine trees dripped icy branches. There were a few horses, underweight and scratching at the ground for fodder. Had they belonged to the Seventh, they'd likely have been destroyed.

A stocky chief emerged from his teepee, probably in his late forties but looking ancient. It could have been an older version of Slow, but I wasn't sure. Waiting for him were three men, two wearing the uniforms of Canadian Mounties, the third in civilian dress. They appeared grim.

"Sitting Bull, the Queen Mother can do no more," the civilian said with a British accent.

"My people are not starving," Sitting Bull replied.

The Indian agent looked around at the blank faces. Worn out. Dispirited. Homesick.

"They soon will be," the Brit said.

Sitting Bull nodded his head. It was true.

"Mr. Walsh, the bluecoats still seek revenge for Yellow Hair," Sitting Bull protested.

"The Americans have agreed to your return," Walsh said. "When the snow melts, go to Fort Buford. You will not be harmed."

"This is not the path Tunkasila Wakantanka seeks for my people," Sitting Bull stubbornly resisted.

"The buffalo are gone. The deer are few. Elk are rarely seen," Walsh said. "I do not think your Great Spirit wishes death for your people."

"To surrender is death for my people."

"The Queen Mother will not force you to leave her domain. This is a thing you must decide for yourself," Walsh said.

As the three white men left, a woman cradling a baby emerged from the teepee. She looked worried.

"Can the Blackfeet not help?" she asked.

"No, wife. They have done all they can," Sitting Bull said.

"You named our son for Crow Foot."

"The Blackfeet and the Lakota were once bitter enemies. Now Crow Foot is my friend. We have smoked the pipe. But the Blackfeet are poor, as are we."

"Will you surrender?" Sitting Bull's wife asked.

"I will go south when the snows melt," Sitting Bull said.

It wasn't Canada anymore. I recognized the city. Pittsburgh. And I recognized the man in the elaborate buckskin outfit. It was Bill Cody. A stagecoach drove at a rapid pace around a crowded dirt arena, chased by fierce mounted Indians in war paint. Bonnets flew, lances were waved. Indian war cries filled the air. A brave guard on the stagecoach fired his shotgun as women screamed.

And then there was a bugle call. A charge. U.S. Cavalry rushed from a gate to the rescue at a full gallop. After a brief, bloodless skirmish, the Indians rode off through the same gate the cavalry had appeared from. A thousand spectators rose in their seats, clapping and cheering.

What the hell? I thought.

Then Bill Cody rode into the arena on a magnificent white stallion, the silver saddle glistening. Next to him, on an impressive mount, was Sitting Bull dressed in white fringed leather, a feathered war bonnet draped down his back. I guessed him in his mid-50s. He posed like a cigar store Indian. A mockery of his former self.

"Thank you, ladies and gentlemen, thank you!" Cody shouted. "And thank you, Sitting Bull, and the braves of the noble Sioux Nation."

Most of the people cheered, but not all. Some grumbled in anger. Sitting Bull showed no reaction, remaining stone-faced until he and Cody rode from the arena.

Outside the gate was a colorful collection of tents, almost like a circus. Horses were being watered by young boys. Many of the Indians, and some of the cavalry, were sitting together at a long table eating fried chicken. A black minstrel wandered around playing lively tunes on a banjo. A tiny woman dressed in red leather trimmed with black fringe was surrounded by eager admirers. She wore a large floppy hat and held a small gauge shotgun under one arm.

"Don't let them bother you," Cody said to his companion. "That ruffian who threatened you yesterday got worse than he bargained for. It was good publicity."

"The white man cannot hurt me," Sitting Bull said. "I feel sad for your people. But for a few, they have no wealth. The children go hungry. Money has replaced the Great Spirit in their hearts."

"Nothing wrong with money. I'm paying you fifty dollars a week plus expenses, ain't I?" Cody bragged. "And I don't take any of your autograph money, do I? You get what? Five dollars a scribble?"

"I do not charge the children," Sitting Bull answered.

"Sure would like to sign you for the '86 season," Cody urged. "We'll do the whole Eastern seaboard. New York, Philadelphia, Boston."

"A red man belongs in his wigwam," Sitting Bull said with a touch of satire. "I will go home and tell my people to reject the gifts of the white man."

"You're going home a rich man. You got enough cash now to buy horses and cattle," Cody said.

"And a cabin," Sitting Bull said. "I would like a cabin."

Sitting Bull walked away from Cody, but not in anger. They seemed to get along well enough. Then I saw Sitting Bull smile as he approached the young woman in red leather. I heard him call her Watanya Cicilla. Little Sure Shot.

The scene abruptly changed. I was feeling tired. Crockett stood alongside me, equally weary. I glanced down to see if he held the jug of corn whisky, but his hands were empty.

A few years had passed, or so I supposed. Sitting Bull was in a warm log cabin on a cold day, surrounded by half a dozen family members. A wood burning stove in the corner was frying wheat cakes. Modern cooking utensils hung on the kitchen wall. Nearly everyone was draped in store-bought wool blankets. A small maple cabinet held boxes of sugar, tins of coffee, and several bottles of medicinal cures. Which, in my experience, usually contained grain alcohol. Two of the young men wore the heavy canvas pants popular in the mining camps.

There was a knock on the door.

"Come out, old man. Come out," a Sioux voice demanded.

Sitting Bull wrapped a shawl over his drooping shoulders and went to the door, opening it slowly. There were forty armed Indians dressed as reservation policemen, their blue jackets and gray pants similar to cavalry uniforms. Their black boots were machine-cut leather. A few wore heavy woolen coats. The young policemen were nervous, looking to their leaders for guidance.

"What do you want, Bullhead?" Sitting Bull asked.

"The soldiers at Fort Yates want to see you. They want to know if you encourage the Ghost Dancers," Bullhead said, forcing his way into the cabin.

237

"I will come later," Sitting Bull promised.

"You will come now, before your followers gather," Bullhead insisted.

"You were once my follower," Sitting Bull said.

"That was long ago. Red Tomahawk is getting your horse. We must hurry," Bullhead said.

The tall Indian policeman held the door open, a hand on his holstered pistol. It was an Army Colt .45. His uniform bore lieutenant's bars on the shoulders.

Sitting Bull reluctantly went outside, followed by his wife and older son. The village was made of cabins with stone chimneys, teepees, and slat board shanties. A corral held several horses, and in a pasture beyond was a small herd of cattle. It had snowed recently, the ground slushy. One group of Indian policemen, a dozen or so, stood near Sitting Bull's cabin, the others lingering back.

Before long, Sioux were arriving from all over the Hunkpapa village, possibly two hundred men, women and children, most but not all bundled against the cold. The Indian policemen grew worried, outnumbered five to one. A burly private brought a horse from the corral that looked like the same one Bill Cody had ridden, though it probably wasn't. The horse was fitted with a sturdy western saddle like those made in St. Louis.

"Get on your horse," Bullhead said.

"I will not," Sitting Bull answered.

Several of the Indian police readied their rifles. Ironically, they carried Springfield carbines. The crowd grew angry. They had weapons, too. A few carried Winchesters.

"Do not cause trouble, old man. You will go to the fort," Bullhead demanded.

"Maybe, but not now," Sitting Bull said, turning back toward the cabin.

"And you will not make him," Sitting Bull's son said, about fifteen years old and holding a pistol.

"Make no trouble, Crow Foot," Sitting Bull said to the hot-head. "These slaves of the white man have no power over me."

Sitting Bull's wife stood in the cabin doorway looking fearful. Two of the Indian policemen moved in closer, prepared to seize the old medicine man if necessary.

"If Agent McLaughlin wishes to know of the Ghost Dancers, he should speak with Kicking Bear," Crow Foot said.

"Your father is their leader," Red Tomahawk said, pointing an accusing finger.

"My father is not leader of the Ghost Dancers. He only asks questions," Crow Foot replied.

I noticed Red Tomahawk was a sergeant, better dressed than most, and more determined than his lieutenant to make the arrest.

"They must not take Tatanka Iyotake," a woman shouted, waving a mallet.

"Bullhead, do not do this," another Indian pleaded, trying to get in the way.

"No more talk. I will put you on the horse," Red Tomahawk said.

The crowd surged forward, pushing and shoving the Indian policemen. I could not understand everything they were saying, but threats were being made. The Indian policemen shifted into a line, but they didn't have much space to deploy. A fistfight broke out.

"Shave Head, drive them back," Bullhead ordered a subordinate.

"My husband, come back into the lodge," Sitting Bull's wife pleaded.

Suddenly a rifle shot rang out. Bullhead spun around, holding his side in pain.

"Catch-the-Bear, do not shoot!" Sitting Bull shouted.

It was too late. Bullhead drew his pistol and shot Sitting Bull in the chest. The surprised leader staggered backward, falling to the ground in a sitting position. Another bullet hit Bullhead, killing him, and then Shave Head was shot as well. The Indian policemen quickly raised their rifles, firing into the crowd. Crow Foot went to help his father and was shot in the back. Several other men were shot. Even Sitting Bull's horse was shot. In the confusion, the sergeant stepped forward pointing a small pistol.

"No, Red Tomahawk, do not shoot my husband!" his distressed wife cried.

Red Tomahawk snarled, took aim at Sitting Bull's head, and pulled the trigger.

The vision seemed over, or so I thought. There was darkness, but no mysterious mist. Crockett and Slow were gone, and I stood alone on a high place. Exalted? No, but I felt a sense of satisfaction. Was I still alive? I couldn't tell. Then light broke from the east, and I saw a huge crowd on the steps of an ornate marble building. There was a podium at the top of the steps, banners, bunting, a band, and a dozen flags waving in a light breeze. The largest flag bore the image of a buffalo. Another also featured a buffalo, but with a bear added to the upper left quadrant. Other flags bore a similar design, the buffalos joined by an eagle, an owl, a stag, and various noble animals.

Then there was movement on the steps of the great building. Distinguished men in fine suits, some with gray beards, emerged from the interior to form a line behind the podium. One was my brother, now an elder statesmen, with Morning Star at his side. Next to him stood Juan Almonte, slightly bent and holding a cane. Algernon Smith followed, then Juan Seguin and many I didn't recognize.

One younger man I did recognize. Dressed in a long gray frock coat and black tie, he looked like an Eastern banker except for his long black hair and a yellow feather in his headband. Holding his hand was a handsome Spanish woman, and with them were five mixed breed children of various ages. The younger man took his place behind the podium as if preparing to give a speech. It was Slow.

The band played a song I didn't know. Thousands stood solemnly with hands over their hearts. And then the band played "Garry Owen", making many cheer. Slow smiled and shook Tom's hand, whispering something confidential. I couldn't hear it, nor could I read his lips, but suddenly I knew. I knew it all.

The sun was rising in a cloudy red haze when my final vision came to an end. The strange blue smoke coming from the campfire had dissipated. Crockett looked exhausted. I could barely move my legs. Slow looked angry, and confused.

"The white man cannot be stopped," he muttered under his breath. "The People will not give up the white man's temptations. They will even kill their own."

Slow jumped to his feet and climbed up the rock facing, standing on top of the cliff in the morning light. I couldn't tell what lesson he had taken from the vision. I wasn't sure what lesson I should take.

"Ain't done that in awhile," Crockett said, finally beginning to stir.

"You've done it before?" I asked.

"Cherokee gots many a trick in thar medicine lodges. Sat down with 'em a time or two, but ne'er quite like that."

"What did you see? Or thought you saw?"

"Back in '12, saw a big forest. Bigger than the world. An' anything in it were mine," Crockett wistfully said. "Didn't turn out that way."

"And now?"

"And now I'm lucky to be here, George. Lucky to get a second chance. But I already knew that."

"I didn't," I replied.

John approached with two cups of hot coffee, giving one to me and the other to Crockett. Autry was making breakfast.

"I was worried, sir," John said.

"No need. Let's have some food. And I'd like to shave," I said.

John heated water to soak my beard, which was a luxury, while Autry made omelets stuffed with goat cheese and peppers. Crockett dunked his head in the creek, returning a few minutes later looking refreshed. I noticed Sergeant Fuentes readying the horses.

"We should do some huntin' on the way back," Crockett said, taking a seat near the campfire.

"That's it? Go hunting? No backwoods wisdom about our journey?" I asked.

"Guessin' you an' the boy will figure that out. If ya ain't already."

"You already know, don't you?" I said.

"It ain't for me to say," Crockett answered.

Fuentes and I were packing the mule when Slow finally came down from the mountain. He looked older. And grim.

"I made a mistake," Slow said.

"Bigger than the one I made at the Little Big Horn?" I asked, hoping to cheer him up.

"You lost an army. I lost a nation," he answered.

"Maybe you should think on gettin' it back?" Crockett said, walking up with his freshly cleaned rifle. He wasn't joking about the hunting trip.

"I don't understand," Slow said.

"Boy, yer nation ain't lost. No yet. And George ain't lost 'is army. You all should think on that," Crockett advised.

Crockett didn't elaborate, getting on his horse and slowly riding out of camp. I sent Fuentes to join him. The country could be dangerous for a lone rider.

"David speaks strangely," Slow complained as we mounted our

horses.

"We just traveled backward, and forward, and sideways in time. Don't you find that a little strange?" I asked.

"No," he replied.

We rode through green valleys, camping near a gorgeous blue lake. John and Fuentes went fishing while I built a fire. John and the sergeant made an interesting pair, for John's Southern accent was thick and Fuentes only knew the basics of English. They returned with a fat string of trout. Slow made the coffee, which surprised me. Just before sunset, we heard a rustling in the meadow. A herd was approaching the lake, possibly deer or elk. Hopefully not moose.

"Finally," Crockett said, reaching for his rifle.

I found my sporting rifle and followed Crockett to the meadow, Slow just a few paces behind.

"Quiet, boys, don't wanna spook 'em," Crockett warned.

We stopped at the edge of the trees, and then stared. We were not stalking deer or elk. Or moose. It was a small herd of shaggy beasts not often seen in California.

"Tatanka," Slow whispered, pushing Crockett's rifle aside.

"Buffalo," I repeated in awe.

It could not be a coincidence. As much as I rejected mysticism, or spiritualism, or any of the nonsense charlatans use to fleece common folk, this seemed too great a coincidence to ignore. And, admittedly, I do believe in Custer's Luck.

"I understand now," Slow said. "We have delayed too long already."

"Yes. Let's get back to headquarters," I agreed. "We must start for Texas at once."

————————

"You must seduce the Indians," Slow answered, entering *La Sirena* dressed in a gray business suit. His dark brows were bent in thought, the long black hair brushed back.

"Do what?" Crockett asked.

Crockett, Santa Anna and I were deep in conference. Plans were being made.

"If the Indians of this land are to remain free, they must live with the white man, for there will soon be too many to fight," Slow

242

explained. "I once thought we must reject the white man's ways to preserve our traditions, but I was wrong. To keep our land, the People must have wealth. Banks. Mines. Ranches. Lawyers. Instead of fighting the government, we must be the government."

"It is the only way to guarantee liberty," Santa Anna agreed. "When the monarchy in Spain no longer served the Mexican people, we established our own laws and institutions."

"In'dans kin be stubborn 'bout changin' ther ways," Crockett warned.

"Women like iron pots and knives. And shovels and blankets. Warriors want guns. Metal shoes for their horses. Cloth shirts," Slow said. "We will take gold from the mountains to build towns."

"The Sioux prefer to chase the buffalo," I said.

"Without strength, the buffalo will disappear. And the People will lose their land," Slow answered. "Is this not correct?"

"I'm afraid it is, but you're asking a lot," I said.

"It will not be easy, but Wakan Tanka has made the new path clear," Slow said.

I paused to look out the window toward San Francisco Bay. The harbor was filled with trading ships. The town was bustling with white immigrants, Indians, Californios, Chinese, and freed slaves. It was a new empire, beholding to none. And if fortune was kind, it was an empire that would stretch to the Gulf of Mexico, its liberties safe under the Kellogg Code. Could the Sioux be brought into such a union?

"Slow, if that's what you want, I'll help anyway I can," I offered.

"Me, too," Crockett promised.

"It is why you are here," Slow said. "And I must no longer be Slow. I am now a man. My name is Tatanka Yotanka."

Custer was a man of many flaws. Where a great chief keeps the People first in his thoughts, Custer saw only himself. Where a great hunter sees a vast horizon filled with bounty, Custer saw only his next kill. And where a great leader inspires followers to a noble cause, Custer would summon those about him as servants. I did not think Custer completely at fault for these failures, for it is the white man's way to dismiss the Great Spirit's wisdom. But in one respect, Custer was unequaled. When it came time to fight, none pursued battle with more desire for victory.

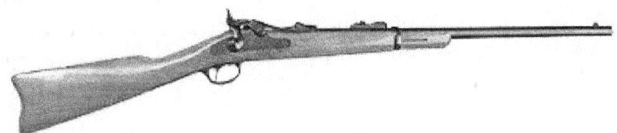

Chapter Nine
RIDING EAST

Three days after returning to San Francisco, a new proclamation was issued calling for volunteers. Each would receive six hundred acres of prime land for a year of service and full citizenship for their families. And able-bodied men who did not volunteer might find an unfriendly government when I returned. Turnout was good, for I only had enough horses to mount three hundred troopers. The remainder of the volunteers would stay behind to garrison California, bound by oath to our flag. Within the week, we were ready to march.

"Gots my boys ready," Crockett reported.

"Antonio wants to go, too. Who's going to govern our country?" I asked.

It was my last night in the Presidio. Everyone had been busy gathering supplies and readying the equipment. We would take no cannon, and the wagon train would only go as far as Warner Ranch. From there we would move fast on the Custer Road.

"I'm still president of Texas. It's my job ta git back thar," Crockett said, quite correctly.

"Maybe Slow can govern California?" I said.

"Bet he could, but 'e's got 'is own command," Crockett said.

"His own what?"

"Gathered fifty Indians, an' 'bout twenty squaws off his own lands. Theys ready ta come with us," Crockett explained.

"Guess I shouldn't be surprised," I said.

Santa Anna entered my office. Rather than the elegant blue and gold uniform he wore during office hours, or the trim business attire that I often envied, he was dressed in frontier leather. He looked a bit silly, for unlike myself or Crockett, Santa Anna simply could not shuck off his air of sophistication so easily.

"My battalion is formed, General Custer," Santa Anna said, saluting.

"No salutes from you, General Santa Anna," I protested. "If we ride together, it will be as equals. But I would rather you stay and govern this ungovernable city."

"There is no need. Señora Richardson will rule the council while we are gone," he replied.

"Maria Antonia?" Crockett said.

"Señora Richardson is the wife of San Francisco's most prominent merchant. Her father serves as commandant of Sonoma," Santa Anna said. "She has the respect of the Californios, the Indians, and the Church. As a woman, she will not cause rivalries among the administrators we leave behind. And she does not suffer fools."

"It's a brilliant choice," I praised.

"Of course," Santa Anna agreed. "Inés is preparing dinner for us at the Black Swan. A final banquet before the heroes leave for Tejas."

"Tony, I respects ya an' all, but I gots ta ask. What are you a wantin' in Texas?" Crockett asked.

"If the Americans seize Tejas, my people will be oppressed," Santa Anna said. "If the Buffalo Flag prevails, my people will come and go as they please. They will share in the wealth. They will have a voice. Isn't this true, George?"

"Do you hope to be their voice?" I asked.

"I already am," he replied.

"Antonio, if you want to run against Crockett for president of Texas, that's your right," I said. "I might even vote for you. One of you might want to run for president of California someday. As long as I'm still the general, I don't much care."

"What about civilian authority?" Crockett inquired.

"Ask me again in twenty years," I answered.

Soon we had another visitor, a very young man in a blue cavalry uniform and a Colt .45 strapped to his waist.

"Hello Tatanka Yotanka," I said, still trying to pronounce it correctly.

246

"Tatanka is easier to say," he suggested.

"I hear you've raised your own army," I said.

"My family is in Texas. Morning Star, Walking-In-Grass, Spotted Eagle," Tatanka explained. "For my people to be free, Texas must be free."

"Guess we've all got work to do," I replied.

We rode at dawn to the sound of the regimental band playing "The Girl I Left Behind Me". The townspeople cheered, for despite the Buffalo Flag's stringent laws, the land was at peace. I rode at the head of the column, tipping my hat.

"Ya did a good job here, General Custer," Crockett said, riding at my side.

"It wasn't so hard," I replied. "My officers and I maintained martial law in the South after the Rebellion. Suppressed the Ku Klux Klan. We instilled order on a lawless frontier. Those were difficult challenges."

"And these ain't?" he asked.

"The 1830s are a simpler time, David. Tom, Fresh, even Bouyer, we've all remarked on it. People are less bloodthirsty."

"Seems we've had our share of trouble," Crockett disagreed.

"Not like Antietam, or Shiloh. Or Cold Harbor. You've never fought a real war. Not like the war we fought. Hell, Meade lost more men at Gettysburg than died in the entire War of 1812."

"Let's hope people never need to know of a Shiloh or Gettysburg," Crockett said.

The Camino Real had been a crude merchant road on our arrival, now it was a thoroughfare of ranches, stables, farms and taverns. Fresh horses and mules were provided along our route, in accordance with set contracts. Within a week we were in Los Angeles, and then turned southeast for Warner Ranch. It was there that I said goodbye to Vic.

"Why do you leave Vic behind? He has never failed you. He will not fail you now," Tatanka said.

"My old friend has done his duty," I said, feeding Vic apples as I hugged his neck. "He has carried me from Fort Lincoln to Crockett's Fort across forty years. I don't want to lose him on some Texas battlefield."

"He wishes to serve," Tatanka protested, for he had spent more time riding Vic in the last year than I had.

"And I wish him to live," I said.

"Is Tejas to be your last stand?" Tatanka asked.

"I still have Custer's Luck," I answered.

Warner Ranch was a small town with a fort now, a key step along the road to Yuma, but it remained informal. The mission had reestablished some of the farm land, vaqueros continued to herd cattle, and prospectors searched the hills for gold. Father Tomás had procured a nice little ranch for me off the main road near the hot springs. Someday I would build a sanitarium where victims of consumption could come for a cure.

Orders had been issued to clearly mark the trail, but the extent to which the order had been carried out surprised me. Beyond the stakes pounded into the ground every twenty yards were rock cairns, dyed leather markers hanging from trees, and white-washed crosses. Apparently marking the trail had become a sort of game for the travelers, each seeking to make their contributions.

When we reached the edge of the desert, I ordered all of the horses unsaddled. They would be walked, not ridden, with mules our primary form of transportation. Several vaqueros suggested this was an unnecessary precaution, the long gaps between waterholes now peppered with cisterns, but I wanted to take no chances. We needed healthy mounts for the long march though west Texas.

The trail from Warner Ranch to Yuma was uneventful. The Indians of southern California tended to be tame, more interested in farming than ambushing strangers. Reports from the commandant of Los Angeles, and Father Tomás of the San Gabriel Mission, gave favorable reports of local conditions. As we approached the Colorado River, a cannon shot announced our arrival.

"Trouble, George?" Santa Anna asked, once again mounted on his tall Spanish gelding while I was riding Traveller.

"Standard practice, Antonio," I said. "Sergeant Santos, answer with a six-gun volley."

Fort Yuma was on a small elevation guarding the ferry on our side of the river. It wasn't a big fort, but boasted two 6-pounders and a staff of twenty, most assigned to patrol duties. The town of Yuma on the opposite bank had grown considerably since my visit eighteen months before. Near the confluence of the Colorado and Gila Rivers, it had become a hub for New Mexico trade.

And there were docks. Someone had figured out that supplies could be brought upriver from the Gulf of California and started a shipping business with a small steamboat. Of course, I knew this had been standard practice in the 1870s when Yuma had been a Quartermaster Depot for the U.S. Army, but I hadn't thought to exploit it myself. I didn't know if Robinson's Landing or Port Isabel had been founded yet, but guessed they soon would be.

We received a hardy welcome by the thousand or so residents, mostly Quechan Indians and Mexicans. A Catholic mission been established by some ambitious Franciscans, and the hills were filled with cattle brought in from the west. The town seemed peaceful, the people were well armed with muskets and even a few Baker rifles. Desperados would think heavily before raiding such a settlement. A Buffalo Flag flew proudly from the presidio.

We stayed a day to rest the animals, enjoying a fiesta where Santa Anna was the guest of honor, and then headed east. We were thirty miles short of Tucson, in the heart of Apache country, when a group of horsemen approached from the southwest. At first I thought they were cavalry, wearing blue jackets and flying a guidon, but I soon realized that was not the case.

"Chiricahua, Gen'ral. Looks like they has massacred one of our troops. Took their uniforms," Bouyer said.

"Skirmish line, sir?" Captain Autry asked, looking nervous by their rapid approach.

It was probably the smart move, but something about them didn't speak of a hostile force. I'd ridden the Great Plains for years. One gets a feeling for such things. Besides, the land was flat and open, the only protection sagebrush and cactus. The thirty or so riders could not hope to prevail against a force of three hundred.

"It is Cheis," Tatanka said, riding next to me on a sturdy sorrel Crockett had bought for him. Not that Tatanka couldn't afford to buy his own horses.

"I remember. He was the young chief in the village that Carson attacked," I said.

"It was not an attack. We took back that which was stolen," Tatanka said, insulted by the implication. Which struck me as strange, for the Sioux are notorious horse thieves.

249

"Crockett, take the men on to Tucson, I will speak with our strange comrades of the trail," I ordered.

"Think'in that's a good idea?" Crockett asked, his Springfield laid across his lap.

"I reckon so, David," I responded, my weapons holstered.

"I will stay with General Custer," Tatanka announced.

The command rode on, kicking up dust now that the spring rains were gone. Tatanka and I waited for the riders, our mounts impatient. I dismounted and gave each a handful of grain, whispering encouragement. Tatanka glared at the newcomers. He had not liked the Apache on first acquaintance, and nothing had changed since.

"General Custer, greetings," Cheis said, leaping from his stout mustang to shake hands. His English had improved.

"Greetings, Cheis. Have you married the daughter of Mangas Coloradas?" I asked.

"Dos-teh-seh is my wife," he replied, thumping his chest.

Again I was impressed with this man. Six feet tall, broad-chested, with classical features and piercing gray eyes. I wondered if there was a Spaniard in his family tree, possibly an aristocrat. His blue woolen jacket had silver buttons down the front and captain's bars on the shoulders. The trousers were gray, reinforced in the seat with white canvas.

"You ride as a cavalry battalion. May I ask why?" I said.

"We are Company B, 8th Cavalry, reporting to Governor Sharrow," Cheis replied, partly in English and partly in Spanish. "We are summoned to Tucson for the Great War."

Cheis raised a Springfield rifle and shouted. His men shouted even louder. They were all young and eager for adventure.

"Texas is a far distance, my friend. Far from the land of the Chiricahua," I warned, for I had doubts such volatile warriors could be controlled.

"We will win glory in battle," Cheis said. "We will take many rifles and many horses from our enemies. We will steal cattle from the Mexicans. We will return with boots, blankets, tobacco and coffee. And the silver promised by Governor Sharrow."

Cheis waved to his color bearer, who unrolled a swallow-tailed version of the Buffalo Flag. I suddenly realized these were my soldiers, riding under my colors, like the Apache scouts who had served General Crook. I glanced for Tatanka's reaction, expecting him to be displeased, but his mood was one of contemplation.

"All men seek glory," Tatanka said.

"Captain Cheis, it will be my honor to ride with you," I said. "But your men must maintain order. *Mantener el orden*. The reputation of the Apache is fierce. Many will be afraid if you do not show proper discipline."

"General Custer, we trained for six moons in El Paso with Governor Sharrow," Cheis said. "Company B can outride any troop, outfight any unit, and outdrink any man in the army. We know our duty."

I sensed he did. He was a proud young man at the head of a proud unit. It reminded me of my 5th Michigan Wolverines.

"Then let us move on to Tucson. We can be there by nightfall," I said.

"Sooner, General. We know a quicker route than the road taken by wagons," the chief said. "And now that we serve together, you should use the name given me by my white allies."

"And what would that be?" I asked.

"I am known as Cochise."

My detachment reached Tucson in the late afternoon, an hour before the main column. The fields were rich with spring planting, but only a few women and children were working the crops. A handful of old men armed with muskets watched from the presidio walls. They did not acknowledge our approach. As I was riding with the Apache, I could not fault them.

The town was in disarray, the north side of the river virtually deserted. I found scattered wagons near a pontoon bridge formed in a circle, but saw no horses and few mules. The citizens of Tucson appeared holed up on the south side of the river. A Buffalo Flag flew from the roof of the church.

"Mexicans hide from the Chiricahua," Cochise said.

"They fly the Buffalo Flag, my friend. You must earn their trust," I scolded.

"This Governor Sharrow has taught us, but it is not an easy lesson," Cochise agreed, reining in near the river.

After a few minutes, Señor Jose Juarez came out from the main gate and walked across the plank and barrel bridge, bobbing up and down with the rough spring run-off. He looked worried but composed, unhappy about the company I was keeping.

"General Custer, I have word from Santa Fe," the alcalde said, reaching into the pocket of his green frock coat.

The note was from Bill Sharrow. I gave it a quick read.

"What is it?" Crockett asked.

"Sharrow needs help in Santa Fe. Seems a large wagon train has arrived from Missouri filled with unruly immigrants," I said, reading the note again.

"Should I take a few of the boys?" Crockett offered.

"No, David. We have more urgent business. Captain Cochise, please bivouac your men upriver," I said. "Rest the horses. Tomorrow, you must ride for Santa Fe."

"We would ride to Texas," Cochise said.

"My friend, Governor Sharrow needs you to protect this land. Can I count on you to keep the peace?"

"Company B will help Governor Sharrow keep the peace," Cochise promised. "I will ride to Texas with Custer."

"Cochise—"

Cochise put up his hand, the sharp gray eyes focused. He waited until I was forced to listen.

"I have told my people that I will go to Texas. I have told my wife," Cochise said.

There was no use in arguing, so I waved Cochise on to inform his company they would be riding to Santa Fe without him.

––––––––––

West Texas is an empty place except for tumbleweeds and rattlesnakes. The tall mesas can be beautiful, but they get monotonous after a while, and thick scrub brush often inhibits access to the rivers, especially in the late spring. Fortunately, the Custer Road was well built, the way stations adequately stocked, and water readily available. We moved fast, but not so quickly as to exhaust the mounts. I'd finally learned my lesson on that score.

It was early May when we finally reached the Medina River and found the first evidence of trouble. The tiny village of Castroville had expanded with the tents of refugees from San Antonio, which we learned was under siege. Most were women and children, with just enough men to discourage the Comanche. Their ammunition was low but we had none to spare. I could only promise that if they were attacked, the Seventh Cavalry would seek revenge. And then we moved on.

Nearly twenty miles later, just short of Leon Creek, we saw smoke rising from the east. It was not a small fire. I guessed the San Antonio was being burned but could not be sure. Being late in the day, and with eight miles to go, we would not be there before nightfall.

"We should press on," Santa Anna said.

"A night movement could be dangerous," I disagreed.

"If General Sesma had seized Béjar on the 22nd like I ordered, the rebel garrison would not have taken shelter in the Alamo on the 23rd," Santa Anna recalled. "The Army of Operations suffered hundreds of casualties instead of a handful. That mistake should not be made again."

"What do you think, Crockett?" I asked.

"Shot more bears at night than in the day, George," Crockett answered.

"Then we march. Order the command to tie down everything that makes noise, especially their sabers," I said. "Column of fours, maintain separation between the units. And no shooting without orders. If the rebels have occupied the town, I don't want them to know we're nearby."

"May I have the honor of the lead?" Santa Anna requested.

"You may, sir, and good luck," I agreed.

We crossed the creek in good order. The night was fairly clear and we had the benefit of a waxing moon. I looked for Tatanka, for I did not want him lost in the confusion. Or riding ahead with Antonio, as he was inclined to do. He surprised me by returning just before sunset with a band of Lipan Apache.

"This is Chief Flacco and his first-born, Flacco the Younger," Tatanka introduced. "They have fought the Mexicans, and they have fought Comanche. Now they wish to fight for Texas."

"Greetings, warriors," I said, not sure if they spoke English.

"This is a time to stand with friends," Flacco said with a rough accent.

The elder chief was a vigorous gray-haired man about fifty years old. His son appeared about twenty and every inch a horseman. I knew the Lipan to range southwest of San Antonio, sometimes as far as the Rio Grande. Flacco had a good reputation with white settlers in the region, and I had read stories of him riding with the Texas Rangers.

"You are welcome allies," I said, shaking his hand. "We have food and drink to share. Your horses may graze with ours."

As the Apache went to make camp, I turned to Tatanka.

"Where did you find them?" I asked.

"They have found us. I will ride with them to Béjar," Tatanka said.

"Those Indians are brave, but they have no training," I complained. "Stay with the regimental staff. I may need you to ride messenger."

"I will learn how to fight in the badlands of Texas," Tatanka insisted.

"Flacco will be a good teacher, I'm sure. Be careful," I said.

As Tatanka disappeared into the dark, Crockett rode up. I had attached my staff to his troop, following a few hundred yards behind Santa Anna.

"Guess we is ready. What do you reckon we'll find?" Crockett asked.

"Bears," I said.

The farms leading into San Antonio were deserted, the fields stripped clean of crops and livestock. A cannon sounded in the distance, and flames were seen as we crested a hill overlooking the river valley. Some were bonfires, at least one was a building near the plaza.

"Crockett, Cochise, Chief Flacco, you'll ride with me," I decided. "Autry, advance on La Villita. Hold the ford open in case we get in trouble."

I motioned for our group to make a right oblique, leaving the main road toward a river crossing a few miles downstream from Béjar, then riding northeast through pastures until reaching the Alameda.

The Alameda was long dirt road running east and west, heavily lined by cottonwoods. In my own time, it had been known as Commerce Street. Using the trees to screen our movement, we soon reached the top of a hill where Tom, Kellogg and I had first seen the besieged Alamo two years before. It was besieged again, but not with the force I expected.

"What do you make of it?" Crockett asked, squatting next to me in the tall damp grass. I studied the scene with my binoculars.

"There's an army camped north of the Alamo, and I see a battery posted on Powder House Hill," I observed. "Can't tell who is who."

"Do we still hold Béjar?" Crockett asked.

"Santa Anna is about to find out. He's only a mile from San Pedro Creek," I said.

I waited to hear if there'd be gunfire. I hadn't thought what the reaction would be to a largely Mexican force approaching in the dark. Would Santa Anna suffer the same fate as Stonewall Jackson?

"Who goes there?" a voice shouted from our right. It was a Southern accent, possibly Georgia.

"Who's askin'?" Crockett shouted back.

"Fannin's Volunteers," the picket announced.

"Are we holdin' that Alamo?" Crockett deceptively asked.

"Fer awhile longer. General Fannin's got us pullin' back to Goliad," the sentry explained.

"Why's that?" Crockett persisted.

"Scouts say an army is coming this a way. Mostly Mex'cans and In'dins. Where ya been?" Fannin's man said.

"Californy," Crockett answered, firing a shot in the air.

There was a burst of activity all along the ridge. We could hear officers calling for their men. I stood up and fired my pistol into the dark, and then Crockett's company fired a volley.

"Charge!" I shouted, running forward with my sword drawn.

We were only sixty strong, with no idea of our opposition's strength, but we were on their flank, like the Rebs at Chancellorsville, and under cover of darkness. I could see movement against the light of their campfires while we were just shadowy phantoms.

We crossed the Alameda toward Powder House Hill, covering ground quickly toward the old weather-beaten watchtower that spied down on the Alamo a thousand yards away. A guard post was overrun, two men surrendering and two others killed. I tried to stay in the lead but some of the younger boys were getting ahead, slashing with swords and jabbing with lances. One daring private had a bayonet mounted on his Baker rifle and drove it though a surprised picket's chest. I wished it had been Fannin.

The enemy began shooting back, but the resistance was sporadic, without structure. I supposed they thought us an army of Mex'can and In'dins. When two gray-garbed militia suddenly loomed on my right, I drew a Bulldog and shot both of them. One went down forever, the other started to crawl off, then twisted around and pointed a pistol at me. Corporal Garcia shot him in the head.

"Occupy the ridge!" I shouted, for I didn't want my men spreading out toward the cemetery in the dark.

We pushed on toward the campfires of the ridgetop outpost. There was some hand-to-hand fighting, grunts and groans, and the occasional wounded man, but no organized resistance. I noticed Cochise and several Lipan Apache rounding up horses.

The watchtower was abandoned by the time I got there, two bronze 8-pounders having been captured. The rebels had broken northeast into the wilderness, leaving most of their supplies. Even their bedding, which Crockett's men quickly scooped up.

"Should we mount a pursuit?" Crockett asked, out of breath.

"No, Colonel. Custer's luck got us this far. I'm not going to press it," I said.

I climbed up on a low adobe wall to look at San Antonio. Our action on the ridge had been noticed, but the garrison in the town were not sallying out. Much closer, the Alamo could be seen by the light of a large bonfire. There was activity around the corral. I guessed enemy militia still had a force occupying the battered mission.

"Crockett, have your men hold this position," I ordered. "Garcia, you're with me."

I returned to the thicket where we had left our horses and mounted Traveller, sheathing my sword and putting the Bulldog back in the holster. My regimental staff was helping Captain Badillo secure the hill, but I only needed one orderly.

"Pedro, will you carry my personal guidon?" I offered.

The young Tejano smiled and took the flag, mounting his spirited stallion to ride at my side. The skirmish had been his first real battle, and he'd performed well. His parents would be proud.

We rode down the Alameda slowly, the Alamo off to our right, the tall cottonwoods on the left. The ground leveled out as we crossed over an irrigation ditch and approached the bridge. But it was no longer the crude suspension bridge I had known. Keogh had replaced it with a log bridge made of cypress and cedar, sturdy enough for freight wagons. I saw a redoubt on the other side.

"*Quién va allí?*" a sentry shouted.

"*Custer de la séptima caballeria,*" Garcia answered, halting twenty feet back of the bridge.

"*Tomas?*" the voice said.

"George," I replied.

"What's that?" a Virginia voice asked.

"That you, Baugh?" I asked.

"General Custer?" Baugh said.

"Thought you deserted on me," I replied.

"Came back, sir. Brought a company New Orleans Grays with me," he boasted.

"Glad to hear it, John. May I pass?" I requested.

"Be careful. Town's all shot up," he warned.

The bridge appeared weakened by cannon shot, creaking under the horse's hooves, but there seemed no danger of collapse. The sentries we saw in the struggling moonlight were bedraggled. Worn out. Several had been wounded but were still on duty. Baugh was once again in his gray uniform, though tattered.

"My compliments, señors," I said, offering the brave men a salute.

Garcia and I rode up the muddy road toward the plaza. Many of the small farm houses were wrecked, the fences torn up. I saw where Green Jameson had erected a wall around the plaza enclosing the church, presidio and many of the old adobe buildings. On the far side of town, I saw Santa Anna's troops walking their horses in our direction. There was no formal gate, but several men pulled open a barricade for us to enter. Campfires and lanterns lit the area.

"George, this is a surprise," Keogh said, rushing up as I dismounted. The man looked like hell, thin, ragged and bearded. His command looked equally stressed.

"General Keogh, looks like you've had a time," I said, reaching to shake hands.

"Two weeks of hard fighting, sir. Burleson's men came in from the east, Fannin from the south. I think they were going to make a final effort until they heard you were coming," Keogh said.

"We found Fannin's rearguard on Powder House Hill. Did Burleson leave without him?" I asked.

"Our spy says the two of them have been fighting like cats and dogs," Keogh said. "Houston hates Burleson so much, he refused to come. Lucky for us these Texians spend more time fighting each other than us."

"Losses?"

"Eighty-seven dead at last count. Close to two hundred wounded," he reported. "Damn Rebs got it worse, most likely, but no way of knowin' for sure."

"Where's my brother?"

"*La Casa de Caminar-en-la-Hierba*," Keogh said, pointing toward Main Street.

"Where?"

"Your old headquarters," Keogh explained. "Walking-in-Grass started a dormitory there for orphans. They make blankets. At the moment, it's a hospital."

"Tom's wounded?"

"Early in the fight, but he should make it," Keogh said. "Young Harrington weren't so lucky. Shot though the heart. Smith may lose his arm. Bill Cooke led a raid behind the enemy lines. We haven't heard from him in several days."

I felt like this was my fault, but disguised my thoughts. This was no time for introspection.

"Thanks, Myles," I said, gripping his shoulder.

I heard a cheer go up. Or was it a jeer? Santa Anna rode into the light of the bonfires, much to the surprise of all. The Tejanos in our numbers were encouraged, old wrongs forgotten. I must admit, the dictator looked grand on his white horse wearing a cocked hat, the gilt sword hanging at his side. He smiled graciously, especially to the ladies.

"We heard you took him in," Keogh whispered.

"Best we gather every ally we can," I quietly replied, for Keogh's army looked more defeated than victorious. "Help Santa Anna quarter his troops. Officer call at dawn."

I went to my former headquarters, a fine hacienda across the street from the San Fernando Cathedral, dreading what I might find. Tom had been wounded before, most seriously at Sailor's Creek, where a Reb had shot him while the daring scalawag was seizing a Confederate battle flag.

"General," Sergeant Voss said, jumping from a chair at the door of the hacienda.

"Henry, you hurt, too?" I said.

"Just lost a finger, sir. I'll still be sounding my trumpet," he said, holding up the bandaged hand streaked with blood.

Without thinking, I embraced my young subordinate, happy to see him alive and with such courage. Voss was surprised and uncomfortable with the gesture.

"General Custer is inside, sir. Should be awake," Voss said.

I entered slowly. The hall was lit with oil lamps. I heard the moans of the wounded. There were a dozen women, Mexican, Indian and a few whites, tending thirty or forty soldiers in the former dining room. One looked up, her eyes growing wide, and she rushed toward me.

"Autie, you've come," Isabella said, keeping her voice low despite obvious excitement.

"Not too late, I trust. How is your father? Your brother?" I asked, giving her a hug.

"My father is well. He moved what he could of the armory to Bowie's *casa*," Isabella said. "Juan rode away with Bill. We haven't heard from them in days."

"They'll be fine. Cooke's come through worse than this," I said.

"Tom is in the master bedroom with Morning Star. He'll be glad to see you," Isabella said.

"I can only hope," I replied.

We passed through the outer rooms, stopping among the men to whisper encouragement. I recognized many, some of them from the original Seventh Cavalry, some from the Alamo garrison who had once served Bowie and Travis. The majority I did not recognize, volunteers Keogh had recruited during my absence. I paid them my attentions, too.

"Autie?" Morning Star said, looking up from a chair next to a quilt covered bed.

I saw Tom propped up in the candlelight, his face pale and chest wrapped in bandages. He was holding a Spanish bible. Morning Star rushed to embrace me, tears in her eyes. Odd, I thought, for I'd always thought her more stoic. I took the red scarf from around my neck and dabbed her face.

"It's going to be all right," I said.

259

Tom seemed half asleep until noticing me at his side.

"Forgot to duck?" I asked.

"What are you doing here?" Tom weakly replied.

"Ghost walk."

"Long way for that," he said.

"We've made longer journeys," I replied.

"Come alone?"

"Brought Crockett, Santa Anna, and three hundred good men. What's our assignment, sir?"

"Conquer Texas," Tom said, resting back and closing his eyes.

I quietly went to the far side of the room. Walking-in-Grass was sitting by the fire with three young apprentice nurses, the ancient toothless woman looking at me with large black eyes. She had become the mother of my regiment after our transition from another place and time, and now she was revered by hundreds more. I knelt at her feet, taking her wrinkled hand.

"Como estás, madre?" I asked in Spanish, for I'd never learned to speak Lakota.

"I am well, George," she answered in English.

"Thank you for taking care of my brother."

"One accepts no thanks for helping family."

"How is Spotted Eagle? I hoped he could come to California," I said, for I'd grown fond of the young lad in our travels.

"My grandson is to the east, riding scout for Colonel Seguin. There is much danger in this land," she said.

"I'll bring him back safe," I promised, possibly foolishly.

I caught a catnap near the back door to the stables and was up before dawn, finding a water bowl to wash my face. An early morning mist rose from the river, invading the downtown streets. There was the rank smell of decaying bodies not yet moved to the cemetery.

"How is the husband of my sister?" Tatanka asked, emerging from the fog in a mud-streaked buckskin outfit. He had Bowie's knife in a sheath on his belt and a carbine slung over his shoulder, looking older than his years.

"Thomas should be fine if there is no infection. Morning Star and Walking-in-Grass sit at his bedside. Where have you been?"

"My command has taken position north of the Alamo, awaiting orders," he replied.

"Burleson?" I asked.

"Running for Gonzales," Slow reported. "Only the Alamo stands against us."

We walked across the plaza, past the looming church, and into the presidio, finding the surviving officers gathering outside the hundred-year-old governor's palace. Though, in fact, the single-story hacienda wasn't much of a palace, nor was it used by governors, normally housing Béjar's garrison commander. Nevertheless, it had room for our meeting and a kitchen to prepare breakfast.

Thirty of us found space in the grand dining room, twenty on fine wooden chairs, and the rest on benches or milling about. I saw Keogh, Crockett, Santa Anna, Smith with his wounded arm in a sling, Brister, Baugh, Cochise, and many others, all gritted with determination. I was sorry to hear of young Harrington's fate, having been killed defending the Alamo armory.

"With President Crockett's permission, I now assume command of our country's army," I announced, standing at the head of the table.

I did not cut the best figure, having slept in my clothes, but few looked much better. This was not the spit and polished Union Army enjoying our well supplied bivouac on the Potomac, but a battle-hardened force ready for more. Or so I hoped and expected.

"General Keogh, a report for those of us newly arrived," I requested.

The Irishman stood up, not tall but broad-shouldered, his hair cut close. He'd taken time to clean his uniform and patch the tears.

"The Brazos Convention has moved to San Felipe. They are offering gold to recruits," Keogh said. "Gold they plan to take from California. Thousands of Southerners poured in after the Patricio Massacre, taking Galveston back from the Mexicans. Winter was quiet, but come spring they moved down the coast and occupied Victoria.

"Harrington and I rode to Copano and met with General Filisola, still licking his wounds. We agree to give up Goliad until the rebels were defeated so the army could concentrate on defending Gonzales."

"That worked out fine," Captain Forsyth sarcastically said from the back of the room, accompanied by muttering agreement.

"I'm not entertaining criticism at this time, Mister Forsyth," I rebuked, looking at the other complainers with a glare of warning. No soldier likes to give away a position that was honestly won.

"When Refugio fell to Fannin, Seguin reported that Goliad was in trouble, too," Keogh continued. "On March 22nd, the Rebs took La Bahia and put the garrison to the sword. Two hundred of Filisola's men died, but he escaped to Matamoros. We've heard he's going to abandon Texas entirely. We were forced to fall back on San Antonio and prepare for an attack."

"That's when Tom and I arrived," Smith said, sitting opposite me at the far end of the long table. I hoped Dr. Lord had managed to save his arm, but remembered that General Phil Kearney still had a noble military career even after losing an arm at Churubusco. Until he was shot in the back by rebels in '62.

"Please report, Colonel Smith," I said.

"Señor Seguin had the armory established in the Alamo's barracks, and General Keogh had tightened the fort's perimeter, but Tom wasn't convinced," Smith said. "We started transferring the arsenal to Veramendi House. The powder, shot and molds for the cartridges were already safe when Burleson's cavalry arrived. Henry—that is Major Harrington—thought the tools for making the Springfields could still be saved, but when Fannin launched a night attack, the Alamo was overrun. We lost forty good men, and Tom was wounded trying to save them. Henry died on the south bastion covering the retreat."

Smith appeared spent, resting back in his chair. I wished Cooke was here. No one could present a more comprehensive report than Bill Cooke. Or Tom, who Dr. Lord would not release from his sick bed. I suddenly realized Juan Almonte wasn't here, either, and no one had even mentioned him.

"Captain Forsyth, I believe you had something to say?" I requested.

Forsyth was sitting with Brister, Baugh and Blazeby, all good men who had served at the Alamo. I sensed Forsyth regretted his intemperate words. Something I rarely did.

"The Goliad army was led by Fannin, Tom Rusk and Mirabeau Lamar, sir," Forsyth said. "Two thousand strong. Maybe more. Eight cannon. Burleson came from Gonzales, mostly cavalry and some militia. Three or four hundred. We barely had five hundred men under arms, but proved better than the odds."

A soft cheer rose from the assembly. This was not a beaten army.

"Fought the bastards good for thirteen days, sir," Sergeant Hughes said, side-by-side with Butler, Voss, French and Williamson. "They finally ran out of powder. Ran out of food, too. Most pulled back to Gonzales for supplies, but they left a hundred men in the Alamo, so we expect them back soon enough. A prisoner says Houston is comin' with another thousand men."

Every face in the room suddenly turned in my direction. Béjar was also low on powder, the food nearly gone. And an army of thousands might soon be knocking on our door again, with a legendary commander leading them. I stood up, adjusted my jacket, and walked thoughtfully around the room, a hand on the hilt of my saber. In the past, I might have bristled with arrogance and declared a plan to attack. I still wanted to.

"This has been a noble fight, gentlemen. The Third Battle of San Antonio will go down in the annals of history, but I don't propose a fourth engagement on this ground," I said. "Colonel Crockett, prepare your men to storm the Alamo this afternoon. General Santa Anna, you will command the assault. Lull the garrison into a sense of complacency, then move on them late in the day."

"Thank you for the honor, General Custer," Santa Anna said, departing with his staff. Crockett and Cochise followed, for they had much to do.

"We would have taken the fort in a day or two," Keogh said.

"My men are fresh, General Keogh. We have a good supply of ammunition," I said, for my desire was not to insult him. "Now that the batteries have been chased off Powder House Hill, the Alamo has no flanking protection. How soon can your command be prepared to march?"

"March?"

"I'm not staying here waiting for Houston, or waiting for our enemies to find new lines of supply," I explained. "You have Cooke, Juan Seguin, and I assume Almonte out in the field?"

"Yes, they have orders to harass and delay reinforcements. That's what cavalry does," Keogh said.

"Then we'd better get out there and help," I decided.

The battered town took new energy from my arrival. I had Chief Flacco ride about the streets with his Lipan Apache, reassuring all they were on our side. His warriors were flattered by female attention. I visited the church where dozens of wounded soldiers lay, offering encouragement as General McClellan had done during the Peninsular Campaign, for I needed their loyalty.

Before noon, I went to Veramendi House on Soledad Street just west of the river, passing through the large doors into the entry hall. Parlors lay to the left and right, a large courtyard just ahead. The Veramendi family had been prominent in Texas politics, inspiring Jim Bowie to marry Ursula Veramendi and become part of the Tejano community. Ursula, her parents, and her children died in the cholera epidemic of 1833, but Bowie had kept his prominence. His last words to me as he lay dying in the Low Barracks were to take care of his people. A task I had neglected.

"*Señor Seguin, es bueno verte bien,*" I said, finding the elder statesman near the rear door. Beyond were wagons filled with tools, barrels, and a forge, all hurriedly loaded.

"I am not so well, George. I am a tired old man. It is good to see you," Erasmo Seguin said, embracing me. I noticed Isabella in the courtyard and gave her a smile.

"You rescued the ammunition, and the Springfields," I complimented.

"They did not get the weapons we already made, but they have the molds for the breechblocks," Erasmo explained.

"Don't worry. We'll get them back," I assured him, for if the molds were not still in the Alamo, they could not have gone very far. Not on these muddy Texas roads.

"I have enjoyed your letters from California. You must be very rich now," Erasmo said.

"In time, perhaps we will both be rich. Are we not still partners?"

"We are," he said, glad to be reassured. "What of you and my Isabella?"

"I mean to talk with you of that once we have the time."

"There is something here for you. I had hoped to present it under more auspicious circumstances," Erasmo said, going into the next room and reemerging with a leather rifle sheath. He opened the flap and pulled out a brand new Winchester, complete with silver inlays.

"This is marvelous," I said, testing the rifle's weight and looking down the sights.

"The armory has produced forty of them," Erasmo proudly said.

"Myles has one, and we have one for Colonel Crockett. Before the siege, we had six thousand rounds of ammunition. Most of that was expended, but there are still eight hundred rounds left."

"Are you able to make more?" I asked.

"My shop boys produce two hundred cartridges a day, but more powder would be helpful," he said, pointing to a separate building on the back of the lot, possibly once used as servant quarters. And his workers were boys, most of them barely teenagers.

"We brought a good supply from California, and there's more on the way," I assured him, and hoping it was true. Transporting heavy loads over thousands of miles never comes with a guarantee.

As Señor Seguin resumed rebuilding his armory, I looked for Isabella, but she had disappeared. We had not spoken much since our argument in San Francisco, nor did she seem anxious to speak now. I went into the street, studying the defensive positions Keogh had established to protect the town. Many of the redoubts had been built by General Cos in December of 1835, though he lacked the ability to man them properly. Keogh had done better.

I soon found Jimmy Butler, Bobby Hughes and Henry Voss following in my footsteps. I showed them my new Winchester. Voss was similarly armed, though Butler still preferred his Sharps and Hughes his lever action Henry.

"We formed a new unit, sir," Hughes said. "Had to reorganize with so many casualties. We saved C Company for you."

"Tom's company?" I said.

"Young General Custer will be laid up for a bit, and we have places to ride. Don't we?" Butler said.

"Yes," I replied.

"Got a plan, sir?" Voss asked.

"Remember General Stoneman?" I said.

All three smiled. After all, at heart we were still the Seventh Cavalry, and we would do what cavalry does best.

———————

At four o'clock, a cannon roared from the riverbank behind Veramendi House. It was the 18-pounder threatening the partially demolished west wall of the Alamo. Powder was limited, so I did not expect a full scale bombardment, but it would provide a useful

265

distraction.

My first instinct was to find Traveller and join the attack, but this was Keogh's station. It would be poor form for me to overshadow his authority.

I did return to the river just upstream from the bridge, looking again at the old mission where two-hundred and fifty men had held off Santa Anna's three thousand on a cold March 6th morning. The fortress had been greatly altered since I left. The north wall where Travis, Bonham and Cos had died was gone, as was most of the west wall. Green Jameson had shortened the perimeter, enlarged the southwest bastion, and built a gun emplacement on the north end of the long barracks. Where a wooden stockade had once defended the south wall, a raised platform with three guns now defended the prairie extending toward the Alameda.

But the Alamo still had irretrievably fatal flaws. Supplying a large garrison was difficult in this part of Texas, and the adobe walls could not be sustained against a persistent barrage. The enemy cannon on Powder House Hill had softened the east wall enough for an attack through the corrals, and that portion of the fort remained a shambles.

I could not help wonder what the enemy holding force was thinking. As long as they held the hill, they had a secure line of retreat, but Captain Badillo and K Company were now occupying the position, supported by a hundred Tejano volunteers. Unable to withdraw, surrender seemed the garrison's only option, but no white flag had been seen. If they were expecting help, they would be disappointed.

"Shouldn't be much longer," Crockett said, joining us in the redoubt. "Gots plans for the prisoners?"

"Recommendations?" I asked.

"Santa Anna wants ta shoot 'em, 'specially after want happened in Goliad," Crockett said, though he sounded unconvinced.

"Wish I could shoot them, David," I replied. "But Señor Seguin says our enemies are divided into three or four different factions. Burleson, Fannin, Houston, and many who don't support the rebels at all. I can't do anything that will unite them."

"Doesn't mean we can't hang the ringleaders," Butler suggested.

Badillo's artillery on the hill fired several shots while Santa Anna's troops formed up south of the Alamo in full view of the garrison.

Chief Flacco was demonstrating east of the fort, his Apache riding back and forth waving their feathered lances. I saw the rebels moving to protect the main gate and manning the southwest bastion, leaving the north wall weak. Keogh appeared on the bridge with his staff. The 18-pounder roared again, the solid shot ripping a piece from the west wall. Standing only sixty feet away, we were forced to cover our ears.

Santa Anna's company moved forward, then stopped and prepared for volley fire. The former dictator of Mexico sat behind the line on a fine white charger, resplendent in his gold-braided blue uniform, personally directing operations. Scattered musket fire came from the fort, most falling short.

As the firing grew general along the south wall, commotion erupted on the far side of the fort. I could hear the rebel sentries yelling warning, though little inside the compound could be seen. I raised my field glasses to see Cochise's company coming over the north wall, scaling the end of the long barracks to seize the idle cannon. Apparently the Rebs had run out of powder for the gun.

Bugles blew on all four sides of the fort, Keogh coming from the west, Santa Anna from the south, Cochise on the north, and Badillo closing off escape to the east. It took little time for the encroaching forces to take and walls, the armies disappearing from view.

"General, shouldn't we get in there?" Butler asked, for it was hard to resist such a battle.

"Wish I could, Jimmy," I answered, continuing to watch.

Within twenty minutes, the blue rebel flag with a white star was hauled down, replaced with the Buffalo Flag. The fighting ceased. Prisoners began to emerge from the gate, marched toward the Alameda in ragged bunches. They wore no specific uniforms and looked well spent. A messenger rode in our direction.

"General Santa Anna's compliments, sir," Sergeant Allen said. "He requests your instructions on the captured pirates?"

"Detail the officers to the presidio. Confine the enlisted men to La Villita under guard pending further orders," I said, offering a salute.

Hughes came up with our horses and we rode across the creaking bridge up the gentle slope to the Alamo. Men were coming and going through the south gate, helping injured friends and rounding up stray horses. I noticed the acrid smell of burnt gunpowder. Bits of adobe littered the ground where cannon shot had torn holes in the wall. I went inside, finding that casualties were light, perhaps two or three dead on our side, and a dozen of the enemy. The wounded were being tended in the quadrangle before the old chapel.

I made a few acknowledgements and went into the long barracks to check on the armory where our Springfields were being manufactured. The entire lower floor looked like a factory turned upside down. Several of Señor Seguin's Tejanos were starting to clean up. Two of Fannin's teamsters were sitting on the floor with rifles pointed at them.

"They got greedy," Crockett said, inspecting several crates stacked near the door.

Tools, molds and spare parts were boxed, stuffed with straw for protection. A dozen wagons sat in the corral already loaded.

"They were going to take the wagons out last night," Autry speculated. "We showed up just in time to stop them."

"It's a wonder Fannin left without them," Butler said.

"Not if you know Fannin," I said.

The sun was beginning to set on what had been a blue spring day. A light wind was blowing. Erasmo Seguin was back in his shop, urgently resuming the production of ammunition with what little powder remained. I would need all he could make.

"What are ya thinkin', George?" Crockett asked as we walked back to town, giving our mounts a rest.

"Béjar sure is a mess, sir," Butler said.

"No time to worry about that, Jimmy," I said. "The rebel attempt to seize San Antonio has been repulsed, just like Lee's attempts to invade the North at Antietam. The Army of the Potomac under McClellan failed to pursue. I will not make the same mistake."

"You're going to attack?" Voss said.

"The Seventh Cavalry is going to attack, but we're going to be smart about it," I replied.

"That will be a change," Hughes said.

The command was not ready to move out immediately. We had seven hundred men spread over many miles of territory, some scouting, others gathering food from ranches north and west of town. The region to the south and east was largely stripped by encroaching armies. There was only one thing to do.

"A grand review?" Keogh said at the officer's call.

"You've won a splendid victory, general," I congratulated. "Each troop will form up in their finest, parade down Main Street, and then we'll have a fiesta to wake the angels. When the Seventh moves out at the end of the week, everyone will know we're the finest fighting force in Texas. Maybe the world. And where we ride, victory will ride with us."

The room filled with officers and sergeants cheered. I pretended my speech was spontaneous, but I'd been rehearing it all morning, waiting for the right moment. I put Crockett in charge, for the man knew how to throw a shindig.

It came time to visit our prisoners, two officers and seventy-five volunteers, from what I'd heard. I took Keogh and Santa Anna with me, Keogh being the garrison commander and Santa Anna feeling aggrieved from the murder of Mexican soldiers in Goliad. I had made no decision on the enemy's fate, and preferred to postpone one if possible.

"The criminals should be shot," Santa Anna said, walking beside me as we crossed the plaza toward the presidio.

"Hangin' is better. Spare the powder," Keogh said.

Keogh was not normally a vengeful man, but he'd taken young Harrington's death hard. I could not blame him. And I remembered the murderous raids of John Mosby in the Shenandoah in 1864. I'd executed as many of the skulking killers that could be caught, returning evil for evil, and when General Sheridan ordered me to burn rebel homesteads to the ground, I did so with relish.

San Antonio's presidio, located behind the cathedral, was surrounded on three sides by barracks and storerooms. Officers generally lodged in the hotels, but there was a commandant's office used by Keogh. The captured officers were being held in the saddlery, a narrow windowless room that smelled of oil and leather.

"Gentlemen," I said, bursting through the door first without introduction.

The two jumped to their feet, both dressed in blue wool uniforms absent decoration.

"We beg for nothing," the younger said in an Irish accent, tall with thin shoulders and a stubby red beard. I guessed him at twenty-five years.

269

The other was older, about Tom's age, with light wavy hair and the build of a cavalryman. By his bearing, I assumed he'd had formal military training. He looked at me with curiosity, but not the contempt of his youthful subordinate.

"Colonel Albert Johnston, sir. Houston's Rangers," he said, offering to shake hands. The accent was Kentucky, mostly.

The name could mean nothing to Santa Anna, but Keogh and I looked at each other in surprise. In another time, this man had once commanded the Texan Army during Houston's first term as president. He would later lead the U.S. 2nd Cavalry, fight in the Mexican War, command troops in California, resign to become a Confederate general, and bleed to death at the Battle of Pittsburgh Landing. Jefferson Davis thought him the most talented Southern general of the war, though Lee's admirers disagreed. By reputation, Keogh and I considered Johnston the ideal soldier.

"You graduated West Point, Class of '26," I said, shaking his hand as if touching a ghost.

"I've heard General Custer claims to be a West Point graduate, but I don't remember that name on the rolls. Either does Jim Fannin. Fannin may be an ass, but he's not a liar," Johnston said.

"It's a complicated story," I replied, sad that I couldn't explain. "Fannin and Burleson attacked this town, but not Houston. What are you doing here?"

"Emissary," Johnston said.

"Let us send his head back to Houston in a box," Santa Anna said, reaching for his sword. The younger officer stepped forward, fists clenched. Johnston merely stood his ground.

"Captain McCormick, please control yourself," Johnston said, pulling him back.

"Mr. Johnston, the Buffalo Flag does not recognize the Brazos Convention," I emphatically said. "Nor have your commanders been kind to their prisoners. You place me in a dilemma."

"And your solution?" Johnston asked.

I glanced to Keogh for confirmation, for we shared the same experience.

"If we may have your parole, you may remain here in Béjar until the war ends or you are properly exchanged," I said, much of Santa Anna's displeasure.

"You will accept my word, sir?" Johnston said.

"I know your reputation," I answered.

We waited patiently, for such a decision is important to a man's honor.

"You have my parole, sir," Johnston finally agreed, standing at attention.

"You won't get mine, ya lying Yankee scum," McCormick said. "I will fight your kind to the bitta' end."

Again I glanced at Keogh. He nodded.

"Officer of the guard," I summoned.

Lieutenant Sebastian entered with three *soldados*. They had joined me after the surrender of General Castrillón and served well ever since.

"*Sí*, General Custer," Sebastian reported.

"Escort this man to La Villita, Lieutenant Sebastian," I ordered. "Give him five minutes with a priest, and then hang him in the square."

"*A la vez, general*," Sebastian said, motioning for the prisoner to be bound. There was a brief struggle, but resistance proved useless.

"General Custer, may I intervene?" Johnston requested in distress.

"I'm sorry, sir. You may not," I replied, motioning for McCormick to be removed. "Have you changed your mind about the parole?"

"I gave my word," Johnston answered.

McCormick was led away. If he thought I was bluffing, he was soon proved wrong.

Tom was restless, wanting to ride out with the command three days later, but he wouldn't be ready for another week. I held a final conference in his sick room with Keogh, Santa Anna and Erasmo Seguin.

"Kit Carson is bringing as many men as he can from New Mexico," I said, having just received another message. "Myles, you need to reinforce Béjar, then join us in a final campaign to suppress the rebel governments."

"Where will you be, George?" Keogh asked.

"Hard to say. March to the sound of the guns," I said. "Antonio, you'll take three companies and move south. Retake Goliad and go on

271

to Copano. If Filisola will ally with us, take command of the forces and march east toward Galveston."

"Vicente may resist such a proposal, if he still commands the army," Santa Anna said. "How do you know I won't seize control for myself?"

"I don't," I replied, for it was something I'd worried about. "But I do have one request. If you capture Fannin, save him for me."

"No promises, George," Santa Anna replied.

"Where are you going, Autie?" Tom asked, sitting up in bed as best he could.

Morning Star was nearby should he need help, and Tatanka sat in the corner, just watching. Walking-In-Grass was busy in the next room treating some of the children injured by stray artillery fire. Two had died.

"I'm taking five companies in pursuit of Burleson," I explained. "He's heading for Gonzales to resupply, but there can't be much left they haven't already scavenged. If I can catch him unprepared, it will be a short fight."

"He still outnumbers you, Autie," Tom warned.

"They are a rabble," I said.

"So was the Continental Army," Tom said.

"I'm not Lord Cornwallis, and there's no French Navy to save them," I said.

"There might be in Galveston," Santa Anna suggested.

"Let's worry about that when we get there," I replied. "Does everyone understand their assignments?"

"I would rather ride with the command," Keogh said. "Señor Seguin can rally San Antonio without my help."

"That is true, general. I would not see Myles denied his rightful place," Erasmo agreed.

They had worked together for two years and grown close. I wondered if Erasmo had another daughter that Myles might marry. Or he might choose Isabella, who had ignored me at the review.

"General Keogh and I will have a talk," I said. "Gentlemen, you are dismissed."

Santa Anna and Seguin left, having much to prepare. I caught Keogh by the elbow.

"Myles, if Burleson tries to hold Gonzales, where will he find supplies?" I asked, already suspecting the answer.

"Nothing left in San Felipe or Victoria. He'll try to get food from the Cherokee," Keogh answered after a moment of thought.

"And I'd like to get there first," I whispered. "If I bypass Gonzales, can you keep Burleson pinned down while I cut the legs from underneath him?"

"Going Stoneman on me?" Keogh said.

Myles knew much of such things. He had been at John Buford's side on July 1st, 1863, when Lee's armies were invading Gettysburg. A year later, he served as George Stoneman's aide de camp during the failed attempt to free Union prisoners at Andersonville.

"It's my turn, isn't it? I let you take Béjar while I was holding the Alamo," I recalled, still jealous of his glorious feat.

"I'll be riding with Myles," Tom insisted.

"You be careful, little brother. That's an order," I said.

The wars in Texas had burdened the people, robbed them of possessions, and now many faced starvation. It was thought the Cherokee, who had done no fighting, were rich in food, and without their help no army could thrive. Custer spoke of another army, in a place called Appomattox, that had fought bravely only to fall into destitution. Custer admired this army and was proud to have defeated it, but he no longer admired the white men who brought death to his empire.

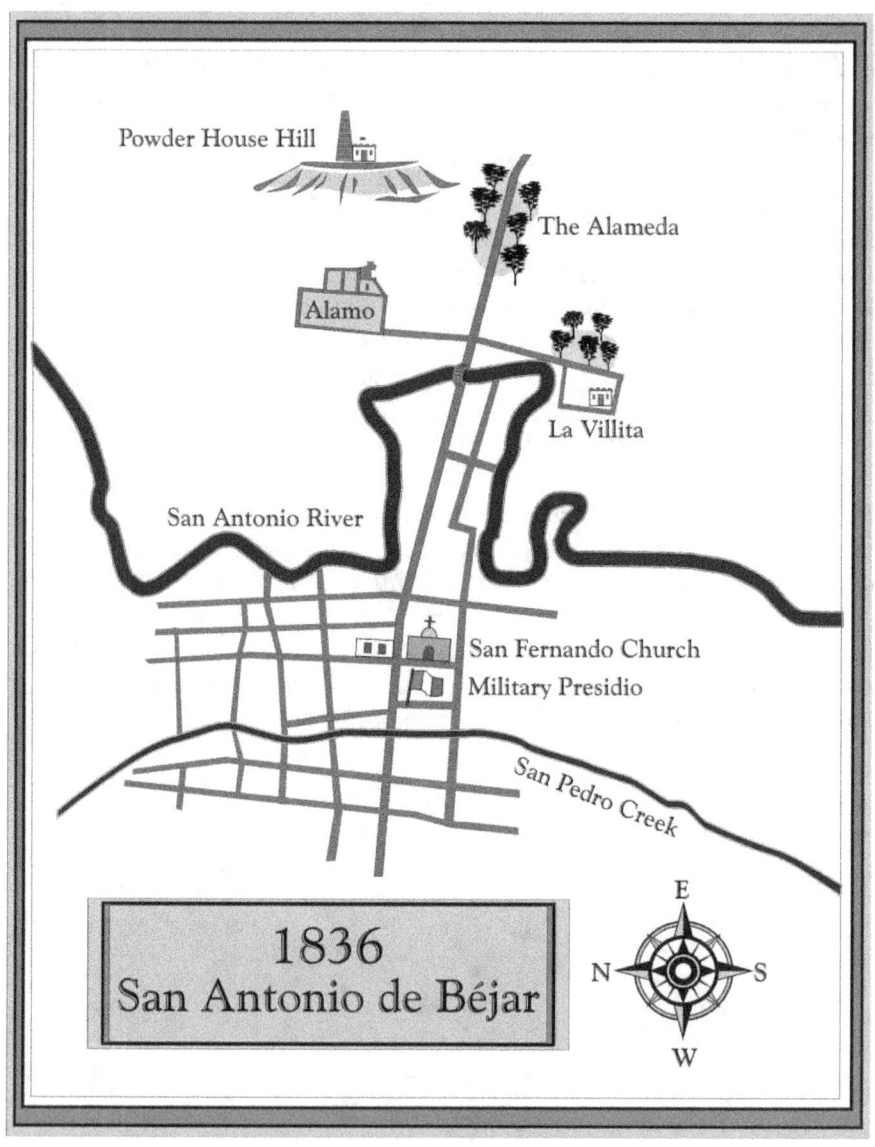

Powder House Hill

The Alameda

Alamo

La Villita

San Antonio River

San Fernando Church
Military Presidio

San Pedro Creek

1836
San Antonio de Béjar

274

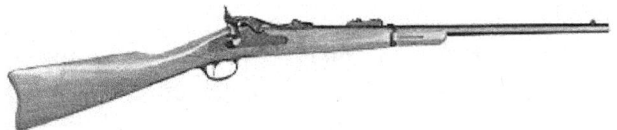

Chapter Ten
A RIVER AND A RECKONING

We were marching east on the trail again, organized in five units. Four were Seventh Cavalry: Crockett's Company A, Brister's Company B, Company C with me, and Company K commanded by Juan Badillo. The fifth was Chief Flacco, who was surprising me with his discipline. Not typical of an Indian, let alone an Apache. I promoted Cochise to aide-de-camp, for I could not let him ride home without glory. Because Tatanka's people were the least experienced, they had been left behind to repair Béjar, though the boy rode with my staff.

A hard ride would get us to Gonzales in a day and a half, but we had wagons and two 6-pounders, so our progress was slower. The road was good, however, well-trod and dry. I had no desire to attack the town. George Kimble and thirty-one mounted volunteers had ridden to the aid of the Alamo in 1836. William Irvin was good friends with Keogh and Seguin. Galba Fuqua was serving in Santa Fe with Sharrow. There were no slaves in Gonzales, and they had been loyal friends to the Buffalo Flag. I had no intention of burning the town as Houston had threatened to do.

Crockett found us a strong position with rivers on our flanks and an open pasture to the rear. We threw up a log barricade and placed the cannon to good effect. The fortification was necessary, because I had no intention of keeping the command together.

"Captain Badillo, you will remain here with the wagons until General Keogh comes up," I instructed. "Major Brister, you and Captain White will demonstrate to the north and south of town. I

275

want Burleson to think he's surrounded by a thousand men."

"Where are you going, sir?" Brister asked.

"Crockett and I are going to see Chief Bowles. We have word the Cherokee are camped on the Trinity River near Dallas," I said.

"Dallas?" White asked.

"If someone hasn't built it yet, they soon will," I explained.

"*Qué pasa con la segunda caballería?*" Flacco the Younger asked.

The eager warrior, tall with long black hair like his father, was learning English quickly, but Spanish was still his preferred form of communication. I responded so everyone would understand.

"My friend, in another war, there was a cavalry officer of great fame," I said. "His name was James Ewell Brown Stuart. He rode circles around enemy armies, captured supplies, killed unlucky stragglers, and then reported back to his commander. I want you to be my Jeb Stuart. Ride around Gonzales, scare the hell out of them, and then join me on the Trinity. Can you do that?"

"Yes, General, I can do that," Young Flacco said, pleased with the assignment.

"Riders coming in!" a sentry shouted from our picket line.

We stood from our campfire to see. There were eighty tents mixed into the forest housing three hundred and sixty men, thirty women, and sixteen stubborn boys impressed as wood gatherers. Between the horses, mules, oxen and cattle, there were better than six hundred animals. It was a busy camp, and we made no effort to be quiet, for I wanted the cowards in Gonzales to fear every movement we made.

"George, it's Tatanka and Spotted Eagle," Crockett said, the old man's eyes still better than mine in the dark.

They dismounted at the picket line, turned their horses over to the orderlies, and ran in our direction. It was good to see Spotted Eagle again, though he was no longer the teenager who had bravely kicked over the trench planks at the Alamo. He was a young man, my height and broad-shouldered, wearing a blue cavalry uniform. His long black hair was tied back with a red silk scarf. There were sergeant stripes on his sleeves. Tatanka wore fringed rawhide and a gray kepi hat.

The shine in Spotted Eagle's eyes showed he was glad to see me, but halted at attention, saluting. I returned the salute.

"Sir, Colonel Seguin's complements," Spotted Eagle said, his Lakota accent still thick. "The Béjar Mounted Rangers will be here before midnight. He wants to know if he should position south for an attack on the town."

If I was going to attack Gonzales, which would be a standard tactic, Seguin's plan would be appropriate. But that wasn't the plan.

"My compliments to Colonel Seguin," I said. "My instructions are for him to move east of town. Colonel Crockett and I will join forces with him before noon tomorrow. He should be rested and ready to ride."

"Yes, sir," Spotted Eagle acknowledged.

"Sergeant, how many men does Colonel Seguin command?" I asked, for no one had word of them in two weeks.

"Forty-seven volunteers, sir. And ready to fight," Spotted Eagle said.

And it sounded like he'd already seen his fair share. That was one thing I liked about the Sioux. They love glory as much as I.

Without another word, Spotted Eagle returned to the picket line, grabbed a fresh horse, and rode off into the darkness. I had wanted to ask him to supper.

———————

We found the younger Seguin a few miles east of Gonzales. His company was made up of Tejanos, who were rapidly being dispossessed of their lands, and original Texan colonists unhappy with the invasion of mercenaries from the east. They had been scouting the enemy and raiding where they could. Most were dressed in worn leathers and bits of uniforms. They carried few supplies, and their horses had seen hard service.

"Want you to know we freed our slaves, General," Captain Isham Philips of the Austin Colony said. He pointed to half a dozen Negroes riding with their company, all armed. "We aren't happy about it, but better to lose our slaves than our land. These filibusterers are carving up Texas like a Christmas goose."

"Have you sworn allegiance to the Buffalo Flag?" I asked, mounted on Traveller and giving these frontiersmen a careful inspection.

I saw they were farmers, ranchers and shopkeepers, not the fortune hunting horde pouring in from the states.

"We will if you confirm our land grants," Philips said.

I glanced at Seguin. He had apparently made promises but needed my approval. I didn't care for the circumstances, but could ill afford to reject their help.

"Those who ride with the Seventh Cavalry will have their rights protected," I agreed.

"Then we are your men, General," Philips said.

"News from Victoria, sir," Seguin reported. "Fannin caught General Filisola. Shot him. Urrea is falling back on Copano."

"Any news of Santa Anna?" I asked.

"What about him, sir?" Seguin said.

"He's marching on Goliad with two hundred men."

"I didn't know the dictator was in Texas," Seguin said.

"He's just a general now, Juan. Crockett is the president," I replied.

"Sir, until three days ago, we didn't even know you were in Texas. Or that the Texians had retreated from Béjar. Many thought our cause lost," Seguin explained.

"So Fannin is in the south, Burleson is behind us, Houston is in front of us," I summarized. "Any other rebel armies I should know about?"

"Burnet is raising a force at Galveston, but he's lost the confidence of Fannin, and Houston hates him," Seguin said.

"And he's from New Jersey. The Southerners call him a damn Yankee horse thief," Philips added.

"He probably is," I said.

With the extra men, I was able to reform my headquarters command, taking those I knew best and giving C Company to Major Baugh, who was once again in my good graces.

We went east away from the Guadalupe River, then turned north to the Colorado, crossed below Bastrop, and then used the Old San Antonio Road to cross the Brazos before reaching the Trinity River. The ranches we found along the way had been plundered of their stock, the small towns nearly deserted. Fortunately, the unpredictable Texas weather was kind to us, possibly due to Tatanka's intervention with his Great Spirit.

I expected to find the Cherokee villages where they had been two years before, for the Cherokee were not nomads like the Cheyenne or Comanche. They liked to build towns, irrigate farms, and cultivate the riches of civilization. I was looking forward to meeting Chief Bowles again. Maybe he would believe me now that the Brazos Convention had proven unreliable allies.

We found no evidence of a force riding ahead of us, and finally concluded that whatever foragers Burleson had sent out for supplies decided to go south instead. Mercenaries are not famous for their loyalty, and the war was proving less than profitable.

Seguin fell in with Hughes and Butler, swapping tales of the last two years. All had struggled, but Texas had the harder case. I spoke to few, and then only when necessary. There was a boiling anger that in my younger days I would have expressed with inappropriate behavior, but now I feared the repercussions.

We neared the Cherokee villages, close enough to see the smoke of their chimneys. Because the pack animals were slowing our progress, I crossed the Trinity with my regimental staff and scouts, moving quickly along a wide river road. The summer crops were wheat and corn. We saw shacks used for storing hay and pens for the stock, though they were empty. The smoke up ahead grew thicker, and then we heard gunshots.

"On the gallop," I ordered, giving Traveller a kick.

A branch road turned up toward the nearest village surrounded by large pastures. The cows were rushing in the other direction, fleeing the noise. I saw a log building on fire.

Butler started to move ahead of me, his Colt drawn. Then Seguin and Allen. I pushed Traveller harder, drawing a Webley. There was a fighting force off to our right, white men in rough gray leather. A few were mounted, most were on foot. I guessed two or three hundred in all. The Cherokee had retreated to the woods on the far side of the clearing, though many had fallen during the escape. Their return fire was sporadic. Had the Cherokee been taken by surprise?

"Wheel right!" I shouted. "Voss, sound the *Charge!*"

Though only forty in number, we were cavalry, and better armed than our adversaries. Crockett and Baugh were still on the back trail but close enough to hear the muskets. They would be along quick enough.

It's a known fact that a few dozen cavalry look like hundreds to a man standing in knee high grass holding a single shot rifle, especially one not formed into a disciplined unit. As we closed on the enemy line, they fired a few shots but fearfully.

I realized that most of the marauders were grouped near the Cherokee store houses, no doubt plundering grain and jerky. Wagons were being loaded, and one ambitious frontiersman was attempting to catch a chicken. A score were still firing at the villagers, who had barely managed to gather up their women and children. I saw ten wounded or dead Cherokee in the pasture and at least of pair of white men.

When the raiders saw us coming, they abandoned the wagons and began to withdraw toward the south road. A bugle replied to Voss, but I didn't recognize the call, likely a retreat. We only rode that much harder.

Small groups of stragglers attempted to make stands, usually in groups of three or four, much as I'd seen my own men do in my vision of the Little Big Horn. Hughes took ten troopers and veered toward the largest batch. Cochise and the Lipan Apache broke in the other direction, swinging around their flank.

Down by the river, I saw a tall man in buckskins take a bead on Hughes with his Pennsylvania long rifle and I made for him, giving Traveller an extra kick. The man turned and fired as I aimed my Colt. He missed, and so did I. He spun to the ground with my second shot, clutching his chest.

The fighting in the pasture became general. I saw Private Lopez get wounded but remain mounted, teaming with Voss to drive several riflemen from a ditch. Butler with half a dozen troopers captured the supply wagons. Eight of Seguin's scouts, and Tatanka, dismounted into a skirmish line and opened fire on the trees, firing several volleys. Seguin's men were armed with Springfield carbines that they reloaded with great speed, but Tatanka held a Winchester, getting off eight quick rounds. The raiders in the trees faded from view, no doubt running for their horses.

I guided Traveller back toward the main road leading to the village. Many of the Cherokee were now rushing back to join the fight. Voss rode up, his bugle ready, and then Tatanka rejoined us, having run out of shells. With the enemy on the run, I was reluctant to risk more casualties, but the battlefield was still in chaos. Attempting to disengage could be more hazardous than not.

"My compliments to Colonel Crockett," I said to Cochise. "Tell him the rebels are retreating south. He is to harass them where he can, but rejoin the command before sunset."

"Yes, General," Cochise said with a salute.

"Cheis?" I said.

"Sir?" he answered.

"Stay with Crockett. Come back with blood on your hatchet."

He saluted again, anxious to find another fight.

"How are you, Tatanka?" I asked. "That was brave work, and timely performed."

"Thank you, General," Tatanka replied.

"I need an aide-de-camp. Want the job?" I offered.

"Yes, sir," Tatanka said.

"Tell Voss to sound *Recall*. We'll reform outside the village."

I turned Traveller back toward the pasture where the Cherokee had made their fight, dismounting and walking through the stubby grass. Traveller paused to graze and I let him go. I kept my pistol ready but doubted I'd need it.

The first two I saw were wounded Cherokee dressed in red and black dyed wool, more festive than work wear. Their women folk kneeled at their sides rendering aid. The next two I saw were dead, unattended in the confused aftermath. One of them was white. Then I looked forward and saw a strange sight. It was Sam Houston, apparently uninjured, sitting on the ground with a wounded Indian. It was Chief Bowles, covered in blood, the eyes glazed over.

"They shot him," Houston said, his voice choked with emotion. "We were negotiating. Duwa'li only wanted what's fair for his people. Suddenly my own men opened fire."

I looked about the field. There were more wounded than I'd originally been able to see, perhaps thirty, most seeking shelter in ditches or behind logs. Not all were men. The attack was not a massacre, but might have become one. And though Houston had not wanted it, I don't know that he'd done much to prevent it.

"Where is your army now?" I asked.

"It's not my army anymore. Lamar took them. That sneaking bastard planned it this way," Houston answered. "And if it's the last thing I do, I'll cut his goddamned throat."

"Sir, you can start by getting up off your knees," I said, finding such behavior unseemly for a white man. "The village is on fire, the people need help. Try to make yourself useful."

With the danger over, hundreds of Cherokee returned to suppress the fires. The store houses were standing, but many of the smaller huts were in flames. I saw the village elders approach where my staff was regrouping on the road under my guidon. Several looked familiar, and they all seemed to remember me.

"General Custer, thank you," Chief Gatunwali said, reaching to shake my hand.

"I told you the Seventh Cavalry will stand with the Cherokee," I said. "We do not want your land, only your friendship."

"Which you have earned," another distinguished chief said.

I was reassured by these words, for I had not ridden hundreds of miles merely to be rebuffed again. Had the Cherokee decided to support the rebel cause, it would have been the Seventh Cavalry robbing their warehouses.

Crockett, Baugh and Flacco the Younger rode in an hour before sunset carrying two enemy battle flags. Tom would be envious. While their men were billeted, we met in a council of war with the Cherokee chiefs.

The long log meeting house still smelled of smoke, but had not suffered much damage. I sat with the leaders in circle with Tatanka on my left, much to the curiosity of the Cherokee. Crockett and Seguin were on my right. Together, we represented Indians, whites, Tejanos, and the Seventh Cavalry. How my command had turned into such a mongrel army I didn't know, but it had worked for the kings of Persia, so it would have to work for me.

"We have summoned our brothers from the north," Chief Gatunwali said.

Though an older man, the war chief still made a vigorous presence. Gatunwali appeared to be in charge now that Bowles was dead.

"Got friends to call on?" Crockett asked.

"Plácido of the Tonkawa comes with a hundred warriors," a younger chief said.

"We made an treaty with the Raven, but he could not keep his promises," another chief complained. He had been wounded in the fighting. I heard his son was missing.

"We will have no more false allies," Gatunwali agreed.

"Your future failed, as the future of my people failed," Tatanka said. "Now Wakan Tanka has offered a different path. Custer has fought

Indians. He has fought Mexicans. He has fought the white man. Custer will fight all of those who oppose his flag. If you make Custer's flag your flag, he will fight for you."

The chiefs looked at me with inquiry. I had never thought of my situation in such terms, but Tatanka had boiled me down to the essentials.

"We kinda got this plan," Crockett said, using gestures to emphasis his words. "America is a group a states, each with its own gov'ment, but united by a Fed'ral union. We kin do that same here, with a empire that stretches to the Pacific Ocean. And we'd be right proud ta have the Cherokee as our kinsmen."

"The Five Tribes had friends in our own country, but not enough," Gatunwali said. "Jackson forced us on a trail of death to this new land, and even here, enemies seek to destroy us. We would like more friends, but it is hard with Duwa'li lying dead in the field."

"I know your fear," Tatanka said. "My own people have friends among the Arapaho, Black Foot, and our cousins, the Cheyenne. But the whites are too strong. The end of the trail are the reservations unless we seek a new way. You must follow Custer. You must fly the flag of a new nation."

"The boy speaks strong words," a young chief remarked.

"The boy speaks truth," Seguin said. "My own people supported the Brazos government. Lorenzo de Zavala and José Navarro signed the declaration of independence. But as Americans have come from the east, they take our property. Fine old families are shown no respect. Burleson's government even accuses us of betrayal. These invaders are not like the Texians of Stephen Austin. If we do not fight now, it will be too late."

"And what does Custer say?" Gatunwali asked.

"Whites will continue to come from the east," I replied, pausing to let the suspense build. I looked each chief in the eye. "They want land. They will hunt game. This country will change. Maybe, if we work together, the change will be good. As Colonel Seguin wants, and Tatanka hopes. I am not so optimistic, but I'm willing to try. Crockett is a good man. So are my friends Erasmo Seguin and Myles Keogh. And my brother, Tom. You must do what is best for your people, but you must decide soon."

The conference ended. The Cherokee had much to discuss, and my

283

command needed relief from the hard ride. We were low on food, the men tired, and the mounts exhausted. Hughes found us a good campsite among elm trees near the river where we pitched our tents.

"What do you think, George?" Crockett asked.

Women had come down from the village with fish and corncakes. Furs had been provided for our bedding, and several large tents had been loaned to us. Crockett and I ate by our campfire, letting the other troop captains stay with their men.

"We'll wait for the scouts following Lamar to report back, and send messengers to Gonzales," I answered. "If Keogh needs our help, we'll need to go back."

"And if he doesn't?"

"We'll strike south," I said.

"Strike at what?" Crockett asked.

"Whatever gets in our way. Our opponents have three, possibly four armies separated by quarreling commanders and hundreds of miles," I explained. "If Santa Anna can take Victoria, Fannin will fall back on San Felipe. Burleson will need to do the same if Gonzales falls. They'll be short of supply."

"And their only source of supply is Galveston," Crockett realized.

"That's our mission, David."

"It's a mighty big mission," Crockett said, stirring the fire with a stick.

"Then I guess we'll need some Custer luck to see it through," I replied.

———————

We lingered near the Cherokee towns for a week, partially due to heavy rains. Information from the west was sparse and somewhat contradictory. Burleson was slowly withdrawing from Gonzales, but to where? In what numbers? Was Keogh in pursuit? And Santa Anna had apparently declined to march on Victoria. Why? And where was Fannin?

"Start'in ta feel kinda 'lone out here," Crockett said early one morning as we prepared to ride south.

"During the Rebellion, the army had telegraph lines. Railroads. Maps for the dispatch riders. Texas is a land of many rumors and few facts," I complained.

"We gots three well-armed companies an' plenty a scouts. More than our enemies got," Crockett said.

"That's what I thought at the Little Big Horn," I remarked. "Where is Tatanka? Maybe we can ask what his damn birds have to say."

"I hope you're a jokin'," Crockett said.

"I hope so, too," I answered.

We walked from our camp, the ground now drying out under a summer sun. The mounts were fed and rested, our equipment repaired. The men were saying goodbye to new friends among the villagers.

"We're ready, General," Butler said, organizing the march.

"Keep them jumping, Jimmy," I said.

"*General, mis guerreros están listos?*" Flacco the Younger asked.

"Tell them we ride to glory, my friend," I said, patting the fine Spanish sword on my hip.

Crockett and I inspected the preparations, offering encouragement. It wasn't the manner in which I preferred to command. A general should issue orders, not cajole and flatter. But this wasn't a professional army.

"Turning on the charm, George?" Crockett asked.

"I can't afford desertions, and volunteers are notorious for running from a fight," I said.

"Catch more flies with honey than vinegar," Crockett said.

"I'll be satisfied to catch Lamar before he regroups with Burleson," I replied. "Tell your company to mount up. You have the lead."

Crockett moved out in mid-morning. I sent Flacco the Younger and Cochise with him. They got along well, though Crockett seemed to get along well with everyone. And the Apache made the Cherokee nervous. Chief Gatunwali sent half a dozen guides with them.

"Company C is mounted, sir," Major Baugh said with a salute.

"As are the Béjar Rangers," Seguin reported, doffing his wide brim hat.

Both were dressed for the trail in leathers, as was my regimental staff, our blue uniforms no longer suitable for a long day's ride.

"Proceed, gentlemen," I ordered, staying behind for a final chat with Gatunwali. I had come to admire the old chief.

"All the chiefs are gathering on the new moon," Gatunwali said. "If they will not fight, my own people will. We will ride under this flag."

Gatunwali motioned to two young warriors. They unfurled a red cotton flag with a large black buffalo sewn in the middle and a white owl mounted in the upper left quadrant. The design was striking, and I instantly decided the other nations under the Buffalo Flag would use the same model.

"It's a noble banner, my friend," I said, shaking Gatunwali's hand. "From this day forward, we are brothers. I will not disappoint you."

"We must struggle together now, General Custer. Your people and mine," Gatunwali said.

I turned to mount Traveller. Butler, Hughes, French and Voss were already mounted with the rest of my staff, twenty in all. Tatanka was overseeing our teamsters and two dozen unruly mules.

Before we could ride out, I noticed a distraction coming in our direction. It was Sam Houston. I'd not seen him since Diwali's funeral, nor spoken with him since the day of the battle.

"General Custer, may I have a moment of your time?" he asked, reining in next to me on a tall brown sorrel. Nearly forty Cherokee were riding with him, well-armed with muskets and outfitted for the road.

"How may I serve you, General Houston?" I coldly replied.

"*Colonel* Houston, sir. I am resigned from the Army of Texas, but feel entitled to my rank in the Tennessee militia," Houston said.

"Militia?" I said.

"You've not contested Crockett's title," Houston protested.

It was true. Crockett had only been a third sergeant under Andrew Jackson during the Creek War, his more exalted rank came when he was elected lieutenant colonel of Tennessee's 57th militia regiment. And my own title was honorary as well, for general was my brevet rank during the Rebellion. I had ridden to the Little Big Horn as a lieutenant colonel, though I had no intention of telling Houston that.

"What may I do for you, Colonel Houston?" I asked.

"I wish to join your army. Me and my warriors," Houston said.

"Permission denied," I said, preparing to leave.

"Sir, I am a proud man," Houston said, sitting erect.

And he was impressive, at least six inches taller than I. I looked him over carefully. A heavy drinker, but not drunk. At the moment. Intelligent, determined, but with the wits of a fox. Could I trust him?

"We will not let Texas be annexed to the United States as a slave

286

state," I said. "Why would you want to join us?"

"To protect my people," he said, indicating the Cherokee.

Tatanka rode up, already dusty from organizing the cantankerous mules. He smiled to see Houston.

"Has *Colonneh* finally heard the ravens?" Tatanka asked.

"Yes, young chief. Though it took the death of my father to see it," Houston replied.

Houston's statement was sincere. I looked back to see my men nodding their heads. Though I had ignored Houston as best I could, many others had not been able to resist this living legend.

"Sir, Sam here has lots of friends in Texas, and we need all the friends we can get," Butler whispered.

He was right, damn it.

"Colonel Houston, you may ride with us, if you take oath to the Buffalo Flag," I said.

"I take oath," Houston said, holding up his hand.

My men cheered. The Cherokee cheered. Houston grimly smiled, looking for my reaction. I reluctantly shook his hand. After all, the son of a bitch was Sam Houston.

With experienced scouts leading the way, the command made good time going down the Trinity River Valley. Where the river abruptly turned east, we continued south through a pass and over low foothills to the headwaters of the San Jacinto River. Unlike west Texas, this land was green, and many of the more remote ranches were yet to be raided by desperate mercenary armies. We even found a small cattle herd that we paid for in script and a handful of California dollars. When Crockett's company raided a modest cotton plantation, freeing eight slaves, the overseer fled for his life.

"Comin' up on Buffalo Bayou, General," Seguin reported. "Signs show a few of Lamar's men headed for the Sabine, but most are going toward Harrisburg."

"Keep watch on their position, Juan. They may attempt to block our march," I decided.

"San Felipe is close by. Just on the other side of the Brazos," Seguin warned.

"The Brazos is a tricky nut," Houston said. "Runs high, runs low. Lots of swamps. Be hard to cross if we burn the ferry crossings at San Felipe and Fort Bend."

287

"Small group a good men kin burn 'em both," Crockett urged.

I took out one of the hand-drawn maps Cooke had made, for nothing published in Texas was remotely adequate for military operations. Without word from Keogh or Santa Anna, I was on my own, and possibly outnumbered. A chance for glory?

"Colonel Houston, you and the Cherokee detachment will destroy ferry at Fort Bend, but I want the ferry at San Felipe left alone," I decided. "Let the rebel army cross if they wish."

"If Lamar and Burleson link, and Fannin joins them, they'll have the biggest army in Texas," Houston said.

"Yes, I suspect they will," I agreed.

"Kinda risky, don't ya think?" Crockett said.

"I like the odds. Gentlemen, you have your instructions," I said.

I waved to my staff and gave Traveller a kick, galloping off toward the muddy creek a few miles distant. Crockett shrugged and motioned for A Company to follow.

I was not overly concerned with Harrisburg, or even San Felipe. In my time, due to the railroads, the largest towns in Texas were San Antonio, Galveston, Austin and Houston. Harrisburg was a hamlet when I visited in 1865, and no one even knew where San Felipe had once been. Neither town boasted sufficient resources to support an army.

"Chief Flacco," I summoned.

"Yes, General," Young Flacco said, his English continuing to improve.

"As we approach Buffalo Bayou, I would like you to scout the San Jacinto River," I said. "Major Baugh will be on our right. You'll encounter a marsh, then a creek that empties into the bay. Rejoin us there before sunset."

"Thank you, General," Flacco said, for he liked to act independently. And as the Apache hadn't massacred any settlers yet, I was willing to trust his judgment.

As we got closer to the bayou, ranches began to appear. Nearly all were deserted. Butler found a suitable ford, though we would still need to swim the horses for a short distance. A flatboat was appropriated for the pack mules. When I reached the far shore, I found Tatanka in conversation with a local farmer.

"Sam Watkins, sir," the tall lean fellow said in a thick Southern accent.

"Armies have taken their crops," Tatanka explained.

"That they have, sir. That they have. Left us a bit, but not much," Watkins said. "Sure be glad when this war is all over."

"Any slaves on your plantation, Mr. Watkins?" I asked.

"Plantation?" he answered with a laugh. "Ain't no plantations round 'ere. Few to the east, and one on the lower Brazos. We mostly got swamps and alligators."

"But no slaves?" I persisted.

"Mr. Jenkins got six slaves, but he took 'em to Harrisburg when he heard you was comin'," Watkins confessed. "None left that I know of."

"His property will be confiscated, and worse if we're resisted," I said.

"That's what people say. Been published in the newspapers," Watkins confirmed.

This I already knew. Northern newspapers had been supportive of the Buffalo Flag's efforts, while Southern newspapers had condemned us for abolitionists. I wondered if Galveston was publishing a paper, for it had been two years since I stole their printing press.

Crockett emerged dripping wet from the bayou leading his horse by the bridle. Watkins's eyes lit up with recognition and he rushed to shake hands. Whatever story Watkins shared with his neighbors, I could bet Crockett would be part of it.

We shook water out our equipment and dried off near some river shacks. A few miles to the west, Brister's company was coming in our direction. It was midday when a fast rider approached from the east, one of the young Apache lads.

"*Hombres blancos, en el río. Luchan,*" Kuruk reported, out of breath.

Kuruk was one of the Lipan Apache, a cousin of Flacco, with clear eyes and a ready spirit.

"What's that?" Crockett asked, the lad's accent strong.

"Tall Bear says there's a battle at the river. White men," I translated.

"Best we get a goin' then," Crockett said. "Corporal, *Boots and Saddles*, if you please."

As the bugle call sounded, troopers ran for their horses. Tatanka ran up.

"There is fighting," Tatanka said.

"Yes, I've had a messenger from Flacco," I said.

"There are many enemies. You will need Major Baugh," Tatanka said.

The boy rushed off to find his horse, and before I knew it, he was riding out to fetch C Company.

"Kind of decided, isn't he?" Hughes said, coming alongside me with my guidon unfurled.

"Probably some heathen foolishness," I said. "Let's get Baugh up here before Crockett has all the fun."

Though the mules were sent forward, I held back until sure that Captain Baugh knew to follow, not wanting another Benteen episode. Baugh waved from the front of his troop and I motioned my staff on at a brisk gait. We soon heard cannon fire.

"Must be near the bay, sir. The way the sound echoes," Butler said.

"Close on, too," French agreed.

"It could be the old San Jacinto battleground," I said. "Tom and I visited there with my father after the war. If so, the bayou will be on the left, Peggy Lake on the right, and the river beyond. Could be a small bridge or two, but water on all four sides."

"Possible ferry landing?" Butler asked.

"Don't know about that, but a couple of riverboats could do as well," I guessed.

"Who can be fightin'? Way out here?" French wondered.

"That is a wonderful question. No Mexican army in the area that we know of," I said.

"Maybe the Texians are fighting each other?" Butler speculated.

As Baugh's troop caught up, the rate of gunfire from the river increased. It was not intense, but steady enough to signal an engagement. At first all I heard was musket fire, but gradually, the sound of Springfields filtered through the trees. Crockett had just arrived as we came up on the Apache scouts. They were dismounted among the trees near an old wooden bridge. Heavy foliage screened whatever was happening on the island.

"*Corporal Kuruk, donde está su Capitán?*" I inquired.

"*El jefe Flacco está siguiendo a los hombres blancos,*" Cochise said.

Hardly a moment later, Flacco returned from his scout, walking quickly across the bridge. Though wide enough for a wagon, it creaked under his weight. The water was running low, but it would still take time to ford the creek if the bridge was destroyed. The swampy green water could easily be a death trap.

"General," Flacco acknowledged, kneeling to draw a map in the dirt with his finger. "There are two groups of white men. The larger is closest with their backs to the creek. They are Texians, perhaps three hundred. They have a cannon. Beyond a big pasture are a hundred more white men. They fly the Buffalo Flag."

"Is either side entrenched?" I asked.

"No. They battle at rifle range, but the Texians prepare to move forward. Their cavalry is mounted in the trees on the right," Flacco reported.

"Any idea who's flying the Buffalo?" Crockett asked.

"I believe it is General Custer," Flacco said.

"I am General Custer," I said.

"The other General Custer. The husband of Morning Star," Flacco replied.

It hardly seemed possible, but Flacco was unlikely to be wrong. I saw Tatanka running for his horse.

"Tatanka, where are you going?" I asked.

"To attack," he said.

Clearly the boy had been exposed to bad influences, but soon everyone else was heading for their horses, too, and I hadn't even given an order.

"First on the bridge," Baugh said, his troop already mounted.

I doubted Baugh had ever seen the field before, for it wasn't any kind of landmark in 1838. But the confined area would hold few mysteries.

"John, move left around their flank, then roll down their line," I said. "Flacco, charge the enemy cavalry on the right. *Carga de la caballería enemiga.* Break them up. Crockett, Brister, when both flanks are engaged, our trumpeters will sound the *Advance*. We'll attack the center. Any questions, gentlemen?"

"No questions, sir," Baugh said, leading C Company across the bridge.

"Tatanka, you are my aide-de-camp. Stay close to my guidon," I ordered.

The lad nodded, anxious for battle. We all were.

A rough overgrown trail led toward the pastures. I couldn't

remember if there had been a ranch or small town on the battlefield. There should be something. Why else would anyone build a bridge?

Flacco disappeared into the trees on the right, seemingly familiar with his destination. Apaches are good at that. Crockett rode to my side, our horses at the walk. We were surrounded by flags and trumpets.

"What do you think, George?" Crockett asked.

"Only one explanation," I decided. "Tom followed Santa Anna to Copano and took ship for Galveston. I can't image why, but the rascal got here before we did."

"You figured Galveston out. Why couldn't he?"

"Because to get here this quickly, he'd have thought of it before I did. I'm the general."

"He's a gen'ral now, too, George. Better set your mind on that," Crockett said.

The ground was much as I remembered it, overgrown with tangled trees, prickly cactus and sawgrass. Birds rustled in the branches all around us.

"Captain Cochise, we will soon reach a clearing," I said. "Have the teamsters secure the mules. Those who aren't needed will come forward as horse holders. Crockett, Brister, when we dismount, prepare to advance in skirmish formation. Hughes, Butler, French, spread out among the men. Keep them steady. Voss, Allen, Williamson, you'll stand by the flag."

The firing in the meadows had paused. I saw smoke rising only a few hundred yards ahead. And then the trees gave way, revealing tents, wagons, and campfires. The smell of roasting beef filled our nostrils, making us hungry. A gentle wind blew in from the bay. We dismounted, the holders taking the mounts in charge as the command moved quietly forward through the brush.

"Camp followers," Butler said, pointing to groups of women and children.

I counted two score, young and old, dressed in cotton and wool. Half a dozen were slaves. A few of the older boys carried muskets, but seeing eighty armed men suddenly emerging from the woods, they were unsure how to respond. When one raised his gun, he found twenty guns pointed in his direction. The lad wisely set the musket down.

"Ladies, please retire to the tents and stay there," I said, passing through the campground.

Beyond the tents and wagons, we found a long row of armed men some two hundred yards further on. Some wore makeshift uniforms, most simply wore their common everyday clothes, made tired by a lack of care. They were formed into several units behind a thrown up barricade of tree branches and scrub wood.

"Looks like we found Lamar," Hughes said, cocking his rifle.

The enemy was so focused on their opponents across the pasture that we remained unnoticed until one turned to see we were not his fellows.

"Mr. Voss, sound the *Advance*," I ordered.

As the trumpet blew, I drew a pistol and stepped to the front of our line, but Williamson drew me back.

"Can't let you get killed, sir," the sergeant admonished.

The rebel line began to shift, both our forces well within range of each other. Then Voss' bugle was answered on the left as Baugh's troop rode forward firing their pistols. The enemy on that flank were forced to give way, firing a few shots as they fell back.

Horsemen began to pour from the woods on our right, disorganized and bewildered, with howling Apaches on their heels. One man took a spear in the back. Two more were shot from their saddles. They tried to rally only to find the warriors among them shooting at close quarters. And then the hatchets came out.

"Fire men! Open fire!" I shouted.

Our entire line let loose a volley, gray smoke blanketing our front. Half of the enemy seemed to go down, though I suspect most of them were ducking rather than wounded. A few stood their ground and returned fire. One of Crockett's men was hit, and Jimmy Allen took a nick on the shoulder. Our line fired again, and within seconds, fired a third time. Butler, Hughes and French busy with their Winchesters, each holding fifteen rounds.

The center of the enemy line, based near a wagon flying a blue flag with a white star, appeared to be the command post. A man in a fine gray suit staggered back, seriously wounded. Another in a tall beaver hat was waving a sword. Three men were trying to turn around a 6-pounder, but a pile of cannon shot was in the way. One brave gunner was soon hit, falling over the wheel. A comrade who went to help him was hit as well. An officer in a fine blue uniform with rows of gold buttons was yelling at all about him with feverish emotion.

There was another bugle call. A Seventh Cavalry bugle calling the *Charge*. Across the meadow, sixty or more men began riding toward the enemy position at a steady gallop. I saw the blue and red silk guidon of E Company, a swallowtail Buffalo Flag, and two banners I didn't recognize.

The rebel force had no place to go, under attack from four sides. There was so much noise and smoke that the officers seemed unable to take any sort of control. One group of enemy militia managed to form a line, fire, and reload to fire again. Their action drew return fire from all over the field. Soon effective resistance began to collapse. The flank falling back from Baugh's charge disintegrated first, running wildly to and fro. The right wing had tried to help their beleaguered cavalry, but the swirling dust had reduced visibility to a blur, obscuring friend and foe. The center of the line appeared frozen, unable to commit in any direction. The thundering of E Company made the task even harder, for they would be among them within minutes.

"Volley fire!" I heard Hughes shouting from my right.

"Lay into them, boys," French said on the left.

For the first time, I started worrying more about the expenditure of ammunition than winning the battle. Perhaps Crockett was thinking the same thing. He'd holstered his pistol and was walking the line, seeking to slow the rate of fire.

I saw part of the enemy cavalry finally break free and ride for Peggy Lake. Some were riding double. At least a dozen bodies lay in bloody heaps. Riderless horses milling at the edge of the woods were being gathered by the Apaches.

Far to my left, I noticed the militia nearest the trees ducking past Baugh's charge, making for the bayou. Baugh wisely let them go, keeping pressure on the enemy flank. The remainder began throwing down their arms.

"Cease fire!" I ordered, the command being repeated down the line by the sergeants. "Voss, sound *Recall*."

The recall was met with similar calls across the field, the rapid firing quickly dying to an occasional shot, and then an eerie silence. The sound of victory.

"Hughes, Butler, disarm the prisoners," I said. "Tatanka, where are you?"

"Here, General," he answered, standing only a few feet away. A trace of blood dripped from a scalp wound.

"Good work, my young friend. Good work," I complimented, slapping him on the shoulder.

The aftermath of a pitched battle is excitement, melancholy, fear for the wounded, and a sense of relief. And in this case, surprise, for I had blundered into triumph as surely as I had once blundered into defeat.

"Orders, George?" Crockett asked, his face smudged with powder.

"Round them up. Weed out the officers. We'll take over their camp for the night," I said.

I looked around for Traveller, wanting to find my brother and needing to speak with Flacco. Corporal Vasquez brought my horse forward, but when I went to mount, my leg grew stiff.

"You are wounded, sir," Vasquez said, pointing to my boot.

Son of a gun if I wasn't. I thought for a moment of General Johnston, killed at Pittsburg Landing, when a bullet cut the artery behind his knee. And I remembered Sam Houston at the Battle of San Jacinto, lying under an oak tree with a shattered ankle while accepting the surrender of Santa Anna. I looked about for the famous tree, but all the oaks looked alike.

French and Vasquez soon had me sitting on the ground, cutting off the boot and calling for a doctor. The injury didn't look serious, a flesh wound in the calf, but there was no point in bleeding out. I looked up as Tom was jumping from Athena.

"Autie, what happened?" he said, kneeling at my side.

"Just a stray. How are you? Last I saw, you were bedridden."

"Weren't that bad," he answered. "Looks like I got to Galveston first."

"Looks so. E Company. Is Smith with you?"

"Gathering up the enemy flags. His arm's kinda stiff, but he rides well enough. Let's find you a tent."

I would not be put in a tent, there were too many decisions to be made, but we did find a sturdy wagon bed that would let me see the camp. Tom rushed off to find a doctor, always scarce after a fight.

"General Custer, what should we do?" Flacco the Younger asked, reining up but not dismounting. His painted mustang was covered in sweat. He'd removed his shirt, a half-empty cartridge belt slung over his shoulder. I looked to see if he'd taken any scalps, and was relieved that he had not.

"Casualties?"

"Three wounded. Bipin was stuck with a sword," Flacco said.

"Bipin must report for treatment. Pursue the rebel horse as far as the creek and then return," I ordered.

Flacco saluted and rode off. He was not one for long conversations.

"George! What the hell?" Crockett shouted, rushing up with a dozen men on his heels. Only two were Seventh Cavalry. The rest looked like recent enemies.

"Who are your friends?" I inquired.

"Few old neighbors from Tennessee," Crockett said, though he didn't seem personally familiar with them. "This is John Moore. Friend of Chief Flacco. He's got a ranch on the upper Colorado. This 'ere youngster is Jack Hayes, born back home in Cedar Lick. They got 'xperience fightin' the Comanche."

"And fighting the Seventh Cavalry," I pointed out.

"Jack and I weren't fighting the Buffalo Flag, sir," Moore said, a man of middle height, about forty years old, with long brown hair and hazel eyes. "We're Texas Rangers, and we haven't taken sides in this war."

I vaguely recalled something about Moore and the Texas Rangers, but the details escaped me. The younger man, which I guessed at twenty years old, looked like a younger version of Crockett, though shorter.

"We don't own no slaves, and there ain't a government in Texas worth a pitcher a spit. Except maybe Colonel Crockett's," young Hayes said. "Our job is fightin' Indians, not white men."

"What do you expect of me, gentlemen?" I asked.

"My wife Eliza is in this camp," Moore said. "We only joined Burnet to protect families against the Comanche. We ask for pardon."

I looked to Crockett. He would not have brought these men before me had he not expected a favorable decision.

"May President Crockett and I confer for a moment?" I requested.

The crowd backed off, leaving me alone with the old bear hunter. And Corporal Vasquez, who was wiping down my leg with murky river water.

"We need ta figure on this," Crockett said. "Some of these men come fer free land and booty. But thar are others, like Moore, who been settlin' this land fer years. Good folks. We done beat this batch, now we gotta decide what ta do with 'em."

"Did we capture Burnet?" I asked.

"Yeah, an' Lamar. Houston be glad to hear that," Crockett reported.

"Put the ringleaders under guard," I said. "The freebooters who offer no resistance can return to the states. As for colonists like Moore, you should decide which neighbors are worth keeping."

"Thanks, George," Crockett said, offering a lazy salute.

He strolled back to the prisoners with the good news. Moore looked in my direction with a nod and ran to find his wife. Jack Hayes stood by Crockett earnestly asking questions, pleading his case, and after a suitable delay, he was handed a rifle. I suspected Crockett had just signed up a new recruit. What young man from Tennessee wouldn't want to serve with Davy Crockett?

Tom returned with a middle-aged man in a fine cloth suit carrying a black leather satchel. He was tall but tended to slouch, the eyes studious. A gray week old beard covered his chin.

"Autie, this is Doc Virgil Goodfellow, all the way from Boston," Tom introduced.

"You've traveled far, sir," I said.

"Not alone, General. There are forty-five of us, all fit and ready to serve your cause," Goodfellow boasted. He peeled back the cloth over my leg and made a face. "What is this?"

"Calf wound. Looks like it went all the way through," Tom said, taking a close look.

"Not the wound, this filthy water," Goodfellow said.

The doctor reached into his bag, took out a quart-sized bottle of clear liquid labeled carbolic acid, and poured it on the bullet hole.

"Goddamn! What in the living god of hell?" I shouted, the pain so bad my eyes rolled back in my head.

Goodfellow poured more of the horrid fluid into a clean cloth, grabbed my leg, and began to scrub deeply into the wound. Only a need for dignity prevented me from disgracing myself.

"Just an antiseptic, sir. Haven't you read Dr. Lord's paper?" Goodfellow said.

"Dr. Lord? The Seventh Cavalry's Dr. George Edwin Lord?" I asked.

"One and the same," Goodfellow said. "When Lord's thesis first appeared in the Boston medical journals, his theory was treated with disdain. As one would expect. But trials on test subjects have proven sterilization fights infection, especially during surgery. Every physician in New England is now adopting the practice."

I knew Lord subscribed to the theories of Joseph Lister, who probably hadn't been born yet. But even the U.S. Army still had its doubts.

"Has Dr. Lord submitted any papers on pasteurization?" I asked, for I had read of Pasteur's experiments in *Harper's Weekly*.

"That's a crazy theory, too, but we're looking at it," Goodfellow admitted. "Anything that fights child-bed fever would be a blessing."

As Goodfellow was wrapping my leg, I saw Algernon Smith walking in my direction.

"Glad to see you, Fresh. How's the arm?" I asked.

"Dr. Pollard says I'll get full use eventually, if I keep exercising it," Smith said, flexing the muscles. He looked good, bronzed from the sun and healthy. His uniform, a dark blue jacket and tan trousers, was well-tailored.

"Casualty report?" I requested.

"We'll have that in a minute," Smith said.

"I have it now," a voice said with a Canadian accent.

"Queen's Own? I was wondering when you'd turn up," I said. "I was afraid you might have gotten yourself killed."

"I don't think so, sir," Cooke answered. "As for my report, thirty-two dead on their side, six on ours. We have about twenty wounded, including a careless general."

"I wasn't careless, just unlucky," I responded.

"We're still counting, but French thinks there are two hundred prisoners in all," Cooke continued with barely a pause. "We've captured three hundred rifles, one cannon, and two hundred pounds of powder. We're not unhappy about the tents and wagons, either."

"I saw some new flags out there," I remembered.

"Juan Almonte brought a battalion from southern Texas, the Goliad Rangers," Tom said. "Mostly Tejanos and a few Mexican recruits."

"Almonte? Here?" I asked, looking around.

"Juan is still gathering supplies in Galveston," Smith explained.

"We drew lots to see who would stay behind, and he lost."

"The other company are New Englanders under Captain Bill Garrison. Call themselves the Boston Liberators," Cooke said. "Garrison's got no military experience, so Tom put me in temporary command."

No one said it, but we all knew who William Garrison was. Or would be, in another time. Some blamed him for bringing on the Civil War rather than let slavery die out naturally, especially my father. But none of that mattered now. And it was good to know there were those in the North rallying to our cause.

"Dr. Goodfellow, what does President Van Buren have to say about all this commotion?" I asked.

"Sir, if Texas were to sink into the sea, no man would be more pleased," Goodfellow replied.

We camped that evening near the battlefield, several blazing bonfires marking our celebration. Whiskey found in the captured wagons was shared, though not in great quantities. I finally found my oak tree and lay under it on a blanket, setting about making plans for the upcoming campaign. Crockett wanted to discuss the captured officers, but I put it off until morning. When I noticed Tom and Tatanka huddling together, I waved them over.

"Take a seat, brother," I offered. "Is there anything you want to tell me?"

Tom sheepishly sat on the blanket, Tatanka next to him. Tom poured a finger of whiskey into my empty coffee cup.

"Been tryin' to avoid it, Autie. Not sure what you'd say," Tom hedged.

"Morning Star? Well, Indian marriages aren't all that formal," I said.

"They are when conducted by a priest," Tom replied.

"A priest?" I said.

"My sister was educated by the Catholic sisters in St. Louis," Tatanka explained. "They made her one of their faith."

"I'm sort of a Catholic now, too," Tom admitted. "I know Pa would skin my hide, but we're Texans now. Father Francis converted me. Morning Star and I married just before you returned from California."

"And you neglected to tell me?" I said.

"Everyone was kind of busy," he answered. "Anyway, this makes

Tatanka my brother-in-law. Which I guess makes him your family, too. Sort of a little brother."

I was a bit peeved. It was one thing to take up with an Indian girl, quite another to marry one. But Tom never was one for conventions. I reached out my hand.

"Congratulations, brother, you've married above your station," I said. "So who else knows? Smith? Cooke? Crockett?"

"Yes," Tom said.

"All of them? Everybody except me?"

"Tough subject to bring up, Autie," Tom repeated.

"I hope you'll tell me when to expect a nephew," I insisted.

"Well, now that you mention it," Tom said.

"That's enough for now, Mr. Custer. Tatanka and I need to talk," I said, pointing for him to leave.

Tatanka sat cross-legged looking at me, sipping coffee. For some reason he seemed pleased by my discomfort.

"We are brothers. You must help the People," Tatanka finally said.

"Did you think I wouldn't?"

"You are Custer. No one knows what you will do."

————

The next morning dawned cool and clear. I slept well after Dr. Goodfellow administered a mild opiate, for the leg had a tendency to throb. I soon choose to ignore it, for the day would begin grimly.

"Bring the prisoners forward," I commanded before a large gathering.

We assembled in the green pasture where the battle had been fought the day before. Company C and the Apache scouts were mounted, positioned behind the surrendered rebel army should any decide to cause trouble. Company E and the Boston Liberators, on foot, were stationed on the flanks, weapons loaded. Crockett's Company A acted as orderlies of the court. I sat in session with Juan Seguin and Miciagh Autry.

The first defendant was David G. Burnet, a fifty-year-old New Jerseyite and former president of Texas. His republic had crumbled when other rebel leaders formed into rival groups, but he had remained to cause trouble.

"Mr. Burnet, we see that you have taken up arms against the

Buffalo Flag even after our declaration," I said. "Can you offer some defense?"

He was a lawyer. Of course he could offer a defense. But would it be good enough?

"General Custer, gentlemen of the court," Burnet said. "I come humbly before you. I've had a busy life. As a young man I lived with the Comanche. I joined General Francisco de Miranda to liberate Venezuela from Spain, though we failed. Then I fought in Chile, and again in Venezuela, always in the name of liberty. When I came to Texas, Stephen Austin welcomed me. In 1836, I answered Travis's plea to aid the Alamo, but arrived too late. I have meant no disrespect to the Buffalo Flag. I own no slaves. All I seek is freedom for the people."

There were many cheers from the crowd, and even a few from my own troopers. I glanced at Seguin, who was not impressed by the speech. I wasn't, either.

"Mr. Burnet, how does your quest for liberty reconcile with the massacre at the Cherokee village?" I asked.

"I did not order that," Burnet vehemently protested. "The army was sent to make a treaty. To secure food and horses. The Cherokee have lived in peace with us."

"Until you murdered Chief Bowles," I said.

"I was not there. I was in Harrisburg when I learned of Bowles's death," Burnet said. A convincing alibi.

"Then you blame your subordinates?" Baugh inquired.

"I blame no one. I only say what I know to be the truth," Burnet responded.

Awaiting their turns were six more belligerent officers, all of low rank. Except for Lamar, who styled himself a colonel. Houston had said it was Lamar who gave the orders at the Cherokee village, and he was yet to return from burning the ferry at Fort Bend. I had no specific knowledge of the others.

"Thank you, Mr. Burnet," I said, calling the judges back to confer in private. Crockett, Tom and Tatanka joined us, unofficially.

"What do you think?" I asked.

"He makes a good case," Autry said.

"He is a good liar," Seguin said.

"Being a lawyer, he kin likely talk the feathers off a goose, but I

301

kan't see that he's a criminal," Crockett added.

"Tom?" I asked.

"Burnet's pretty much been out of sight since I got back to Texas," he said. "Fannin and Burleson attacked Béjar. Fannin allowed the Goliad massacre. Houston and Lamar marched against the Cherokee. Burnet is more of a quartermaster than a general."

"Tatanka?" I requested.

"It would be good to shoot all of the white captives, but it might cause trouble," Tatanka said. "The Buffalo Flags should have friends as well as enemies."

"I guess this is Burnet's lucky day," I concluded.

The court reconvened. I stood while Seguin and Autry remained seated. Burnet was brought before us.

"Mr. Burnet, this court finds you guilty of misdemeanors against the legitimate government of Texas. You are sentenced to ten years exile," I announced. "Return to Galveston and take ship to New Orleans, and thank God for your life."

"Yes, General. Thank you. Thank you members of the court," Burnet said, bowing as he withdrew.

I pointed to the other five officers standing next to Lamar and motioned them forward.

"Would any of you gentlemen like to join Mr. Burnet, or take your chances at trial?" I asked.

They looked at each other, whispered, and one stepped forward.

"Captain von Blücher got family in San Felipe, sir," the spokesman said. "If he could go home, he promises to cause no more trouble. The rest of us, we take whatever you give us."

"What is your name, sir?" I asked, impressed with his loyalty.

"Silas Beecher, sir. I served in the Nashville Battalion under Parsons Miller," Beecher answered.

"You're a Tennessee man?"

"Yes, sir, I am."

I began to wonder if there was anyone in this war that wasn't from Tennessee.

"Colonel Crockett, please come forward," I summoned.

Crockett hurried over and stood next to Beecher.

"Colonel Crockett, this court suspends the charges against these men and places them in your charge," I said.

302

"Thank you, George. General. That's mighty generous," Crockett said, slapping Beecher on the shoulder.

The entire group looked relieved, and I saw among the faces of the other prisoners that they approved. Tom was giving me his devil's eye, believing it a cagy gesture on my part.

"Mr. Lamar, you face serious accusations," I declared as the forty-year-old Georgia lawyer was pushed forward.

"I am a colonel of cavalry for the Republic of Texas, serving under General Sam Houston," Lamar answered. "I have done no more than my duty."

"Last I heard, Sam wasn't too pleased with you," I said.

"The heathens fired first. We were just defending ourselves," Lamar replied.

The man was well-spoken. Educated. I had no doubt he could argue his way out of a deep hole if given the chance, but I knew him well by reputation. As the second president of Texas, he had started a long and bloody war against the Comanche that lasted into the 1870s. He not only murdered Chief Bowles, but stole the Cherokee land more ruthlessly than Andrew Jackson had. He was a bold politician and brave soldier. He had even been appointed Minister to Nicaragua by President Buchanan while I was attending West Point. In every respect, Mirabeau Buonaparte Lamar was a dangerous man.

"This court has heard enough," I abruptly decided, standing up.

Tom, Crockett and Tatanka started toward our conference area, but I held up a hand to stop them. I whispered to Seguin, who looked back in surprise, and then whispered to Autry, who nodded reluctant agreement.

"Colonel Lamar, you are found guilty of murder and treason against the Buffalo Flag. The sentence is death, to be carried out at dawn," I declared. "Sergeant of the guard, take the prisoner to Father Rodriquez that he might forgive his sins."

Sergeant Knowles of Crockett's command hesitated, for the sentence was unexpected. Hughes elbowed him aside.

"We got the duty, sir," Hughes said, Butler and French at his side.

"Jimmy," I whispered as Lamar was led away.

"Yes, General," Butler said.

"If Lamar were to escape during the night, he'll want to rejoin Fannin. Assign a scout to follow him," I suggested.

303

Among the People, leaders earn respect through their wisdom. The People may follow such a leader, or they may not. None may be told what to do. This is not so among the white men, where a powerful few appoint the leaders, and punish those who will not obey. Except in Texas, for the white men of that land were difficult to rule, and they would not follow a chief they did not believe in. Crockett and many others realized this truth, but Custer resisted such a thought. Custer believed a leader should be obeyed, and Custer believed he should be the leader.

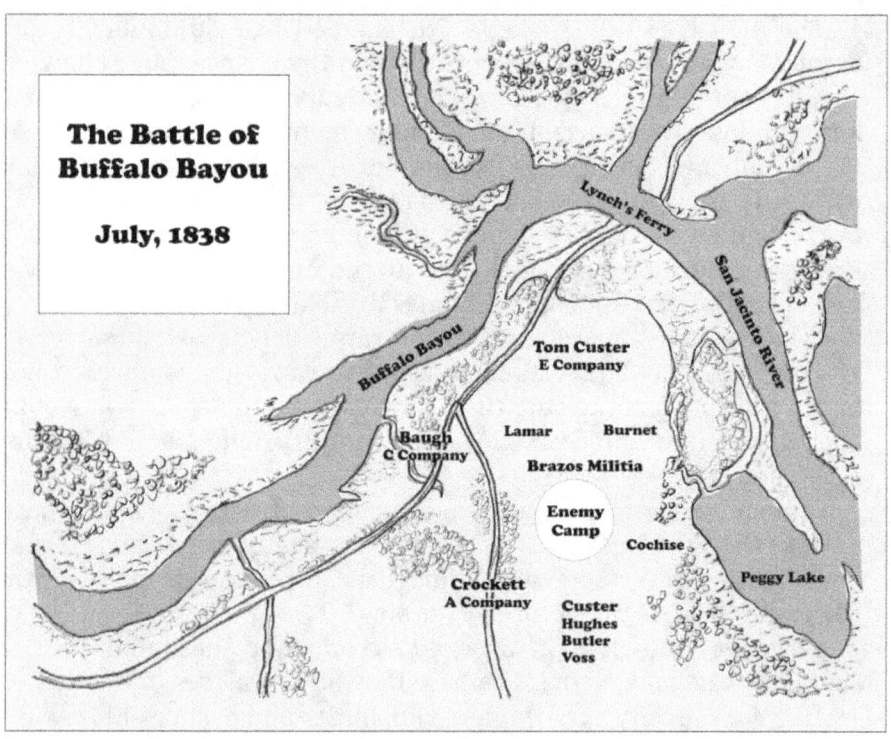

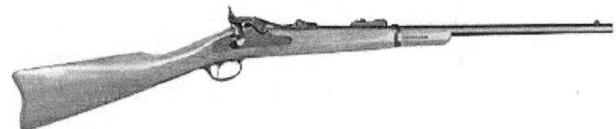

Chapter Eleven
THE TRAP CLOSES

We spent four days at Buffalo Bayou treating the wounded, burying the dead, and deciding what to do next. The aggressive move was toward Harrisburg, which I'd still had no word from, but cooler heads urged a return to Galveston.

"Burleson can't go west because of Keogh," Cooke said, his finger on a hand drawn map. "If he goes east to Lynchburg, he'll be caught between us and the Cherokee. If he goes south to Velasco, Santa Anna will be waiting for him."

"Antonio's in Velasco?" I asked.

"After taking Goliad, we found the Mexican Navy at Copano. What's left of it," Tom explained. "Santa Anna sent two companies under Castrillón to chase Fannin, and took the other two to Velasco. We stayed with him while the troops landed, then sailed on to Galveston."

"Our old friend Admiral Cochrane is there," Cooke said. "The rebels didn't want to pick a fight with England, so they've sort of left the town open."

"Very wise of them," I approved.

"You knew Cochrane would be patrolling the gulf, didn't you?" Tom asked.

"We discussed it last year," I admitted. "The King's government doesn't want the United States annexing Texas, and they're not too happy with Mexico because of the unpaid debts. At least we pay in gold."

"Some of the time," Cooke said, knowing much of our commerce was still being conducted in notes.

"Galveston has a Buffalo Flag over it now," Smith bragged. "And it won't be coming down again. The port is ours."

"If Galveston is safe, maybe we should march on Harrisburg?" I suggested. "Fannin and Burleson combined can't have more than two thousand men, and I suspect their real number is closer to fourteen hundred. Our force alone is sufficient to finish the rebellion."

"No, Autie, Harrisburg isn't the right move," Tom said with some impatience. "Almonte is gathering supplies in Galveston. Cochrane will wish to confer with you, and that's where Houston expects to rejoin the command. And if Myles is sending a messenger, he'll need to come by sea to Galveston. When we know what Myles and Santa Anna are doing, we can coordinate for a final campaign."

"We're going to win this war, George," Smith said. "I wouldn't have said that two months ago, but now I can."

"We'll squeeze the rebels out of whatever shelter they've found, like Lee at Petersburg, and then run them to ground," Cooke added.

It suddenly dawned on me the plans were already made. They weren't asking my permission, they were telling me what would happen. It was a revolt. Insubordination, at the very least. And it was a *fait accompli*.

"Very well, gentlemen, we move at sunrise," I agreed.

I went outside my new campaign tent, formerly used by the provisional president of Texas, and met up with Crockett. He had his hands full with the prisoners, and though I'm sure they all weren't from Tennessee, it felt like they were.

"Keep them in the center of the line," I advised. "The women can ride in the wagons. Let the older boys mind the mules. We'll ship the mercenaries back to New Orleans."

"And the colonists? Those who were 'ere 'fore the war?" Crockett asked.

"They can't stay and own slaves, David," I said. "The whole point of a free Texas is to blunt the slavery issue. The Missouri Compromise, the Compromise of 1850, the Kansas-Nebraska Act, all led to war. That can't happen this time."

"Tom already give me that lecture. And Bill, and Algernon. Pretty strong in thar 'pinions. Can't say I'm always sure you believe it."

"The Gang thinks they can control the future. I learned the hard way that we can't. But it's our best course for now."

"I'm still needin' wiggle room. No slaves, but we should give some of these folks a chance ta live under our laws. Be peaceable neighbors."

"Caesar gave clemency to his enemies, and look what happened to him."

"George, ya ain't Caesar," Crockett said.

Tom had made that clear.

"President Crockett, do what's right. They are your responsibility," I granted.

I figured it was about three days to Galveston by foot and wagon. Maybe four, with women and children in tow. Faster for the cavalry, though most would stay with the battalion. I decided to take my staff ahead, leaving Tom in charge of the column, fielding complaints, tending mules, and searching for lost strays. If he was going to be the general, it was time to learn that rank isn't all privilege.

We headed southwest, crossing several rowdy creeks. On our left, the San Jacinto River gave way to Galveston Bay, though the locals just called it the Bay. The countryside was hilly, filled with oak trees, and good for cattle, though there were few to be seen. We camped near a clear blue lake and were off again the next morning. I needed a little help from Allen getting on and off my horse, for the leg was stiff, but I was determined to shake off the pain. French cut me a maplewood staff to lean on.

The land eventually grew flat down near the water where we would find the ferry station.

"General, look," Butler said as we paused above a new settlement.

"Refugees," Hughes observed.

It was a shanty town of tents, shacks and hovels. Ragged people of all ages, burned out or chased out of their homes. Two years of war had not been kind, but I had seen worse in Virginia during the Rebellion. They would rebuild.

"Hughes, Allen, unfurl our colors," I ordered. "Voss, play us a tune as we ride through. Something to reassure them."

"Dixie?" Voss asked.

"Don't be smart," I rebuked. "But you don't need to play "Marching Through Georgia", either."

Neither song had been written in 1838, but that wasn't the point.

307

The forty of us proceeded down a gentle slope, the ruddy road well-beaten, and acknowledged the dispossessed mob who watched us in silence as we rode by. I took off my wide-brimmed trail hat, tipping it at the women folk, and tried not to look too grim. My men were relaxed, offering a few smiles. Corporal Vasquez paused to give a pouch of bread rolls to a group of waifs.

Riding on my right, Tatanka did not share our mood, often glaring.

"What's wrong there, lad?" I asked.

"This was the future of my people. It still could be. I did not know the white man lived in such a way," he answered.

"The poor are everywhere," I said. "Some work hard and rise above it. Most don't."

"These white men did not work hard?" Tatanka asked.

"They probably did," I conceded.

"My people are not the only ones who need a new path," Tatanka concluded.

We reached the ferry and dismounted. A log fort of sorts had been established, with stables and a storeroom, but no cannon. There were plenty of cannon on the island protecting the approaches.

"General Custer, sir!" the sergeant of the guard said, snapping to attention.

"Sergeant Mendez, how fares the command?" I asked.

"Standing tall, sir. Standing tall," he said, squaring his thin shoulders.

A score of soldiers, all in blue uniforms and looking sharp, had lined up to greet us. They were a mixture of white and Tejano, with an Indian or two and several freed Negroes. Morale was high. I noticed two British warships anchored in the harbor, and our flag flying over the town.

"Return to duty," I said with a salute.

Stable hands unsaddled our mounts and led them to a grassy field to graze. I gave Traveller a hug, for he was a superb horse, worthy of the best treatment. A boy came forward to give Traveller an apple, earning my appreciation.

Near the fort was a new mercantile run by a vigorous pioneer named Samuel Parr, who wanted to call his small outpost Parrsville. The league of land he was claiming seemed somewhat excessive, but I promised to consider his petition.

We wandered down to the dock, the ferry boats much improved since my previous visit, being wider and more stable. Out in the bay, I saw *HMS Lydia* bobbing quietly at anchor with her colors waving in a gentle breeze. Nearby was an armed British brig that I didn't recognize. The spray of the cold salt air contrasted sharply with the dusty trails we'd ridden the last month, though after a while, I sheltered in the steering house. Powered by a small steam engine and a crude sail, the voyage took about thirty minutes. A rushed but respectful delegation awaited us at the Galveston Pier.

"General Custer, you're alive," Juan Almonte said, giving a salute. "We heard you were killed by Comanche. Or Sam Houston."

Almonte was looking fit. Now thirty-five years old and growing mature.

"I wasn't killed by Houston, but I did consider hanging him," I replied.

Almonte went to greet Butler and Hughes, for they'd served together in the days after the Alamo. Galveston was still the weather-worn beach town I remembered, though somewhat larger. One of the old warehouses had burned down, but two more had been built. There was a sense of prosperity, for in every war, some areas will thrive while others suffer. Being the busiest port west of New Orleans had its benefits.

I saw Lord Thomas Cochrane emerge from the King's Arms Hotel. He fully looked the admiral, dressed in a formal blue navy jacket covered in brass buttons, a velvet collar, white trousers and a cocked hat. I didn't know if his lost knighthood had been restored yet, but he seemed happy. There was a beautiful woman hanging on his arm that I recognized.

"Good to see you again, Custer. Afraid you were going to miss the show," Cochrane said, gripping my hand.

"Another week and I might have missed the whole war," I replied.

"Still have some war left," Cochrane said, giving me a knowing look. It wasn't something to discuss on a crowded dock.

I gazed at Isabella, so happy to see her that I nearly rushed into her arms, but I still wasn't sure where we stood. I had left Béjar without saying goodbye.

"Miss Seguin," I said, for she preferred her maiden name when not visiting her late husband's family in Mexico City.

"George, I am pleased to see you still have your scalp," she replied, possibly in jest, for my hair continued to thin.

"Is your father well? And your mother?" I inquired.

"They are, thank you. Have you seen my brother?"

"I have. He is scouting east of Harrisburg, earning a name for himself."

She gave a charming smile, and then stepped forward, offering both hands. I drew her close, feeling her breath against my face, and though we would not kiss in public, I had hopes of her affections.

I wanted an immediate briefing. What was the situation in Galveston? What had Cochrane discovered? What were newspapers in the east saying? Would Van Buren send troops across the Sabine? Where was the Mexican army? Was there a Mexican army? But that all had to wait, for I needed to greet the garrison first. Shake hands. Give compliments. Tip my hat. I would never be a Davy Crockett, or a Sam Houston, or even a Tom Custer, but if I wanted the loyalty of this army, I would need to win hearts.

––––––––––

Isabella joined me for a brief walk around town, though there were too many spectators for us to talk. I leaned on my maplewood cane and managed to get along well enough. Isabella remarked on my bravery, and appropriate concern for the wound, but did not embarrass me by dwelling on it.

I learned Cochrane's squadron had arrived two weeks earlier escorting several sloops from Boston and Philadelphia. The small rebel garrison under Burnet had fled, leaving Galveston to the Yankee abolitionists. Tom's arrival a few days later had insured control of the port. Having changed hands several times during the war, the locals seemed to take it all in stride.

The New Englanders were a disparate group, their outfits reminiscent of the Second Cavalry Dragoons. Much like the New Orleans Grays had been. But these uniforms were dark blue wool with off-white trousers and tall black boots. The officers carried dashing sabers on their wide leather belts, each highlighted by a red sash.

Reverend Danforth of the Boston Brigade told me that not all of the volunteers were Northerners. One troop of thirteen had joined them in New Orleans from west Tennessee, and I sensed Danforth held some suspicion of their motives. Thomas Morris, leader of the Philadelphians, declined to offer an opinion. I would draw my own conclusion when the Tennesseans returned from duck hunting on the far side of the island.

After making the customary rounds, particularly with the merchants and their womenfolk, Isabella went to visit with Hughes and Butler. Several years before, they had helped me rescue her from a roaming band of Comanche. I went to the Golden Eagle Tavern up from the docks, making sure I'd have their best room, and then limped down to the customs house. The commandant's office was at my disposal.

Someone had done a diligent job of gathering newspapers from different parts of the country. A crate on the office floor held recent issues of *The Picayune* from New Orleans, the *New York Herald*, the *Weekly Register* out of Baltimore, a few copies of the *Edgefield Advertiser* from South Carolina, and even the *Times of London*. I had spent fifteen minutes perusing the major stories when Tatanka entered.

"Is it as you expected?" he asked, taking a seat across the desk from me.

"I believe so. At West Point, we learned the country had bitter divisions over the annexation of Texas," I recounted. "The North did not want another slave state in the Union. The South wanted to expand slavery into the territories. Several times they came close to war. Even during my days as a cadet, there were bitter arguments, and three score of my classmates left the academy when the Southern states seceded."

"What does this mean for Texas?" Slow asked.

"I'm not sure. The South may have to give up their dreams of expansion. Or they may challenge the North now instead of twenty years from now," I speculated. "From what these newspapers say, both sides are passionate for their cause."

"Then you expect war?"

"There is always going to be a war somewhere," I said.

Admiral Cochrane announced a grand dinner for us that night, taking over the entire dining hall at the King's Arms. Included were the town fathers who had stayed after Burnet fled, Isabella and

Almonte, the British sea captains, and the leaders of the new volunteer contingents. An hour before sunset, a Mexican brig received approval to drop anchor and several officers rowed to shore. I rushed down to meet them.

"General Castrillón," I said. "It's a pleasure to see you so well."

"We heard you were in Alta California hanging horse thieves," Castrillón said, his deep brown eyes twinkling with mischief.

"Duty called," I responded. "I heard you were fighting Fannin outside Victoria."

"The pirates retreated. We had no supplies for pursuit," he explained.

"Will you take dinner with us?" I invited.

"Gladly, though I may need a moment to gain my land legs."

I led him away from the wharf, past the warehouses, and beyond the farthest workshop, walking along the beachfront until we were alone.

"Are you here as Antonio's emissary, or Mexico's?" I asked. "Or are they again one and the same?"

"It is true General Santa Anna has been invited back to Mexico City," Castrillón admitted. "The Congress has proven corrupt. The country is in chaos. But he has not yet been offered a return to power."

"And if he is?" I pressed.

"George, such directness," Castrillón chided. "Have you no diplomacy?"

"You've been his best friend for twenty years. I have been your friend. And I have been Antonio's friend. I think I deserve a straight answer."

"General Santa Anna has taken Velasco with two hundred men. He expects Urrea to bring a thousand more. If he destroys the pirate army first, he may lay claim to all of Texas."

"And California?"

"No, he is not a fool. Alta-California is lost to Mexico."

"So is Texas."

"He is not sure of that."

"Then I will need to convince him," I decided. "What do you think?"

"I am just an officer in his army."

"Manuel, what do you think?"

"I think if you leave Texas, the Americans will come in, and that is not good for Mexico," he said.

"When the time comes, I will call upon you," I warned.

"That will be a difficult day," he replied.

We walked back toward the King's Arms slowly, enjoying the sunset. I was glad some history had been changed, for on another day in another time, this fine gentleman had been murdered on the battlefield at San Jacinto.

Just as we passed the docks near the hotel, a lanky thirty-year-old in buckskin came in my direction. He was tall and sandy-haired with a bold smile. Every inch a politician, albeit a familiar looking one. He rushed to greet me.

"General Custer, I just heard you were here," he said with a Tennessee drawl. "How is my father?"

"Who is your father?" I asked.

"David Crockett, sir. My name is John Crockett, his oldest son."

"I heard you were running for Congress?" I said.

"A few of the voters didn't take kindly to Pa's stand against slavery. But it was a close election. Only lost by a hundred votes."

"Well, John, I was with your father just two days ago," I said, shaking the offered hand. "The old bear-killer never looked better. He'll be here day after tomorrow."

Crockett the Younger let out his breath with relief.

"I was worried. We haven't had word in months," he said.

"Mr. Crockett, General Castrillón and I are preparing for dinner. Care to join us?" I invited.

"That I would. Thank you, sir," he answered.

The formal state dinner at the King's Arms was splendid. Cochrane had his silver plate brought over from his ship, and the room was lit with dozens of elegant candle holders. A small army of servants served three courses of beef, fish and poultry, along with an excellent onion soup spiced in just the right way. It reminded me of Delmonico's. Later, a Marine band played music and many of the participants danced, though I was forced to watch, leaning on my cane.

Afterwards, the men retired to the smoking lounge. Present were Admiral Cochrane, Captain Bush, Almonte, Crockett, Castrillón, Dr.

Anson Jones of Massachusetts, Tatanka, and half a dozen others. I enjoyed a fine Havana cigar, a small taste of brandy, and got down to business.

"Where do we stand, Sir Thomas?" I asked.

Cochrane leaned back in his padded chair, his ruddy cheeks flushed, letting the question hang for a moment of mischievous drama.

"No one knows what to think of Texas, George," he finally replied. "Every time it looks like the Republic and Mexico are reaching a decisive moment, the Buffalo Flag appears to upend the situation. Between the sectional conflict and financial panic, Van Buren's administration is paralyzed. France is afraid to alienate Mexico, for a great deal of money is owed them. Spain has hopes of resurrecting their empire if Mexico falters."

"Few believe you can hold Texas with such a small army," Captain Bush added. "But until a victor emerges from the chaos, none are likely to intervene."

"And after a victor emerges? What happens then?" Dr. Jones asked.

"George has the power of the British Navy, as long as our alliance is firm," Bush said. "It is firm, isn't it?"

"Yes, William. The promises we made in San Francisco will be kept," I assured him. The British officers were satisfied by my answer, for we all knew where our best interests lay.

"And what of the South, Mr. Crockett? The stream of volunteers seem to have lessened in the last six months," Castrillón asked.

"The promise of free land has not been forthcoming," John said. "And the more adventurous souls have gone to California. But the big plantation owners still see promise in Texas."

"And you?" I asked.

"I stand with my father," John replied.

"The Missouri Compromise limits the South's ability to expand," Jones said. "After Florida and Arkansas, they will have no new territories, unless they seek conquest overseas."

"Cuba?" Almonte asked.

"It's been spoken of," John said.

"The grip of Spain is strong in Cuba. I know. I grew up there before joining Ferdinand VII's army," Castrillón said.

"The South could aspire to the Indian Territory," Cochrane

suggested, for he was well-versed in Washington politics. Tatanka looked at him, then over at young Crockett. He was not pleased.

"The Five Tribes have little land left. They will not let the white man take it from them," Tatanka said. "If they must, they will call upon the Sioux and Cheyenne. The Kiowa and Comanche. The Cherokee and the Creek. They will call upon the Seventh Cavalry."

All heads turned to see my reaction, for none thought the Buffalo Flag capable of waging war against the United States.

"The Indian Territory is safe for now," I said. "Let's not look for more trouble than we already have."

It was late when I returned to the Golden Eagle. Though I had begun to drink again during the last few years, after a decade of abstinence, I was still not good at holding my liquor. A good night's rest would help.

There was nothing cosmopolitan about a Galveston hotel. The clapboard rooms were drafty, the floors creaked with every step, and there was the persistent scent of a barnyard. But there was a bowl for washing on the dresser, and a bedpan for use in the middle of the night. A cloth screen covered the open window to keep out mosquitoes. I had half undressed when there was a knock on my door.

"*Disculpa que te moleste tan tarde,*" Isabella said.

"You aren't disturbing me, and it's not that late, sweetheart. Please come in," I said.

Had she never been married, or was still a young girl, I would have been more circumvent. But as a widow and of age, Isabella had the right to make up her own mind about entering a man's room.

"We need to talk," she said, sitting on the bed.

I would have pulled up a chair, but there were none to be had, so I leaned against the dresser instead.

"I had hoped to talk in Béjar," I replied.

"Many brave men died in Béjar defending the town. And some brave women. I was disappointed you were not there. I was heartbroken you did not leave California when Texas needed you."

"I should have. I offer no excuses."

"What changed your mind?" she asked.

I was tired, and my leg bothered me. I moved to sit on the bed and she made room for me. I dared to take her hand.

315

"Sweetheart, I grew up dirt poor in Ohio. The son of a struggling blacksmith," I explained. "So poor, my Pa sent me to live with my sister in Monroe because he couldn't afford to feed me. I gained fame in the war, but not the success I wanted. My career stalled. The money I made was invested badly, and when I rode off to Montana for the last time, I left my Libbie in debt. My life was a failure.

"In California, I had a second chance. I was in command, beholden to none. I had finally started making the money I'd always dreamed of. And then Texas called me back. I didn't want to give up what I'd fought for. For what I'd earned. Not even for glory."

"But you did come back?" she said.

"Yes, because a vision taught me there are some things more important than wealth or fame," I said, squeezing her hands.

"You might be a great man someday," Isabella said, a twinkle in her eyes reflecting the candlelight.

"Not without a great woman to stand beside me," I replied, leaning forward for a kiss.

———

By the time Tom and Crockett rode in two days later, I had put all of Galveston on a war footing, much like City Point in 1865. Warehouses were being reorganized, a hospital established, and official government offices opened for business. The Buffalo Flag would be buying supplies, selling land grants, and confiscating the property of traitors. Dr. Anson Jones was appointed the civil magistrate, and William Garrison was detached from his militia unit to publish a newspaper. After pleading for a pardon, David Burnett was allowed to stay as a surveyor.

"Juan Seguin sent a messenger from Harrisburg," Tom said, coming up to the roof of the customs house. "Counts about five hundred men under Thomas Jefferson Rusk. He thinks Rusk is trying to make it back to his family in Nacogdoches, but most of his army wants to link with Fannin at San Felipe."

"Rusk. South Carolinian. Senator from Texas," I remembered. "He opposed secession and advocated for railroads."

"Does that mean we don't need ta hang 'em?" Crockett asked.

"David, I'd rather not, but let's not get ahead of ourselves," I said.

Old Crockett and I had been watching ships in the harbor, and the fort being expanded across the bay at the ferry landing. I decided to let Samuel Parr keep most of his league of land, but it wasn't going to be called Parrsville. I couldn't name the new town Fort Custer, as I was trying to appear humble, and Crockett already had his own fort. We finally settled on Fort Austin, the pioneering *empresario* who had brought hundreds of settlers to Texas. Austin had died of pneumonia a few months after the Brazos Convention, before the war began to ruin reputations.

"This 'ere operation would be a heap much easier if we knew where Myles was," Crockett said.

"We have Kid Flacco out looking for him. He's got to be somewhere east of Gonzales," Smith speculated.

"Maybe on the Colorado or San Bernard," Tom said.

"Or following Burleson?" I speculated.

"Following Burleson where? Why in hell does Texas have to be so big?" Tom complained.

I noticed Cooke walking up from the dock, and he had some surprise visitors with him.

"Maybe we'll get a few answers," I said.

A moment later, Cooke came up the stairs with Mitch Bouyer, the venerated scout looking a bit green. Morning Star was with him, looking beautiful as always.

"Gen'ral, I ain't ever getting' on a boat a'gin," Bouyer said, not even bothering to salute. "Up 'an down, up 'an down. Like a big jerky horse, but ya can't git off."

"Where have you been, Mr. Bouyer? Before the boat?" I asked.

"With General Keogh," he answered.

———

Four days later, the command was on the trail to Velasco. Knowing the British had blockaded Galveston, the rebels had come up with a new strategy, and it was a good one. Fannin had struck at Victoria, breaking that portion of Santa Anna's army, and was now countermarching east. Burleson was coming down the Brazos River from Gonzales, and Rusk taken sudden flight from Harrisburg, burning the town in the process. All were converging on the port Velasco while a flotilla of supply ships were coming west from New Orleans. With a large, well-supplied force, they could then strike in any direction, defeating their opposition piecemeal. I'd had no word from Houston.

"You sure about this, Autie?" Tom said, looking back.

Our column stretched for a mile. Cavalry, infantry, wagons, carts, and cannon. Our force numbered nearly five hundred and fifty, made up of seven companies and militia units, three score teamsters, and eighty women recruited for camp labor and hospital duty.

"It's true we could have ridden out two days ago with three hundred troops," I said. "And when we met the enemy, we would be poorly supplied and without artillery. If Fannin and Burleson are waiting in strength, what then?"

"We might have gotten to Velasco first," Tom suggested, for he had wanted to move quickly on Bouyer's news.

"No, Burleson kept us guessing, knowing all along what he needed to do," I argued.

Colonel Crockett rode up to the head of the column. I had my staff around me, guidons and banners furled. The day was warm, our march kicking up a cloud of dust on the dry road.

"How are your new volunteers?" Tom asked.

"Most gots some 'xperience, army or militia," Crockett said. "Thanks, George, fer lettin' me deal with 'em in my own way."

Crockett's force was large now. In addition to the sixty troopers of A Company, he commanded the baker's dozen his son had brought from Tennessee, and forty-five colonists who had switched sides to keep their land grants.

The hundred and fifty troops Tom had brought to Buffalo Bayou were now supplemented with the Massachusetts men and Pennsylvanians. I retained two companies along with Seguin's Béjar Mounted Rangers and the Apache scouts.

Regimental Saddler George Howell, promoted to sergeant major, was placed in charge of the supply train, with our borrowed Royal Marines assigned to guard duty. I did not want them in combat if I could help it, and the sea dogs didn't much care for cavalry duty.

Dr. Goodfellow was given the task of training the medical corp. It would be a challenge, but I'd learned during the Civil War how valuable women could be, freeing men for more important duties. His department was made up of Tejano camp followers, freed slaves, and two dozen white women. The white women were the most controversial, for such duty was not expected of them. Despite the example of Clara Barton's nurses in Virginia. If the Angels of the Battlefield could do it, these women could, too.

"Bouyer should have word for us as we approach the port," I said. "If Santa Anna has held the fort, we might catch Fannin out in the open. If not, we may need to lay siege until Keogh comes up."

"Maybe we'll find out now," Crockett said, spying a group of Mexican lancers riding toward us. They looked dirty. The mounts exhausted. There was a sense of desperation about them.

"*Tenemos que ver General Custer*," their sergeant said, halting before us.

"*Yo soy General Custer*," Tom and I said at the same time.

"*General Tomas Custer*," the sergeant clarified.

Tom dismounted and walked forward. The sergeant handed him a rolled up letter, frayed at the edges. Tom read it and frowned.

"This is Sergeant Bernardo, messenger from Santa Anna," Tom said. "Fannin arrived outside Velasco four days ago, and a flotilla of six schooners are blockading the harbor. Santa Anna only has garrison troops, and he's low on powder. He bids me to march with all possible speed."

"What other support does Santa Anna have?" I asked, for surely the small force Tom brought to Buffalo Bayou would be of little help, and Santa Anna could not know we had linked forces just a week before.

"Santa Anna has summoned General Urrea from Copano," Tom said, reading more of the letter. "It doesn't look good, Autie."

Voss blew *Officer's Call*, and within twenty minutes each of the troop commanders and their subordinates had gathered under a grand sycamore tree. I had the commissary provide lunch, for there might not be time later.

"What do we know of Velasco?" I asked.

Cooke unrolled a map. It was sparse on detail, but I knew the town was fairly small, with a customs house and a wooden palisade fort.

"The fort is on the east bank of the Brazos, upriver from the bay. That's good," I said. "I see a road along the coast, and woods to the north. The river takes a sharp turn west just past this creek."

"Is that a moat around the fort?" Smith asked.

"Mostly dry now," Seguin said. "The fortifications were neglected after the fight in 1832."

"Unless Burleson has concentrated his forces, he may still have men in Brazoria acting as a rear guard," Cooke warned.

"I'll take the artillery north of town. The woods will provide cover," Tom said. "From there, I can threaten the fort and block reinforcements from coming down river. Howell, you'll stay with my command until we take position. Set our supply camp along that creek. Goodfellow will go with you. Have the teamsters fortify the encampment."

"Yes, sir," Howell said, glancing around for the elusive doctor. Who was normally found providing instructions among the señoritas.

"I'll move along the coast, possibly draw some attention off Santa Anna," I decided. "Crockett, your militia are the least trained. Form a skirmish line with Tom on your right, my battalion on the left, and your sturdiest men in the center."

"Them is my Tennesseans, George," Crockett said. "They won't never let me down. Or you, neither."

"Make sure each man has a hundred rounds for the rifles, fifty rounds for the pistols," Tom said to the gathered officers.

"That will strain the supply," Howell warned.

"The ammunition won't do us any good if we lose," Tom replied.

I thought the allocation excessive, too. Under the circumstances. But we had run short at the Little Big Horn, and that had been my fault.

"Watch your flanks. Stay within supporting distance," I advised.

We rode on a few more miles, the artillery moving off to the right, Crockett keeping the main trail, and my battalion drifting toward the gulf. Before we were within sight of our objective, a band of hard riding Indians emerged from the woods to our left.

"Captain Cochise and some Cherokee," Major Baugh said, leading with C Company.

Cochise had found thirty or so of Gatunwali's warriors and brought them back to the column. I recognized them as the scouts who had accompanied Houston to burn the ferry at Fort Bend, but I didn't see Houston among them.

"Where is the Raven?" I asked the Cherokee leader, a tall gray-eyed warrior wearing a blue campaign jacket with sergeant stripes.

"White men came to speak with him yesterday," the sergeant said. "The Raven was troubled by their talk. He told us to go away, and went west with the white men."

"To Velasco?" Baugh asked.

"We could not see. There is an enemy camp blocking the way," the sergeant explained.

"Are you going home?" I inquired.

The Cherokee seemed miffed by my question. A young brave in leathers rode forward and unfurled their Buffalo Flag, the sea breeze letting it flap in the wind.

"We will have vengeance for Duwa'li," their leader said, straightening tall in his saddle.

"Colonel Crockett can use your help. He is just north of here, preparing to fight those who seek to steal you land," I said, pointing the way. They rode off without another word.

"Orders, General?" Cochise asked.

"Report to Crockett. See if you can find good ground for a fight," I said.

"What about Houston?" Baugh asked.

"I don't know, John," I replied. "He was angry about Bowles's murder, but he has also schemed with Jackson to annex Texas."

"If he's turned traitor, will you hang him?" Tatanka asked.

"I don't know that, either. My father loved Houston. He was my childhood hero," I said. "That's the hardest part of a civil war, fighting men you admire on the wrong side."

I finally saw smoke on the horizon. Campfires. I did not hear any muskets or cannon. It was growing late in the day, but there were a few hours of light left. If Velasco was under siege, immediate action might prove necessary. If the town had already fallen, I would want to attack at dawn to retake it.

"There they are, sir," Butler said, pointing to a guard post stationed five hundred yards up the road.

In the distance, hundreds of small tents were arranged haphazardly in a meadow, and beyond was a larger town than I expected, mostly adobes but with a few wooden buildings. The fort rose near the Brazos River, a tall timber enclosure big enough for a modest garrison. The sky was too hazy to make out the flag even with my binoculars. I guessed the enemy force between fourteen and sixteen hundred, spread out in an arc from east to north of town. Easily twice our number.

"General, my scouts find only a light guard along the beach, and they say a schooner is unloading cargo at the dock," Colonel Seguin reported, riding in with twenty of his rangers. They had been on the move for days. Their mounts were tiring.

"The fort?" I asked.

"There has been fighting. We don't know who won," Seguin said.

I studied the enemy crouching behind their hastily erected barricade. They were ill prepared for a rapid assault, but what then? Overrunning a sentry post would prove futile if a thousand or fifteen hundred rebels launched a counterattack. Tom and Crockett still needed time to get in position before we started a general engagement.

There wasn't time to scout the ground. The road was wide and dry, good for quick movement but without cover. We had a grassy prairie on our right, thick woods growing on the left. And beyond the woods was the Gulf of Mexico. I noticed seagulls and wondered what Tatanka would say.

"Baugh, Badillo, your companies will hold the road," I said. "Threaten their barricade, then fall back and establish a line. Flacco, you will follow Seguin and I down to the beach, then hold in support. You are the guardian of our flank. Colonel Seguin, we'll move along the surf, then turn toward the dock. If we're able, we'll capture their supplies and relieve the fort. Gentlemen, this is the time to be steady. We are the Seventh Cavalry, and we are destined for glory."

I let the officers relate my speech before riding out, for such eloquence should not be wasted, and then broke off with the Béjar Rangers and Lipan Apache to begin my raid. Belatedly, I remembered that I was riding with very few white men, mostly my regimental staff, but it no longer mattered. They were all my men. My army.

The trail down to the gulf was lined with oak trees, ash trees and mesquite. There were so many large birds that a good hunter wouldn't even need a shotgun. We burst out on a broad sandy beach, surprising half a dozen men and boys fishing in the surf. None raised a weapon, so Seguin and I bypassed them, leaving Flacco to protect our rear.

The churning sea was now on our left, dunes and woods to the right. A few small ships lay at anchor near the mouth of the river up ahead. We could not see the fort or the town but would as we closed on the Brazos. There were only sixty of us, well-armed with Springfields, Baker rifles, Colts, and six of us carried Winchesters. What we lacked in numbers we made up in firepower, speed and determination.

"They're in a bad place, sir," Hughes said. "Rebs got the river to the rear, cuttin' off their retreat. If General Keogh were here, we'd trap 'em and carve 'em up."

"Then for us, the greater share of glory," I said.

"Shakespeare?"

"Henry V."

"I hope he won that battle," Hughes said.

"He won all his battles, Bobby," I replied.

Before we reached the Brazos, a trail cut northwest over the dunes. The top of the fort was visible through the trees, but no alarm had been raised. Gunfire from the east indicated Baugh and Badillo were keeping the enemy's attention, and artillery from the north spoke of Tom's arrival near the bend in the river. No doubt Crockett would be demonstrating, threatening the enemy center.

"Column of twos. No bugle, Voss, let's see if we can catch these bastards by surprise," I said.

Our trail turned north up a narrow dirt road running parallel to the river. A two-masted schooner was tied to a short dock, the lane filled with boxes and barrels. Several wood plank buildings, possibly warehouses, were coming up on our right. I saw half a dozen burly men unloading the ship, taking their time. Two armed guards saw us approach but seemed to have no idea who we were. It all seemed too easy, and it was. Suddenly dozens of leather clad soldiers rushed from the fort, running down a slight hill to intercept us.

"General?" Seguin asked.

"Charge the fort, I've got the dock," I said, giving Traveller a kick while drawing my sidearm.

Voss blew the *Charge* for my staff. Corporal Garcia joined in for the Béjar Rangers. As the command burst into a gait, a few of the men shouted. I tried to stay in the lead, but Traveller was more stout than quick, and several passed me. Both dockworkers dropped their bundles and ran. Two guards raised their muskets, only to be shot down before taking aim. A group of sailors on the schooner hurried to ready a cannon but came under fire from Butler and Hughes.

In an instant we had reached the docks. I dismounted among the stacked supplies, still not having fired a shot. There were boxes of rifles, lead shot, powder charges, food and powder. There was even a cannon, though it wasn't mounted on a gun carriage. Seguin had cut through the infantry coming down the path, then swung around for another charge, taking some pressure off our right flank. I spotted two wagons just a bit farther on.

"Allen, Voss, with me," I said, racing to seize the harnesses on the mules before they could drag the wagons away.

Allen got there first, taking hold of the lead mule. Voss climbed up on the seat, using the reins to halt the wagon. We didn't need the rifles, though I wanted them. We did need the powder. Cooke, Butler, Hughes and French arranged a skirmish line, keeping a steady fire on any enemy who tried to approach. We couldn't stay long, not outnumbered a ten to one, but we sure were causing a distraction for Tom and Crockett to take advantage of.

"Sir, look out!" Allen shouted, pointing at the river.

I turned in utter surprise, and dread. Another schooner had appeared, drifting upriver on a light breeze, the mainsail and jib providing movement. On the top deck, three cannon were pointed in our direction, the crews busily preparing them for action. And standing on the deck, giving the orders, was Colonel Sam Houston.

"Oh my God," I muttered, for if the cannon were loaded with grapeshot, they would sweep my entire command away. And me with them.

"Allen, get down. Everybody scatter!" I shouted.

I waved to the men, tossed Voss under the wagon, and turned back toward the schooner as the cannon fuses were lit.

"General, duck!" Butler yelled.

But I refused, standing my ground, shoulders straight. If this was my moment, I would go down fighting, like I had at the Little Big Horn. Without regrets, and without apologies.

The cannons roared, smoke engulfed the dock, and burning lead poured past me, but I was not dead. When the smoke cleared, I saw the schooner had fired on the stockade.

"Custer, you damn fool!" I heard Houston bellow. "The gate is down! Take the fort!"

I saw Houston was right. The gate facing the river was hanging on broken hinges. The defenders not routed by Seguin were retreating north, leaving the path open except for a brave few who couldn't or wouldn't run.

"Voss, the *Charge* if you please," I said in a calm voice, drawing a Colt and limping up the path as quickly as I could go.

Seguin's men were there first, some riding through the open gate, others dismounting and taking rifles from their sheaths before entering. Butler and French were right behind them, all greeted by a brief storm of gunfire. By the time I reached the enclosure, the shooting was sporadic. Apparently, most of the garrison was out in the meadow dealing with Crockett.

"Secure the fort," I ordered, quite unnecessarily, for my troopers were already taking positions on the ramparts.

Cooke and French took time to disarm the prisoners, and two of the wounded who continued to resist were shot dead on the spot, discouraging others.

"Four dead, four wounded," Cooke reported.

"Us or them?" I asked.

"Us. Fourteen dead rebs, about a dozen wounded," he replied. "Are you hit, George?"

"Me? No, why would you ask?"

"You don't seem as lucky as you used to be," he said, pointing at my sore leg. And my limp had grown more pronounced with all the exertion.

"I'm about to conquer Texas, Bill. Seems pretty lucky to me."

The battlefield grew quiet. Helped to the top of the wall, I saw men, women and children dashing about in the streets of the town, but no soldiers. Farther out on the plain, a knot of rebel leaders were gathered around a big tent. No doubt they were trying to come up with a plan, for they were now surrounded. They still outnumbered us two or three to one, but there was no way for them to know that.

"Orders, sir?" Seguin asked.

I looked to the flag pole, seeing a blue banner with a five-pointed white star in the middle.

"Take that flag down, raise ours," I said. "Get that gate back up. See if this fort has any cannon worth using. Some food and coffee for the men would be good, too."

I remained on the wall a few minutes more, tempted to order an attack. Maybe chase off their horses. But decided against it. We had been on the march since dawn and achieved advantageous positions. I would not turn a marginal victory into a rash defeat.

"Help me down," I asked Cooke, descending the ladder with difficulty.

The headquarters was a log cabin surrounded by a barracks, blacksmith, supply depot and stable. As I walked across the compound looking forward to a chair and tall glass of cold water, I saw a dozen prisoners being removed from a woodshed. They were dirty, their uniforms torn, and most spattered in dried blood. They were not rebel prisoners, but survivors of the Mexican garrison. One was Antonio López de Santa Anna.

"Anthony," I said, hobbling faster to shake his hand.

The man looked like hell. Gaunt, unshaven, and his right arm in a rag sling.

"George, I should have known it would be you," Santa Anna said, embracing me with his good arm. "Have you beaten the pirates?"

"Not yet, but we're working on it," I replied.

We retired to the headquarters where I found Santa Anna clean clothes and an orderly to scrub out his wounds. I needed his presence on the ramparts with me, as a general, standing tall and ready to fight. He knew this as well as I.

Half an hour later, as the sun was setting over the trees beyond the Brazos, Houston entered the fort with thirty armed river rats. They were disheveled, boisterous, and drunk. Houston and Santa Anna had been enemies for years, but until now, they'd never met. I wasn't sure what would happen.

"Colonel Houston, let me introduce General Santa Anna," I said, standing slightly between them with a hand on my sword.

Santa Anna straightened up, reluctantly offering his hand. Houston looked Santa Anna over and grunted, ignoring the gesture.

"Fog comin' in," Houston said. "Best get the rest of our supplies off the dock 'fore they get stole."

After Houston left, I sat down at a small table in the corner near the fire. It reminded me of the table Grant had used to write out the terms of surrender for Lee at Appomattox. Phil Sheridan quickly bought the table from Mr. McLean and gave it to Libbie, saying no officer in the Union army had done more to bring about the country's victory than her husband. I opened a bottle of wine and waved Santa Anna over.

"Houston still wants Texas for the United States," I said. "If it would be a free state, I might sympathize, but the South will never permit it. We need to decide how this is going to work."

"My country still wants Texas," Santa Anna said.

"Then you need to decide which country is yours, Mexico or the Buffalo Flag," I replied. "But before you answer, you should know I've had a vision."

"You? A vision? When did George Custer start believing in visions?" he asked.

"I've always believed in Custer's Luck."

"Which took you to the Little Big Horn."

"And the Little Big Horn brought me here," I persisted. "Antonio, the Buffalo Flag will be a nation. The clock isn't turning back. In my vision, I saw Slow being inaugurated president, all grown up with a family."

"Do you mean Tatanka?" Santa Anna asked.

"Yes, among other names," I said.

And speak of the devil, if Tatanka didn't suddenly walk into the room, covered in trail dust and tired from a hard ride.

"General Custer, dispatches," Tatanka said, coming to our table and handing me a packet. I recognized Crockett's handwriting and Tom's scrawl.

"Take a seat, lad, we were just talking about you," I said.

"I know. The birds have been generous," Tatanka replied, accepting a glass of watered wine.

I doubted the birds had revealed my conversation with Santa Anna. More likely he'd gotten word from Voss, for they were close friends.

"Antonio has a divided loyalty," I explained. "You have also, between the old ways of your people and the New Path. What advice can you give?"

I was teasing. I doubted there was an easy solution, or any solution at all. My family had not supported Lincoln, or many of his administration's aims, but I had been an officer in his army. My oath

327

to uphold the Constitution overruled personal sentiments. Santa Anna and Tatanka did not have such a luxury.

"Houston may not have his way. Mexico will not keep Texas," Tatanka said. "For my people to have a future, they need powerful allies. They need the Buffalo Flag, and because the Buffalo Flag has many enemies, it needs my people. In this manner are nations forged."

"We don't have that many enemies," I objected.

"Your army is small, the land vast. On this field, you stand with white men, Indians, Tejanos, and Europeans, none of whom trust the others," the young wise man said. "If Mexico rises against you, the Americans will conquer all."

"I fear this is true," Santa Anna said.

"We must be one nation. A nation forged by Custer," Tatanka said. "It is he who brings unity. A crazy man chosen by the gods for an uncertain destiny. He belongs to none, and therefore he belongs to all."

"And what of my people?" Santa Anna asked.

"They must have trust in our future, as I now have trust in mine," Tatanka said. "To show this trust, I will marry your oldest daughter, that our families may be one."

"Marriage?" I said.

"To my María de Guadalupe?" Santa Anna said, equally surprised.

"Is this not how your people may be reassured?" Tatanka said.

The boy had certainly figured us out. Marriage alliances are as old as history itself. Though I deeply cared for Isabella, her connection to Erasmo Seguin and the Tejano community had not escaped me. Tom truly loved Morning Star, but his marriage would give us standing with various Indian tribes. Houston had married a Cherokee girl. Even Cochise had married the daughter of Mangas Coloradas, affirming his prominence among the Apache.

"It would be a good match," I said. "Tatanka grows in wealth. He has the respect of the army."

"That he does," Sergeant Voss said from the door.

We turned to see Voss, Butler and Hughes watching our conversation. Inappropriately, but in such close quarters, difficult to avoid. The three made an impression, for they were the very soul of the Seventh Cavalry.

"I will let you marry my daughter," Santa Anna agreed.

"Good. Now we can discuss the dowry," Tatanka replied.

————————

The fog rolled in just as Houston predicted, a thick river soup that reduced visibility to a few yards. We shored up the damaged gate, fed the horses, and settled down for a tense night. There was sporadic gunfire from the east, probably nervous sentries. Houston returned after Santa Anna retired to the barracks for some sleep. Fannin had threatened to shoot him a dawn, which must have been distressing.

"I've had a letter from President Jackson," Houston said, sitting next to me at the fire.

Having had time to sober up, Houston was congenial and somewhat contrite. The consummate politician. He didn't realize I'd spent a career being flattered by congressmen and senators, and I didn't enlighten him, for I'd learned how empty their promises are.

"I have dispatches from my brother and Colonel Crockett," I said, laying the rushed messages on the table. "They think Fannin and Burleson are hemmed in. They want instructions for ending this quickly."

"I can help," Houston said. "Most of those boys out there don't own slaves, but they're mighty offended by you abolitionists. They say you insult our Southern way of life. Still, most of them might set slavery aside for admission to the Union. President Jackson agrees."

"Former President Jackson," I corrected.

"Yes, former president," Houston acknowledged.

"Sam. May I call you Sam? There may come a time when Jackson's dream will come true, but I can make no promises. My men and I, we've seen the future. Being a proud white man, I once thought it was a good future. I saw an America where our civilization ruled from the Atlantic to the Pacific. But I was mistaken. This world is bigger than such an ambition."

"You speak like a Boston preacher," Houston said.

"And it embarrasses me," I conceded.

"Custer, I didn't know what kind of half-baked plans you Yankees got in mind," Houston said. "Tejanos are civilized some, and the Cherokee can rule their own, but you'll never make a nation without white men in charge. And they need to be the right kind of white men."

"Are you extending an invitation?"

"You'll have position. Support. When Texas becomes a state, you can be the first senator. Maybe even President of the United States someday."

Houston's words were well-spoken. Even elegant. And without doubt, it was a tempting bribe. But what would Tom say? Or Isabella?

"One day I may take you up on that, Sam. But today I have other obligations," I answered.

Houston nodded with resignation. He had thought me a weaker man, and didn't know how close he'd come to being right.

Santa Anna entered, a warm summer breeze following him through the door. He'd found a clean captain's uniform and a servant to polish his boots. He had not shaven, his narrow chin sprouting gray whiskers.

"Cooke reports we have a hundred and ten men under arms," Santa Anna said. "All but the sentries are bedded down. When the fog lifts in the morning, this fort will be under attack."

"Unless we attack first," I said.

It was not a quiet night. Gunfire continued from the east, and just past midnight, there was a brief exchange of artillery. The horses in the stable were spooked, few of them trained for battle conditions. I spent half an hour with Traveller stroking his long gray neck. Later, I met with Cooke on the rampart, though we could see nothing in the gloom.

"This stronghold was their fallback position," Cooke said. "Food, powder, shot. They're in trouble if they can't take it away from us."

"I want to take the whole town," I replied. "With Crockett and Tom on their flanks, they'll have no place to go. We can finish this up in one day."

"Dreams of San Jacinto?" Cooke said.

"I already won San Jacinto, but that just was a skirmish. If we win here, we win the war. This is where the monuments will be built."

"A monument to who?"

"To whoever wins, Bill. No one build monuments to the losers."

Velasco was not a good fort. Not like the ones the Americans built on the Missouri River, or even the Alamo. This fort was made of dank timber and smelled of rot. The barracks leaked in the summer rain. The parade ground turned to mud, and the stables were not fit for Crows, let alone our horses. When I rode in, I thought the fort too big for our force, for we had but a hundred warriors and needed twice that number. But I soon realized my mistake. Now that Velasco held Custer, Houston and Santa Anna, the fort felt very small.

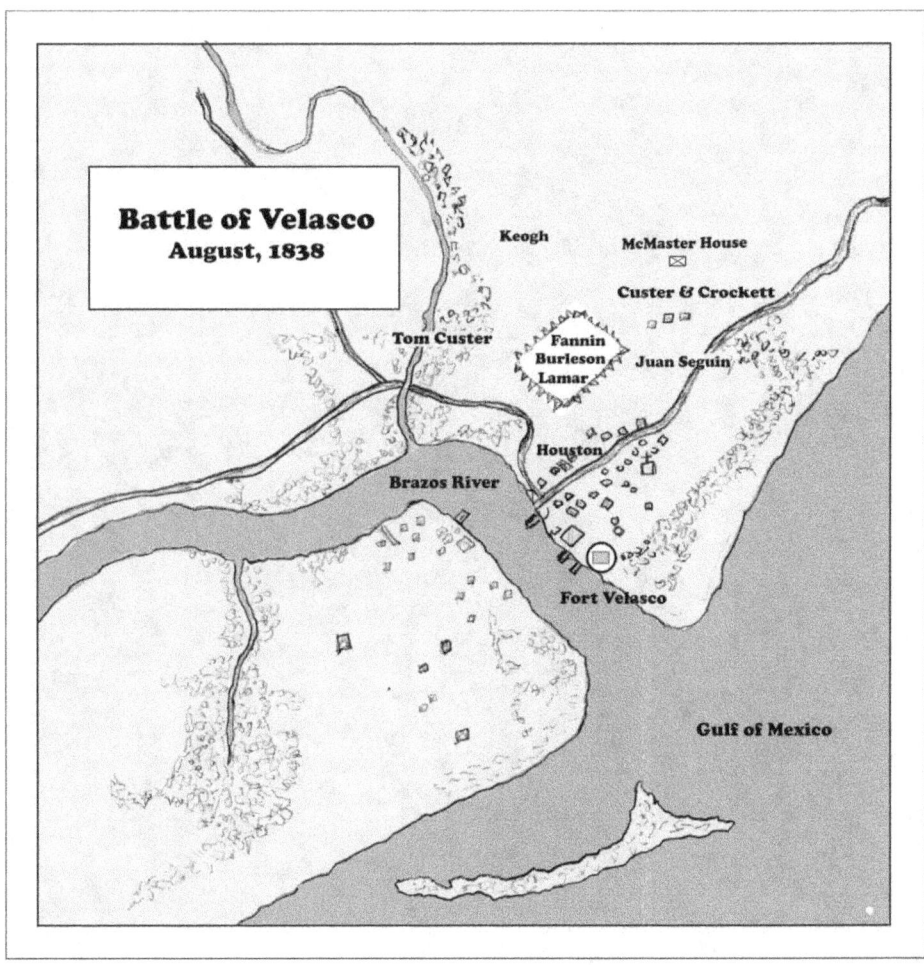

Custer and Crockett

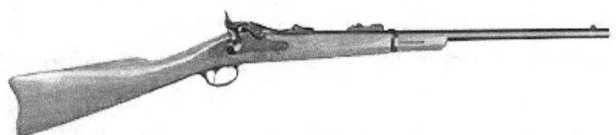

Chapter Twelve
Velasco

Dawn could not come soon enough, though I managed to snatch a few hours' sleep. The fog settled like a shroud, as it often does near oceans and rivers, leaving us blind. Even after the morning sun should have been rising, all we saw was murky gray. A few musket shots were heard from the north, and then from the east. I became nervous, pacing the courtyard, wondering what the enemy was doing. When sporadic cannon fire resumed, I couldn't take it anymore.

"We've got to get out there," I said to Cooke, going toward the stables.

"Can't ride in this soup, George. We'll only hurt the horses," he replied.

I paused, and then the solution occurred to me.

"We don't need the horses," I said. "Gather the command. We'll sally out the gate on foot. The fog will break at some point and let us see the battle."

"And if a thousand of them are coming at a hundred of us? What do we do then?" Cooke asked.

"Better than hiding here like a bunch of cowards," I decided.

Voss blew *Assembly*, the men rushing into the courtyard. We were Seventh Cavalry, Tejanos, Mexicans and Texans. Even a few Indians. None with a temperament to stand aside while there was a fight going on. Houston came up, sword in hand. Santa Anna appeared, riding his stallion. Two lancers and a bugler rode with him. Outside our walls, all could hear the near continuous gunfire.

"Soldiers!" I shouted, my sword drawn. "The battle rages without us! The enemy may be trying to break out, or maybe they have the numbers. It matters not. Strike hard! For victory. For glory!"

The north gate swung open and I led the charge, Cooke at my elbow, Hughes, Butler and Voss on my heels. The gray mist swirled around us as our boots caused the wooden bridge over the dry moat to creak. Flashes of musket fire flinted about like fireflies. There was a clammy smell to the air.

"Flankers," I called out, sending skirmishers to the left and right.

Then we began moving forward again, probing for opportunity in the mist. The marshy ground was flat, cleared of brush. We reached a low rock wall, possibly a breakwater protecting the town from high tides.

"George, I still don't see anything," Cooke said, pausing next to me. "It's just like that fog at the Little Big Horn. The one that brought us to Texas."

"What are you trying to say, Bill?" I asked, staying low, for we could feel the wild musket balls cutting through the air.

"What if we're going back? What if this fog is taking us back to Dakota? Back to the Little Big Horn?"

"Don't be ridiculous," I snapped.

"Because nothing strange has ever happened before?"

I looked around at the murky landscape. The scrub-covered dirt and occasional spiny plant. The shouting in the distance was not so much different than Sioux war cries. And for a moment, I began to wonder. A light from the edge of the haze revealed a tall pointed structure. A teepee? Could...?

"Hell, George, I'm only joking," Cooke said.

Cooke stood up, waved to those around us, and advanced with his Winchester ready for action. I followed, relieved to find the mysterious teepee was actually a pile of hay.

A few old wooden storage buildings lay before us, but most of the town was laid out to my right along a single avenue going east, the largest adobes surrounding the plaza. As we emerged into the morning glare, I saw an effort had been made to blockade the street, but most of the defenses were facing Crockett's men in the eastern woods. As the town was too cramped for deployment, the enemy was camped farther on, occupying the flat prairie to the north. There was steady fire coming from both sides, though still long distance, creating a gray haze over the battlefield.

"Take the high ground," Butler said, pointing to a two-story tavern on the south side of the plaza.

"This way!" Hughes shouted.

I tried to keep up, but stumbled, and then stumbled again. The wounded leg would not allow me walk quickly, let alone run. I was finally forced to sit on a flour barrel outside a bakery as the men poured past, cursing in frustration. Finally Lieutenant Mendoza, an aide to Santa Anna, came by with a mule and helped me mount.

"*Gracias, Señor,*" I said, allowing Mendoza to lead the animal.

At the edge of town, my men had stopped to form a skirmish line in a corral while sharpshooters took positions on the roof of a tavern. I was helped up the staircase, puffing for breath.

"It's a magnificent sight," I said to Cooke, who had graciously returned to my side.

"I've only read about this in story books," Cooke observed.

Before us on the plain was the rebel army formed in a great square, much like the formations of Wellington at Waterloo. The four long lines of supply boxes and hay bales, a hundred yards to each side, were well organized, the soldiers alert. A variety of flags and banners indicated dozens of different militia groups, the dress varying from formal uniforms to store bought broad cloth and even some rough rawhide. Hundreds of horses, mules and oxen were kept in the middle of the formation within a wagon park. I counted eight cannon, mostly 4-pounders and one 8-pounder.

The side nearest our position was hurriedly thrown together, surprised by our sudden advance. A weaker wing faced the river where two lightly gunned schooners were at anchor. I could not tell if the ships were enemies or friendly. Facing east was a strong force with three cannon, supported by forty or fifty dismounted cavalry. I could not see Crockett's force, they being dug in among the woods about fifteen hundred yards away.

The strongest segment of the square enjoyed the protection of a creek or half dug canal, probably a thousand men in all. More than a mile away, Tom's banners were flying in a morning breeze.

"George, look," Cooke said, handing me binoculars and pointing to the northeast.

"Keogh," I said.

"Must have arrived during the night," Cooke guessed. "We should have equal numbers on them now, or close to it."

"Officer's call, I want Houston and Santa Anna here on the double," I ordered.

The firing along the lines had died to an occasional warning shot, both armies waiting to see what might happen.

"Fannin has to break out," I said. "Either break out or surrender."

"He tried to break out last night. Lost his nerve," Houston reported, for he had spies all over the field. "Now he'll ask for a parley. Try to talk his way out of this."

Houston was right. A few minutes later, a white flag was waved and a score of rebels emerged on the eastern side of their square. I recognized Fannin and Lamar among them.

"What's that building?" I asked, watching through my binoculars.

"It's a trading post. McMaster House," Houston said.

"Colonel Houston, you have the command here. Cooke, gather the regimental staff. We're going to the parley," I ordered.

"I should come," Houston said.

"These were your friends, Sam. I think its best you stay back until we have a resolution," I insisted.

"What about Santa Anna?" Cooke asked.

"Antonio should come, too. And call Tatanka," I said.

While Cooke gathered up my command, I gave instructions for the men in town to fall back on the fort if necessary. If the rebels decided to push south, the eighty troops with Houston wouldn't hold the streets, but they could hold the stockade long enough for the other wings of the army to close in. I shook Houston's hand before riding out, for I'd decided he'd make a better ally than an enemy.

Sixteen of us rode from the central plaza along the line of militia facing us. We were well armed with Colts, Winchesters and Springfields.

"We could just sit four hundred yards off their square, out of musket range, and shoot into their lines," Butler suggested.

"We could. But that would force them to charge one direction or the other," Cooke said. "And they just might overrun whoever gets in their way."

"There must be blood," Tatanka said.

"That's something I expected Antonio to say," I remarked, though it was not out of character.

"The boy is right," Santa Anna said. "If the pirates are allowed to surrender and go home, they will come back. Fortune may not favor us a second time."

It had been my intention to accept surrender on terms, but now I wasn't sure. This wasn't the Civil War, where high codes of conduct were expected among honorable men. It was an invasion of marauders who had plagued Texas for two years.

"Let's see what's being offered," I decided.

We skirted the southeast corner of the square. McMaster House stood on a knoll above a creek surrounded by open fields. The ground floor was adobe brick, the second floor made of pinewood slat board. I guessed the observation post on the roof was used to watch for Comanche. The corrals that had once kept horses or cattle were empty, most of the fences broken down. If the owner of the trading post was nearby, I never saw him.

Fifty or more leaders and officers were gathering for the parley. Fannin and his staff milled around the west of the building near a stable while Crockett, Tom and Keogh waited just to the east by a smokehouse. Juan Almonte stood on the broad covered porch waiting to act as arbiter. I choose to avoid our adversaries, taking a wide loop through the fields.

"Autie, heard you got shot again," Tom said, helping me down from my horse.

"Looks like no one shot you," I said, embracing him.

"Not yet," he answered.

Keogh and Crockett came forward, none looking worse for wear. The campaign had been pursuit and containment so far. Everyone wondered if that was about to change.

"Did you hang Houston?" Crockett asked, half in jest.

"Not yet," I said.

"Don't 'pect ya need to. He's been a sendin' us regular reports," Crockett said, relieved his old friend had not betrayed him.

"What's our strength?" I asked.

"Figure we got about eleven hundred," Keogh said. "But there's a Mexican force under Urrea coming up from Copano. We'll have three hundred more by tomorrow night."

"We?" Santa Anna asked.

"Official alliance," Tom said, taking a parchment from his blouse.

I looked the document over quickly, my Spanish fairly good. The thrust of the message was clear. Mexico did not want Texas becoming part of the United States, and the Buffalo Flag seemed less of a threat. Maybe we'd find ourselves at odds someday, but not today. I handed the paper to Santa Anna, who seemed surprised. And a little disappointed.

"*Que es lo que se*," Santa Anna said, not knowing he would be quoted for years afterwards.

"What's that, sir?" the younger Crockett asked.

"*It is what it is*," I said. "And it is. What are we going to do with these trouble-makers?"

"They're in a tough spot, but digging them out will cost us," Keogh said.

"Tom?" I inquired.

"We've been offering them terms since the Seventh rode back from California, and the sons of bitches have spit in our faces," Tom complained. "I think the time for terms is over."

"We have the artillery to break their square. A steady advance followed by a charge will run them over," Smith advised.

"Colonel Seguin? Your thoughts?" I requested.

"The Tejano people have been driven from our homes," Seguin said. "Our stock stolen. Promises broken. We are tired of these interlopers."

"Tired enough to let it rest? Or angry enough to seek retribution?" I asked.

"A price should be paid," Seguin replied, gripping the butt of his pistol.

I noticed that, as we spoke, Tom, Cooke, Smith, and Seguin had gradually grouped themselves together, and when Almonte wandered down from the porch, he joined them. All similar in age, ambition, and even temperament. Keogh stood apart, but not very far apart. Crockett, Santa Anna and I were the old men.

"Crockett?" I asked.

"Hate ta kill them that don't need killin'," Crockett said. "Maybe some of them fellers ain't too fixed on fightin'?"

"Let's see what they've got to say," I decided. "General Santa Anna, Colonel Crockett and I will do the talking, but if someone needs to jump in, don't be shy. We've all earned a voice today."

We walked around to the front of McMaster House. It wasn't the McLean House by any means, but it reminded me of that April day at Appomattox when General Lee had surrendered the Army of Northern Virginia. Lee's horse was named Traveller, too.

The rebel leaders came forward from the stable, stopping in the middle of the dirt courtyard. I recognized James Fannin and Mirabeau Lamar. Two I knew by reputation, Ed Burleson and Colonel Albert Horton. The others were strangers, though I guessed them to be Thomas Rusk, Frank Johnson, and some recent arrivals from the States. All were wearing new blue uniforms, most decorated with silver buttons and gilded thread. Fannin was the youngster at thirty-four. Burleson and Lamar were my age, about to scrape forty.

"General Fannin, you are in arms against the Buffalo Flag. You were warned of this," I said, standing with one hand on my sword.

"Texas must be free, General Custer," Fannin said, his Georgia accent more pronounced than I remembered. "Your flag suppresses liberty. Robs the people of their natural rights as Americans."

"You claim land that isn't yours," Burleson added, his bearing that of a military man. I understood him to have fought in the War of 1812 and had a long history as an Indian fighter. He had certainly given Keogh many sleepless nights.

"I've seen your army, Custer. Nothing but a rabble of Mexicans, Indians and Frenchmen," Lamar said. "They won't hold up in a real fight."

"We kicked your tails at Buffalo Bayou," Tom said, stepping forward with clenched fists.

"Ya snuck up on us in the dark. That Yankee trick won't work twice," Lamar retorted.

"This 'ere arguin' ain't gettin' us nowhere," Crockett interjected. "You boys is in a spot, and we got more a comin'. Insults ain't gonna help ya none."

"What is it you want?" Burleson asked.

"Unconditional surrender," I replied.

"No surrender," Fannin said. "We march out, rifles on our shoulders, and take ship for the states. For now. We keep our flags."

"Your flags shall decorate my palace," Santa Anna said, also gripping his sword.

"You got no power here, tyrant. Not even an army," Fannin said. "Bustamante holds you in contempt."

"Santa Anna commands three hundred Tejanos," I exaggerated. "How many of your militia groups are bigger than that?"

"The regular army is eight hundred strong, and we have seven hundred more in reserve," Fannin lied.

"One white man is as good as any ten Mexicans," Lamar added. "And better than twenty of your dirt-digging Indians."

"There's only one way to prove that, gentlemen," I said. "I will make one concession. Any enlisted man who lays down his arms will be spared. For the rest of you, no promises."

"You offer us nothing," Burleson said.

"I made a promise to General Fannin at Goliad, and I intend to keep it," I replied. "You have an hour to make a decision."

My command retreated to McMaster House, except for Crockett, who lingered speaking with Captain Philip Dimmitt. I knew Dimmitt to be a thirty-seven-year old Kentuckian who had led the first assault on La Bahia in 1835 and later served with Crockett at Béjar.

While Crockett and Dimmitt were still conferring, Fannin and his other officers stormed back to their lines in a fury, waving their arms and shouting.

"You didn't give them much choice, Autie," Tom said.

"Should they be allowed to march out under arms? Is that how we beat down the Rebellion?" I asked.

"I ain't against a fight," Tom said. "After all, I did win all the medals."

"Try not to win one today, little brother," I urged.

Crockett eventually returned with a wink, but declined to explain. Tom rejoined his command on the northern flank, taking Smith with him, while Santa Anna and I stayed with Keogh in a forested glen. Crockett lingered for a bit, having loyal subordinates to command his militia before wandering off with Juan Seguin. I saw the Buffalo Flag flying over Fort Velasco, though Houston still had most of his men occupying the town. Just before the hour was up, we noticed some movement.

"There, General," Cooke said, handing me his binoculars.

I saw commotion along the southern side of the enemy square opposite Houston. Several flags abruptly came down and a hundred or so rebels climbed over their barriers, a few holding muskets over their heads. Most held no weapons at all. They were soon followed by a second wave of fifty or so. I saw Captain Dimmitt in the lead and realized why Crockett had been grinning. Houston went out to meet them halfway, shaking Dimmitt's hand.

"That can't be good for morale," Butler said, standing at my elbow.

"We should get ready, General. Fannin's got no choice but to break out now," Hughes said, cocking his rifle.

I glanced at Keogh, who already had his men dug in and supported by a mounted reserve. Three cannon were loaded with grape shot, and the open ground offered a wide field of fire. To my left, Crockett's men were stationed among the trees, two cannon on the far end of the line near the waterfront road. Seguin's cavalry was patrolling the beaches. Houston's position was the weakest, but recapturing the fort would still leave Fannin trapped against the river, and the few schooners he might gather wouldn't be enough to evacuate his army.

"They have to cut north along the river," I decided. "If they hit Tom's right flank in strength, they might break out."

"Should we warn him?" Cooke asked.

A warning became unnecessary. Tom's entire line suddenly erupted in cannon fire, at least six guns that I could count. The cannon were followed by rapid volley fire—Springfields, Baker rifles and muskets that raked Fannin's front. The enemy tried to return fire, but they didn't have the range. And then the field was covered in smoke, obscuring the battle.

We heard the cannon being fired again, moving sequentially down the line. I looked through the binoculars, seeing Fannin and Burleson in the center of the square desperately trying to rally their men. Burleson was hit and went down. I could not tell how serious the wound was. Lamar was getting his men mounted, moving toward the Brazos River. A sudden push by the rebels could have Tom outnumbered three or four to one.

"Voss, *Boots and Saddles*," I ordered.

As the men rushed for their horses, Keogh ran up to me.

"George, what the hell?" he shouted.

"They're running for the river, Myles," I explained. "Keep men on the guns, but prepare to charge."

"Tom won't let them out," Myles protested.

"This battle can last five hours or fifteen minutes. I prefer fifteen minutes," I said. "We're cavalry. We'll act as cavalry."

Keogh grudgingly called his mounted reserve forward. Crockett's men heard the bugle call and were also racing for their horses. The rebels watching us from behind their boxes and hay bales seemed confused by our preparations, for the open ground acted to their benefit as well. Some looked back to see Lamar's men going the other direction. I knew Lamar was seeking a favorable angle to attack Tom's flank, but to his infantry, it surely looked like a retreat. One of the officers from the parley ran along the line trying to keep order, but they were militia and undisciplined.

"They're nervous, George," Cooke said, flushed with excitement. "Let's demonstrate just out of range as if ready to charge."

"It's my intent to charge, Bill," I said.

"Give them time to see what they're up against. Blow the bugles. Let the sharpshooters open a gap in their line," Cooke urged.

Despite my best instincts, I thought Cooke might be right. If even a few of the enemy broke from their line, the rest might fall into disarray.

"See to it," I agreed.

It was a beautiful fight. Fannin was keeping his north line engaged, the sound of rolling gunfire filling the meadow. Cannon continued to duel, though without the ferocity of the early bombardment. As I Company rode back and forth as if ready to attack, the enemy's east line was gradually breaking up, and since the departure of Colonel Horton, the south flank had all but disappeared.

"Houston is getting ready to charge," Santa Anna said, riding up on his fine white stallion with a naval spyglass in his hand. "If we wait too long, the glory will be his."

"Houston only has a few horses. No charge on foot can rob glory from a cavalry charge," I disagreed.

"I've gathered thirty lancers. Let me have the lead," Santa Anna requested.

"No, you'll get yourself killed," I said.

"Are you so concerned?"

"*Sí, amigo mío, tú eres un buen hombre para perderte.*"

"No more valuable than you. We shall ride together," Santa Anna persisted.

"And I, too," Tatanka said, coming to my side on a borrowed mare, his Colt already drawn.

"The charge of the Light Brigade?" I said.

"Did they win?" Tatanka asked.

"That's not important. At least there's no valley of death."

In truth, sitting on the horse made my leg hurt. I was getting impatient, and I wasn't the only one.

"General, what the hell are we waiting for?" Hughes said.

I looked around to see my entire staff ready for action, their horses snorting and pawing the ground in anticipation. A bugle sounded to my left, the *Forward* echoing off the trees. I saw Seguin's mounted rangers coming up from the beach at a gallop, their flag flying.

Another bugle. Crockett's men emerged from the woods, forming a long line. The younger Crockett rode at his father's side along Chief Flacco the Younger. Forty Lipan Apache and dozens of Cherokee were with them flying their Owl decorated Buffalo Flag.

"George, por Dios!" Santa Anna complained.

Cooke had a dozen skirmishers before us raining hot fire on the center of the rebel line. Keogh had abandoned his cannon, seeing they weren't going to be needed, and was rapidly mounting two companies on my right. Houston's men slowly moved out from the town, firing, stopping to reload, and then firing again. There was just enough resistance to slow him down, but the smoke was beginning to drift over the field, hampering visibility.

"Bill! How much longer?" I shouted.

Cooke saw the command was ready to move, and though he still thought it premature, recalled his sharpshooters, who ran for their horses. Voss brought Cooke's horse forward, letting him mount in time to join us.

As firing slackened on our side of the field, the intensity grew near the river. Lamar was making his move, the bulk of his army trying to move up the Brazos along the beach and trees. Closer to us, Fannin's men were still on foot, slowly falling back.

"General, are we attacking or making camp?" Butler asked.

"Damnit, Jimmy ..." I started to say.

Crockett's corporal blew the *Charge*, causing a hundred and

343

twenty-five horses to surge across the field. The old bear hunter was stealing my thunder.

"Voss, sound the *Charge*," I ordered, giving Traveller a kick.

The call was hardly begun when Santa Anna drew his saber and started forward, followed closely by Tatanka, the Tejano lancers, and my own staff. Traveller hesitated, almost leaving me behind. Slightly closer, Keogh's command rushed ahead on our right, striking toward the corner of the square.

"For glory!" I shouted, waving my sword as Traveller broke into a gallop. The ground was flat, at first, then grew cluttered with shell holes.

"General, watch out!" Hughes shouted as the rebels prepared to volley fire.

A cavalry charge must absorb such things, and we rode forward into a wave of red flashes and gray smoke. Half a dozen horses went down. Half a dozen men were knocked from their saddles. There was no time to stop and help the wounded. No time to tally the dead. I urged Traveller on before the enemy could reload, following Butler and Hughes through a hole blown in the barricade. The air was thick. Choking. I pointed my revolver and shot the first leather clad man I saw.

We were among them, Colts firing right and left at the desperate defenders, for they could not reload fast enough. I saw Cooke raise his Winchester and get off eight rapid shots, hitting three or four unlucky foes. Butler emptied his revolver and drew another, rarely missing at such close range.

When I halted to reload, I suddenly discovered a wounded man staggering toward me with a fixed bayonet. At first I thought he was trying to run me through the belly, but at the last moment, I realized it was Traveller the scoundrel was aiming at. I stuck out my wounded leg just in time for the bayonet to drive through the calf, catching Traveller in the shoulder. The proud old horse bucked up, throwing me off against a wagon with the broken end of the bayonet still protruding from my leg.

The reb backed away from Traveller, then came at me with his hunting knife. My pistol was gone, lost somewhere on the field. I struggled to draw the sword, but found myself sitting on the bent scabbard. There was a hateful glare in my attacker's eyes as he lunged, and a great deal of satisfaction. And then his head exploded.

"General, are you hurt?" Cochise asked, a Colt in his hand.

"Ride on, Captain," I ordered, slowly drawing up my leg to pull the bayonet free. I hoped not to lose the leg.

Private Engle found Traveller, bleeding but not seriously wounded, and after quickly wrapping my seeping injury, had me back on the horse. I was well behind now, the charge of the Seventh Cavalry having disappeared into a churning dust cloud. Through the drifting mist, I was able to see Keogh's men flanking the north front, and Seguin was overwhelming the struggling defense to my left. A few rebels began falling back toward their wagon park, and then more.

I borrowed a Colt from Engle and resumed the pursuit, Traveller now forced to pick his way through broken supply boxes and lost equipment. I heard another bugle. The *Charge.* Our attack was now general throughout the square, the enemy running for the river in full flight. They simply didn't have the firepower to stop us.

When I reached the circled wagons, I found that some of the men were forced to rein in. Keogh and Seguin had us squeezed, and the oxen trapped among the wagons blocked our path. A few of the defenders had taken shelter there, but none were pointing their weapons. I saw no officers, only bewildered militia.

"Autie, some of them are surrendering," Cooke said, coming up beside me.

Cooke was splashed in blood, but it wasn't his blood. His eyes were lit with excitement. Sweat dripped from his long sideburns.

"Spare any man who throws down his arms," I said, not wanting a massacre.

"I think they killed Santa Anna," Cooke said.

"Antonio? Dead?"

"Went down just short of the barrier. Looked bad," Cooke explained.

I hoped it wasn't true, but there was no the time to find out.

"Drop your guns," Cooke shouted, riding up to the wagons with his Colt ready.

Soon my sergeants were doing the same, waving at the enemy to lay down their arms. The men there needed no more convincing, especially with wives and camp followers cowering among them.

With a better view than I had from the barricade, I watched

345

Crockett's men pour over the last resistance on the eastern side of the field. The ground around us subsided to moans and groans, the braying of wounded horses, and the thuds of muskets being thrown down. I turned Traveller to the right, trying to see where the main fighting was. I heard gunshots and screaming from the river, but could see nothing in the cloudy confusion.

"Voss, sound *Recall*," I ordered, anxious to get back in the fight.

Forty men rallied around my guidon as we skirted the wagon park, following Keogh. I saw the old bear hunter, now on foot, hurrying his company along. Young Crockett was with him, faces grim and black with powder.

We passed a few wounded and dead scattered from place to place, though not so many as one might think. I found Keogh's adjutant seated on a barrel, his left arm in a bloody sling, his good hand holding a pistol on several prisoners. He saluted as we moved on.

Several minutes later, I finally caught up with Keogh. His men were dismounted in skirmish formation. There was little if any gunfire. What remained of the rebel force was crouching in the smoke a hundred yards away trapped against the river. There were so many troops around us that I was forced to halt. Voss held Traveller's reins.

"George, what happened to you?" Keogh asked, his blouse torn and hat lost.

"The general fell off his horse. Broke his leg," Engle said.

"Fell off your horse?" Keogh asked.

"I didn't fall off my horse," I protested.

"What happened?" Butler asked, busy with several prisoners.

"General Custer fell off his horse. Broke his leg," a militia sergeant said, spreading word among his men.

"We'll win this fight without you, sir. Don't worry," Voss insisted.

I wanted in on the last phase of the battle, pushing forward until reaching the skirmish line. Seguin was there, his head wrapped in a bandage, but otherwise no worse for wear. Rather than press the issue, he was holding his rangers back, satisfied to contain the situation. I saw the enemy at our immediate front was milling around, neither fighting nor surrendering.

"We can end this now, Myles," I said.

"They've got no place to go, George," Keogh said, sensing my

346

eagerness. "No reason to get more men killed. Not now."

"It would only take one volley," I insisted, for the collapse of the militia before us would surely spread throughout the surviving rebel horde.

"It's not what Tom wants," Keogh said.

"Tom? It's not what Tom wants?"

"He has command of the field."

"I'm still the general," I insisted.

"Tom's a general, too. And it was Tom who returned from California in time to save Texas," Keogh explained. "No disrespect, George. It's the way things are."

Five minutes later, the shooting stopped. Hundreds of muskets were dropped at our feet. Seguin's men began rounding up prisoners, taking them back to the wagon park that was now empty of animals. My leg began to ache again, so I found a supply box to sit on. Doctors were soon roaming the field looking for patients, of which there were plenty. I ordered them to care for our own first.

The battle was over, and I'd hardly fired more than a few shots. Younger and quicker men had won the glory, and I was forced to settle for victory. Or was it Tom's victory?

———

Dusk came sooner than expected. I was resting in a large campaign tent overlooking the Brazos when Tom, Crockett and Cooke came calling. They had been busy while a crude Boston butcher scraped my wound and applied a new dressing. I could only hope that infection didn't set in.

"Seven hundred and fifty prisoners," Cooke reported. "We've counted two hundred and fifty-eight dead. Some of the survivors took boats across the river. Kid Flacco is looking for them."

"Our losses?" I asked.

"Forty-two dead, another hundred wounded," Cooke said.

"Sam Houston's in bad shape," Crockett added. "Musket ball shattered 'is ankle. He kan't walk none. Lost him a good horse, too."

"What about Santa Anna?" I inquired.

"You should go see him, Autie," Tom urged. "He's hanging on, but probably not much longer."

I was reluctant. After Stonewall Jackson had been mortally

wounded at Chancellorsville, Bobby Lee had declined to visit him. The thought of losing Jackson was too painful. I was having similar emotions about Santa Anna, who had taught me how to be more than a general.

"Where's the boy?" I asked, suddenly remembering I hadn't see Tatanka since the start of the fight.

"Laid up with a broken arm," Crockett said. "His mare got shot out from under him. Doc Pollard says he be fine."

"He's the hero of the charge," Cooke added. "First one to jump the barrier. Shot Rusk in the neck. Almost grabbed a rebel flag."

"I'm giving him a medal of honor," Tom announced.

"Let him sleep in my tent tonight," I offered. "I can watch him while writing my report."

"What report is that?" Cooke asked, for he was the one who usually wrote the reports.

"I'm sending dispatches to the newspapers," I explained. "Now that the war is over, Mexico will know to stop sending troops. The plantation owners will learn their dreams of empire are defeated. Van Buren's government will be informed that the Buffalo Flag flies proudly from the Gulf of Mexico to the Pacific. And our own people should know it's time to rebuild."

"Pretty darn ambitious," Crockett observed.

"I had a good teacher. What's being done with the prisoners?" I said.

"Gonna parole 'em, 'cept the leaders. 'Lessen you gots objections," Crockett answered.

"No, no objections. We can't shoot them all," I replied.

"But we will shoot some of them," Tom said, the scar on his jaw turning red.

"It would be criminal not to," I agreed.

Near midnight, I went to visit Santa Anna, who had been grievously shot through the lung. Dr. Pollard gave him morphine to make him comfortable. Morning Star and Isabella did what they could to help, but there seemed little hope. Tatanka joined us, assisted by Voss. They were business partners, after all.

"I asked you to be careful," I complained, sitting on a canvas chair at his bedside.

"You wanted all the glory," Santa Anna replied.

"I have plenty of glory."

"And now I do, too," he said.

"Your daughters will be taken care of," Tatanka announced.

"You must still marry Guadalupe," Santa Anna said, reaching to take Tatanka's hand. The boy returned the grip firmly.

"She will be my first wife," Tatanka promised.

"Isabella and Inés are close friends. I will make a home for her in San Francisco. She'll want for nothing," I said, glancing up to see if she'd heard.

"Can you still trick Isabella into marrying you?" Santa Anna said, offering a weak smile.

"Yes, Isabella will still marry me. It just might take a little longer," I responded. "I'm just sorry you won't be there."

"I will be there, George. I will be there," he said.

General Antonio López de Santa Anna died just before dawn, surrounded by many friends.

After the priest finished saying the Last Rites, I walked from the tent holding Isabella's hand. We found a log to sit on, for I could only get around on crutches. The night was misty but not cold, a few stars poking through the gloom.

"I was wrong last winter. In San Francisco, when I turned coward. I'm sorry," I apologized.

"You were not a coward. I see that now. You had grown tired of battlefields," she said.

All around us were the moans of the latest battlefield. Bodies were being carried to the small cemetery adjoining the Velasco church. Catholic priests and Baptist ministers were having a busy night.

"When I was a young man, little of this had an effect on me," I confessed. "I thought only of the fight. What I had done, how I would receive credit. What the newspapers would say. Then the war ended, and for ten years after, I thirsted to recapture the glory of my youth."

"And now?" Isabella asked.

"I don't know if a leopard can change its spots, but I want a different life. One without cannon fire and weed-covered hillsides. And I want that life with you."

"Autie, I've loved you since we first met at Casa Blanca. And then you learned Spanish, just so you could ask my father for my hand in his own language. You are bold, and crazy, and face the world with a full heart. But my people have a heritage, too. Deep faith. Ties of family. Can a white man from Ohio embrace such a life?"

"It would be hard, if I was still a white man from Ohio. But I don't care about such things anymore," I said, surprised to discover it was true. "I've grown to love your father as my own. Lived with Mexicans, Negroes and Indians. And the Irish. There comes a time to outgrow the conceits of our youth."

"I think maybe you have," Isabella said, leaning forward to give me a gentle kiss. "We will marry in Béjar, if my father gives permission. Then we will return to California, and you will build your empire. We will have ranches, donate to the church, and leave our children a rich heritage."

I reached into my campaign blouse, ripped from falling against the wagon, and found the gold ring I'd given her once before. I slipped it back on her finger. It was my greatest victory of the day.

A moment later, Tatanka emerged from the tent, his arm in a sling. We told him the good news.

"Then you will be my sister, as Morning Star will be your sister," Tatanka said, giving her a hug. "When I marry the daughter of Santa Anna, our children will be cousins, and our family will reach from Mexico to the Black Hills."

"A Custer dynasty?" I asked.

"Morning Star is married to your brother. Her sons are my nephews. Her sons are your nephews. Her nephews are the cousins of all. Why would it not be Morning Star's dynasty?" Tatanka asked.

We both laughed. In a man's world, women do not have dynasties. Tatanka took a flask from his back pocket and unscrewed the cap. I could smell a fine brandy.

"Shall we toast your engagement, in the tradition of your people?" Tatanka offered.

"That's strong drink for a youngster," I warned.

"I am not so young as you believe," Tatanka said.

The next morning dawned clear for the first time in weeks. The rebel leaders wished to meet, but I declined, and ordered Tom and Crockett to decline as well. There would be time to hear their excuses later, but we needed order first. They were confined to the same dank storeroom where Santa Anna had been held after the fall of Fort Velasco.

"Wagons coming in, sir," Voss reported just after breakfast.

I was under Goodfellow's care in a large tavern at the end of town, my balcony giving me a good view of the surrounding fields. I saw Crockett, Baugh and Brister all busy speaking with our former enemies, attempting to win them over. I was not enthusiastic about their efforts, but Tom insisted on taking Lincoln's approach to the problem by letting them up easy.

"Galveston?" I asked.

"No, sir. General Keogh's train," Voss said.

With some help, I stood up at the railing. Twenty wagons guided by a hundred scouts and teamsters were bringing in supplies from San Antonio. The army would welcome more ammunition. I recognized Kit Carson leading the scouts, fifty rough men looking for a fight.

"Is that Erasmo I see?" I asked, pointing at the lead wagon.

Dr. Pollard, consulting with Goodfellow, came to my side for a look.

"That's Mr. Seguin, all right," Pollard said. "And that's Lorenza de Zavala with him. Looks like the Tejano leaders finally made peace."

"I know Señor Seguin holds him in high regard," I remarked, glad to see they were friends again.

Just after noon, a meeting was called at McMaster House. Letting Traveller recover, I rode a borrowed mare to the eastern plain, passing a thousand soldiers, along with hundreds of camp followers, townspeople, teamsters, ranchers, hunters and sailors. It occurred to me that this was possibly the largest gathering ever in Texas up to that time.

The new rulers of Texas were already assembling in the courtyard where planks had been laid across water barrels to make a long conference table. Chairs and boxes had been taken from the town. I noticed Tom sitting at the head, accompanied by Bill Cooke, Algernon Smith, Juan Seguin, Juan Almonte, Nathanial Brister, Kit Carson, Captain Cochise, and even the younger Crockett.

"Feelin' left out, George?" Crockett asked, approaching with Tatanka and Morning Star.

"Remember when we sat around the dining table the night before the Alamo?" I wistfully recalled. "We tried to convince Santa Anna to let us settle the question of Texas."

351

"We're the old men now. You, me an' Myles," Crockett said.

"Not that old," I protested.

"Thomas has big plans," Morning Star said. "We are going to start a new city to be the capital. He will call it Austin, to please the Texians. He says we will have many children."

"Texas will be strong," Tatanka added. "So strong that if the Americans threaten to steal land from the People, they will know the Lakota have powerful allies."

"Might be awhile 'fore the States threaten anyone," Crockett said. "Newspapers say South Carolina is ready for secession. Maybe Alabama, too. That fool Van Buren don't know what ta do. He ain't no Andy Jackson."

I wondered if the United States might break up in 1838 instead of 1861. Would there still be a Civil War? Certainly not the devastation that my generation saw, where the industrial revolution had created mechanized slaughter. And if the United States did dissolve, would that leave the Buffalo Flag as the most powerful nation in North America?

"We shouldn't give up leadership to the kids yet," I said to Crockett. "Find Myles and Señor Seguin. Invite Señor de Zavala. And I want the Cherokee here, too. Ask Chief Gatunwali to join us."

The old men, though none of us were really that old, barged in on Tom's meeting, taking the best seats and forcing the adjutants to set up another table. Those without chairs were forced to stand. I took the head seat, Crockett on my right, Tom to the left. Erasmo Seguin, de Zavala and Gatunwali sat close by.

As word of the meeting spread, even Sam Houston insisted on being carried from his tent, the pain of his shattered ankle offset by morphine and corn whiskey. After a moment of frustration, Houston demanded a bench near Crockett. Cooke stood behind me, ready to issue directives, while Tatanka took a tall stool just behind my shoulder, close enough to whisper his cryptic advice.

"What is this, Autie?" Tom asked, his voice gruff with displeasure.

"We have business to conduct, little brother," I responded. "It's time to reward our friends, punish our enemies, and form a real government. Isn't that right, Tatanka?"

"The General speaks truth," Tatanka agreed, staring at Tom with impatient black eyes. I could not say exactly what passed between them, but they now had a long history. And they were brothers-in-law.

"What do you think, David? Shall we punish our enemies first?" I asked.

"What ya got in mind, George?" Crockett said.

"Just enough justice to make a point," I replied, standing for attention and then motioning to Cooke.

It was time for a reckoning with the rebel leaders. Hughes raised his hand and five bedraggled prisoners were led forward under guard. The uniforms were tattered. They wore no hats. A large crowd gathered, some having fought the rebel leaders, others having fought for them. I had a special squad of troopers under Butler and French to maintain order, for I would not have the proceedings interrupted.

"General Custer, sir. These men were taken under arms against the Buffalo Flag," Cooke announced, acting as my adjutant-general.

"Their names?" I requested for the official record.

"James Fannin, Mirabeau Lamar, William Ward, Albert Horton, and Dr. Jack Shackelford," Cooke called out, indicating each villain as they lined up before us.

I moved around the edge of the conference table to face them, followed by Crockett and Tom. It had been more than two years since we had confronted Fannin at Goliad, and I had not forgotten my promise.

"Edward Burleson?" I asked.

"Dead on the field, sir," Cooke confirmed.

"Just as well," I said. "Mr. Fannin, have you anything to say before I pronounce sentence?"

"Sentence? What about my trial?" Fannin stuttered.

The man looked pale, his hair turning prematurely gray. The shoulders were bent, not in fear, but weary from losing a war he might have won.

"You had your trial yesterday when you failed to lay down your arms. Now dozens of my men are dead, and you will answer for it," I replied.

I glanced back at Crockett, my expression firm. Tom nodded agreement. A look at Houston showed no particular reaction either way. They had not been on good terms since Houston ordered Fannin to abandon Fort Defiance and Fannin refused.

"I am a soldier, sir. Fighting for my country and my constitution," Fannin said, raising his voice so all could hear. "Our cause is just, for we ask no more than our forefathers earned at Cowpens and Yorktown. You have no right to judge me."

"Be that as it may, you raised a rebel flag to fight a free land, and rejected an honorable surrender," I said, in no mood for hollow politics.

I paused to allow the surrounding multitude a moment to consider my words, studying the faces of Señor Seguin, my own captains, and our Indian allies, some of whom needed time for translation. When I was sure all eyes were on me, I turned to my sergeant-at-arms.

"Sergeant Williamson, please have your detail escort Mr. Fannin over to that oak tree and shoot him," I ordered, pointing to the spot where Santa Anna had been treated after his fatal wound. "And take Mr. Lamar with him."

"George..." Crockett began to say.

"You've pardoned enough treason, Colonel Crockett. You've been pardoning treason since Buffalo Bayou. It's time to show that not all scoundrels may expect mercy."

French needed no extra prodding. This war had cost us enough already. He positioned eight men armed with Springfields around the prisoners and marched them the eighty yards to the old oak. Butler and Hughes followed a few steps behind should they be needed. A few minutes later, the shots rang out.

"General Custer, 'bout these others?" Crockett asked, indicating Ward, Horton, and Shackelford. There was great suspense, and I was enjoying it.

"Mr. Ward, at the urging of Colonel Crockett, you may lead what remains of your Georgia Battalion back to Georgia. Do not return," I sternly said.

"For my men, I thank you, General," Ward said, pretending he wasn't relieved.

"Dr. Shackelford, what of your Red Rovers?" I respectfully asked, for I had heard good stories of their conduct, unlike many of the militias.

"They just as soon go home, sir. And me with 'em," Shackelford said, his accent educated. "But my son, Fortunatus. He's married.

Laid down roots. Appreciate if he could stay."

The son, a second lieutenant, had not strayed from his father, standing nearby among the captured officers. He was a tall good-looking lad. I walked over.

"Will you take the oath?" I asked. "Will you swear allegiance to the Buffalo Flag?"

"Yes, sir. I'll take the oath," Fortunatus replied.

"Say it loud, boy," I insisted.

"I'll take the oath, sir!" the boy shouted.

"Dr. Shackelford, your Rovers may go home. And your son may stay," I said. "And as for you, Mr. Horton. What are we to do with you?"

Horton could not have known it, but I knew he had lived a distinguished life, having visited with his family during my trip to Texas in 1865. The year the old man died.

"Rather not give up on Texas," Horton replied.

"Are you ready to give up on slavery?" I demanded.

"Rather not die for it," he said, shrugging his thin shoulders.

"Crockett?" I asked.

"Reckon we kin give 'em a chance," Crockett said.

"Reckon we'll give you a chance then, Mr. Horton," I agreed.

"Thank you, sir," Horton said, offering to shake hands.

It was the first opponent's hand I'd shaken all morning.

We adjourned for supper. I heard General Castrillón had arrived from Galveston and wanted to consult with him. When Tom took his allies aside for a talk, I waved Crockett and my sergeants over.

"Still think leniency is the best course, David?"

"Rightly do. Fightin' is over, time to make the peace," Crockett replied.

"Put on your coonskin cap," I said. "Butler, Hughes, French, Voss, take your best men. Circulate among the prisoners. Let them know those who want a life in Texas or California can still petition the new government. Have them address their petitions to me."

"You?" Crockett said.

"I am the Lieutenant General of the Army, and they are prisoners of war," I explained. "Every name I approve will be forwarded to you for the final decision."

"Do I got a choice?" Crockett asked.

"We can ask Butler and Hughes what they think. Boys?" I asked.

"Hang 'em all sir. Every last son of a bitch," Butler said.

"Hangin' is cheaper than shootin', sir," Hughes remarked.

"David?" I inquired.

"Ya made yer point, George. We'll git goin' on them petitions," Crockett said.

"Cooke," I summoned, drawing him away from Tom's group.

"Yes, George," he reported, wondering what the twinkle in my eye meant.

"We need more tables. Lot's more. And flags. Find every pole you can and put a flag on it," I ordered. "The fate of Texas is about to be decided. We should make it a grand event. Where is the band?"

"I understand," Cooke said, and I know he did. He rushed off to organize the event as only Bill Cooke could.

General Castrillón and I met briefly near the dock for cigars. He had already heard of Santa Anna's fate, and we raised a glass to Antonio's memory, planning a formal ceremony before his body was taken back to Mexico. I also asked Castrillón to stay as my personal advisor. He was reluctant to live north of the Rio Grande, but agreed to think it over.

The meeting reconvened under a light cloud cover, protecting us from the late August sun. Crockett had the head chair, with Tom and I at his elbows facing off across from each other. Otherwise the seating was the same, though Castrillón now sat next to Señor Seguin.

"We have letters from Béjar to San Francisco. Newspapers, too," Cooke announced, showing half of dozen of them. "The war has united the Buffalo Flag. More militias are forming. The Kellogg Code is being posted in every church and plaza."

"This one is from Señora Williamson," Tom said, reading one of the missives. "It seems even the Californios are suddenly thinking we're the best bet. Los Angeles is sending a battalion to reinforce Santa Fe."

"Sounds like the gold is safe," Smith remarked.

"Of course it's safe," I said. "Who's going to challenge the army that beat both Mexico and the Brazos militias?"

"We didn't defeat the Mexican army. We didn't even fight them," Tom corrected.

"Says we did, right here," I said, holding up a copy of the *San Francisco Examiner*. "Second column. *"Buffalo Flag Triumphs."*

"The story is wrong," Tom protested.

"The story is already history, Tommy," I replied.

"With the troubles over, it's time to resolve the governing issues that have bothered so many," I announced, standing so the large crowd could see me. "President Crockett, what would you recommend?"

As I took my seat, Crockett stood to the cheers of the mob, raising his coonskin cap before laying it on the table before him.

"Seems it's time to form a Congress," Crockett said. "Military rule's got its place in time of war, but war's over. For now."

There was cheering, Crockett basking in the glow of their admiration. The old bear hunter had come to Texas for a fresh start, but I doubt he ever envisioned a moment like this. He had, after all, lost as many runs for Congress as he'd won.

"What sort of Congress would this be?" de Zavala asked. "Under the Brazos constitution, the Tejano people lost the right to vote. Our lands were stolen. Our stock was taken without payment. This is not a government we can respect."

"Señor de Zavala was not the only victim," Chief Guatimini also protested. "Houston promised our land claims would be confirmed, but Lamar came to rob us. We have seen the Americans steal our land in Alabama. In Georgia. Our people put on a trail of tears. What protection will a white congress offer the Cherokee?"

"We can't have no dictators," John Wesley Crockett said. "This may be Texas, but we're still Americans. Can't live under nothing less than liberty."

"Liberty to let lawyers steal farms from humble folk? Liberty for a few rich men to tell the rest of us how to live?" Brister said, defiantly pounding the table.

It surprised me. I'd served with Nathaniel since he was my aide at the Alamo, shared hard days and long rides, and knew he came from a prosperous Virginia family. But didn't know he was such a radical.

"*Necesitamos una constitución*," Juan Almonte said.

"Yes, we need a constitution," Tom agreed.

"Excuse me, esteemed delegates," General Castrillón said, rising with great dignity. "But your Buffalo Flag waves from Galveston to San Francisco. You are Americans, Tejanos, Mexicans, Cherokee, Apache, Comanche, Californios, and a dozen others. How will you manage such an empire?"

"Through the voice of the people!" some miscreant yelled from the mob.

"It's white man's country!" someone else shouted.

"Let's vote!" a recently pardoned rebel yelled, as if we would let any of them have the franchise fresh from arms against us.

The meeting wasn't out of control, but was tending in an awkward direction. Crockett leaned over, motioning with his hands.

"What are ya thinkin', George?" he whispered.

"It took our forefathers twelve years to come up with a constitution, and it was so badly flawed it led to war," I answered. "We don't have such luxuries."

I looked at Tom and saw he had no ready answer for our dilemma. As I knew he wouldn't. He had led a company of forty troopers for ten years, and often acted as my aide-de-camp, before winning his star. Nothing in his experience prepared him for forming a government.

"Tommy?" I said.

"We've got to be fair, Autie," was his only answer.

I stood up and raised my hands for attention. Had my leg not been wrapped from ankle to knee, I'd have looked for a sturdy cracker barrel to stand on. Voss blew his bugle. As the wind picked up, I noticed our banners flapping in the breeze.

"My friend General Castrillón is correct about our challenges," I said, suppressing a high-pitched tone to my voice. "We are a vast empire, filled with diverse constituencies. We have been at war. We may be at war again. Texas has few resources other than land. The farms have been plundered, the ranches stripped. The treasury is empty. But Texas does not stand alone. We have friends in California. Horses and cattle to restock this land. Silver in Nevada. Treasure in Utah and Colorado.

"In the days after the Alamo, David Crockett and I envisioned a new Texas, one where every man could rise on his own merits. To accomplish this, we need a federation. A federation of states, wielded into an empire. Like the empires of Rome and Persia, we need a strong centralized state to take us through these difficult times. I propose our government be placed in San Francisco. I know the people there. It's where the gold is. We have the protection of distance and the sea."

The crowd remained silent. I had hoped for cheers. Agreement that California offered stability, and that my leadership would be recognized. I glanced toward Tom, who was whispering to Cooke and Smith. They did not seem enthusiastic. Señors Seguin and de Zavala were vested in their own homeland. Chief Guatimini and Chief Flacco the Elder were unimpressed by a land far removed from their hunting grounds. Houston was smiling, as if I'd finally made the blunder he'd been hoping for. I turned to Crockett, who shook his head.

"Now that everyone's had their say, let's get this over with," General Keogh suddenly said, walking between the tables where all could see him. Until then, I hadn't realized he had been watching from one of the wagons rather than sitting in counsel.

"Myles?" I said, surprised.

"George, you got good ideas, but California is too far away. That's a simple fact. Some of you want a congress, and say a constitution will protect the rights of the people. Well, no one knows better than an Irishman how worthless paper can be. So this is what we're gonna do."

Keogh motioned to the crowd. Captains, lieutenants and sergeants came forward by the bushel, including members of my regimental staff. I should not have been surprised. While Tom and I had been gallivanting around the country, Keogh had been left to hold Texas against steep odds, and performed his duty superbly. He had earned the loyalty of this army.

"Now good old George ain't much of a talker, but he likes readin'," Keogh continued. "An' he give me this book on the Archimedies."

"Achaemenids," I corrected.

"These Achaemenids was a big empire in Persia, lots of land and of lots of folks, just like we got. They had to make some tough decisions. So do we," Keogh explained.

Keogh strolled around the tables, smiling and slapping a few backs. I noticed Crockett discreetly put his coonskin cap back on.

"From what I understand, their empire had a king. We can't have no king, but we can have a president," Keogh elaborated. "This king governed his land with a bunch of stirrups."

"Satraps," I corrected again.

"Each district had a satrap, sort of a governor, along with a general," Keogh said. "And that's what we need here. Tom, you're gonna be the governor of East Texas. Chief Guatimini will watch over the Cherokee lands. Señor de Zavala, you are the governor of West Texas. You can set up a council, or a Congress, or whatever you need. People still get to vote. That ain't gonna change.

"Bill Sharrow's done a good job in New Mexico. I'll be sending him his commission, and askin' that he appoint this Cochise fella to be his general. General Castrillón, I don't know that an officer here commands more respect than you do. We need help watching over Southern California. Can you do that for us, until we find someone more inclined?"

Castrillón stood up to the acclamation of the crowd. He bowed to the mob, bowed to Keogh, smiled in my direction, and then saluted. Keogh walked over and shook his hand.

"George, you've done fine in the north of California. I'd like to see you keep it up," Keogh urged.

"Who is going to be president?" I asked.

"We already have a president, and his name is David Crockett," Keogh replied. "Isn't that right, boys?"

"Crockett! Crockett!" the men shouted.

Shots were fired, bugles blared, and my own band began playing "For He's a Jolly Good Fellow". Crockett was helped up on the table, waving and bowing. Tom, Cooke, Almonte and the younger Seguin surrounded him, offering their support. Keogh wandered over to stand at my side.

"Sorry, George. Had to do what's best," he whispered. "And you did leave me in charge."

"That I did, Myles," I said. "Are you the Lieutenant General of the Army now?"

"I deserved a promotion," Keogh answered.

A chief will say that great problems are not settled by great councils, only great leaders. It surprised many that General Keogh emerged as the leader on this day, and that his words would form a government that lasted many years. Like the tribes of the People, the Buffalo Nations determined to be cousins. To assume a warrior's responsibility while sharing a brother's burdens. I thought Custer would be angry that he was not the great chief, and for a time, I think he was. But as all things with Custer, the disappointment soon faded. California was about to be overrun with gold hunters, the Comanche would rise in revolt, and the Americans in the east would soon be fighting amongst themselves. But those problems awaited another time. At the town of Velasco, on a sunny afternoon in August of 1838, a nation arose that would one day be the allies of my people. Wakan Tanka's vision was at last becoming clear.

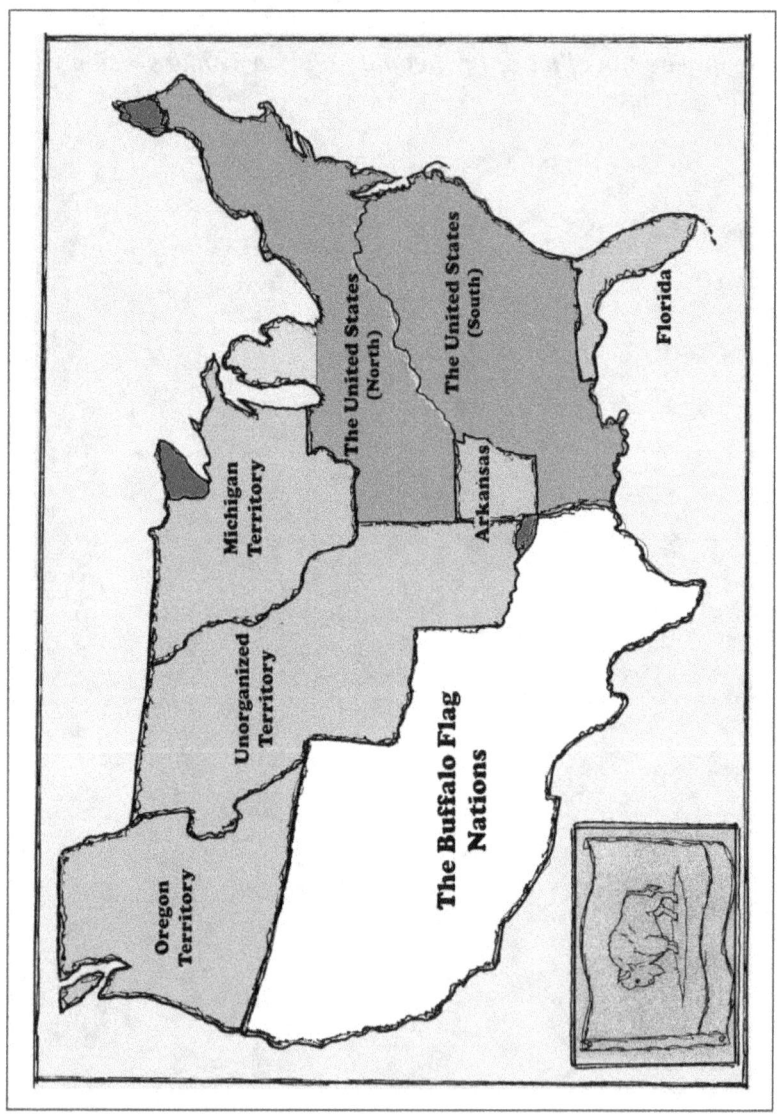

Map of the Buffalo Flag Nations, 1838

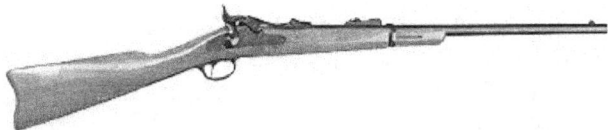

Epilogue
OLD SOLDIERS

Three years after the Battle of Velasco, I woke up on a rainy June morning, gave Isabella a kiss, and strolled down Nob Hill from Custer House to Juanita's Catania near the docks. San Francisco continued to grow like no other city in the world, now boasting forty thousand people. Ships filled the harbor, merchants hawked their wares, and tradesmen sat in coffee houses crafting deals. Uniformed police officers walked the streets in pairs, asking questions and checking permits, for strict laws were need to maintain order. Antonio López de Santa Anna had taught me that, and the new city hall was named in his honor.

Taking my usual seat at a window overlooking the bay, I gave the newsboy a nickel for the *San Francisco Examiner* that I read while waiting for breakfast. French troops had landed in Vera Cruz, just as Louis Philippe's government had threatened. Queen Victoria and Prince Albert finally had a male heir, who they'd named Edward. South Carolina had declared independence from the United States, again, but this time they were being ignored by the Clay administration. Preparations continued in Texas for the Velasco Day celebrations, reminding me that I had a long trip ahead.

After a quick meal of pork sausage and fried eggs, I limped along the Embarcadero toward the stable where my carriage awaited, doffing my hat and waving my cane at friendly passersby. Some mornings I rode Vic up to the fort, but my leg tended to hurt on damp days, urging the warmth of a closed cab and leather seat.

"Good morning, General," John said, emerging from his quaint house on 2nd Street to join me, as he always did. His wife waved goodbye, holding their baby in her arms.

"Good morning, Mr. Armstrong," I returned. "Ready for a boat ride?"

"And the stagecoach, after that," John said with a grin. "Me and Martha is lookin' forward to seein' Texas again."

"Isabella is excited, too. It's been a year since she's seen her father. Longer since I've seen Tom," I said, for such long distances can be difficult. "A few years from now, we'll be taking the train instead. We'll get there in three days instead of four weeks."

"That be nice, sir. Mighty nice," John agreed.

Ben Travane joined me at the carriage house, for I liked to be briefed on the day's business during the ride up to my office at the Presidio. Ben was a civilian now, well-dressed in a fine brown suit, but continued to act as my financial manager. I never did learn to handle money well, but I did learn to trust those who could.

"George Hearst got good news from Virginia City," Ben reported, flipping through a thick stack of letters. "Another rich vein. Town might be growing faster than San Francisco."

"Do we own any of the hotels there?" I asked.

"Of course, George. At least, I do."

I knew he was joking. Sort of. Ben often made the initial investments and then brought me in as a partner. I didn't mind as long as Isabella and I got our share.

"Looks like I got Egypt," I remarked.

"Sir?" Ben asked.

"When Alexander the Great died, his generals carved up his empire," I explained. "Ptolemy was given Egypt, which proved the richest province. Maybe I didn't become president of the Buffalo Flag, like Crockett was, but I didn't get cheated."

"President de Zavala still looks to you for advice. Some even say you are the true power of the Nations," Ben observed.

"Like I said, I got the richest province."

We reached The Point, passed the new Fisherman's Wharf, and made the final turn to the Presidio. The tall white stone walls loomed like a guardian over the bay. The guard post there was alert, inspecting the credentials of office seekers, while the tower recorded the ships sailing through the Golden Gate. The rush of prospectors had created chaos for a period of time, but quick justice and the occasional hanging now ensured proper respect for authority.

We left the carriage on the parade ground and I hobbled up the stairs to my office on the second floor. The walls were decorated with captured enemy flags and portraits of famous men. The oak desk was a gift from Admiral Cochrane, made from the timber of a retired ship-of-the-line. A potbelly stove in the corner allowed me to remove my wet coat and work in shirtsleeves. From the window, I could see all the way to Sausalito on a clear day.

"Good morning, brother. You are late again," Tatanka said, entering before I even had a chance to sit down. He wore a wool suit and tie, as always, his long hair held back by a red head band.

"Isabella and I were kept awake by your nephew's crying," I said. "Emanuel Erasmo Custer has strong lungs. Complain to me again when you have your own growing brood."

"Babies are women's work. Our work is here," Tatanka said, for he was a hard taskmaster.

He unrolled a new map, showing lands from the Mississippi to the Pacific Ocean. Many areas were highlighted, most particularly our disputed northeastern border, for the Buffalo Flag rightly claimed large swaths of Utah, Colorado and Wyoming. Lands occupied by Indians tribes but sought after by American politicians.

"We have a new treaty with the Lakota," Tatanka said. "The Travane Mining Corporation & Trust will extract the gold from the Black Hills, but the hunting grounds will be managed by the People."

"The Sioux live in the United States. You know we have no authority there. Not without a war we're not prepared for," I mildly objected.

Tatanka opened a notebook, ran his finger down the page of the congressional records, and pointed to a particular clause.

"It says here, the tribes are granted sovereignty of their lands by the American Congress. Is this not correct?" he said.

I glanced at the passage, though I already knew what it said. Such articles were common in my own day, though rarely honored for very long.

"Yes, technically that's true. The tribes are sovereign on their own land," I confirmed.

"Then tell me why the Buffalo Flag may not make trade agreements with sovereign tribes?"

He had me there. Though I was no lawyer, it seemed to me a case could be made for his argument. And if Washington sought to interfere with such trade? I looked Tatanka in the eye and saw what he was thinking.

"Send the treaty to the State Department. If Secretary Almonte approves, we'll take it to the next step," I suggested.

"The proposal was telegraphed to Austin this morning. Tom promises to discuss it at the cabinet meeting," Tatanka said.

"One less thing for me to worry about," I concluded.

My staff gradually arrived and the day was spent planning for the Texas trip, deciding who would stay behind to keep an eye on California. Mayor Richardson and Francisco de Haro had the official responsibility, but I still placed my trust in Señora Martínez. Bill Richardson was a conscientious administrator, but his wife was tougher.

And I knew if there were serious problems, Crockett would come down from Sacramento to serve as magistrate. Having declined to run for reelection, David was now spending his days overseeing the Gold Country. A few weeks away from his mansion on Plum Creek, now overflowing with children and grandchildren, would come as a welcome distraction. Isabella and I had spent Christmas with them, and I could tell the Old Bear Hunter was getting restless.

Toward the end of the day, my secretary announced a surprise guest.

"General Custer, the ambassador is here," Lieutenant Allen said.

"Which one is that, Jimmy?" I asked, for diplomats usually arranged their meetings at Kellogg House on State Street.

"Mr. James G. Birney, sir," Allen said.

I stood up and put on my official dress coat as the Kentuckian entered, a tall man with good visage, dressed in an elegant black suit.

"President Clay sends his greetings, General Custer," Birney said, shaking my hand.

"I did not expect him to send a Southerner," I remarked, for many plantation owners in Congress were still hoping to claim Texas one day. Something the Seventh Cavalry would never allow.

"An abolitionist Southerner, sir," Birney replied, showing no offense.

"That's different. Would you care for a cup of coffee? Or something stronger?" I asked.

"Coffee would be fine, General," he said, making himself comfortable. "I just finished reading your book. *The Conquest of California.* Quite the adventure story."

"It sells well," I said.

"How much of it is true?" Birney asked.

"Enough," I replied. "What brings you all the way up here on a rainy day?"

"I required an informal meeting. Not one ready for the newspapers," Birney explained. "The panic of 1837 is still affecting my country, and the tensions along our borders are not helping."

"And how does this concern me?"

"It is said that Thomas Custer will be the next president of the Nations," Birney explained. "He is young and popular. My government would like influence, and what better way than to make friends with his famous brother?"

It was not the first time such an approach had been made, but at least Birney was more honest than most.

"What is President Clay proposing?" I asked, taking a deep breath.

Birney reached into his pocket for a letter, stained and folded from a long trip.

"Written in his own hand," Birney said, handing the envelope to me with grim determination.

I was not wearing my spectacles, nor did I want to expose such a weakness before a man I barely knew.

"May I have the gist of it?" I requested.

"It's an invitation for the Buffalo Flag Nations to join the United States," Birney said.

I went back to my desk, found my spectacles, and read the offer carefully. It was generous enough, but hardly acceptable.

"I'm sorry, sir," I said with genuine contrition, giving the letter back to him. "Please ask President Clay to have patience. In time, we will ask the United States to join us."

General Custer was not the same man after the war in Texas. When white men would object that he treated Indians, Negros and Mexicans with too much deference, and this happened often, he would sit back in his chair and ask if they knew of the Persian Empire. He spoke of Darius and Xerxes, of Assyrians, Phoenicians, Babylonians, and other strange tribes that live far away. He would rise from his desk, lean on his cane, and say that no such land as the Buffalo Flag had been created since the time of Alexander the Great. There were some who believed Custer still sought power, perhaps even war with the United States, and wrote of him in a disparaging manner. But in his heart, Custer did not believe himself exalted above all others. He spent quiet evenings with his wife, indulged his children, and sought to govern with a justice that surprised those who knew him in harsher days. I once asked him of this, and with a whisper, he said that a tranquil life was his reward for achieving glory.

Keogh's Marker, circa 1877, by Coffeen-Schnitger

Acknowledgements
Some may consider *Custer and Crockett* an alternate history book, or simply a time travel book more akin to fantasy, but this has not prevented a good deal of historical research. In May 2014, I drove through Texas visiting Fort Stockton, San Antonio, Goliad, Austin, and Fredericksburg. This was an excellent opportunity to see the countryside, visit with locals, and purchase research materials. On the trip back to California, I was able to see some of the western trails that were close to non-existent in 1836, but would be thriving a mere ten years later. In Custer's time, General Stephen Kearny's route to California, and the Butterfield stage line, would have been old history, well-known to army officers and travelers alike.

George Custer was a staunch believer in railroads. He believed in their economic power, and their power to bring civilizations together. The country believed in railroads, too, which is why the United States made the Gadsden Purchase in 1854 to lay tracks from Texas to California. Custer did not live to see the first segment of the Southern

Pacific laid between Los Angeles and Fort Yuma, completed in 1877, but he was very aware of the progress. One of his best friends at West Point, Thomas Rosser, scouted routes for the Northern Pacific Railroad. Both envisioned a day when multiple routes would connect the Atlantic Ocean to the Pacific.

Prior to researching this novel, I did not realize that California was in revolt against Mexico City at the same time Texas was having its revolution. The revolt has never received much notice by historians, and the biographies of the participants are often vague. This can be useful when writing fiction, for it imposes fewer restrictions, but I still wanted to capture the important elements of life in California before the gold rush.

A few readers of *Custer at the Alamo* have questioned Custer's abilities as an army officer. It should be noted that, as today, there is more to leading men (and women) into battle than jumping on a horse and shouting 'charge.' As Lt. Colonel of the Seventh Cavalry, Custer spent most of his days writing reports, ordering supplies, overseeing training, passing judgment on infractions, and treading the treacherous political waters of the post-war U.S. Army. As an example, I will cite the 1873 Yellowstone Expedition, where Custer organized 1,600 cavalry and infantry, thousands of horses and mules, and 275 supply wagons. Accompanying the expedition were surveyors, railroad engineers, newspaper reporters, photographers, geologists, zoologists, botanists, and Indian scouts. And the expedition was successful. When Custer makes his move from Texas to California in *Custer and Crockett*, I am not providing him with leadership skills he didn't have.

We should also remember that Custer learned his craft during the Civil War under General George McClellan who, in the words of historian M. John Lubetkin, "had one of the best organizational minds in the country." McClellan may not have known how to wage war with an army, but he certainly knew how to build one.

Writing books is often not as easy as it looks. I am indebted to many people for the completion of this work: to Matthew Bernstein, my story editor, who helped keep it on track, and my wife, Kwei-lin Lum, for her artistic advice. But most of all, I need to thank the readers of my previous book, whose positive remarks were an inspiration to write a sequel.

References

13 Days to Glory by Lon Tinkle, McGraw-Hill, 1958

Alamo Traces by Thomas Ricks Lindley, Republic of Texas Press, 2003

Archaeology, History, and Custer's Last Battle by Richard Fox Jr.,
    University of Oklahoma Press, 1993

A Ride with Kit Carson, Geo. Brewerton, Harper's Magazine, Aug. 1853

A Terrible Glory by James Donovan, Little-Brown, 2008

A Time to Stand by Walter Lord, Bonanza Books, 1987

Béxar Family Connections and the Alamo by Dr. R. Bruce Winders

Boots & Saddles by Elizabeth Custer, Harper & Brothers, 1885

California Land of Promise, Maidee Nelson, Caxton Printers, 1962

Cochise by Peter Aleshire, Castle Books, 2005

Custer by Jeffrey D. Wert, Simon & Schuster, 1996

Custer and the 1873 Yellowstone Survey, M. John Lubetkin,
    University of Oklahoma Press, 2013.

Custer, A Soldier's Story by D.A. Kinsley, Promontory Press, 1992

Custer in Texas by John M. Carroll, Sol Lewis & Liveright, 1975

Custer Victorious, Gregory J.W. Urwin, Associated Univ. Presses, 1983

Custerology by Michael A. Elliott, Univ. of Chicago Press, 2007

Custer's Gold by Donald Jackson, Univ. Nebraska Press, 1966

Custer's Luck by Edgar I. Stewart, Univ. of Oklahoma Press, 1955

David Crockett, Lion of the West by Michael Wallis, Norton 2011

Eye Witness to the Alamo, Bill Groneman, Republic of Texas, 1996

Following the Guidon by Elizabeth Custer, Harper & Brothers, 1890

History of the Presidio of Monterey by Kibby M. Horne,
    Defense Language Institute Foreign Language Center, 2007

Kit Carson by David Remley, Univ of Oklahoma Press, 2011

Old Trails West by Ralph Moody, Promontory Press, 1963

Sutter's Fort by Oscar Lewis, Prentice-Hall, 1966

Sword of San Jacinto by Marshall De Bruhl, Random House 1993

Texas in 1837, Andrew Forest Muir, Univ. of Texas Press, 1963

The Alamo Remembered, Timothy Matovina, Univ. of Texas, 1995

The Apaches by Donald E. Worcester, Univ. of Oklahoma Press, 1979

The Custer Reader, Paul Andres Hutton, Univ. of Oklahoma, 2004

The Custer Story, Marguerite Merington, Devin-Adair Company, 1950

The Last Stand by Nathaniel Philbrick, Viking, 2010

With Santa Anna in Texas, Jose De La Pena, Texas A & M Univ., 1975

Custer and Crockett

Novels by Gregory Urbach

———

Custer at the Alamo

Sent 40 years into the past by a spell of Chief Sitting Bull, General George Custer and the Seventh Cavalry join Davy Crockett to defend the Alamo against Mexican forces under the command of General Antonio López de Santa Anna.

Magistrate of the Dark Land

A cowardly lawyer seeks two kidnapped
girls in a war-torn medieval land.

The Waters of the Moon Series

Born on the moon and raised by computers, young Grey Waters struggles to survive in a world ruled by machines.

————

Tranquility's Child
Tranquility's End
Tranquility's Heirs
Tranquility Besieged
Tranquility In Darkness
Tranquility Down
Tranquility Divided
Tranquility Under the Eagles
Tranquility's Last Stand

Slave of Akrona

Discovered by an alien salvage ship outside the Laros Stargate, a mysterious castaway is sent to the mining camps of Akrona, there to live his final days as a slave. But this survivor from another world is no slave, and the Arikhan Empire will never be the same again.

About the Author

An avid student of history, Gregory Urbach has been writing science fiction and fantasy for nearly 30 years. From his days working for a campus newspaper, he has also pursued an interest in politics and popular culture. His degree in Urban Studies proved useful when writing the nine book Tranquility science fiction series. In 2013, he published his first fantasy novel, *Magistrate of the Dark Land*, followed by *Custer at the Alamo* and *Slave of Akrona*. All of the author's books reflect alternate worlds where the concepts of good and evil are challenged by complicated realities.